挑战六级

710分 新题型

综合测试

主编：金 莉

编者：何 静 苏蕴文

其他参编人员：

蒋志华 周利芬 宋李戈 丁 哲 关晓蕙

张利辉 胡 薇 王 珂 刘晓光 展 萍

外语教学与研究出版社
FOREIGN LANGUAGE TEACHING AND RESEARCH PRESS
北京 BEIJING

图书在版编目(CIP)数据

挑战六级 710 分. 综合测试／金莉主编 . — 北京：外语教学与研究出版社，2006.10
ISBN 7 - 5600 - 6034 - X

Ⅰ. 挑… Ⅱ. 金… Ⅲ. 英语—高等学校—水平考试—习题 Ⅳ. H310.42

中国版本图书馆 CIP 数据核字 (2006) 第 108784 号

出 版 人：李朋义
责任编辑：韩　蜜
封面设计：王　薇
出版发行：外语教学与研究出版社
社　　址：北京市西三环北路 19 号 (100089)
网　　址：http://www.fltrp.com
印　　刷：北京市鑫霸印务有限公司
开　　本：787×1092　1/16
印　　张：15
版　　次：2006 年 11 月第 1 版　2006 年 11 月第 1 次印刷
书　　号：ISBN 7 - 5600 - 6034 - X
定　　价：22.90 元
＊　　＊　　＊

前 言

2004 年初教育部高教司组织制定并在全国部分高校开始试点实施《大学英语课程教学要求（试行）》（以下简称《教学要求》）。《教学要求》规定，大学英语课程的教学目标是：培养学生的英语综合应用能力，特别是听说能力，使他们在今后的工作和社会交往中能用英语有效地进行口头和书面的信息交流。针对这样的要求，教育部在多年实践的基础上，开始对大学英语四、六级考试进行改革。改革方案中，六级考试各部分测试内容、题型和所占比例如下表所示：

试卷构成	测试内容		测试题型	比例
第一部分：听力理解	听力对话	短对话	多项选择	35%
		长对话	多项选择	
	听力短文	短文理解	多项选择	
		短文听写	复合式听写	
第二部分：阅读理解	仔细阅读理解	篇章阅读理解	多项选择	35%
		篇章词汇理解	选词填空	
	快速阅读理解		是非判断＋句子填空或其他	
第三部分：综合测试	完形填空或改错		多项选择	15%
			错误辨认并改正	
	篇章问答或句子翻译		简短回答	
			中译英	
第四部分：写作	写作		短文写作	15%

上表中的第三部分即"综合测试"，这一部分的题型较多，组合也比较灵活，以一种全新的方式测试考生综合运用英语词汇、语法、篇章结构知识的能力。

为了帮助那些即将参加六级考试的考生熟悉和掌握改革后六级综合测试的形式、内容、试题特点、内在规律和应试技巧，我们编写了本书。本书特色如下：

内容全面，分类讲解

本书依照改革方案和最新样题编写，涵盖了六级综合部分的所有题型——完形填空、短文改错、汉英翻译和短句问答。全书共四章，每章一种题型，给出技巧讲解和针对性训练，为大家备考新六级中的综合部分提供切实有效的帮助。

总结技巧，指点迷津

本书的编者为多年活跃在大学英语教学一线的教师，丰富的教学经验使得本书每一章中针对题型的技巧讲解和点拨都极具实效性。讲解部分思路清晰，逻辑性强，为帮助大家在较短的时间内迅速地提高综合部分的答题速度和准确率提供了有力保障。

仿真模拟，实战性强

针对每一种题型，编者精心挑选，编写了 20 篇到 40 篇不等的模拟练习。所有练习的选材

（包括题材、体裁、长度、难度等）及题型设置都严格按照《教学要求》中的相关规定进行，不仅符合现有真题的考试难度和特点，也体现了改革后新题型的变化趋势。试题考点分布均匀且涵盖全面，经测试验证，信度、效度极高。相信通过这些模拟练习，大家一定能够"熟能生巧"。

归纳考点，边练边记

本书的另外一个重要特点在于解析后的"考点归纳"栏目，即针对该题所涉及的相关词条、短语、重要语法等命题者容易出题之处进行扩展归纳，详解考点，荟萃精华。考生做完本书的模拟题后，不仅可以对六级综合测试的主要考点有比较全面和系统的掌握，还可以举一反三，对历年的出题点进行比较，把握出题的类型和脉络。

方寸之间皆显匠心，愿大家在感受到本书的实用性和使用的便利性的同时，在综合运用英语语言的能力上有长足的进步！最后，预祝大家在即将到来的六级考试中取得好成绩！

编者

目　录

第一章 完形填空

第一节 现状与趋势

完形填空是大学英语六级考试的一个组成部分，主要考查考生综合运用语言的能力，即理解篇章和使用词汇和语法的能力。大学英语六级考试采用的完形填空题的形式是在一篇题材熟悉、难度适中的短文（约280词）内留有20个空白，每个空白设一题，每题有四个选择项，要求考生在全面理解短文内容的基础上选择一个最佳答案，使短文的意思和结构恢复完整。它考查的范围涵盖词、句、语篇和语法知识，因此能达到各个单项测试难以达到的测试目的。

在教育部高教司组织制定并在全国部分高校开始试点实施的《全国大学英语四、六级考试改革方案（试行）》（以下简称《改革方案》）中，完形填空属于"综合测试"的第一部分，占总分的10%，和短文改错构成二选一题型。从测试手段和测试形式来说，和旧题型相比没有太大变化。

大学英语六级考试中的完形填空具有如下特点：

- 文章题材所涉及的文化背景知识为考生能够接受的内容。
- 体裁上大多为说明文，篇章的逻辑性较强，结构严谨，文体特点突出。
- 对词汇的考查占主导地位（见下表），主要测试单词的用法、搭配和辨析，而对单词的语法形式，如时态、语态等的考查较少。
- 对篇章逻辑的考查比重较大（见下表），且其中相当一部分的题目综合考查篇章逻辑和词义辨析。由此可见，六级的完形填空属于"篇章—语义型"完形填空，主要测试考生在语篇中理解和运用词汇的能力。换句话说，就是要求考生从篇章入手，结合词汇和语法知识来答题。

六级完形填空全真试题题型分布表

年份 \ 题型	词义辨析	固定搭配	篇章逻辑	语法结构	题材	体裁
2005. 6	9 (5)	4	12 (5)	0	科技	说明文
2003. 1	12 (7)	2	12 (7)	1	管理	议论文
2001. 1	13 (8)	2	10 (8)	3	教育	说明文
1999. 1	13 (5)	4	7 (5)	1	旅行	说明文
总计	47 (25)	12	41 (25)	5		
比率	59% (31%)	15%	51% (31%)	6%		

注：括号中为词义辨析和篇章逻辑两种题型的交叉题数及其所占比例。

第二节 对策与技巧

前面提到，六级考试中的完形填空属于"篇章—语义型"完形填空，因此它的考查点主要集中在词汇运用和篇章理解两个方面。在词汇运用方面，考查的主要内容是词义辨析和固定搭配；在篇章理解方面，主要考查考生对篇章逻辑关系的理解。在实际考试中，往往是在考查对篇章理解的同时测试考生对四个选项进行词义辨析的能力，因此这两个方面不是孤立的。此外，在该题型中还有少量的语法结构题，主要从句法角度测试考生运用代词、关系词、限定词等的能力。

简言之，六级完形填空包含两个主要切入点——词汇和篇章，四种题型——词义辨析、固定搭配、篇章逻辑、语法结构。下面我们就对这四种题型的应试技巧进行剖析。

一、词义辨析题

六级完形填空中的词义辨析题主要考查考生根据上下文选择合适的实词（名词、动词、形容词、副词）的能力。选项设置有两种方式：一是四个选项毫无关系，只要认识，并对上下文的理解正确，就可以正确选择。实际上，这种题是在篇章逻辑的基础上对词义辨析加以考查，具体内容将在本节"篇章逻辑题"中加以介绍。二是四个选项为近义词或近形词。在六级完形填空的选项设置中，对近义词和近形词的考查远远多于四级，在真题中所占的比例达到了 28%。在这里，我们着重对近形词和近义词辨析题进行分析。

📝 命题规律

1. **近义词**：选项词义虽相似，但是其他特性，如词法特性、语义特性等不同。词法特性指词性、名词单复数、及物动词还是不及物动词等。语义特性指词义的内涵和外延、用于人或者用于物等。有时，近义词的考查会结合固定搭配进行，如，同为"谴责"之意，accuse 和 charge 的用法却不同，通常的搭配为 accuse sb. of，charge sb. with。

   例 1：

   Wise buying is a positive way in which you can make your money go further. The 67 you go about purchasing an article or a service can actually save your money or can add to the cost.

   67. [A] form   [B] fashion   [C] way   [D] method

   > 这是一道典型的考查近义词的词义辨析题，选 C。根据上文 Wise buying is a positive way in which... 和空后的 you go about purchasing an article 可知，这里应该填一个表示"方法、途径"的词。form（形式）和 fashion（时尚）在含义上均不符，method 虽然有"方法"的意思，但是一般指的是解决某个问题的方法，并不能用来指"购买东西的途径"这层含义，所以选项 C 是最佳选择。

2. **近形词**：四个选项通常具有相同的词缀或者相同的词根，但是含义区别较大，因此只要认识单词，对上下文理解正确，就可以正确解题。

例2：

Now a new anti-jetlag system is __68__ that is based on proven __69__ pioneering scientific research. Dr. Martin Moore-Ede has __70__ a practical strategy to adjust the body clock much sooner to the new time zone through controlled exposure to bright light.

68. [A] adaptable   [B] approachable   [C] available   [D] agreeable

69. [A] broad   [B] inclusive   [C] tentative   [D] extensive

70. [A] devised   [B] recognized   [C] scrutinized   [D] visualized

> 这三道题测试的都是近形词辨析。
>
> 68. 选 C。空格所在的句子说："现在_____一种抗时差问题的方法"，应该填入表示"有"的意思的单词，只有 available（可利用的）最合适。其他几个选项 adaptable（适应力强的），approachable（可接近的），agreeable（令人愉快的）均不符合题意。
>
> 69. 选 D。空格所在的短语要说的是："_____的具有开拓性的科学研究"。根据上下文，extensive（广泛的）最符合句意和英语的搭配习惯。其他几个选项 broad（广阔的，宽的，一般指具体的东西），inclusive（包括的）和 tentative（尝试性的）均不符合题意。
>
> 70. 选 A。空格所在的句子的意思是："Martin Moore-Ede _____了一种实用的方法"，可见应该选表示"设计、发明"之意的 devised。其他几个选项 recognized（认出），scrutinized（仔细检查）和 visualized（想象）均不符合题意。

📖 答题技巧

1. 近义词辨析：不要死抠单词汉语意思上的细微差别，而要从单词的其他特性入手加以区别。

1）仔细辨别近义词的词法特性，如词性、单复数、动词的及物或不及物等。

2）熟悉词语搭配（collocation）。这里所说的词语搭配，不是指我们通常所说的固定搭配（本节第二类题型），而是指形容词和名词或者名词和名词的修饰搭配、动词和名词的动宾搭配、及名词和动词的主谓搭配。实践证明，在这样的搭配中大家很容易搞清楚很多近义词的区别。例如，通过 blank paper，vacant position，bare hill 这一组修饰搭配，大家就清楚了 blank，vacant，bare 这三个单词虽然都有"空的"之意，但是 blank 指"空白的"，vacant 指"空缺的"，而 bare 指"光秃秃的"，记住了搭配，就不用费力去记词义的区别了。在本章模拟练习的解析部分，我们在"考点归纳"中给出了一些这样的搭配，供大家参考。

3）注意选项所处的位置是否与前面或者后面的某个词构成特定短语或者固定搭配。例如，空格后有介词 of，那么在 approve 和 agree 间进行选择的时候就无需辨别两个单词的含义，直接选择 approve。

2. 近形词辨析：透彻分析词义和词性，根据词根词缀进行推断。

1）对于具有相同词缀的单词（简称"同缀词"），大家不妨根据它们的词根词缀的含义进行推断。例如 approachable，available，adaptable，agreeable 这样一组单词，后缀均为 -able，意为"可以被……的"，它们分别来自不同的动词：approach（接近），avail（利用），adapt（调整）和 agree（同意）。结合词缀的含义，就很容易推测出这几个形容词的意思了。

2）对于起源相同，但是含义却大不相同的单词（简称"同源词"），大家要在平时的学习中注意它们的区别，考试时切莫张冠李戴。例如：ashamed，shameful 和 shameless 虽然都源自名词 shame，而且都是形容词，但是第一个用来指人"感到羞愧的"，第二个用来形容某种行为是"可耻的"，第三个形容人是"无耻的"，用法大不一样。

二、固定搭配题

这里说的固定搭配，是指由主词（包括动词、名词和形容词）结合副词或者介词构成的短语及其惯用法，这也是六级完形填空考查的一个重点。

命题规律

1. 选项中给出介词或副词，要求选出一个能和原文中的主词搭配且符合原文含义的选项。
例 3：

When the Trip Guide calls __78__ bright light you should spend time outdoors if possible.

78. [A] off   [B] on   [C] for   [D] up

> 本题选 C。短语 call for 的意思是"要求，需要"，代入句中，句意为："当这份旅行指南表明需要光亮时，你就应该尽可能地呆在户外"，符合题意。而由其他几个选项构成的短语 call off（取消），call on（号召）和 call up（打电话，召集）均不符合文意。

2. 原文中给出介词，要求选出一个可以与其搭配且搭配之后的意思符合原文含义的主词。这类题往往结合词义辨析题进行考查，这一点已经在"词义辨析题"中说明。

3. 选项中给出搭配好的短语，要求考生分辨其正误并选择与原文意思相吻合的一个。

答题技巧

1. 明确空格前后的搭配关系。常见的介词及其搭配有：

单词	词义	搭配
about	关于	concern about 关心，挂念；speak about 谈到
	产生	come about 产生；bring about 产生，发生
	周围	hang about 闲荡，乱逛
across	穿过	cut across 抄近路穿过；get across 通过
	偶然	run across 快速跑过，偶然遇到；come across 偶遇
against	反对	fight against 和……斗争；hold against 责备；insure against 投保以防……
	支撑，靠着	lean against 靠着

（续上表）

单词	词义	搭配
at	向，朝某个方向，在……方面	look at 看；be good at 善于
	不友好的（对待）	smile at/laugh at 嘲笑；come at 袭击
away	离开，去掉	get away 逃脱；break away 脱离
	消失，终止	pass away 停止，死亡；wear away 损耗，减弱
	在远方	far away 遥远
by	按照	abide by 遵守；go by 遵守
	从……旁边	get by 通过，度过；stand by 站在一旁，袖手旁观
down	向下	hand down 代代相传，传下去；break down 毁坏
	倒	lie down 躺下；pull down 推倒
	减少，减弱	turn down 调小；let down 减速，放低
in	带入，进入（地点，状态等）	engage in 从事，忙于；involve in 卷入
	在……方面	differ in 在……方面不同
of	关于，对于	approve of 赞成；dispose of 处理，安排
	由……	consist of 由……组成；by means of 依靠，以……方式
off	离开，去除	pull off 脱去；set off 出发
	停止	go off 停电；call off 取消
	向外	give off 散发出；let off 释放出
on	在……之上	impose on 强加给
	处于（工作）状态，进行中，一直	carry on 继续；wait on 等待
	关于，涉及，用	live on 靠……为生；rely on 依靠，依赖
out	向外；发生（含有突然之意）	set out 出发；out of hand 失控；break out 爆发
	完，完全	wear out 耗尽；sell out 售完
	去掉	clear out 去除
over	超过	boil over 煮沸；get over 克服
	反复（含有大量之意）	think over 仔细思考；worry over 担心
	从一端到另一端；在……正上方	look over 从……上面看，目光看过……；run over 跑过
through	从头到尾（强调过程或艰难或轻松）	live through 经历，活过；glance through 浏览
	破	break through 突破；see through 看透，识破
to	朝，向，对	apply to 应用于；adjust to 适应于
	达到	amount to 合计，等于
with	与……，对……	connect with 与……相连；deal with 处理；popular with 受……欢迎

2. 明确要选择的介词或者副词的概念性含义，根据介词与副词的含义推测搭配的意思。如：区分 hang on 和 hang up。介词 on 意为"在……之上，一直"，表示一种静态，介词 up 表

示一种动态的"向上",这样,hang on 就可理解为"在……之上挂着,坚持(一直挂着)",hang up 就可理解为"把……挂起来"。考生在复习时,应尽量熟悉常用介词或副词的含义,注意在语境中把握易混淆的短语或搭配之间的不同含义。

3. 明确要与之搭配的主词的基本含义。如果被考查的搭配中的介词或副词相同,而主词不同(即空格后已给出与之搭配的介词或副词),就可根据主词所在句子的语境和该词本身的含义来推测搭配的意思。

三、篇章逻辑题

既然完形填空是从篇章的角度考查词汇,那么篇章逻辑类的题目就必不可少。近年来,六级完形填空中对于逻辑类题目的考查力度逐步加大,因此大家一定要对此类题型加以注意。

命题规律

1. 考查逻辑衔接,也就是句与句之间或者句子内部的逻辑关系。一般题目会要求考生根据上下文选择合适的逻辑连接词(包括连词和副词)。

例 4:

　　The symptoms of jetlag often persist for days __67__ the internal body clock slowly adjusts to the new time zone.

67. [A] while　　　　　　[B] whereas　　　　　　[C] if　　　　　　[D] although

> 本题选 A。句子的意思应该是:"当体内的时钟慢慢地适应新时区时,时差反应的症状常常持续好几天"。两个分句之间应当是主句和时间状语从句的关系,而非其他,所以只能选 while。

具体说来,完形填空中涉及到的逻辑关系主要有以下几种:

转折关系(but, however, though, whereas, nevertheless 等)

因果关系(so, therefore, thus, because, for, since, as 等)

顺序关系(before, after, first, second, in addition, then, next, finally 等)

让步关系(though, although, despite, in spite of 等)

条件关系(if, unless, once, provided that 等)

解释关系(that is to say, in another word, in other words 等)

并列关系(and, while 等)

2. 考查语境理解,即对上下文的理解。这类题目实质上是词义辨析和篇章逻辑的交叉题型,这一点前面已经说明。它要求考生根据上下文在四个选项中选择最合适的词语,而这四个选项的含义区别较大,不涉及近义词或者近形词的辨析问题。

例 5:

　　Data on a specific flight itinerary (旅行路线) and the individual's sleep pattern are used to produce a Trip Guide with __77__ on exactly when to be exposed to bright light.

77. [A] directories   [B] instructions   [C] specifications   [D] commentaries

> 本题选 B。instruction 意为"指令、指导",因为我们使用旅行指南的目的就是获得指导。而 directories(姓名住址簿),specifications(规格、说明书)和 commentaries(实况报道)均不符合题意。

📖 答题技巧

1. 掌握篇章主旨大意。篇章的主旨决定了所有的细节,换句话说,一切细节都是为主题服务的。这给考生答题,尤其是解答篇章逻辑题中的语境理解类题目,提供了很多依据。请看下面这个例子(中间的无关部分,用省略号代替):

例 6:

    Something else was needed to start the industrial process. That "something special" was men— __74__ individuals who could invent machines, find new means of power, and establish business organizations to reshape society. The men who __76__ the machines of the Industrial Revolution come from many backgrounds and many occupations. Many of them were __78__ inventors than scientists... Most of the people who __87__ the machines of the Industrial Revolution were inventors, not trained scientists.

74. [A] generating   [B] effective   [C] motivation   [D] creative

76. [A] employed   [B] created   [C] operated   [D] controlled

78. [A] less   [B] better   [C] more   [D] worse

87. [A] proposed   [B] developed   [C] supplied   [D] offered

> 这是一篇讲英国工业革命中人的重要性的文章中的一部分。第二句话中说到"人类是_____的个人,他们发明了机器"。74题的四个选项中只有 creative 有"有创造力的"之意,和后面的"发明"相对应,是正确答案。而后,人类"发明、创造"的概念贯穿全文,因此76题的答案是 created(发明),87题的答案是 developed(创造)。78题略有不同,因为这里并没有要求直接选择具有"发明、创造"之意的单词。然而空格后面的连词 than 意味着这里不是 less 就是 more,那么究竟是哪个呢?既然文章中心是"发明、创造",可见要说的是这些发明机器的人"与其说是科学家,不如说是发明家",所以78题选 more。

2. 把握篇章逻辑关系。通过把握篇章的逻辑关系,考生不仅可以准确掌握句与句之间的关系,正确解答篇章逻辑题中的逻辑衔接类题目,而且可以迅速地确定文章的中心思想和基本结构,从而准确理解上下文语义,提高答题速度和质量。还以那篇英国工业革命中人的重要性的文章为例:

例 7:

    A land free from destruction, plus wealth, natural resources, and labor supply — all these were important factors in helping England to become the center for the Industrial Revolution. __72__ they were not enough. Something else was needed to start the industrial process. That "something special" was men ... Many of them were more inventors than scientists.

72. [A] But   [B] And   [C] Besides   [D] Even

> 这是一道典型的篇章逻辑题，考查逻辑衔接。由于前文说了英国成为工业革命的中心有很多因素，空格后面又说它们并不够，可见两者是转折关系，故答案是 A。
>
> 此外，这部分的最后一句话说这些人与其说是科学家，不如说是发明家。由此我们可以判断下文一定是讲科学家和发明家的区别：科学家重理论，发明家重实际。顺着此思路做题，准确率会很高。

3. 寻找词汇同现和词汇复现线索。**词汇同现**就是指有着某种关系的单词同时出现在同一语篇中。它可以分为场景同现、修饰同现、因果同现和反义同现。**场景同现**指同一场景下的相关单词同时出现，例如在 university 这个场景下，professor 和 student 这两个单词就会同时出现。**修饰同现**是指具有修饰关系的两个或者多个单词同时出现，例如提到 high-way，那么 smooth，fast，straight 等修饰性的词语就很有可能出现。**因果同现**指原因和由此导致的结果同时出现在篇章中，例如前文若说了杰克早上 got up late，那么后面出现的结果就极有可能是 late for school，而不会是 early。**反义同现**指意义相反的两个单词同时出现在语篇中，例如前文说杰克很 lazy，接着说大卫和他不同，再下面要填一个形容词形容大卫，就应该是 lazy 的反义词 hard-working 了。所谓**词汇复现**就是指以某个词为中心，这个单词的原词，或者它的近义词、指代词、衍生词和上下义词（上义词指某单词的上一级概念性单词，下义词则指其下一级概念性单词，例如 animal 就是 tiger, lion, monkey 等的上义词，而 tiger, lion, monkey 则是 animal 的下义词）反复出现在同一语篇中。

由于语篇本身的逻辑性，在同一语篇中各种相关词汇必会同时出现或反复出现，而利用这一特点，通过在上下文中寻找词汇的同、复现信息来做题，可以帮助大家迅速解答语境理解类的篇章逻辑题。

例 8：

    Wise buying is a positive way in which you can make your money go further. The way you go about purchasing an article or a service can actually __68__ your money or can add to the cost.

68. [A] save   [B] preserve   [C] raise   [D] retain

> 通过空格后的 or 我们可以判断空格内的单词和 add to the cost 是对比关系，所以答案是 save。save money 正好和 add to the cost 构成强对比关系。这里是典型的词汇反义同现。

例 9：

    Before you buy a new __82__, talk to someone who owns one. If you can, use it or borrow it to check if it suits your particular purpose. Before you buy an expensive __84__, or a service, do check the price and what is on offer. If possible, choose from three items or three estimates.

82. [A] appliance   [B] machinery   [C] utility   [D] facility

84. [A] component   [B] element   [C] item   [D] particle

> 82 题选 A，appliance 是这段话倒数第四个单词 item 的近义词，这是近义词复现；84 题选 item，属于原词复现。

来看一个长一点的段落：

例 10：

A successful time zone shift depends on knowing the exact times to either __73__ or avoid bright light. Exposure to light at the wrong time can actually make jetlag worse. The proper schedule for light exposure depends a great deal on __75__ travel plans. Data on a specific flight itinerary（旅行路线）and the individual's sleep pattern are used to produce a Trip Guide with __77__ on exactly when to be exposed to bright light.

73. [A] attain   [B] shed   [C] retrieve   [D] seek

75. [A] unique   [B] specific   [C] complicated   [D] peculiar

77. [A] directories   [B] instructions   [C] specifications   [D] commentaries

> 这个段落讲如何避免时差反应。第一句话说："要想有效地避免时差反应，就要知道什么时候应该避免接触强光，什么时候可以_____强光。"73 题空格后面有个 or avoid，可见该空格和后面的这个 avoid 是对比关系，所以选择 retrieve（再次获得），这是典型的反义同现。75 题选 specific，根据是后一句话中的 specific flight itinerary，有了具体的旅行路线，当然就会有具体的旅行计划，所以是 specific travel plans，这里是原词复现。77 题所在句子的意思是："……旅行指南里面有关于何时可以接触强光的_____。"旅行指南里面有的当然是"指导"一类的东西了，所以 77 题选 instructions，这里面运用的是词汇的场景同现技巧。

四、语法结构题

完形填空的考查重点是词汇和篇章，对语法结构题的考查已经越来越少，因此这里仅对其加以简单介绍。

命题规律

1. 对限定词如冠词、物主代词和指示代词的考查。

2. 对定语从句关系代词和关系副词的考查。

3. 对区分各类从句连接词的能力的考查。

4. 对特殊句型如强调句、倒装句等的考查。

5. 对虚拟语气的考查。

答题技巧

1. 认真判断代词在上下文中的指代关系，注意是指人，还是指物，以及单复数的问题。

2. 认真判断从句的类型，是名词性从句、定语从句还是状语从句。

3. 熟悉特殊的句子结构，如强调句 It is...that...。

4. 熟悉各种类型的虚拟语气。

关于以上提到的各类常考语法现象，我们将会在本书的其他章节中陆续讲到，并进行相关总结。

第三节 模拟练习

Directions: *There are 20 blanks in each of the following passages. For each blank there are four choices marked [A], [B], [C] and [D] on the right side of the paper. You should choose the ONE that best fits into the passage. Then mark the corresponding letter on the Answer Sheet 2 with a single line through the center.*

Passage 1

The census of 1851 recorded half of the population of Britain as living in towns—the first society in human history to do so. Over the __1__ 70 years, the population of Britain had risen at an unprecedented __2__, passing the levels reached in earlier period of __3__ when the population had been decimated by epidemics such as the Black Death in the early 14th century.

But was there any reason for __4__? The towns offered a better chance of work and __5__ wages than the countryside, __6__ many families were trapped in dire poverty and seasonal unemployment. On the other hand, the countryside was __7__. A baby born in a large town with a population of more than 100,000 in the 1820s might __8__ to live to 35; in the 1830s, life expectancy was down to __9__ 29. A comparison between a desperately unhealthy large town and a small market town __10__ the costs of migrating in search of work and prosperity. In 1851, a boy born in inner Liverpool had a life expectancy of only 26 years, __11__ with a boy born in the small market town of Okehampton __12__ could expect to live to 57.

Large towns were __13__ desperately unhealthy, with levels of death __14__ a level not seen since the Black Death. New epidemics were __15__ the cities: cholera and typhoid were __16__ by polluted water; typhus was spread by lice; and "summer diarrhoea" was caused by __17__ of flies feeding on horse manure and human __18__. The problem was easy to __19__ and difficult to solve: too little was invested in the urban environment, __20__ sewers, street paving and cleansing, and in pure water and decent housing.

1. [A] early   [B] former   [C] previous   [D] precedented

2. [A] pace   [B] rate   [C] velocity   [D] stride

3. [A] growth   [B] advance   [C] rise   [D] improvement

4. [A] optimism   [B] pessimism   [C] indifference   [D] enthusiasm

5. [A] higher   [B] more   [C] greater   [D] less

6. [A] which   [B] there   [C] where   [D] when

7. [A] better   [B] healthier   [C] cleaner   [D] quieter

8. [A] suppose   [B] assume   [C] postulate   [D] expect

9. [A] tolerable   [B] miserable   [C] understandable   [D] accessible

10. [A] demonstrates   [B] exhibits   [C] presents   [D] shows

11. [A] comparing   [B] comparison   [C] compared   [D] compare

12. [A] who   [B] where   [C] which   [D] that

13. [A] however   [B] therefore   [C] nevertheless   [D] notwithstanding

14. [A] at   [B] in   [C] to   [D] with

15. [A] stroking   [B] stalking   [C] staking   [D] staining

16. [A] motivated   [B] carried   [C] promoted   [D] generated

17. [A] schools   [B] teams   [C] swarms   [D] herds

18. [A] waste   [B] dust   [C] rubbish   [D] disposal

19. [A] distinguish   [B] find   [C] identify   [D] manipulate

20. [A] on   [B] at   [C] in   [D] to

Passage 2

The Mesolithic, or Middle Stone Age, can seem a very remote and "mysterious" time. It started in about 10,000 B.C., as the last Ice Age ended. 1 northern Britain and everything north of this lying under vast ice 2 , with so much water 3 up in the ice 4 sea levels could be 50m (160ft) 5 those of today.

What we now know as Britain was part of the European landmass in the Mesolithic Age, and was 6 to France and Denmark. And the shallow fishing grounds in the North Sea that are now known as the Dogger Bank were then a huge island.

But as the ice melted and retreated northwards, the seas 7 , just as they are doing today, and the newly shaped lands became covered first in arctic tundra and then in 8 mixed forests. Animals returned to graze, and with the animals came people.

The people that returned to these newly 9 lands were not settled farmers, but were hunters and gatherers. It is thought that they must have been 10 on the move in order to survive, scarching for wild foods such as nuts and berries, and 11 wild animals for meat and skins. We 12 that since they were so 13 , they lived in temporary structures that were light, easily dismantled (拆除) and 14 .

Unfortunately, if this is the case, there are unlikely to be many physical 15 for archaeologists to find. So, even though there are a few 16 in Britain and Scandinavia where 17 of some sort have been found, all 18 can usually be 19 of a site where Mesolithic people lived is a scatter of finely worked and very 20 stone tools.

1. [A] Think   [B] Imagine   [C] Suppose   [D] Presume

2. [A] slices   [B] papers   [C] strips   [D] sheets

3. [A] locked   [B] covered   [C] blockaded   [D] stored

4. [A] that [B] so [C] then [D] and

5. [A] above [B] below [C] under [D] on

6. [A] related [B] combined [C] joined [D] unified

7. [A] arose [B] rose [C] raised [D] appeared

8. [A] dense [B] dark [C] thick [D] crowded

9. [A] approachable [B] formidable [C] habitable [D] inheritable

10. [A] contiguously [B] consistently [C] continually [D] constantly

11. [A] tracking [B] transiting [C] retracing [D] trading

12. [A] subsume [B] assume [C] resume [D] consume

13. [A] mobile [B] motivating [C] movable [D] locomotive

14. [A] available [B] portable [C] transferable [D] manipulable

15. [A] details [B] information [C] tracks [D] traces

16. [A] examples [B] cases [C] exceptions [D] irregularities

17. [A] dwellings [B] apartments [C] caves [D] villas

18. [A] which [B] that [C] those [D] what

19. [A] foresaw [B] predicted [C] expected [D] imagined

20. [A] distinct [B] distinctive [C] separate [D] individual

Passage 3

When Queen Victoria opened the Great Exhibition on 1st May 1851, her country was the world's leading industrial power, producing more than half its iron, coal and cotton cloth. The Crystal Palace itself was a triumph of pre-fabricated __1__ production in iron and glass. Its contents were __2__ to celebrate material progress and peaceful international competition. They ranged from massive steam hammers and locomotives to the __3__ artistry of the handicraft trades-not to mention a host of ingenious gadgets and ornaments of domestic clutter. All the world displayed its wares, but the __4__ were British.

This __5__ was both novel and brief. It was only half a century earlier __6__ Britain had wrested (夺取) European economic and political __7__ from France, at a time when Europe itself __8__ far behind Asia in manufacturing output. By 1901, __9__ , the world's industrial powerhouse was the USA, and Germany was challenging Britain __10__ second place. But no country, even then, was as __11__ as Britain in manufacturing: in 1901 under ten per cent of its labor __12__ worked in agriculture and over 75 per cent of its wheat was imported, __13__ from the USA and Russia. Food and industrial __14__ materials, __15__ from around the globe, were paid for by exports of manufactures and, __16__ , services such as shipping, insurance and banking and income from overseas investment. __17__ was any other country so __18__ : already in 1851 half the population inhabited a town or city; by 1901 three-quarters did so. Yet even in 1851 only a minority of workers was employed in "modern" industry (engineering, chemicals and factory—based textiles). They were __19__ concentrated into a few regions in the English north and Midlands, South Wales and the central belt of Scotland-where industrialization was __20__ by 1800.

1. [A] scale [B] mass [C] range [D] quantity

2. [A] intended   [B] tended   [C] aimed   [D] focused
3. [A] elegant   [B] exquisite   [C] special   [D] distinctive
4. [A] minority   [B] popularity   [C] prosperity   [D] majority
5. [A] dominance   [B] prominence   [C] existence   [D] evidence
6. [A] when   [B] which   [C] that   [D] since
7. [A] power   [B] authority   [C] priority   [D] leadership
8. [A] kept   [B] lagged   [C] remained   [D] upheld
9. [A] therefore   [B] however   [C] then   [D] so
10. [A] for   [B] with   [C] to   [D] on
11. [A] special   [B] specific   [C] specialized [D] professional
12. [A] vigor   [B] force   [C] strength   [D] might
13. [A] mostly   [B] roughly   [C] rarely   [D] essentially
14. [A] original   [B] crude   [C] coarse   [D] raw
15. [A] resourced   [B] sourced   [C] originated   [D] dated
16. [A] increasingly   [B] decreasingly [C] constantly   [D] frequently
17. [A] Or   [B] Nor   [C] Only   [D] Either
18. [A] rural   [B] urbanized   [C] modern   [D] suburbanized
19. [A] predominantly [B] heavily   [C] largely   [D] particularly
20. [A] evident   [B] distinguished [C] intricate   [D] projecting

Passage 4

African elephants have been slaughtered at alarming rate over the past decade, largely because they are the primary source of the world's ivory. Their population   1   been dwindled from 1.3 million in 1979 to just 625,000 today, and the rate of killing has been   2   in recent years because many of the older, bigger tusked animals have already been   3 . "The poachers (偷猎者) now must kill times   4   many elephants to get the same quantity of ivory," explained Curtis Bohlen, senior vice president of the World Wildlife Fund.

  5   its record on the environment has been spotty so far, the government last week took the   6   in a major conservation issue by   7   a ban on ivory imports into the US. The move came just four days after a consortium (联盟) of   8   groups, including the World Wildlife Fund and Wildlife Conservation International, called for that kind of   9 , and it made the US the first nation to   10   imports of both raw and   11   ivory. The ban, says Bohlen, sends a very clear   12   to the ivory poachers that the game is over.

In the past African nations have resisted an ivory ban, but   13   they realized that the decimation (大批杀害) of the elephant herds poses a   14   threat to their tourist business. Last month Tanzania and several other African countries called   15   an amendment to the 102 nation Convention on International Trade in Endangered Species   16   would make the ivory trade illegal worldwide. The amendment is expected to be   17   at an October meeting in Geneva and to go into effect next January. But   18   now and then, conservationists __19__ , poachers may go on a rampage, killing elephants __20__ , so nations should unilaterally (单方有义务地) forbid imports right away.

1. [A] have [B] has [C] had [D] having
2. [A] accelerating [B] decelerating [C]descending [D] ascending
3. [A] damaged [B] hurt [C] ruined [D] destroyed
4. [A] as [B] of [C] that [D] with
5. [A] But [B] While [C] Though [D] Since
6. [A] head [B] lead [C] first [D] advance
7. [A] forcing [B] imposing [C] making [D] publishing
8. [A] protect [B] security [C] preservation [D] conservation
9. [A] act [B] activity [C] action [D] behavior
10. [A] forbid [B] allow [C] exclude [D] frustrate
11. [A] assembled [B] finished [C] polished [D] processed
12. [A] information [B] sign [C] message [D] notice
13. [A] increasingly [B] surprisingly [C] recently [D] seemingly
14. [A] severe [B] sharp [C] serious [D] subtle
15. [A] on [B] in [C] at [D] for
16. [A] what [B] that [C] who [D] as
17. [A] appraised [B] adjusted [C] approved [D] altered
18. [A] from [B] in [C] at [D] between
19. [A] contrive [B] contemplate [C] contend [D] compromise
20. [A] greatly [B] internationally [C] wholesale [D] fast

Passage 5

When Kathie Gifford's face was splashed across the newspapers in 1996 after her lucrative line of Wal-Mart clothing was exposed as the work of underpaid laborers in New York City's Chinatown, the Department of Labor and the White House teamed up to condemn such __1__ . With much fanfare, President Clinton's administration __2__ the "No Sweat" campaign, which pressured retailers and manufacturers to __3__ to periodic independent inspection of their workplace conditions.

This campaign __4__ manufacturers to sign the Workplace Code of Conduct, a __5__ to self-regulate, that has since been __6__ by a handful of retailers and many of the nation's largest manufacturers, including Nike and L.L. Bean. __7__ , the Department of Defense, which has a $1 billion garment business that would make it the country's 14th largest retail apparel outlet, has not signed the Code of Conduct. __8__ , it has not agreed to demand __9__ its contractors submit to __10__ inspections.

__11__ the Department of Defense has not agreed to adhere __12__ the code, the job of stopping public sector sweatshops falls to the Department of Labor. Federal contractors that persist in __13__ wage laws or safety and health codes can lose their lucrative taxpayer __14__ contracts. But Suzanne Seiden, a deputy administrator at the Department of Labor, says that to her __15__ , the department has never __16__ that rule to government apparel manufacturers. "I just assume that they are __17__ to safety and health __18__ ," she says. According to records obtained by Mother Jones, through a Freedom of Information Act request, the Occupational Safety and Health Administration has __19__ Lion 32 times for safety and health __20__ in the past 12 years.

1. [A] things   [B] activities   [C] practices   [D] performances
2. [A] issued   [B] launched   [C] ordered   [D] stimulated
3. [A] observe   [B] subject   [C] agree   [D] submit
4. [A] needed   [B] urged   [C] motivated   [D] pushed
5. [A] promise   [B] file   [C] way   [D] rule
6. [A] adapted   [B] accustomed   [C] altered   [D] adopted
7. [A] Though   [B] However   [C] Thus   [D] Furthermore
8. [A] On the contrary   [B] On the other hand   [C] In addition   [D] At last
9. [A] what   [B] that   [C] which   [D] if
10. [A] temporary   [B] periodic   [C] permanent   [D] constant
11. [A] Because   [B] Since   [C] Although   [D] Even if
12. [A] with   [B] in   [C] to   [D] for
13. [A] damaging   [B] destroying   [C] ruining   [D] violating
14. [A] financed   [B] paid   [C] provided   [D] offered
15. [A] information   [B] knowledge   [C] mind   [D] message
16. [A] applied   [B] implemented   [C] used   [D] imposed
17. [A] ensuing   [B] alleviating   [C] heading   [D] sticking
18. [A] requests   [B] reconciliation   [C] recreation   [D] requirements
19. [A] cited   [B] illustrated   [C] mentioned   [D] referred
20. [A] speculation   [B] breakdowns   [C] violations   [D] deterioration

Passage 6

An important new industry, oil refining, grew after the Civil War. __1__ oil, or petroleum, a dark, thick ooze from the earth had been known for hundreds of years, __2__ little use had ever been made __3__ it. In the 1850s, Samuel M. Kier, a manufacturer in western Pennsylvania, began __4__ the oil and refining it into kerosene. Refining, __5__ smelting, is a __6__ of removing impurities from a raw material.

Kerosene was used to light lamps. It was a cheap __7__ for whale oil, which was becoming __8__ to get. Soon there was a large __9__ for kerosene. People began to search for new __10__ of petroleum.

The first oil well was drilled by E. L. Drake, a retired railroad conductor. In 1859 he began drilling in Titusville, Pennsylvania. The __11__ venture of drilling seemed so __12__ and foolish that onlookers called it "Drake's Folly". But __13__ he had drilled down about 70 feet (21 meters), Drake __14__ oil. His well began to __15__ 20 barrels of crude oil a day.

News of Drake's __16__ brought oil prospectors to the __17__ . By the early 1860's these wildcatters were drilling for "black gold" all over western Pennsylvania. The boom __18__ the California gold rush of

1848 in its excitement and Wild West atmosphere. And it brought far more wealth to the prospectors than any gold rush.

Petroleum could be refined into many products. For some years kerosene continued to be the __19__ one. It was sold in grocery stores and door-to-door. In the 1880's and 1890's refiners learned how to make other petroleum products such as waxes and lubricating oils. Petroleum was not __20__ used to make gasoline or heating oil.

1. [A] Raw   [B] Original   [C] Crude   [D] Coarse
2. [A] but   [B] because   [C] and   [D] if
3. [A] at   [B] in   [C] from   [D] of
4. [A] gathering   [B] collecting   [C] augmenting   [D] saturating
5. [A] like   [B] as   [C] or   [D] with
6. [A] procedure   [B] process   [C] proceeding   [D] progress
7. [A] replace   [B] supplement   [C] surplus   [D] substitute
8. [A] higher   [B] cheaper   [C] cleaner   [D] harder
9. [A] need   [B] demand   [C] request   [D] necessity
10. [A] supplies   [B] offers   [C] origins   [D] traces
11. [A] all   [B] complete   [C] whole   [D] total
12. [A] fantastic   [B] gorgeous   [C] empirical   [D] impractical
13. [A] when   [B] while   [C] before   [D] as
14. [A] touched   [B] obtained   [C] struck   [D] reached
15. [A] produce   [B] yield   [C] assemble   [D] provide
16. [A] failure   [B] advance   [C] venture   [D] success
17. [A] scene   [B] scenery   [C] sight   [D] view
18. [A] competed   [B] rivaled   [C] encountered   [D] acquainted
19. [A] principle   [B] fundamental   [C] important   [D] principal
20. [A] meanwhile   [B] now   [C] then   [D] latter

Passage 7

Design of all the new tools and implements is based on careful experiments with electronic instruments. First, a human "guinea pig" is tested using a __1__ tool. Measurements are taken __2__ the amount of work done, and the buildup of heat in the body. __3__ joints and stretched muscles cannot __4__ as well, it has been found, __5__ joints and muscles in their __6__ positions. The same person is then tested again, using a tool designed according to the suggestions made by Dr. Tichauer. All these tests have shown the great __7__ of the new designs over the old.

One of the electronic instruments used by Dr. Tichauer, the myograph (肌动描记器), __8__ visible through electrical signals the work done by human muscle. Another machine __9__ any dangerous features of tools, thus proving information upon __10__ to base a new design. One __11__ of tests made with this machine is that a tripod stepladder is more __12__ and safer to use than one with four legs.

This work has 13 the attention of efficiency experts and time-and-motion-study engineer, but its value goes far 14 that. Dr. Tichauer's first 15 is for the health of the tool user. With the 16 use of the same tool all day long on 17 lines and in other jobs, even light 18 work can put a heavy stress on one small area of the body. In time, such stress can cause a disabling disease. 19 , muscle fatigue is a serious safety 20 .

1. [A] regular　　　　[B] usual　　　　　[C] common　　　　　[D] constant
2. [A] in　　　　　　 [B] with　　　　　　[C] by　　　　　　　[D] of
3. [A] Distracted　　　[B] Twisted　　　　[C] Exaggerated　　　[D] Tilted
4. [A] act　　　　　　[B] demonstrate　　 [C] behave　　　　　[D] perform
5. [A] as　　　　　　 [B] for　　　　　　 [C] than　　　　　　[D] that
6. [A] average　　　　[B] normal　　　　　[C] standard　　　　 [D] routine
7. [A] increase　　　　[B] rise　　　　　　[C] improvement　　 [D] inclination
8. [A] causes　　　　　[B] makes　　　　　[C] results　　　　　[D] imposes
9. [A] evaluates　　　　[B] estimates　　　 [C] measures　　　　[D] counts
10. [A] which　　　　　[B] that　　　　　 [C] what　　　　　　[D] it
11. [A] inference　　　　[B] conclusion　　 [C] summary　　　　 [D] investigation
12. [A] firm　　　　　　[B] solid　　　　　[C] steady　　　　　[D] stable
13. [A] absorbed　　　　[B] acquired　　　 [C] attracted　　　　[D] assimilated
14. [A] over　　　　　　[B] above　　　　 [C] out　　　　　　　[D] beyond
15. [A] focus　　　　　 [B] view　　　　　 [C] perspective　　　[D] thought
16. [A] repeated　　　　[B] repeating　　　[C] repeat　　　　　[D] repetition
17. [A] product　　　　 [B] production　　　[C] progress　　　　[D] proceeding
18. [A] hand　　　　　　[B] labor　　　　　[C] manual　　　　　[D] mind
19. [A] However　　　　[B] Lastly　　　　　[C] Beside　　　　　[D] Furthermore
20. [A] hazard　　　　　[B] factor　　　　　[C] effect　　　　　[D] occasion

Passage 8

More and more, the operations of our businesses, governments, and financial institutions are controlled by information that exists only inside computer memories. 1 clever enough to modify this information for his own purposes can 2 big reward. Even worse, a number of people who have done this and been caught 3 it have managed to get away without punishment.

It's easy for computer crimes to go 4 if no one checks up on what the computer is doing. But even if the crime is detected, the criminal may walk 5 not only unpunished but with a 6 recommendation from his 7 employers.

Of course, we have no statistics on crimes that go undetected. But it's 8 to note how many of the crimes we do know about were detected by 9 , not by systematic inspections or other security 10 . The computer criminals who have been caught may have been the victims of 11 bad luck.

12 other lawbreakers, who must leave the country, 13 suicide, or go to jail, computer criminals

sometimes __14__ punishment, demanding not only that they not be charged but that they be given good recommendations and perhaps other benefits. All too __15__, their demands have been met.

Why? Because company executives are afraid of the bad publicity that would result if the public found out that their computer had been misused. They __16__ at the thought of a criminal __17__ in open court of how he juggled (诈骗) the most confidential __18__ right under the noses of the company's executives, accountants, and security __19__. And so another computer criminal __20__ with just the recommendations he needs to continue his crimes elsewhere.

1. [A] Everyone [B] Someone [C] Anyone [D] No one
2. [A] acclaim [B] reap [C] reach [D] reclaim
3. [A] at [B] with [C] of [D] by
4. [A] unfound [B] undetected [C] discharged [D] underestimated
5. [A] aside [B] out [C] on [D] away
6. [A] redundant [B] glowing [C] terrible [D] formidable
7. [A] preceding [B] prior [C] former [D] proceeding
8. [A] annoyed [B] deliberate [C] persistent [D] disturbing
9. [A] accident [B] incident [C] coincidence [D] case
10. [A] procedures [B] process [C] progress [D] precedence
11. [A] unluckily [B] uncommonly [C] recklessly [D] subjectively
12. [A] Like [B] Despite [C] Unlike [D] Though
13. [A] commit [B] do [C] make [D] carry
14. [A] avoid [B] violate [C] escort [D] escape
15. [A] usual [B] often [C] much [D] rarely
16. [A] contemplate [B] manifest [C] hesitate [D] contrive
17. [A] elaborating [B] simulating [C] proposing [D] boasting
18. [A] records [B] figures [C] deficits [D] matters
19. [A] stuff [B] facility [C] staff [D] faculty
20. [A] separates [B] divides [C] cuts [D] departs

Passage 9

Statuses are marvelous human inventions that enable us to get along with one another and to determine where we "fit" in society. In our everyday lives, we mentally __1__ to place people in terms __2__ their statuses. For example, we must __3__ whether the person in the library is a reader or a librarian, whether the telephone caller is a friend or a salesman, whether the unfamiliar person on our __4__ is a thief or a meter __5__, and so on. The statuses we __6__ often vary with the people we encounter, and change __7__ life. Most of us can, at very high speed, assume the statuses that __8__ situations require. Much of social __9__ consists of identifying and electing among __10__ statuses and allowing other people to assume their statuses in __11__ to us. This means that we __12__ our actions to those of other people based on a __13__ mental process of __14__ and interpretation. Although some of us find the task more difficult than others, most of us perform it rather __15__ . A status has been compared to __16__ made clothes. Within certain limits the buyer can choose style and fabric. But an American is not free to choose the costume of a Chinese peasant or that of a Hindu prince. We must choose from among the clothing __17__ by our society. Furthermore, our choice is limited to a size that will fit, as well as by our pocketbook. Having made a choice within these limits, we can have certain __18__ made, but apart from __19__ adjustments, we tend to be limited to __20__ the stores have on their racks. Statuses too come ready made, and the range of choice among them is limited.

1. [A] aim   [B] attempt   [C] ascribe   [D] ascertain
2. [A] of   [B] with   [C] at   [D] in
3. [A] prove   [B] depict   [C] judge   [D] exemplify
4. [A] property   [B] owning   [C] possession   [D] estate
5. [A] measurer   [B] counter   [C] evaluator   [D] reader
6. [A] assert   [B] propose   [C] discern   [D] assume
7. [A] throughout   [B] over   [C] on   [D] across
8. [A] similar   [B] various   [C] unanimous   [D] certain
9. [A] confrontation [B] encounter   [C] contradiction [D] interaction
10. [A] particular   [B] adequate   [C] appropriate   [D] authentic
11. [A] relation   [B] relevance   [C] reconciliation [D] reliance
12. [A] take   [B] put   [C] impose   [D] fit
13. [A] continual   [B] constant   [C] consistent   [D] consecutive
14. [A] appraisal   [B] praise   [C] evaluation   [D] measure
15. [A] hard   [B] effortlessly   [C] badly   [D] intricately
16. [A] previously   [B] completely   [C] totally   [D] ready
17. [A] presented   [B] illustrated   [C] demonstrated   [D] fabricated
18. [A] variations   [B] changes   [C] alterations   [D] adaptations
19. [A] major   [B] minor   [C] tiny   [D] big
20. [A] which   [B] that   [C] what   [D] whom

Passage 10

Prices determine how resources are to be used. They are also the __1__ by which products and services that are in limited __2__ are rationed among buyers. The price __3__ of the United States is a __4__ network composed of the prices of all the products bought and sold in the economy as well as __5__ of a myriad of services, including labor, professional, transportation, and public __6__ services. The interrelationships of all these prices make up the "system" of prices.

If one were to ask a group of __7__ selected individuals to define "price", many would reply that price is an amount of money paid by the buyer to the seller of a product or service or, __8__ , that price is the money value of a product or service as agreed __9__ in a market transaction. This definition is, of course, __10__ as far as it goes. For a complete understanding of a price in any __11__ transaction, much more than the amount of money __12__ must be known. Both the buyer and the seller should be familiar with not only the money amount, but with the amount and quality of the product or service to be __13__, the time and place at which the exchange will take place and __14__ will be made, the form of money to be used, the credit terms and discounts that __15__ to the transaction, guarantees on the product or service, delivery terms, return privileges, and other __16__. In another word, both buyer and seller should be __17__ aware of all the factors that __18__ the total "package" being exchanged __19__ the asked—for amount of money in order that they may __20__ a given price.

1. [A] methods   [B] ways   [C] means   [D] forms
2. [A] store   [B] stock   [C] supply   [D] provision
3. [A] system   [B] construction [C] structure   [D] strategy
4. [A] clear   [B] complex   [C] crucial   [D] cumulative
5. [A] those   [B] that   [C] what   [D] which
6. [A] facility   [B] utility   [C] use   [D] utensil
7. [A] freely   [B] voluntarily   [C] readily   [D] randomly
8. [A] on the contrary [B] in other words [C] on the other hand [D] in conclusion
9. [A] upon   [B] with   [C] to   [D] at
10. [A] void   [B] valid   [C] available   [D] vain
11. [A] special   [B] specific   [C] particular   [D] productive
12. [A] mentioned   [B] related   [C] concerned   [D] involved
13. [A] transported   [B] communicated [C] replaced   [D] exchanged
14. [A] payment   [B] cost   [C] fee   [D] fare
15. [A] apply   [B] implement   [C] suit   [D] endow
16. [A] things   [B] factors   [C] elements   [D] matters
17. [A] fully   [B] completely   [C] fundamentally [D] essentially
18. [A] compose   [B] consist   [C] construct   [D] comprise
19. [A] with   [B] for   [C] to   [D] on
20. [A] evaluate   [B] measure   [C] count   [D] value

Passage 11

If by "suburb" is meant an urban margin that grows more rapidly than its already developed interior, the process of suburbanization began during the emergence of the industrial city in the second quarter of the nineteenth century. Before that period the city was a small __1__ compact cluster in which people moved __2__ on foot and goods were __3__ by horse and cart. But the early factories built in the 1840's were located along waterways and near railheads at the __4__ of cities, and housing was needed for the thousands of people __5__ by the prospect of employment. __6__, the factories were surrounded by prolifer-ating mill towns of apartments and row houses that abutted the older, main cities. As a __7__ against this encroachment (侵犯) and to __8__ their tax bases, the cities appropriated their industrial neighbors. In 1854, for example, the city of Philadelphia annexed most of Philadelphia County. Similar __9__ maneuvers (策略) took place in Chicago and in New York. Indeed, most great cities of the United States __10__ such status only by incorporating the __11__ along their borders.

With the __12__ of industrial growth came acute urban crowding and accompanying social stress-conditions that began to __13__ disastrous proportions when, in 1888, the first commercially successful electric traction line was __14__. Within a few years the horse-drawn trolleys were retired and electric streetcar networks crisscrossed and __15__ every major urban area, fostering a wave of suburbanization that __16__ the compact industrial city into a __17__ metropolis. This first __18__ of mass-scale suburbanization was reinforced by the __19__ emergence of the urban Middle Class, whose desires __20__ homeownership in neighborhoods far from the aging inner city were satisfied by the developers of single-family housing tracts.

1. [A] very   [B] increasingly   [C] highly   [D] quite
2. [A] on   [B] about   [C] forward   [D] away
3. [A] transmitted   [B] conveyed   [C] carried   [D] transacted
4. [A] edges   [B] boundaries   [C] margins   [D] lines
5. [A] pulled   [B] drawn   [C] distracted   [D] indulged
6. [A] In time   [B] On time   [C] At time   [D] For time
7. [A] discrimination [B] protest   [C] denounce   [D] defense
8. [A] stretch   [B] enlarge   [C] lengthen   [D] enhance
9. [A] metropolitan [B] urban   [C] suburban   [D] municipal
10. [A] achieved   [B] acquired   [C] arrived   [D] availed
11. [A] neighborhoods [B] places   [C] locations   [D] communities
12. [A] speed   [B] improvements   [C] acceleration   [D] increase
13. [A] facilitated   [B] approached   [C] rectified   [D] subscribed
14. [A] discovered   [B] created   [C] developed   [D] designed
15. [A] related   [B] connected   [C] separated   [D] divided
16. [A] transformed   [B] shifted   [C] switched   [D] altered
17. [A] crowded   [B] dispersed   [C] widespread   [D] compact
18. [A] procedure   [B] step   [C] phase   [D] process
19. [A] similar   [B] same   [C] simultaneous   [D] simulated
20. [A] about   [B] for   [C] of   [D] on

Passage 12

Although Henry Ford's name is closely associated with the concept of mass production, he should receive equal credit for introducing labor practices as early as 1913 that would be considered __1__ even by today's standards. Safety __2__ were improved, and the work day was __3__ to eight hours, compared with the ten-or-twelve-hour day common at the time. In order to accommodate the shorter work day, the __4__ factory was converted from two to three __5__.

__6__, sick leaves as well as improved medical care for those injured __7__ the job were instituted. The

Ford Motor Company was one of the first factories to develop a __8__ school to train specialized skilled laborers and an English language school for immigrants. Some __9__ were even made to hire the handicapped and provide jobs for former convicts.

The most __10__ acclaimed innovation was the five-dollar-a-day minimum wage that was __11__ in order to recruit and __12__ the best mechanics and to __13__ the growth of labor unions. Ford explained the new wage policy in __14__ of efficiency and profit sharing. He also mentioned the fact that his employees would be able to purchase the automobiles that they produced—in effect __15__ a market for the product. In order to qualify for the minimum wage, an employee had to establish a decent home and __16__ good personal habits, including sobriety, thriftiness, industriousness, and dependability. __17__ some criticism was directed at Ford for involving himself too much in the __18__ lives of his employees, there can be no doubt that, at a time when immigrants were being taken __19__ of in frightful ways, Henry Ford was helping many people to __20__ themselves in America.

1. [A] advanced   [B] appropriate   [C] accessible   [D] acute
2. [A] methods   [B] ways   [C] means   [D] measures
3. [A] decreased   [B] reduced   [C] declined   [D] dropped
4. [A] complete   [B] all   [C] entire   [D] total
5. [A] shifts   [B] switches   [C] sections   [D] classes
6. [A] However   [B] On the contrary   [C] In addition   [D] In summary
7. [A] at   [B] on   [C] in   [D] for
8. [A] professional   [B] practical   [C] technological   [D] technical
9. [A] effects   [B] trials   [C] steps   [D] strength
10. [A] greatly   [B] widely   [C] unanimously   [D] generally
11. [A] provided   [B] assured   [C] offered   [D] sponsored
12. [A] maintain   [B] sustain   [C] retain   [D] attain
13. [A] discourage   [B] hold   [C] prohibit   [D] stimulate
14. [A] virtue   [B] aspects   [C] relations   [D] terms
15. [A] inventing   [B] creating   [C] producing   [D] yielding
16. [A] exemplify   [B] demonstrate   [C] improve   [D] verify
17. [A] However   [B] Since   [C] Then   [D] Although
18. [A] individual   [B] routine   [C] usual   [D] personal
19. [A] advantage   [B] use   [C] profit   [D] interest
20. [A] distinguish   [B] identify   [C] establish   [D] settle

Passage 13

The increase in international business and in foreign investment has created a need for executives with knowledge of foreign languages and skills in cross-cultural communication. Americans, __1__, have not been well trained in either area and, consequently, have not enjoyed the same level of __2__ in negotiation in an international arena as have their foreign __3__.

Negotiating is the 4 of communicating back and 5 for the purpose of reaching an agreement. It 6 persuasion and compromise, but in order to 7 in either one, the negotiators must understand the ways in 8 people are persuaded and how compromise is 9 within the culture of the negotiation.

In many international business negotiations abroad, Americans are perceived as 10 and impersonal. It often appears to the foreign negotiator that the American represents a large multi-million-dollar corporation that can afford to pay the price without 11 further. The American negotiator's role becomes 12 of an impersonal purveyor (传播者) of information and cash.

In 13 of American negotiators abroad, several traits have been identified that may serve to 14 this stereotypical 15 , while undermining the negotiator's position. Two traits in 16 that cause cross-cultural misunderstanding are directness and impatience 17 the part of the American negotiator. Furthermore, American negotiators often insist on realizing short-term goals. Foreign negotiators, on the other hand, may value the relationship established between negotiators and may be 18 to invest time in it for long-term benefits. In order to 19 the relationship, they may opt for 20 interactions without regard for the time involved in getting to know the other negotiator.

1. [A] however   [B] nevertheless   [C] furthermore   [D] therefore
2. [A] fulfillment   [B] success   [C] master   [D] privilege
3. [A] enemies   [B] counterparts   [C] cooperators   [D] entrepreneurs
4. [A] procedure   [B] progress   [C] process   [D] proceeding
5. [A] forward   [B] forth   [C] before   [D] towards
6. [A] includes   [B] concludes   [C] concerns   [D] involves
7. [A] participate   [B] take part   [C] attend   [D] blend
8. [A] that   [B] what   [C] which   [D] case
9. [A] arrived   [B] gained   [C] facilitated   [D] reached
10. [A] wealthy   [B] sensitive   [C] poor   [D] rude
11. [A] claiming   [B] communicating   [C] exchanging   [D] bargaining
12. [A] what   [B] that   [C] it   [D] those
13. [A] studies   [B] discussions   [C] investigations   [D] seminars
14. [A] assure   [B] secure   [C] guarantee   [D] confirm
15. [A] concept   [B] perception   [C] realization   [D] feeling
16. [A] special   [B] particular   [C] essential   [D] private
17. [A] on   [B] in   [C] at   [D] with
18. [A] disgusted   [B] willing   [C] likely   [D] easy
19. [A] strengthen   [B] proceed   [C] tighten   [D] solidify
20. [A] direct   [B] indirect   [C] effective   [D] efficient

Passage 14

During the 18th century, more and more families in Britain came to earn a living from industrial work rather than from agricultural work. And this trend 1 in the 19th century, although work providing services rather than in making goods rose to __2__. At the same time, the country's population increased more rapidly than __3__ before, a marked upturn in the rate of growth __4__ from the late 1700s. As a result, a far greater number of people were __5__ in making manufactured goods in early Victorian times than had been the __6__ in early Georgian times.

The __7__ of population growth from the late 18th century caused a great deal of interest at the time and brought no little __8__. Thus the gloomy Thomas Malthus __9__ that, unless checked, such rapid population growth would outstrip food supplies, leading to starvation. __10__ the event this did not happen, but __11__ about population growth led to the first national census of Britain's population taking place in 1801. Since then, censuses have been taken every ten years, except during 1941 when wartime __12__ occurred. The early censuses give some information on __13__ and hence on how people earned a living. But it is only from 1841 __14__ detail of the occupations of __15__ rather than of groups of people is given. This __16__ change arose because, for the first time, households were __17__ with forms (or schedules) on which they were __18__ required to record details of everyone who stayed in the household on census night. In 1851, the schedules required __19__ information, including occupations. This information was usually __20__ by local people.

1. [A] continued [B] declined [C] maintained [D] upheld
2. [A] excellence [B] existence [C] prominence [D] power
3. [A] ever [B] even [C] still [D] yet
4. [A] existing [B] occurring [C] precipitating [D] dating
5. [A] included [B] absorbed [C] indulged [D] involved
6. [A] affair [B] case [C] incident [D] event
7. [A] pace [B] rapidity [C] deterioration [D] increase
8. [A] chaos [B] hit [C] sympathy [D] anxiety
9. [A] predicted [B] supposed [C] anticipated [D] foretold
10. [A] In [B] On [C] With [D] Under
11. [A] passion [B] concern [C] care [D] grief
12. [A] interruption [B] eruption [C] rupture [D] disruption
13. [A] qualifications [B] occupations [C] accomplishments [D] conditions
14. [A] that [B] when [C] which [D] where
15. [A] people [B] everyone [C] individuals [D] households
16. [A] fundamental [B] necessary [C] essential [D] crucial
17. [A] issued [B] exemplified [C] attributed [D] subscribed
18. [A] legally [B] morally [C] legislatively [D] compulsorily
19. [A] longer [B] better [C] fuller [D] broader
20. [A] assembled [B] accumulated [C] segregated [D] collected

Passage 15

The family is the center of most traditional Asians' lives. Many people worry about their families' welfare, reputation, and honor. Asian families are often __1__, including several generations related by __2__ or marriage living in the same home. An Asian person's misdeeds are not __3__ just on the individual but also on the family-including the dead ancestors.

Traditional Chinese, among many other Asians, respect their elders and feel a deep sense of duty __4__ them. Children repay their parents' __5__ by being successful and supporting them in old age. This is accepted as a __6__ part of life in China. __7__, taking care of the aged parents is often viewed as a tremendous __8__ in the United States, where aging and family support are not __9__ highly. __10__, in the youth-oriented United States, growing old is seen as a bad thing, and many old people do not __11__ respect.

Filipinos, the most Americanized of the Asians, are still extremely family-oriented. They are __12__ to helping their children and will sacrifice greatly for their children to get an education. In turn, the children are __13__ to their parents, who often live nearby. Grown children who leave the country for economic reasons __14__ send large parts of their income home to their parents.

The Vietnamese family __15__ people currently alive as well as the spirits of the dead and of the as-yet unborn. Any __16__ or actions are done from family considerations, not __17__ desires. People's behavior is fudged on whether it brings shame or pride to the family. The Vietnamese do not __18__ believe in self-reliance; in this way, they are the __19__ of people in the United States. Many Vietnamese think that their actions in this life will influence their __20__ in the next life.

1. [A] enlarged   [B] extended   [C] expanded   [D] lengthened
2. [A] history   [B] interaction   [C] blood   [D] bond
3. [A] accused   [B] convicted   [C] charged   [D] blamed
4. [A] toward   [B] for   [C] of   [D] on
5. [A] contributions   [B] sufferings   [C] sacrifices   [D] tributes
6. [A] formal   [B] natural   [C] regular   [D] peculiar
7. [A] In comparison   [B] To the same extent   [C] In a way   [D] In contrast
8. [A] relief   [B] responsibility   [C] burden   [D] business
9. [A] rewarded   [B] honored   [C] regarded   [D] complimented
10. [A] In fact   [B] Of course   [C] And yet   [D] As a result
11. [A] accept   [B] receive   [C] deserve   [D] gain
12. [A] confined   [B] dedicated   [C] corresponded   [D] exposed
13. [A] devoted   [B] contributed   [C] indulged   [D] observed
14. [A] occasionally   [B] intentionally   [C] typically   [D] steadily
15. [A] insists on   [B] consists of   [C] persists in   [D] resists to
16. [A] incidences   [B] decisions   [C] accidents   [D] expedition
17. [A] personal   [B] private   [C] individual   [D] own
18. [A] particularly   [B] naturally   [C] especially   [D] mentally
19. [A] counterpart   [B] opposite   [C] competitor   [D] opponent
20. [A] station   [B] status   [C] stature   [D] state

Passage 16

We all know that a magician does not really depend on "magic" to perform his tricks, but on his ability to act at great speed. __1__, this does not prevent us from enjoying watching a magician __2__ rabbits from a hat. __3__ the greatest magician of all time was Harry Houdini who died in 1926. Houdini mastered the art of __4__. He could free himself from the tightest knots or the most __5__ locks in seconds. Although no one really knows how he did this, there is no doubt __6__ he had made a close study of every type of lock ever __7__. He liked to carry a small steel needle like tool strapped to his leg and he used this in place of a key. Houdini once asked the Chicago police to lock him in prison. They __8__ him in chains and locked him up, but he freed himself __9__ an instant. The police __10__ him of having used a tool and locked him up again. This time he wore no clothes and there were chains round his neck, waist, wrists, and legs; but he again escaped in a few minutes. Houdini had probably hidden his "needle" in a wax-like __11__ and dropped it on the floor in the __12__. He stepped on it so that it __13__ to the bottom of his foot __14__ he went past. His most famous escape, however, was __15__ astonishing. He was heavily chained up and __16__ in an empty wooden chest, the lid of __17__ was nailed down. The chest was __18__ into the sea in New York harbor. In one minute Houdini had swum to the __19__. When the chest was __20__, it was opened and the chains were found inside.

1. [A] Generally   [B] However   [C] Possibly   [D] Likewise

2. [A] produce   [B] get   [C] turn   [D] acquire

3. [A] Out of the question   [B] Though   [C] Probably   [D] Undoubted

4. [A] escaping   [B] locking   [C] opening   [D] dropping

5. [A] complicated   [B] complex   [C] difficult   [D] deliberate

6. [A] if   [B] whether   [C] as to   [D] that

7. [A] created   [B] invented   [C] developed   [D] imagined

8. [A] involved   [B] closed   [C] connected   [D] bound

9. [A] at   [B] by   [C] in   [D] for

10. [A] rid   [B] charged   [C] accused   [D] deprived

11. [A] candle   [B] object   [C] material   [D] substance

12. [A] process   [B] isle   [C] passage   [D] room

13. [A] stuck   [B] hold   [C] kept   [D] clang

14. [A] as   [B] usually   [C] maybe   [D] then

15. [A] overall   [B] all but   [C] no longer   [D] altogether

16. [A] included   [B] located   [C] circulated   [D] enclosed

17. [A] it   [B] which   [C] that   [D] him

18. [A] fallen   [B] dropped   [C] declined   [D] waned

19. [A] face   [B] surface   [C] cover   [D] horizon

20. [A] brought up   [B] brought out   [C] broken apart   [D] broken into

Passage 17

Reading involves looking at graphic symbols and formulating mentally the sounds and ideas they represent. Concepts of reading have changed __1__ over the centuries. during the 1950's and 1960's especially, increased attention has been __2__ to defining and describing the reading process. __3__ specialists agree that reading __4__ a complex organization of higher mental __5__, they disagree about the exact __6__ of the process. Some experts, who regard language primarily as a code using symbols to represent sounds, __7__ reading as simply the decoding of symbols into the sounds they stand __8__.

These authorities __9__ that meaning, being concerned with thinking, must be taught independently of the decoding process. Others maintain that reading is __10__ related to thinking, and that a child who pronounces sounds without __11__ their meaning is not __12__ reading. The reader, according to some, is not just a person with a __13__ ability to read but one who __14__ reads.

Many adults, although they have the ability to read, have never read a book in its entirety. By some expert they would not be __15__ as readers. Clearly, the philosophy, objectives, methods and materials of reading will depend on the definition one use. By the most __16__ and satisfactory definition, reading is the ability to __17__ the sound-symbols code of the language, to interpret meaning for various __18__, at various rates, and at various levels of difficulty, and to do __19__ widely and enthusiastically. __20__ reading is the interpretation of ideas through the use of symbols representing sounds and ideas.

1. [A] substantively   [B] substantially   [C] substitutively   [D] subjectively
2. [A] focused   [B] directed   [C] devoted   [D] aimed
3. [A] Although   [B] If   [C] Unless   [D] Until
4. [A] involves   [B] involves to   [C] is involved   [D] involves of
5. [A] opinions   [B] effects   [C] manners   [D] functions
6. [A] quality   [B] nature   [C] meaning   [D] value
7. [A] view   [B] look   [C] agree   [D] think
8. [A] by   [B] to   [C] off   [D] for
9. [A] content   [B] contend   [C] contempt   [D] contact
10. [A] inexplicably   [B] inexpressibly   [C] inextricably   [D] inexpediently
11. [A] interpreting   [B] saying   [C] explaining   [D] reading
12. [A] really   [B] definitely   [C] truly   [D] indeed
13. [A] comprehensive   [B] practical   [C] fundamental   [D] theoretical
14. [A] sometimes   [B] practically   [C] hopefully   [D] actually
15. [A] classed   [B] granted   [C] classified   [D] graded
16. [A] inclusive   [B] inclinable   [C] conclusive   [D] complicated
17. [A] break up   [B] elaborate   [C] define   [D] unlock
18. [A] purposes   [B] degrees   [C] stages   [D] steps
19. [A] such   [B] so as   [C] so   [D] such as
20. [A] By the way   [B] In short   [C] So far   [D] On the other hand

Passage 18

In some countries where racial prejudice is acute, violence has so come to be taken for granted as a means of solving differences; and this is not even questioned. There are countries where the white man __1__ his rule by brute force; there are countries where the black man protests by __2__ fire to cities and by looting and pillaging. Important people __3__ both sides, who would in other respects appear to be __4__ men, get up and calmly argue __5__ violence-as if it were a legitimate solution, like any other. What is really frightening, what really fills you with despair, is the realization that when it __6__ to the crunch (关键时刻), we have made no actual __7__ at all. We may wear collars and ties instead of war-paint, but our instincts remain __8__ unchanged. The whole of the __9__ history of the human race, that tedious documentation of violence, has taught us absolutely nothing. We have still not learnt that violence never solves a problem but makes it more __10__. The sheer horror, the bloodshed and the suffering mean nothing. No solution ever __11__ when we dismally __12__ the smoking ruins and wonder __13__ hit us.

The __14__ reasonable men who know where the solutions __15__ are finding it harder and harder to get a hearing. They are despised, mistrusted and even persecuted by their own __16__ because they advocate such apparently outrageous things as law __17__. If half the __18__ that goes into violent acts were put into good use, if our efforts were __19__ on cleaning up the slums and ghettos, on improving living standards and providing education and employment at all, we would not go a long __20__ to arriving at a solution.

1. [A] imposes   [B] implements   [C] carries   [D] regulates
2. [A] giving   [B] catching   [C] setting   [D] letting
3. [A] at   [B] on   [C] by   [D] along
4. [A] reasonable   [B] reasonably   [C] reasonless   [D] reason
5. [A] for the sake of   [B] for fear of   [C] in case of   [D] in favor of
6. [A] turns   [B] goes   [C] comes   [D] brings
7. [A] improvement   [B] progress   [C] increase   [D] change
8. [A] basically   [B] obviously   [C] necessarily   [D] eventually
9. [A] record   [B] recording   [C] recorded   [D] records
10. [A] severe   [B] depressed   [C] explicit   [D] acute
11. [A] brings to light   [B] bring to light   [C] comes to light   [D] come to light
12. [A] think   [B] consider   [C] contemplate   [D] regard
13. [A] what   [B] that   [C] which   [D] it
14. [A] really   [B] truly   [C] absolutely   [D] entirely
15. [A] lay   [B] lays   [C] lie   [D] lies
16. [A] kind   [B] method   [C] right   [D] rule
17. [A] regulation   [B] enforcement   [C] imposition   [D] reform
18. [A] energy   [B] attention   [C] time   [D] support
19. [A] focused   [B] involved   [C] attracted   [D] absorbed
20. [A] route   [B] path   [C] way   [D] road

Passage 19

In recent years, American interest in all kinds of athletics has greatly increased. Spectator sports are growing in __1__ because Americans have more leisure time to watch them and because TV gives so many athletic __2__ nationwide exposure. Today, women, probably __3__ larger percentage of sports enthusiasts than ever __4__. And, __5__ TV, children are able to understand and enjoy games like baseball and football at a very early age.

About 60 million men and women (55 percent of the nation's adult population) fit twenty-five minutes of exercise out their __6__ at least three times a week. Most Americans have spare time for sports and __7__ money for equipment and instruction. And they can __8__ their bowling, golf, or tennis __9__ as a necessary aid to keeping __10__ fit. Many adults who have no interest in athletic games prefer to keep healthy by __11__ a regular program of calisthenics, perhaps one that has been published in a paperback book or is conducted __12__ on TV. Yoga, isometrics, and aerobics are all popular __13__ both men and women. Walking is the major __14__ of exercise for about 44 million American adults. Jogging one to five miles is part of the weekly __15__ for about six million Americans. People who are __16__ are more likely to __17__ circulatory disorders, says modern medical science. Americans are taking these warnings __18__ and investing more time and money __19__ athletics. The investment is paying __20__ by helping individuals of all ages feel better and stay healthier.

1. [A] prosperity   [B] popularity   [C] density   [D] intensity
2. [A] affairs   [B] cases   [C] incidents   [D] events
3. [A] compose   [B] construct   [C] consist   [D] constitute
4. [A] after   [B] ago   [C] before   [D] since
5. [A] in the aspect of   [B] thanks to   [C] in terms of   [D] by way of
6. [A] schedules   [B] plans   [C] practices   [D] jobs
7. [A] additional   [B] substantial   [C] more   [D] extra
8. [A] verify   [B] justify   [C] demonstrate   [D] intensify
9. [A] costs   [B] payments   [C] fees   [D] expenses
10. [A] mentally   [B] psychologically   [C] physically   [D] emotionally
11. [A] following   [B] observing   [C] watching   [D] simulating
12. [A] regularly   [B] irregularly   [C] daily   [D] weekly
13. [A] in   [B] on   [C] into   [D] with
14. [A] function   [B] form   [C] method   [D] model
15. [A] work   [B] regularity   [C] routine   [D] standard
16. [A] inactive   [B] vigorous   [C] idle   [D] energetic
17. [A] create   [B] develop   [C] form   [D] become
18. [A] severely   [B] seriously   [C] seemingly   [D] sensitively
19. [A] at   [B] in   [C] for   [D] to
20. [A] towards   [B] off   [C] back   [D] out

Passage 20

Perhaps the most startling theory to come out of kinetics (动力学), the study of body movement, was suggested by Professor Ray Birdwhistell. He believes that physical __1__ is often culturally programmed. __2__ , we learn our looks are __3__ us. A baby has generally __4__ facial features. A baby, according to Birdwhistell, learns where to set the eyebrows by looking at __5__ around family and friends. This helps explain __6__ the people of some regions of the United States look so much __7__ . New Englanders or Southerners have certain similar facial __8__ that cannot be explained by __9__ . The __10__ shape of the mouth is not set at birth, it is learned after. __11__ , the final mouth shape is not formed until well after permanent teeth are __12__ . For many, this can be __13__ adolescence (青春期). A husband and wife together for a long time often come to look somewhat alike. We __14__ our looks from those around us. This is perhaps why in a __15__ country there are areas where people smile more than those in other areas. In the United States, __16__ , the South is the part of the country where people smile most __17__ . In New England they smile less, and in the western part of New York state __18__ . Many southerners find cities such as New York cold and unfriendly, partly because people on Madison Avenue smile less than people on Peachtree Street in Atlanta, Georgia. People in __19__ populated urban areas also tend to smile and greet each other in public less than __20__ people in rural areas and small towns.

1. [A] face   [B] complexion   [C] appearance   [D] look
2. [A] Then   [B] In a way   [C] Accordingly   [D] However
3. [A] born with   [B] not born with   [C] granted by   [D] carried out
4. [A] changeable   [B] formed   [C] definite   [D] unformed
5. [A] who   [B] these   [C] person   [D] those
6. [A] that   [B] phenomenon   [C] to   [D] why
7. [A] alike   [B] different   [C] same   [D] like
8. [A] characters   [B] characteristics   [C] specialties   [D] instincts
9. [A] genetics   [B] genesis   [C] generation   [D] genealogy
10. [A] concrete   [B] special   [C] exact   [D] absolute
11. [A] Yet   [B] Finally   [C] In fact   [D] Nevertheless
12. [A] produced   [B] set   [C] made   [D] developed
13. [A] well into   [B] better into   [C] deep in   [D] deeper into
14. [A] know   [B] study   [C] learn   [D] find
15. [A] single   [B] only   [C] separate   [D] lonely
16. [A] what is more   [B] however   [C] that is to say   [D] for example
17. [A] frequently   [B] commonly   [C] usually   [D] regularly
18. [A] still   [B] still less   [C] much more   [D] more
19. [A] crowded   [B] barely   [C] densely   [D] sparsely
20. [A] do   [B] smile   [C] greet   [D] does

答案与解析

Passage 1

【文章精要】

文章描述了19世纪英国城镇人口的健康状况。在城镇中，工作机会较多，且工资较高，但是城镇的人均寿命却远不如郊区的人均寿命长；同时，由于投入到城镇环境建设中的钱很少，因此疾病流行，死亡率高。

【解析】

1. 选 C，此题为词义辨析题。early 意为"早的"，former 意为"以前的"，previous 指时间上"靠前的"，precedented 意为"有先例的"。原句在说（19世纪）前70年英国的人口状况如何，因此 previous 最合适。

【考点归纳】

- early 意为"早的"，如：early 1900s（20世纪早期）。
- former 意为"地点或计划之前的；前任的"，如：former president（前总统）。
- previous 意为"（时间上或顺序上）发生在前的"，如：previous time（以前），previous chapter（上一章），previous experience（以前的经验）。

---

2. 选 B，此题为词义辨析题。pace 意为"步速"，rate 意为"速度，比率"，velocity 意为"（物理学上的）速度"，stride 意为"步幅"。这里指的是英国人口增长的速度，所以使用 rate。

3. 选 A，此题为篇章逻辑题。growth 意为"增长"，advance 意为"先进"，rise 意为"上升"，improvement 意为"提高，进步"。根据上下文，这里指早期人口增长阶段，所以排除 B、D。而这里应该填的是名词，所以 C 也不对。

4. 选 A，此题为篇章逻辑和词义辨析题。optimism 意为"乐观"，pessimism 意为"悲观"，indifference 意为"漠不关心"，enthusiasm 意为"热情"。文章第一段说英国在这段时期人口增长很快，而下文又说其实城镇里面很多人健康状况不好，人均寿命低。由篇章逻辑判断，作者显然对这种现象持否定态度，故句意应为"然而我们有理由乐观吗？"

5. 选 A，此题为篇章逻辑题。文章的第二段对城镇和郊区的生活进行了对比。显然，城镇的工作机会多，工资高，所以选 A。

6. 选 C，此题为语法结构题。这里考查的是定语从句的连接副词。先行词是 countryside，从句中缺状语，所以选 where。

7. 选 B，此题为篇章逻辑题。下文说了郊区的人均寿命长，这里显然是说郊区更"健康"，所以选 healthier。

8. 选 D，此题为词义辨析题。suppose，assume，postulate 均为"假定"之意，expect 意为"期待，预期"。原句意为"19 世纪 20 年代在一个人口超过 10 万的大城镇出生的婴儿可以活到 35 岁"，因此答案是 D。此外，空格后接的是不定式 to do sth.，四个单词中只有 expect 符合。

【考点归纳】

- suppose 意为"假定"，后面跟宾语从句。还可以说 be supposed to do sth. (应该做某事)。
- assume 意为"假定"，后面跟宾语从句。此外，它还有"承担"的意思，此时后面直接跟名词。
- postulate 意为"假定"，和 assume 用法基本相同。
- expect 意为"期待"，可以说 expect that... 或者 expect to do sth.。

9. 选 B，此题为词义辨析题。tolerable 意为"可以忍受的"，miserable 意为"悲惨的，可怜的"，understandable 意为"可以理解的"，accessible 意为"可以接近的"。原句意为"19 世纪 30 年代，人均寿命降低至 29 岁"，这当然是很"悲惨的"。

10. 选 D，此题为词义辨析题。demonstrate 意为"例证，论证"，exhibit 意为"展览，显示"，present 意为"展示"，show 意为"显示，说明"。前三个单词的主语一般都是人，所以只能选 D。

11. 选 C，此题为语法结构题。这里是分词短语作状语。compare 和主句主语 a boy 的关系是被动的，所以用过去分词。

12. 选 A，此题为语法结构题。这里考查定语从句。从句的先行词是 a boy，同时从句缺少主语，所以用 who。

13. 选 B，此题为篇章逻辑题。第二段说了大城镇是不健康的。第三段中，作者首先总结，所以此题填 therefore，意为"因此，所以"。however，nevertheless 均表转折，notwithstanding 表让步，均不合逻辑。

14. 选 A，此题为固定搭配题。at the level 是介词的固定搭配。

15. 选 B，此题为词义辨析题。stroke 作动词意为"抚摸"，stalk 意为"威胁地移动"，stake 意为"冒险，赌博"，stain 意为"玷污"。原句意为"新的传染病_____城市"，显然是"袭击"城市，所以选 B。这里要注意，stalk 本身可以作及物动词，所以可以说 stalk cities。

16. 选 B，此题为词义辨析题。motivate 意为"激发"，carry 意为"携带"，promote 意为"提升"，generate 意为"产生"。原句意为"受污染的水携带霍乱 (cholera) 和伤寒

(typhoid)", 所以选 B。

17. 选 C, 此题为词义辨析题。school 意为 "鱼群", team 意为 "一队 (人)", swarm 意为 "蜂群", herd 意为 "牛群"。其中 swarm 可以指一些昆虫的群, 所以 "一群苍蝇" 用 swarm。

18. 选 A, 此题为词义辨析题。waste 意为 "废弃物", dust 意为 "尘土", rubbish 意为 "垃圾", disposal 意为 "处置, 抛弃"。这里说的是 "苍蝇靠吃马厩中的肥料和人类废弃物为生", 那么只能选 A。另外, rubbish 很少说成 human rubbish。

19. 选 C, 词义辨析题。distinguish 意为 "区别, 辨别", find 意为 "寻找", identify 意为 "识别", manipulate 意为 "操作"。原句意为 "问题要_____很容易, 要解决很难"。根据反义词复现的线索, 后面有 solve, 那么空格应该填 "识别", 即 identify。

【考点归纳】

- distinguish 的两个固定用法: distinguish oneself as... 意为 "作为……而扬名"; distinguish between... 意为 "区别……", 也就是 tell the difference between...。
- identify 还有一个意思是 "把……和……看成是一样的", 固定用法为 identify A with B, 意为 "把 A 和 B 看成是一样的"。

---

20. 选 C, 此题为固定搭配题。这里考查的是介词的用法。表达 "在下水道里", 用介词 in。

Passage 2

【文章精要】

文章讲述了石器时代英国陆地的形成和人们的居住、生活条件。英国最初是和法国、丹麦相连的欧洲大陆的一部分, 随着冰川融化, 陆地逐渐被植被覆盖, 动物、人类开始在此定居。但是为了生存, 人类必须不断地搬迁, 所以居住的也是易于拆除的房子。

【解析】

1. 选 B, 此题为词义辨析题。空格后讲述的是石器时代的事实, 只不过我们现在无法想象, 所以可知空格内要填入一个表 "想象" 之意的词, 故选 B。

2. 选 D, 此题为词义辨析和固定搭配题。"冰层" 用英语说就是 ice sheet, 不能用其他的词。所以这道题与其说是词义辨析, 不如说是固定搭配。

【考点归纳】

- slice 意为 "(从大的东西上切下来的) 一薄片", 如: a slice of bread (一片面包)。
- strip 意为 "一条", 如: a strip of paper (一条纸带)。
- sheet 意为 "一张, 一大片", 如: a sheet of paper (一张纸), a sheet of ice (一块冰)。

3. 选 A，此题为词义辨析题。lock 意为"锁住"，cover 意为"覆盖"，blockade 意为"阻塞"，store 意为"储存"。其中后两个单词不和 up 搭配，首先排除。cover up 的意思是"掩盖（事实等）"，含义不符。lock up 的意思是"封锁住"，符合题意。

4. 选 A，此题为语法结构题。这里考查的是结果状语从句 so...that... 的用法。

5. 选 B，此题为篇章逻辑题。前文说石器时代很多水被锁在冰层下面（locked up in the ice），那么可以推断，其结果自然是水平面比今天低，所以根据词汇因果同现的线索，选 below。

6. 选 C，此题为词义辨析题。四个单词都有"连接"之意，用法分别是：be related to，be combined with，be jointed to，be unified with。首先可以排除 combined 和 unified。be related to 意为"和……有关"，而这里说的是英国和法国、丹麦"相连接"，而不是"有关系"，所以选 C。

7. 选 B，此题为词义辨析题。水平面升高，应该用不及物动词 rise。arise 一般指问题或者现象出现，所以排除。appear 意为"出现"，不符合题意。raise 是及物动词，用在这里是错误的。

8. 选 A，此题为词义辨析题。根据上下文，这里要说的是"浓密的森林"（dense forest），而不是"黑漆漆的森林"（dark forest）。而 thick 和 crowded 一般不用来修饰 forest。

【考点归纳】

● dense 意为"浓密的，稠密的"，常见的搭配有：dense forest（浓密的森林），dense population（高密度人口）。

● dark 意为"黑暗的"，常见的搭配有：a dark corner（黑暗的角落），a dark day（阴天）。

9. 选 C，此题为词义辨析和篇章逻辑题。approachable 意为"可以接近的"，formidable 意为"令人敬畏的"，habitable 意为"适合居住的"，inheritable 意为"可继承的"。原句意为"返回这些新近 _____ 的地方的人却不是固定的居民"，根据反义同现，可知这里要填一个和 not settled farmer 含义相反的形容词，所以选 C。此外，整个第二段都是在说这些地方人口流动性很大，后面的几个题目均可围绕这个段落主旨来解题。

10. 选 D，此题为词义辨析题。contiguously 意为"接触地"，consistently 意为"一致地"，continually 意为"不断地（指频率高）"，constantly 意为"经常性地，总是"。根据段落主旨，应该是说这些人总是在迁移，所以选 constantly。

11. 选 A，此题为词义辨析题。track 意为"追踪"，transit 意为"横越"，retrace 意为"折回"，trade 意为"交易"。这里说的显然是"追踪野生动物"，所以用 track。

12. 选 B，此题为词义辨析题。本题属于近形词辨析。subsume 意为"包括，包含"，assume 意为"假设"，resume 意为"继续"，consume 意为"消耗"。根据上下文，只能选 B。

13. 选 A，此题为词义辨析题。根据段落主旨，这里要说的是这些地方的人口都处于流动状态，所以空格里面的单词应该和前文的 not settled 和 constantly on the move 构成近义词复现关系。mobile 意为 "流动的"，符合题意。motivating 意为 "激发性的"，movable 意为 "可以移动的（一般指物）"，locomotive 意为 "运动的"。

14. 选 B，此题为词义辨析题。available 意为 "可供使用的"，portable 意为 "轻便的"，transferable 意为 "可转移的"，manipulable 意为 "可以操作的"。根据第二段的主旨和前文的 mobile，on the move 等单词和近义词复现的线索，此题选 B。

15. 选 D，此题为词义辨析题。detail 意为 "细节"，information 意为 "信息"，message 意为 "消息"，trace 意为 "痕迹"。根据上文提到的 tracking wild animals for meat and skin（追踪野生动物以获取皮和肉），这里应该是一个能和 track 构成近义词复现的单词，那么只能选 D。

16. 选 C，此题为词义辨析和篇章逻辑题。上一段说这些地方的人口流动性很大，所以他们居住的都是可以移动的简易房，并没有真正的房子。这里又说，在英国等地方发现了一些房子。可见两者不相符，因此这里要用 exceptions（例外）。

17. 选 A，此题为词义辨析题。dwelling 意为 "住处"，apartment 意为 "公寓"，cave 意为 "山洞"，villa 意为 "别墅"。根据上文，这些人有住的地方，所以不是 cave，但是并不固定，再加上在那个时候，人的住所不可能是 apartment 或者 villa。只能选 A。

18. 选 B，此题为语法结构题。定语从句先行词是 all 的时候只用 that，而不用 which。

19. 选 C，此题为词义辨析和固定搭配题。foresee 和 predict 均有 "预测" 之意，expect 意为 "期望"，imagine 意为 "想象"。四个选项中只有 expect 的含义与题意相符。此外 be expected of 是 expect sb. of sth. 的被动形式，是固定搭配。

20. 选 B，此题为词义辨析题。根据上下文，这里要表示的意思是 "有特色的石器工具"，所以只有 distinctive 符合题意。

【考点归纳】
- distinct 指某物与其他东西有显著的区别，如：The warbler is not a distinct species. （刺嘴莺不是那种可清楚辨认的鸟。）
- distinctive 指某个特性或特点使我们能够区分某物与他物，如：The warbler has a distinctive song. （刺嘴莺叫声独特。）

Passage 3

【文章精要】

文章讲述了 19 世纪中期英国工业的特点和发展。那时英国工业处境艰难，前有美国领先，后有德国紧追，但是没有一个国家的工业生产专门化程度和城市化水平高于英国。

【解析】

1. 选 B，此题为固定搭配题。mass production 是一个常见的修饰搭配，意为 "大规模生产"。

2. 选 A，此题为词义辨析和固定搭配题。四个选项均含有"打算，趋向"的意思。从词法的角度来看，tend 作为此意的时候是不及物动词，不用被动语态，首先排除。aim 的用法是 be aimed at，focus 的用法是 be focused on。所以最后只能用 intend。be intended to do 意为"为了……的目的"。

3. 选 B，此题为词义辨析题。elegant 意为"优雅的"，exquisite 意为"精致的"，special 意为"特殊的"，distinctive 意为"与众不同的"。这里讲的是"英国水晶宫内陈设的展品中，有大而重的蒸汽锤 (massive steam hammers)，精致的小配件 (ingenious gadgets)，还有 _____ 的手工制品"。根据上下文，应该是"精致的"，也就是 exquisite。这里是典型的同一场景下，相同性质的修饰性词语同现。

4. 选 D，此题为篇章逻辑题。整篇文章讲的都是英国工业的发展，根据一切细节皆为主题服务的原则，这里应该说的是水晶宫内的大部分展品都是来自英国的，所以选 majority。

5. 选 A，此题为词义辨析和篇章逻辑题。上文说到水晶宫内的大部分展品都是英国的，根据同义词复现的线索，这里要说的应该是"这一统治地位来得并不早"，"大部分"对应"统治地位"。dominance 意为"优势，统治"，符合题意。prominence 意为"突出，出色"，existence 意为"存在"，evidence 意为"证据"。

6. 选 C，此题为语法结构题。这里考查的是强调句 It is/was...that... 的用法。

7. 选 D，此题为词义辨析和篇章逻辑题。power 意为"权力"，authority 意为"权威"，priority 意为"优先"，leadership 意为"领导地位"。根据上下文，此句意为"仅仅半个世纪前英国才从法国的手里夺走了全欧洲经济政治的统治地位"。同时，在第一段的开头提到过英国在维多利亚时期在全世界的工业领域处于领导地位 (leading industrial power)，根据衍生词复现的线索，这里应该选 D。

8. 选 B，此题为固定搭配题。lag behind 是固定搭配，意为"落后"。

9. 选 B，此题为篇章逻辑题。此空前面说英国在工业领域处于领导地位，后面说 20 世纪初，美国处于领导地位，德国也虎视眈眈。可见前后两句是转折关系，所以选 however。

10. 选 A，此题为固定搭配题。challenge A for B 意为"因为 B 挑战 A"。原句意为"德国也开始挑战英国作为老二的位子了"。

11. 选 C，此题为词义辨析题。根据下文，这里要说的应当是"没有国家比英国在制造领域更专业化了"。special 意为"特别的"，specific 意为"具体的"，specialized 意为"专门的，专门化的"，professional 意为"专业的 (指人)"。所以正确答案是 C。

12. 选 B，此题为词义辨析和固定搭配题。几个单词都有"力量"的意思，但是说到劳动力，一般使用的搭配是 labor force。

13. 选 A，此题为篇章逻辑题。根据上下文，此处句意为"英国超过 75% 的小麦是进口的，大部分来自美国和俄国"，故选 A。

14. 选 D，此题为词义辨析和固定搭配题。四个选项均含有"原始的，原来的"之意，但是说到"原材料"，固定搭配应该是 raw material。

【考点归纳】

- original 意为"最初的，独创的"，如：original works（原作）。
- crude 意为"未经提炼的"，如：crude oil（原油）。
- coarse 意为"粗糙的，粗俗的"，如：coarse sand（粗糙的沙子），crude manner（粗俗的行为）。
- raw 意为"未被加工的"，如：raw material（原材料）。

15. 选 B，此题为词义辨析题。根据上下文，这里说的是原材料来自全球，所以选择具有"来源"之意的 source，注意这个单词在这里用作动词。

【考点归纳】

- resource 意为"资源"，如：natural resources（自然资源）。
- source 作名词时意为"来源，源头"，如：source of evil（罪恶之源）。作动词时意为"来自……"，如：They are sourcing from abroad in order to save money.（为了节省开支，他们从国外获得原料。）
- originate 意为"起源，来自"，名词形式是 origin，如：origin of words（词源）。

16. 选 A，此题为词义辨析和篇章逻辑题。空格前面说英国大部分的原材料是进口的，后面说很多服务也进口。可见两者之间是递进关系，所以选择 increasingly。

17. 选 B，此题为语法结构和篇章逻辑题。本句意为"也没有第二个国家像英国这么城市化"，对应该段开头部分的 But no country...was as specialized as... 这两个层次是并列关系，所以选 nor。

18. 选 B，此题为词义辨析和篇章逻辑题。空格的下一句说了在那个时候英国大部分人住在小镇或者城市，根据近义词复现，这里应是表示"城市化"的形容词，所以选 urbanized。

19. 选 C，此题为词义辨析题。predominantly 意为"卓越地"，heavily 意为"沉重地"，largely 意为"主要地"，particularly 意为"尤其"。前一句说到在 1851 年仅有一小部分人在现代工业领域工作，这句说的是他们的主要工作地区。

20. 选 A，词义辨析题。evident 意为"有证据的，显而易见的"，distinguished 意为"著名的"，intricate 意为"复杂的"，projecting 意为"伸出的"。原句意为"这些地方工业化的痕迹在 1800 年已经很明显了"，所以答案是 A。

Passage 4

【文章精要】

　　文章讲述了大规模捕杀非洲象的现象引起了广泛关注，在受到动物保护组织反对的同时，非洲众国也意识到大象对他们的重要性，并开始采取一些保护措施。

【解析】

1. 选 B，此题为语法结构题。population 是集合名词，用作单数，所以谓语用 has。

2. 选 A，此题为词义辨析和篇章逻辑题。accelerate 意为"加速"，decelerate 意为"减速"，descend 意为"下降（指位置）"，ascend 意为"上升（指位置）"。根上下文，这里的意思应该是今年捕杀非洲象的速度呈上升趋势，所以选 A。

3. 选 D，此题为词义辨析题。根据上下文，这里要说的意思应当是年龄较大、象牙较大的大象已经被杀死，所以捕猎者必须要多杀些小象才能弄到足够数量的象牙。四个选项中只有 destroy 有"杀死"的意思。

【考点归纳】

- damage 指物理损坏，但是还可以修复，如：a badly damaged car（一辆损坏严重的汽车）。
- hurt 指从身体上或者心灵上伤害别人，如：His words hurt my feelings.（他的话伤害了我的感情。）
- ruin 指完全毁坏，在这一点上和 destroy 含义非常相似，如：My work was ruined due to his carelessness.（由于他的粗心，我的工作被破坏了。）
- destroy 除了"毁灭"的意思外，还有"杀死"的意思，如：The flood destroyed the village.（洪水彻底摧毁了村庄。）

4. 选 A，此题为语法结构题。这里考查的是倍数的表达方法。"是……的几倍"的说法是 X times as...。

5. 选 C，此题为篇章逻辑题。原句意为"虽然在环境保护方面的记录存在污点，但是美国政府牵头组织了一次会谈，内容是禁止进口象牙"，所以选 though。

6. 选 B，此题为固定搭配题。take the lead 是固定搭配，意为"为首，带头"。

7. 选 B，此题为词义辨析题。force 意为"强迫"，impose 意为"强加"，make 意为"制造"，publish 意为"出版"。从词语的搭配入手，"强制执行禁令"就是 impose a ban，所以选 B。

【考点归纳】

- force 有"强迫"之意，但是一般的惯用法是 force sb. to do sth.。
- impose 可以表示强加政策，或者征税，常见的动宾搭配有：impose a tax on sb.（向某人征税），impose a ban on sth.（颁布关于……的禁令）。

8. 选 D，此题为词义辨析题。根据上下文，这里要说的是"动物保护组织"，下文提到了 conservation，根据原词复现的线索，选 D。

【考点归纳】

- preservation 意为"保管，保持"，如：preservation of food（食物的保鲜）。
- conservation 意为"保护"，如：animal conservation（动物保护）。

9. 选 C，此题为词义辨析题。act 意为"动作"，activity 意为"活动"，action 意为"行为"，behavior 意为"举止"。根据上下文，这里说的是禁止进口象牙这种行为（行动），所以选 C。

【考点归纳】

- action 意为"行为，行动"，但是一般指的是针对某个问题采取的行动，如：take actions（采取行动）。
- behavior 指的是一个人的举止，如：elegant behavior（优雅的举止）。

10. 选 A，此题为词义辨析和篇章逻辑题。前文提到强令禁止进口象牙，那么这里根据因果同现，自然要说这使得美国成为第一个"禁止"进口象牙的国家。forbid 意为"禁止"，符合题意。allow 意为"允许"，exclude 意为"排除"，frustrate 意为"挫败"。

11. 选 B，此题为篇章逻辑题。空格前提到 raw ivory（未被加工的象牙），那么对应的自然是 finished ivory（加工过的象牙），故选 B。process 指通过特殊程序准备、处理或转换，如：process ore to obtain minerals（加工矿石获取矿物质）。

12. 选 C，此题为词义辨析题。information 意为"信息"，但是不可数名词，首先排除。sign 意为"标记"，message 意为"信息"，notice 意为"通知"。比较而言，message 在这里最合适，句子含义为"这个禁令传递给捕猎者一个清楚的信息，那就是游戏结束了"。

13. 选 A，此题为篇章逻辑题。过去非洲国家没有意识到问题的严重性，但是现在逐渐意识到了，可见答案应该是 A。increasingly 意为"逐渐地"，surprisingly 意为"惊讶地"，recently 意为"最近地"，seemingly 意为"表面上地"。

14. 选 C，此题为词义辨析题。severe 意为"严格的"，sharp 意为"尖锐的"，serious 意为"严重的"，subtle 意为"细微的"。原句意为"他们意识到大象的减少给他们的旅游业以_____的威胁"，只有"严重的"最适合。

15. 选 D，此题为固定搭配题。call for 意为"要求"，call on 意为"郑重邀请，恳求"，call in 意为"下令或请求收回（某物）"，call at 意为"（指火车等）停靠"。原句意为"上个月坦桑尼亚和其他几个国家要求修订……"，故选 D。

16. 选 B，此题为语法结构题。这里考查的是定语从句的关系代词。从句的先行词是物，从句缺少主语，所以选 that。

17. 选 C，此题为词义辨析和篇章逻辑题。appraise 意为"评价"，adjust 意为"调整"，approve 意为"通过，批准"，alter 意为"修改"。这里的意思应该是"该修订案将于 10 月日内瓦的会议上通过"，所以选 C。

【考点归纳】

- approve 表示"批准"之意时是及物动词，如：approve a proposal（批准提议），approve an amendment（批准修订案）。
- approve 表示"赞成"时一般是不及物动词，常和 of 搭配，如：approve of an idea（赞成某一想法）。

18. 选 D，此题为固定搭配题。between now and then 是固定搭配，意为"时不时"。

19. 选 C，此题为词义辨析和语法结构题。contrive 意为"设计，图谋"，contemplate 意为"沉思"，contend 意为"主张"，compromise 意为"妥协"。从含义上来说，compromise 显然不对，首先排除。从语法结构上来说，空格后的从句中使用了"should＋动词原形"这种虚拟语气，而几个选项中，只有 contend 后面可以有这种用法，所以选 C。

20. 选 C，此题为词义辨析题。greatly 意为"很，非常"，internationally 意为"国际地"，wholesale 意为"大规模地"，fast 意为"迅速地"。这里说的是捕猎者大规模捕杀大象，所以选 C。

Passage 5

【文章精要】

文章谈论了损害劳工权益的问题。由于劳工权益受到损害，在克林顿政府的要求下，美国很多公司签署了有关保护劳工权益的协议，但有些政府部门，如国防部等在这一点上却没有采取任何行动。

【解析】

1. 选 C，此题为词义辨析题。things 意为"事情"，activities 意为"活动"，practices 意为"实践，惯例"，performances 意为"表演"。此处所填单词对应前文提到的很多公司损害劳工权益的问题，这是一种"办事方式"，四个单词里面只有 practices 有这个意思。

2. 选 B，此题为词义辨析题。issue 意为"颁布"，launch 意为"发起"，order 意为"命令"，stimulate 意为"刺激"。原句空格部分的意思是"发起活动"，所以选 B。

3. 选 D，此题为词义辨析和固定搭配题。observe 意为"遵守"，subject 意为"使屈从于，使受制于"，agree 意为"同意"，submit 意为"屈服，受制于"。根据上下文，此处意为"生产商和零售商要定期接受有关工作环境和条件的检查"。从含义上来说 observe，subject 和 submit 均符合题意。但是只有 submit 符合此处的用法 submit to sth.。另外，在第二段的最后一句话中有 submit to 这个短语，这里属于原词复现。

【考点归纳】

- observe 意为"遵守"，是及物动词，后面直接跟宾语，如：observe the speed limit（遵守限速）。
- subject 意为"使……屈服于"，一般用被动语态较多，如：be subjected to the law（服从法规）。
- submit 意为"受制于"，是不及物动词，后面跟介词 to，如：submit to discipline（遵守纪律）。

4. 选 B，此题为词义辨析题。need 意为"需要"，urge 意为"促使"，motivate 意为"激发"，push 意为"推动"。原句意为"这项运动促使生产商（不得不）签署了《工作环境管理规范》"。这些人并非自愿签署，而是这项运动让他们不得不签署，所以选 urge。

5. 选 A，此题为词义辨析题。promise 意为 "承诺"，file 意为 "文件"，way 意为 "方法"，rule 意为 "规定"。根据上下文，这个《工作环境管理规范》的内容就是一个进行自我约束的承诺，所以选 A。

6. 选 D，此题为词义辨析题。adapt 意为 "调整"，accustom 意为 "调整"，alter 意为 "修改，改变"，adopt 意为 "采纳"。根据上下文，这里说的是这项规范已经被很多公司采纳、接受了，所以选 D。

【考点归纳】

- adapt 意为"调整，使之适应"，如：adapt oneself to... (使自己适应或习惯于某事)。
- accustom 的含义和用法和 adapt 基本一致，如：accustome oneself to... (使自己习惯于某事)。
- adopt 有两个基本含义，就是 "收养" 和 "采纳"，如：adopt a child (收养一个孩子)，adopt a method (采纳一种方法)。

7. 选 B，此题为篇章逻辑题。前面说很多公司签署了这项规范，后面说国防部没有签署，可见两者是转折关系，所以填 however。

8. 选 C，此题为篇章逻辑题。根据上下文，国防部不光不签署协议，而且也不同意要求它的订约人签署协议，可见两者是递进关系，故填 in addition。

9. 选 B，此题为语法结构题。这里考查的是宾语从句的引导词，在句中作 demand 的宾语。

10. 选 B，此题为词义辨析题。temporary 意为 "暂时的"，periodic 意为 "定期的"，permanent 意为 "永久的"，constant 意为 "持续的"。根据上下文，应该是 "定期检查"，故选 B，和上段末句的 periodic 构成原词复现。

11. 选 B，此题为篇章逻辑题。根据上下文，这里考查的是因果关系。原句意为 "由于国防部不支持此规范，制止血汗工厂的工作就落在了劳动部头上"，故选 B。

12. 选 C，此题为固定搭配题。adhere to 是固定搭配，意为 "坚持，拥护"。此句的含义见 11 题。

13. 选 D，此题为词义辨析题。原句意为 "那些执意破坏工资法和健康条例的联邦订约人 (指联邦政府工程的承包人) 可能会因此失去纳税人支持的那些有利可图的合约"。"违反法律" 即 violate laws，其他几个选项均指破坏具体的东西，不能用在这里。

14. 选 A，此题为词义辨析题。finance 意为 "在经济上予以支持"，pay 意为 "支付"，provide 意为 "提供"，offer 意为 "提供"。句意见 13 题。根据上下文可知 finance 为正确答案。

15. 选 B，此题为固定搭配题。to one's knowledge 是固定搭配，意为 "据某人所知"。

【考点归纳】

- "据某人所知" 常见的表达方式有：as far as sb. is concerned，according to sb.，to one's knowledge，as far as sb. knows。

16. 选 A，此题为词义辨析题。apply 意为"应用"，implement 意为"执行"，use 意为"应用"，impose 意为"强加"。从词义上来说，apply 和 use 均正确，但是从词法上来说，只有 apply 后面可以跟介词 to，use 的后面要使用介词 for，故选 A。原句意为"该部门从来没有在政府制服生产商的身上应用过该项规范"。

17. 选 D，此题为词义辨析和固定搭配题。ensue 意为"追求"，alleviate 意为"减轻"，head 意为"前进"，stick 意为"坚持"。原句意为"我以为他们会遵守安全和健康的相关要求"，可知答案应为 stick。再者，从词法的角度，前三个单词作此意讲时都是及物动词，只有 stick 可以作不及物动词，固定搭配为 stick to。

18. 选 D，此题为词义辨析题。request 意为"要求（得到某物）"，reconciliation 意为"调解"，recreation 意为"消遣，娱乐"，requirement 意为"要求（规定）"。根据句意（见 17 题）可知本题选 D。

【考点归纳】

- request 意为"请求得到某物"，如：request for help（请求帮助）。
- requirement 意为"（要求必备的）条件"，如：health requirement（健康要求）。

19. 选 A，此题为词义辨析题。cite 意为"援引，引用"，illustrate 意为"例证"，mention 意为"提到"，refer 意为"提及，引用"。原句意为"在过去的 12 年间，职业安全和健康署 32 次引用了 Lion 条例来惩罚违犯健康和安全规范的人"。首先排除 illustrate 和 mention。refer 是不及物动词，固定搭配为 refer to，所以在这里也不对，只能选 A。

20. 选 C，此题为词义辨析题。speculation 意为"思索"，breakdown 意为"崩溃"，violation 意为"违犯"，deterioration 意为"恶化"。根据句意（见 19 题）可知本题选 C，和本段第三行的 violating 构成衍生词复现。

Passage 6

【文章精要】

文章主要介绍了石油工业的发展历史。19 世纪 50 年代煤油的产生首开石油精炼的先河，从此市场对石油的需求就日益增加，石油勘探业发展迅猛。19 世纪末，人们又通过精炼制造出诸如润滑油等其他石油产品。

【解析】

1. 选 C，此题为词义辨析题。"原油"用英语表达就是 crude oil，crude 意为"未经提炼的"，属于词语搭配中的修饰搭配，所以选 C。

2. 选 A，此题为篇章逻辑题。此句大意为"在美国内战之后，石油为人们所知已经很长时间了，但是却没有怎么加以利用"。空格前后为转折关系，所以填 but。

3. 选 D，此题为固定搭配题。make use of 意为"利用"，句意见第 2 题。

4. 选 B，此题为词义辨析题。gather 意为"聚集"，collect 意为"采集"，augment 意为

"增大"，saturate 意为 "浸透"。原句意为 "19 世纪 50 年代，宾夕法尼亚州西部的一个制造商 Samuel 就开始采集原油，并把它加工成煤油了"，故选 B。

5. 选 A，此题为词义辨析和语法结构题。原句意为 "石油精炼和熔炼一样，是从原材料中去粗取精的过程"，故填 like。

6. 选 B，此题为词义辨析题。procedure 意为 "程序"，process 意为 "过程"，proceeding 意为 "进程"，progress 意为 "进步"。由句意（见第 5 题）可知本题选 B。

【考点归纳】

- procedure 意为 "程序"，也就是 "步骤"，如：a long therapeutic procedure（长期的治疗过程）。
- process 意为 "过程"，即制作或处理某一产品的一系列操作，如：a manufacturing process（生产过程）。
- proceeding 意为 "进程"，一般用复数 proceedings，指 "活动"，如：watched the proceedings from a ringside seat（在看台前排座位上观看活动）。

7. 选 D，此题为词义辨析题。replace 意为 "代替"，supplement 意为 "补充"，surplus 意为 "剩余"，substitute 意为 "代替"。原句意为 "煤油是鲸油的廉价替代品，后者已经越来越难获得"，因此 supplement 和 surplus 均不符合题意。replace 只能作动词，而这里要求填入一个名词，所以只能选 D。

【考点归纳】

- replace 只作动词，固定用法是 replace A with B，意为 "用 B 代替 A"。
- substitute 既可以作名词，也可以作动词。作动词时的固定用法是 substitute A for B，意为 "用 A 代替 B"。

8. 选 D，此题为篇章逻辑题。根据上下文，此处说的应当是鲸油越来越稀少，越来越难获得，故选 D。

9. 选 B，此题为词义辨析题。根据因果同现原则，既然煤油是鲸油的廉价替代品，而后者又越来越难获得，那么对前者的 "需求" 自然越来越高。need 和 request 前面均不用 a，所以不对，necessity 不符合句意，也排除。所以正确答案是 demand。

10. 选 A，此题为词义辨析题。原句意为 "人们开始找寻新的石油供给"。supply 意为 "供给"，offer 意为 "提议，意图"，origin 意为 "起源"，trace 意为 "痕迹"。只有 supply 符合题意。

11. 选 C，此题为词义辨析题。四个单词都有 "完整的" 之意。all 后面要加冠词，所以不对。complete 强调 "完成" 的意思，total 强调的是 "总数"，只有 whole 强调 "从头到尾"，是正确答案。

12. 选 D，此题为词义辨析和篇章逻辑题。fantastic 意为 "奇异的"，gorgeous 意为 "华丽的"，empirical 意为 "实证的"，impractical 意为 "不实际的"。原句意为 "整个采油的过程看起来如此的_____而且愚蠢，以至于旁观者称之为'Drake 的蠢事'"。空格和后面的 foolish 构成同义词复现，四个选项中和 foolish 词义相近的就只有 impractical 了。

13. 选 A，此题为语法结构和篇章逻辑题。原句意为"但是当他钻到 70 英尺的时候，发现了石油"，故选 when。while 虽然含义对，但是后面要用进行时。

14. 选 C，此题为词义辨析题。touch 意为"接触"，obtain 意为"得到"，strike 有"邂逅，发现"之意，reach 意为"到达"。由句意（见 13 题）可知答案是 C。

15. 选 B，此题为词义辨析题。produce 意为"生产制造"，yield 意为"产出"，assemble 意为"加工"，provide 意为"提供"。原句意为"他的井每天产出原油 20 桶"，而不是"制造原油"或者"加工原油"，所以是 yield。

16. 选 D，此题为词义辨析和篇章逻辑题。failure 意为"失败"，advance 意为"先进"，problem 意为"问题"，success 意为"成功"。上文提到他的井开始出油，这是一种"成功"。

17. 选 A，此题为词义辨析题。原句意为"Drake 成功的消息把勘探者们带到了那里"。scene 指有人活动的"场景"，scenery 意为"风景"，sight 意为"景观，名胜"，view 意为"远景"。只有 scene 符合题意。

18. 选 B，此题为词义辨析题。compete 意为"竞争"，rival 意为"竞争，相匹敌"，encounter 意为"遇到"，acquaint 意为"熟悉"。原句大意为"这一热潮甚至可以和 1848 年加利福尼亚州的淘金热媲美"，故选 B。compete 是不及物动词，后面要用介词 with。

19. 选 D，此题为词义辨析题。principle 意为"原则"，fundamental 意为"基础的，基本的"，important 意为"重要的"，principal 意为"主要的"。原句意为"石油产品有很多，但是数年来煤油一直是主要的产品"。

20. 选 C，此题为篇章逻辑题。前面说到了石油经加工后成了煤油，这里又提到了汽油等，可见是递进关系，故填 then。

Passage 7

【文章精要】

　　文章主要介绍了劳动工具的研发过程。首先要有人来使用这个工具，然后在此过程中使用一些仪器记录使用者的肌肉活动并对工具的性能进行评估，这样才能确定该工具设计是否科学。

【解析】

1. 选 A，此题为词义辨析。regular 意为"常备的，合格的"，usual 意为"通常的"，common 意为"普通的"，constant 意为"持续的，不变的"。根据上下文，这里指的应当是使用常规工具，所以是 regular tool。

2. 选 D，此题为固定搭配题。take measurements of sth. 意为"测量，衡量"。

3. 选 B，此题为词义辨析和篇章逻辑题。distracted 意为"心烦意乱的"，twisted 意为"扭曲的"，exaggerated 意为"夸张的"，tilted 意为"倾斜的"。原句意为"当关节扭曲和肌肉拉紧时，其表现没有关节和肌肉都在正常位置的时候好"。根据下文"拉紧的肌肉"，结合同一语义场词汇同现的原则，前面应该是"扭曲的关节"，所以选 B。

4. 选 D，此题为词义辨析题。act 意为"表演"，demonstrate 意为"展示"，behave 意为"举止"，perform 指"做，执行……的功能"。由句意（见第 3 题）可知本题选 D。

5. 选 A，此题为语法结构题。这里考查的是比较状语从句 as well as...，意为"和……一样"。

6. 选 B，此题为词义辨析题。average 意为"平均的"，normal 意为"正常的"，standard 意为"标准的"，routine 意为"日常的，惯例的"。根据上文的 twisted 和 stretched 可知，这里是反义同现，故选 B。

7. 选 C，此题为词义辨析题。increase 意为"增长"，rise 意为"上升"，improvement 意为"提高，进步"，inclination 意为"倾向"。原句意为"所有这一切都显示了新设计比旧设计进步了很多"，故选 C。

8. 选 B，此题为词义辨析和语法结构题。cause 意为"导致"，make 意为"使得"，result 意为"结果是"，impose 意为"强加"。四个选项中除了 impose 含义不合适外，其他三个都行。但是从词法来看，空格后是复合宾语，而 cause 后面直接跟宾语，result 是不及物动词，要使用固定搭配 result in。只有 make 的后面可以使用复合宾语，是正确答案。

9. 选 C，此题为词义辨析题。evaluate 意为"估计"，estimate 意为"评估"，measure 意为"测量"，count 意为"计算"。原句意为"另外一台机器测量了工具的危险性"，evaluate 和 estimate 的主语一般都是人，count 不符合题意，故选 C。

10. 选 A，此题为语法结构题。这里考查的是定语从句的关系代词。空格前面有介词 upon，关系代词在从句中作宾语，所以只能用 which，不能用 that。

11. 选 B，此题为词义辨析和篇章逻辑题。inference 意为"推断"，conclusion 意为"结论"，summary 意为"摘要，总结"，investigation 意为"调查"。原句意为"用该机器进行实验得出的一个结论（或推断）是，三条腿的活梯用起来比四条腿的更安全"，可见 conclusion 和 inference 均符合句意。但是，inference 后面一般用 from，所以选 B。

12. 选 D，此题为词义辨析题。solid 意为"牢固的，结实的"，steady 意为"稳固的，固定的"，stable 意为"稳定的"，原文是说三条腿的活梯更安全、更稳，所以选 D。

【考点归纳】

- firm 指的是信念坚定，如：firm belief（坚定的信念）。
- solid 指的是基础稳固或者质量和质地很好，如：solid foundation（牢固的基础）。
- steady 指平稳，在一个位置或地方不动，是动态的稳定，如：steady increase（稳定的增长）。
- stable 指稳固，保持位置或状态不变化，如：Is the ladder stable?（这梯子稳固吗？）

13. 选 C，此题为词义辨析题。absorb 意为"吸收"，acquire 意为"获得"，attract 意为"吸引"，assimilate 意为"同化"。原句大意为该项工作吸引了相关专家的注意。"吸引注意力"就是 attract attention，故选 C。

14. 选 D，此题为固定搭配题。go beyond 意为"远远超过"。此处句意为"它的价值远远超过了那一点"。

15. 选 D，此题为词义辨析题。focus 意为"焦点"，view 意为"观点"，perspective 意为"看法，观点"，thought 意为"想法"。原句意为"Tichauer 博士最初产生这个想法是为了那些使用工具的人的健康"，故选 D。

16. 选 A，此题为语法结构题。此题考查的是非谓语动词的用法。现在分词表示主动的或者正在进行的动作，过去分词表示被动的或者已经完成的动作。"重复的使用"用英语表达应该是 repeated use，因为"使用"是"被重复"的，故选 A。

17. 选 B，此题为词义辨析题。product 意为"产品"，production 意为"生产"，progress 意为"进步"，proceeding 意为"进程"，这四个词都可以跟 line 搭配。而原句意为"如果每天在_____线和其他工作中重复使用相同的工具……"，只有 production line（生产线）能和空格后的"其他工作"相对应。

18. 选 C，此题为词义辨析和篇章逻辑题。此处所指的工作应该同前文提到生产线上的工作类似，所以排除选项 D，而 labor 不能跟 work 连用，所以排除选项 B。这里并不具体指某种劳动，所以用 manual work（体力劳动）。

19. 选 D，此题为篇章逻辑题。前文说了重复使用同一工具的第一个危害，这里要说的是第二个，故使用 furthermore，表递进。选项 C 若是 besides 也对。

20. 选 A，此题为词义辨析题。hazard 意为"危险"，factor 意为"因素"，effect 意为"效果"，occasion 意为"场合"。原句意为"肌肉的疲劳是一个非常严重的安全隐患"，故选 A。

Passage 8

【文章精要】

文章探讨了利用电脑犯罪的问题。与其他罪犯不同的是，这类犯罪者的罪行很少败露，即使被发现，他们也可以轻易地逃过惩罚，因为雇主们不希望这些人到处宣扬自己如何轻而易举地闯入公司电脑内部窃取机密资料，从而给客户留下不良印象。

【解析】

1. 选 C，此题为词义辨析题。原句意为"任何一个足够聪明，可以为自己特定的目的而修改这些信息的人都可以得到相当丰厚的回报"。根据句意，应该选 C。

2. 选 B，此题为词义辨析题。acclaim 意为"称赞"，reap 意为"收割，收获"，reach 意为"到达"，reclaim 意为"收回"。此处要表达的意思是"获得收获"，故选 B，搭配为 reap reward。

3. 选 A，此题为固定搭配题。be caught at sth./doing sth. 指"在做某事时被当场抓住"。原句意为"更糟的是，很多这样做了而且被当场抓住的人最后都可以设法逃脱惩罚"。

4. 选 B，此题为词义辨析和篇章逻辑题。unfound 意为"未被找到的"，undetected 意为"未被发现的，未被查出的"，discharged 意为"还清的"，underestimated 意为"低估的"。原句意为"如果没有人时刻检查电脑在干些什么的话，电脑犯罪很容易在不被发现的情况下进行"。上段末出现了 get away without punishment，这里根据同义词复现的原则，应该是 undetected，故选 B。

5. 选 D，此题为词义辨析和篇章逻辑题。walk out 意为"走出"，walk away 意为"走到一边去"，walk on 意为"继续走"，没有 walk aside 这种说法。原句意为"即使罪行败露，犯罪者不仅可以不受任何惩罚，甚至还可以从他以前的雇主那里得到一封相当不错的推荐信"。这里的 walk away unpunished 是前文 get away without punishment 的同义词复现，故选 D。

6. 选 B，此题为词义辨析题。redundant 意为"冗长的"，glowing 意为"炽热的，动情的"，terrible 意为"恐怖的"，formidable 意为"强大的，令人敬畏的"。由句意（见第 5 题）可知，本题选 D。

7. 选 C，此题为词义辨析题。preceding 意为"在前的，前述的"，prior 意为"优先的"，former 意为"之前的"，proceeding 意为"进程，行动"。此处要表达的意思是"以前的雇主"，所以选 C。

【考点归纳】

- prior 意为"优先的"，如：prior to（在前，居先）。
- former 意为"时间上靠前的"或者"前任的"，如：former classmate（以前的同学），former president（前任总统）。
- preceding 意为"前述的"，如：preceding chapter（前述章节）。

8. 选 D，此题为词义辨析题。annoyed 意为"烦人的"，deliberate 意为"故意的"，persistent 意为"顽固坚持的"，disturbing 意为"令人厌烦的"。原句意为"令人觉得厌烦的是，很多电脑犯罪是被我们意外发现的，而不是通过系统的检查或其他安全程序发现的"。四个单词里面，deliberate 不符合题意，annoyed 和 persistent 一般用于指人，只有 disturbing 符合题意，故选 D。

9. 选 A，此题为固定搭配题。by accident 意为"意外地"。

10. 选 A，此题为词义辨析题。procedure 意为"程序"，process 意为"过程"，progress 意为"进步"，precedence 意为"优先"。根据句意，这里指的是"安全程序"，故选 A。

11. 选 B，此题为词义辨析题。unluckily 意为"不幸地"，uncommonly 意为"不一般地"，recklessly 意为"不顾一切地"，subjectively 意为"主观地"。原句意为"被抓住的电脑犯罪者都是运气极其不好的"，故选 B。

12. 选 C，此题为篇章逻辑题。整篇文章的中心都是在讲电脑犯罪者即使犯罪，也没有什么严重的后果，因此，这句话要说的意思应该是"不同于其他犯罪者，一旦罪行败露，必须离开国家、自杀或者进监狱，电脑犯罪者有时可以逃避惩罚，要求不但不惩罚他们，还要给他们好的推荐信或者其他的好处"，故选 C。

13. 选 A，此题为词义辨析题。"自杀"就是 commit suicide，为固定的动宾搭配，故选 A。

14. 选 D，此题为词义辨析题。avoid 意为"避免"，violate 意为"违犯"，escort 意为"护送"，escape 意为"躲避"。这里实际上还是对文章中心的重复，即"电脑犯罪可以逃脱惩罚"，也是前文 walk away unpunished 的同义词复现，故选 D。

15. 选 B，此题为固定搭配题。all too often 意为"时常"，选 B。原句意为"他们的要求总是能够得到满足"。

16. 选 C，此题为词义辨析和篇章逻辑题。contemplate 意为"沉思"，manifest 意为"表明"，hesitate 意为"犹豫"，contrive 意为"设计"。这里是在讲为什么公司的管理者不敢惩罚电脑犯罪者。原句意为"他们一想到这些罪犯会在大庭广众之下到处吹嘘他们如何在公司的管理者、会计、安全人员的眼皮底下骗走了最为机密的记录和档案，就会犹豫不决（是否应该惩罚这些人）了"。根据句意，应选 C。

17. 选 D，此题为词义辨析题。elaborate 意为"详细描述"，simulate 意为"模拟"，propose 意为"计划，建议"，boast 意为"自夸"。由句意（见 16 题）可知，simulate 和 propose 意思在这里不合适；elaborate 是不及物动词，要使用固定搭配 elaborate on，也排除。故选 D。

18. 选 A，此题为词义辨析题。records 意为"记录"，figures 意为"数字"，deficits 意为"赤字"，matters 意为"事情，物质"。由句意（见 16 题）可知，选 A。

19. 选 C，此题为词义辨析题。stuff 意为"填充物"，facility 意为"设备"，staff 意为"员工"，faculty 意为"全体教员"。这里指的是公司员工，所以用 staff。

20. 选 D，此题为词义辨析和篇章逻辑题。separate 意为"分开"，divide 意为"分割"，cut 意为"切割"，depart 意为"离开"。原句意为"然后又一个电脑犯罪分子离开了，拿着他想要的推荐信，在另一个地方继续他的罪行"，故选 D。

Passage 9

【文章精要】

文章主要探讨了社会身份在人际交往中的作用。我们总是根据一个人的身份来给他定位，而且我们自身也可以根据环境的变化来选择自己相应的社会身份。但我们的选择是有限度的，只能在这个限度内进行调整。

【解析】

1. 选 B，此题为词义辨析题。aim 意为"打算"，attempt 意为"努力，尝试"，ascribe 意为"归因于"，ascertain 意为"确定，探知"。原句意为"人们总是倾向于按照他人的社会身份来给他定位"。attempt 最符合题意。

2. 选 A，此题为固定搭配题。in terms of 意为"按照"。句意见第 1 题。

3. 选 C，此题为词义辨析和篇章逻辑题。prove 意为"证明"，depict 意为"描述"，judge 意为"判断"，exemplify 意为"例证"。原句意为"我们必须判断图书馆里的人是读者还是图书管理员……"。这里 judge 和前文的 determine 词汇同义词复现，故选 C。

4. 选 A，此题为词义辨析题。property 意为"财产"，owning 意为"拥有物"，possession 意为"拥有"，estate 意为"不动产"。原句意为"……判断在我们财产旁的是盗贼还是抄水表的……"。estate 一般用于比较专业的情况，如：real estate（房地产）。owning 和 possession 虽然都有"财产"之意，但是要用复数。所以正确答案只能是 A。

5. 选 D，此题为词义辨析题。在英语中，查水表、电表、天然气表等的人被叫做 meter reader，属于词语的修饰搭配，故选 D。

6. 选 D，此题为词义辨析题。assert 意为"断言"，propose 意为"建议"，discern 意为"辨别"，assume 意为"承担"。原句意为"我们承担的社会身份会随着遇到的人的不同而有所变化，而且在我们的一生中也会发生变化"。"承担某种身份或者责任"在英语中使用动词 assume。此外，下文其实出现了动宾短语 assume the statuses，这属于原词复现。

7. 选 A，此题为固定搭配题。考查介词的用法，change throughout life 的意思是"一生中有所变化"。

8. 选 B，此题为词义辨析和篇章逻辑题。similar 意为"类似的"，various 意为"各种各样的"，unanimous 意为"一致的"，certain 意为"一定的"。前文出现了 vary 和 change 等词，根据同义词复现的线索，此处应为 various。原句意为"我们中的大部分人都能够快速地呈现不同情况下所要求的社会身份"。

9. 选 D，此题为词义辨析题。confrontation 意为"面对面"，encounter 意为"遭遇"，contradiction 意为"矛盾"，interaction 意为"交互作用"。原句意为"社交就是识别、选择合适的社会身份，并且允许他人选择与我们相关的社会身份"，故选 D。social interaction 意为"社会交往"。

10. 选 C，此题为词义辨析题。particular 意为"特别的"，adequate 意为"足够的"，appropriate 意为"适当的"，authentic 意为"可信的"。由句意（见第 9 题）可知，本题选 C。

11. 选 A，此题为固定搭配题。根据句意，此处为"关于，涉及"之意，相应的固定搭配是 in relation to。relation 意为"关系"，relevance 意为"相关性"，reconciliation 意为"和解"，reliance 意为"依赖，依靠"。

12. 选 D，此题为词义辨析题。take 意为"采用"，put 意为"放置"，impose 意为"强加"，fit 意为"调整，使适应"。原句意为"这意味着我们根据持续的评价和解释的心理过程调整自己针对其他人的行为"。四个选项中，只有 fit 与题意相符。

13. 选 B，此题为词义辨析题。continual 意为"频繁的"，constant 意为"持续的"，consistent 意为"一致的"，consecutive 意为"连贯的"。由句意（见第 12 题）可知本题选 B。

【考点归纳】

● continual 意为"频繁的",意味着不存在间断,如:continual interruptions(频繁的中断)。

● constant 意为"不变的,持续的",侧重于事件发生的稳定性和持续性以及经久不变的特点,如:constant repetition of the exercise(不断重复练习)。

● consistent 意为"一致的",经常使用固定搭配 be consistent with(符合,一致),如:be consistent with the facts(和事实相符)。

● consecutive 意为"连贯的,一个接一个的",如:three consecutive days(连续三天)。

14. 选 A,此题为词义辨析题。appraisal 意为"评估",praise 意为"表扬",evaluation 意为"估价,评价",measure 意为"测量"。此处意为"评估对方的社会身份",故选 A。

【考点归纳】

● evaluate 一般指为查明事情的本质而进行的大量判断与分析,如:evaluate the student's thesis(分析学生论文)。

● appraise 在这里表示评审某物的质量,或估计某人的才能等,如:appraise a student's work(评定学生的作业)。

15. 选 B,此题为词义辨析和篇章逻辑题。hard 意为"困难地",effortlessly 意为"毫不费力地",badly 意为"糟糕地",intricately 意为"杂乱地"。原句意为"虽然有些人会觉得这项任务比较难,但是大部分人都可以毫不费力地完成它"。句子的前半句出现了 difficult,两个分句是转折关系,根据反义同现原则,应填 effortlessly。

16. 选 D,此题为词义辨析题。previously 意为"之前地",completely 意为"完全地",totally 意为"全部地",ready 意为"准备好地"。原句意为"社会身份被比喻为成衣"。"成衣"就是 ready-made clothes,选 D。

17. 选 A,此题为词义辨析题。present 意为"提出,呈现",illustrate 意为"举例说明",demonstrate 意为"示范",fabricate 意为"制作,构成"。原句意为"我们必须从社会提供给我们的衣服中进行选择",只有 A 最符合题意。

18. 选 C,此题为词义辨析题。variation 意为"变化",change 意为"变化",alteration 意为"改变",adaptation 意为"改编"。原句意为"只要在范围内进行选择,我们可以进行一定的修改……",故选 C。

19. 选 B,此题为词义辨析和篇章逻辑题。此处句意为"除了一些小的变动,我们受限于商店货架上给我们提供的东西"。首先排除 major 和 big。tiny 意为"很少的,微小的",指的是大小,而这里指程度,故选 minor。

20. 选 C,此题为语法结构题。这里考查宾语从句的引导词,what 在从句中作宾语。句意见 19 题。

Passage 10

【文章精要】

文章介绍了美国的价格体系、其定义及相关因素。美国的价格体系是一个包括商品和各种服务在内的复杂体系，而"价格"本身就是一个包含了数量、质量等各种不同因素在内的概念。

【解析】

1. 选 C，此题为词义辨析题。原句意为"价格是消费者衡量有限供应的产品或者服务的方式"。空格中应填入表示"方式"之意的单词，故选 C。

【考点归纳】

- method 指具体做某事的方法或详细、有逻辑的计划，如：Our teacher is showing us a new method of writing. (老师告诉我们一种写作的新方法。)
- way 泛指一些方法，如：That's my way of life. (那就是我的生活方式。) 但是在这道题中不应该使用复数。
- means 意为"方式"，指借以成就某事的方法，如：He climbed the tree by means of a ladder. (他用梯子爬上了树。)

2. 选 C，此题为词义辨析题。store 意为"储存"，stock 意为"库存"，supply 意为"供应"，provision 意为"提供"。由句意（见第 1 题）可知，store 和 stock 不符合句意，应排除。provision 虽然意思可以，但是没有 in limited provision 这种说法，故选 C。in limited supply 意为"供应量有限"。

3. 选 A，此题为词义辨析题。system 意为"系统"，construction 意为"建设"，structure 意为"结构"，strategy 意为"策略"。原句意为"美国的价格体系是一个复杂的系统"。根据空格后的单词 network 和同义词复现原则，此处应填 system。

4. 选 B，此题为词义辨析和篇章逻辑题。clear 意为"清晰的"，complex 意为"复杂的"，crucial 意为"关键的"，cumulative 意为"累积的"。空格后解释了价格体系的构成，有多种要素，可见是"复杂的"，故选 B。

5. 选 A，此题为语法结构题。空格处要填入一个指代 prices 的代词，故选 those。

6. 选 B，此题为词义辨析题。facility 意为"设备"，utility 意为"公共事业"，use 意为"使用"，utensil 意为"器具"。此处意指"公共设施"，固定的说法是 public utility。

7. 选 D，此题为词义辨析题。freely 意为"自由地"，voluntarily 意为"自愿地"，readily 意为"欣然地"，randomly 意为"随便地，未计划地"。原句意为"如果让一群任意选择的人来定义'价格'……"，故选 D。

8. 选 B，此题为篇章逻辑题。空格后的部分是对空格前的解释，故选 in other words，意为"换句话说"。

9. 选 A，此题为固定搭配题。agree upon/on sth.意为"就某事达成一致"。agree with sth.意为"（与某事物）相一致"，agree to sth.意为"同意，愿意"。

10. 选 B，此题为词义辨析题。void 意为"无人的，空的"，valid 意为"有效的"，available 意为"可利用的"，vain 意为"徒然的，无用的"。原句意为"这个定义是有效的"，故选 B。

11. 选 C，此题为词义辨析题。special 意为"特殊的"，specific 意为"具体的，不抽象的"，particular 意为"特定的"，productive 意为"生产的"。原句意为"理解一个特定交易中的价格，所要了解的东西绝对不止是涉及的钱"。specific 是和"抽象的"对应的"具体的"之意，用在这里并不合适，所以正确答案只能是 C。

12. 选 D，此题为词义辨析题。mentioned 意为"提到的"，related 意为"相关的"，concerned 意为"有关的"，involved 意为"涉及的"。从含义上来说，后三个选项均可，但是 related 后用介词 to，concerned 后用介词 about，只有 involved 用介词 in，故选 D。

13. 选 D，此题为词义辨析题。transport 意为"运输"，communicate 意为"交流"，replace 意为"代替"，exchange 意为"交换"。原句意为"买卖双方不仅要熟悉涉及的金额，而且要熟悉交换的产品或服务的数量和质量……"。实际上，句子的后半部分再次出现了 the time and place at which the exchange will take place，根据衍生词复现，此处应选 D。

14. 选 A，此题为词义辨析题。此处意为"何时何处付款"，故选 payment。

【考点归纳】

- payment 意为"支付"，指买了东西后的付款，表示一种行为或状态，如：He gave the man £3 in payment for the book.（他为买这本书付给这人 3 英镑。）

- cost 意为"花销，花费"，指为购买而付出的或要求的数量、价格，如：The cost of the house was too high for me.（对于我来说，这房子的价格太高了。）

- fee 意为"费用"，是指一种法律或组织机构规定的为某项特权而征收的固定费用，如：tuition fee（学费）。

- fare 意为"交通费用"，如：taxi fare（打车费）。

15. 选 A，此题为词义辨析题。apply 意为"应用"，implement 意为"执行"，suit 意为"适合"，endow 意为"赋予"。implement 与 endow 不和 to 连用，suit to 意为"相称"，此处句意为"可以应用于本次交易的信用证条款和折扣"，使用 apply to。

16. 选 B，此题为词义辨析题。thing 意为"事情"，factor 意为"因素"，element 意为"要素，成分"，matter 意为"物质"。根据上下文，应选 B。

17. 选 A，此题为词义辨析题。fully 意为"完全地，充分地"，completely 意为"完全地，彻头彻尾地"，fundamentally 意为"基础地，根本地"，essentially 意为"本质地，本来地"。此处要表达的意思是"充分了解"，即 be fully aware of。

【考点归纳】
- fully 意为"充分地，透彻地"，有"深入"之意，如：fully understand（透彻理解）。
- completely 意为"彻头彻尾地"，和 absolutely 含义类似，如：completely honest（绝对诚实）。

18. 选 D，此题为词义辨析和语法结构题。此处要求填入一个表示"组成，构成"之意的单词。四个选项均有此意，但从用法上来说，只有 comprise 符合题意。compose 指"由……材料构成"，一般用被动语态 be composed of。consist 是不及物动词，固定搭配为 consist of。construct 意为"建设，构造"，comprise 意为"包含，由……组成"。

19. 选 B，此题为固定搭配题。exchange A for B 意为"用 A 来换 B"。

20. 选 A，此题为词义辨析题。evaluate 意为"评估，估价"，measure 意为"测量"，count 意为"数，计算"，value 意为"估价，评价"。此处意为"估价"，故 evaluate 和 value 符合题意。但是 evaluate 后面可以直接跟表示价格的词，而 value 后要用表示物的词，就是"给某物估价"的意思。根据空格处的情况，应选 A。

Passage 11

【文章精要】

　　文章讲述了美国城市的郊区化进程。随着工业的发展，越来越多的人到城市寻找工作机会，因此导致了工厂被一排排的住房包围的情况。为了解决这个问题，城市开始吞并周围的郊区；同时，交通的飞速发展也进一步促进了郊区化的进程。

【解析】

1. 选 C，此题为词义辨析题。空格后解释说在以前的城市里，人们徒步走就可以了，可见地方不大，因此应该是 highly compact，故选 C。

2. 选 B，此题为固定搭配题。move about 意为"走来走去"，符合题意。

3. 选 B，此题为词义辨析题。transmit 意为"传播"，convey 意为"搬运"，carry 意为"携带"，transact 意为"交易"。原句意为"货物用马车搬运"，故选 B。

4. 选 A，此题为词义辨析和固定搭配题。at the edge of 为固定搭配，意为"在……的边缘"，其他几个词没有这种用法，故选 A。

【考点归纳】
- edge 指某物的边缘、两个平面相接处的交线：如：cliff edge（悬崖边缘）。
- boundary 指分界、标识界或范围的边界线，如：the boundary of two fields（两块地的分界）。
- margin 指书边的空白处，如：book margin（页边空白）。

5. 选 B，此题为词义辨析和篇章逻辑题。pull 意为"拖，拉"，draw 意为"拖，吸引"，distract 意为"转移，分散"，indulge 意为"纵容"。空格后说有"就业的前景"，那么当然是被这种前景所"吸引"，使用 draw。

6. 选 A，此题为固定搭配题。in time 意为"及时，最后，终于"，on time 意为"准时"，at time 意为"偶尔"，没有 for time 这种说法。前文说了很多人被工厂的就业机会所吸引，来到这里，那么，这里自然是说最终工厂被人们居住的房子包围，从而产生了最早的城市。故选 A。

7. 选 D，此题为词义辨析题。discrimination 意为"辨别，区别"，protest 意为"断言，抗议"，denounce 意为"公开指责"，defense 意为"防卫"。denounce 是动词，首先排除。此处意为"为了防止居住区占领工业区"，可见是一种"防卫"，而非口头抗议，故选 D。

8. 选 B，此题为词义辨析题。stretch 意为"伸长"，enlarge 意为"扩大"，lengthen 意为"加长"，enhance 意为"提高，增强"。此句后半句说到"城市吞并了周边地区。为什么这样呢？是为了_____计税基数"。自然是为了"扩大"计税基数，这里属于词汇的因果同现，选 B。

9. 选 D，此题为词义辨析题。metropolitan 意为"都市的"，urban 意为"城市的"，suburban 意为"乡村的"，municipal 意为"市政的"。前文以费城为例，说它兼并了周边很多县。这肯定属于"市政"的职责和职权范围。故这里又提到芝加哥和纽约采取类似措施时，肯定是"市政策略"，使用 municipal。

10. 选 A，此题为词义辨析题。achieve 意为"达到"，acquire 意为"获得"，arrive 意为"到达"，avail 意为"有利于"。原句意为"实际上，美国的大部分大城市都是通过兼并周边地区才达到现在的规模的"，故选 achieve。arrive 为不及物动词，acquire 和 avail 不符合句意，均排除。

11. 选 D，此题为词义辨析题。neighborhood 意为"住宅小区"，place 意为"地方"，location 意为"位置"，community 意为"团体，社会"。根据上下文，选 D 最合适。

12. 选 C，此题为词义辨析题。speed 意为"速度"，improvement 意为"提高"，acceleration 意为"加速"，increase 意为"增加"。导致后半句说的"城市拥挤和社会压力"的自然是工业增长的"加速"，这属于词汇的因果同现，故选 C。

13. 选 B，此题为词义辨析题。facilitate 意为"使容易，使便利"，approach 意为"接近，逼近"，rectify 意为"调整"，subscribe 意为"赞成，订阅"。此处意为"城市拥挤和社会压力程度之高接近危险比例"，用 approach。

14. 选 C，此题为词义辨析题。discover 意为"发现"，create 意为"创造"，develop 意为"发明"，design 意为"设计"。此处说第一个电力驱动的运输线路的发明，故选 C。

15. 选 B，此题为词义辨析和篇章逻辑题。relate 意为"有关"，connect 意为"连接"，separate 意为"分开"，divide 意为"分割"。电车线路网自然是可以连接主要的城市地区，根据词汇因果同现，使用 connect。

16. 选 A，此题为词义辨析题。此处句意为"郊区化的浪潮把原先紧凑的工业城市转变成了分散的大都市"，故选 transform。

【考点归纳】

- transform 指彻底改变性质、职能或形状等，如：She transformed the room by painting it. (她漆了房间，使它焕然一新。)
- shift 指把某物从一个地方或位置移到或运到另一个地方，如：Shall I shift the chairs? (我把椅子移动一下好吗?)
- switch 指转换或转移，如转变观点或注意力等，如：switch the conversation to a lighter subject (把谈话转移到一个更轻松的话题)。
- alter 指部分地修改以使之不同，如：alter my will (修改我的遗嘱)。

17. 选 B，此题为词义辨析和篇章逻辑题。crowded 意为"拥挤的"，dispersed 意为"分散的"，widespread 意为"普遍的"，compact 意为"紧凑的"。根据反义同现的线索，上文出现了 compact，那么这里应该用它的反义词 dispersed。

18. 选 C，此题为词义辨析题。procedure 意为"进程"，step 意为"做某事的步骤"，phase 意为"阶段"，process 意为"过程"。原句意为"大规模市郊化的第一阶段随着城市中产阶级的出现得到了加强"，故选 C。

19. 选 C，此题为词义辨析题。similar 意为"类似的"，same 意为"相同的"，simultaneous 意为"同时的"，simulated 意为"仿真的"。中产阶级和城市市郊化是同时出现的，故选 C。

20. 选 B，此题为固定搭配题。desire for 的意思是"渴望得到"。

Passage 12

【文章精要】

    文章介绍了亨利·福特率先采取的劳工政策。在这种新政策下，工作环境更加安全，工作时间大大缩短，劳工的待遇和生活质量也得到很大改善。

【解析】

1. 选 A，此题为词义辨析题。advanced 意为"先进的"，appropriate 意为"适当的"，accessible 意为"可接近的"，acute 意为"尖锐的"。这里说"福特在1913年就采取的劳工政策在今天被认为是_____"。根据文章中心，作者对此持肯定态度，故应选 A。

2. 选 D，此题为词义辨析题。method，way，means 均为"方法，方式"之意，而原句意为"安全措施得到提高"，故选 measure，意为"措施"。

3. 选 B，此题为词义辨析题。decrease 意为"下降"，reduce 意为"减少"，decline 意为"下降"，drop 意为"下降"。原句意为"和以前一天工作十到十二个小时相比，工作时间减少到了每天八个小时"。四个单词看似均符合题意，但实际上文中要求填入的是被动语态，而 decrease，decline 和 drop 作为"下降"之意讲时，都是不及物动词，故选 B。

4. 选 C，此题为词义辨析题。这里的意思是"整个工厂"。complete 指一件事情"完整"；all 指"全部"，用在这里应该说 all of the factory；total 指总额上的"全部"，也不对。正确答案只能是 C。

5. 选 A，此题为词义辨析和篇章逻辑题。shift 意为"轮班"，switch 意为"转化"，section 意为"部分"，class 意为"等级"。原句意为"为了适应短的工作日，整个工厂被分成了两至三个班次进行轮班"，故选 A。

6. 选 C，此题为篇章逻辑题。前文讲了新政策的好处之一，这里开始讲其他好处，表递进，故选 in addition。

7. 选 B，此题为固定搭配题。injured on the job 即指"因工受伤"。

8. 选 A，此题为词义辨析和篇章逻辑题。professional 意为"专业的"，practical 意为"实际的"，technological 意为"科技的"，technical 意为"技术的"。原句意为"工厂创建专业学校来训练专门技术门类的工人，并且给移民创办英语学校"。空格后出现了 specialized skilled laborers，根据同义词复现的线索，空格中应该填 professional。

9. 选 B，此题为词义辨析题。effect 意为"效果"，trial 意为"尝试"，step 意为"步骤"，strength 意为"力气"。trial 最符合句意，即"甚至尝试雇用残疾人，并为刑满释放的犯人提供工作机会"，故选 B。

10. 选 B，此题为词义辨析题。greatly 意为"很，非常"，widely 意为"广泛地"，unanimously 意为"一致地"，deeply 意为"深深地"。根据上下文，此处指"得到广泛承认的革新措施"，故选 B。

11. 选 C，此题为词义辨析题。provide 意为"提供"，assure 意为"保证"，offer 意为"提供"，sponsor 意为"资助"。此处指"提供最低工资"，故 assure 和 sponsor 不符合句意，均排除。provide 虽然也是"提供"之意，但是用法为 provide sb. with sth.，不能用在这里。所以正确答案是 C。

12. 选 C，此题为词义辨析题。依据空格前的单词 recruit 和同义词复现原则，应填入 retain，此处句意为"雇用和保留最好的机械师"。

【考点归纳】

- maintain 意为"维持，保持"，如：maintain balance（保持平衡）。
- sustain 意为"支持"，相当于 support，如：sustain the whole family（养家糊口）。
- retain 意为"保留"，如：retain water resources（保留水资源）。
- attain 意为"获得，达到"，如：attain the position of manager（获得经理的职位）。

13. 选 A，此题为词义辨析和篇章逻辑题。discourage 意为"阻碍，使气馁"，hold 意为"掌握"，prohibit 意为"禁止"，stimulate 意为"刺激"。采取了这么多有利于工人的措施，当然是为了阻碍工会的发展，但绝对不是"禁止"，否则就没有必要采取这些措施了。所以正确答案是 A。

14. 选 D，此题为词义辨析和固定搭配题。in terms of 意为"按照……"。其他三个选项的搭配分别为：by virtue of 意为"依靠，由于"，in the aspect of 意为"在……方面"，in

relation to 意为"和……有关"。

15. 选 B，此题为词义辨析题。invent 意为"发明"，create 意为"创造"，produce 意为"生产"，yield 意为"生产"。福特允许工人购买本厂生产的汽车，当然是"创造"了市场，故选 B。

16. 选 B，此题为词义辨析题。exemplify 意为"例证"，demonstrate 意为"展示"，improve 意为"提高"，verify 意为"查证"。原句意为"想要符合拿最低工资的标准，工人必须有和睦的家庭，而且要展现良好的个人素质，包括镇定、勤俭、勤奋和自立"，故选 B。

17. 选 D，此题为篇章逻辑题。根据上下文，这里是转折关系，故选 although。原句意为"虽然有人批评福特过于干涉他的员工的私生活，但毫无疑问，在那样一个移民劳工被压榨到极限的年代，福特帮助了很多人在美国立足"。

18. 选 D，此题为词义辨析题。individual 意为"个人的"，routine 意为"日常的"，usual 意为"通常的"，personal 意为"私人的"。由句意（见 17 题）可知，这里指 personal life"私人生活"。

19. 选 A，此题为固定搭配题。take advantage of 意为"利用"。此处若用 use，则要使用固定搭配 make use of 才行。

20. 选 C，此题为词义辨析题。distinguish 意为"辨别"，identify 意为"鉴别"，establish 意为"使定居，建立"，settle 意为"定居"。distinguish oneself 意为"使扬名"，identify 后面不能跟 oneself，settle 是不及物动词，都应排除。establish oneself 意为"使自己定居下来，立足"，为正确答案。

Passage 13

【文章精要】

文章主要探讨了美国人的谈判风格和在谈判中造成误解的原因。美国人不太懂得谈判技巧，因此往往被认为是拥有大把钞票但却没有人情味的谈判对手。他们往往采用很直接的方式，而且坚持实现短期目标，因而给对方造成了一些误解。

【解析】

1. 选 A，此题为篇章逻辑题。前文说了国际商务交流中需要良好的外语水平和跨文化交际技巧。这里说美国人在这两方面都不在行，可见是转折关系，故填 however。

2. 选 B，此题为词义辨析和篇章逻辑题。fulfillment 意为"实行"，success 意为"成功"，master 意为"掌握"，privilege 意为"特权"。原句意为"美国人在这两个方面都不在行，因此在国际领域的谈判中就没有取得其他国家的谈判者那样的成功"。根据上下文判断，应该选 B。

3. 选 B，此题为词义辨析题。enemy 意为"敌人"，counterpart 意为"对等的人"，cooperator 意为"合作者"，entrepreneur 意为"企业家"。根据句意，这里指其他国家的谈判者，也就是和美国谈判者拥有相同身份的人，故选 B。

4. 选 C，此题为词义辨析题。procedure 意为 "程序"，progress 意为 "进步"，process 意为 "过程"，proceeding 意为 "进程"。原句意为 "谈判就是为了答成同一目的而来回交流的_____"。根据上下文，这里应该指 "过程"，故选 C。

5. 选 B，此题为固定搭配题。back and forth 是固定搭配，意为 "来回地"。

6. 选 D，此题为词义辨析题。include 意为 "包括"，conclude 意为 "总结"，concern 意为 "涉及，关系到"，involve 意为 "涉及"。原句意为 "它（谈判）涉及劝说和妥协"，答案为 D。

【考点归纳】

- include 意为 "包括"，指包括的具体内容，如：Many people went there, including us.（很多人去了那里，包括我们。）
- concern 意为 "涉及" 时，经常使用固定搭配 concern about（涉及），如：The report expressed serious concern about the environment.（报告表达了对环境的严重忧虑。）
- involve 意为 "涉及"，用作及物动词，如：The strike involved many people.（许多人参加了罢工。）

7. 选 A，此题为词义辨析题。participate in 和 take part in 都表示 "参加"，但后者一般指参加某种轻松的活动，这里指谈判，所以不合适，故选 A。attend 为及物动词，后面不用 in，而 blend in 意为 "融入"。

8. 选 C，此题为语法结构题。此处考查的是定语从句的引导词。空格前有介词，从句的关系代词指物，所以只用 which 不用 that。

9. 选 D，此题为词义辨析题。arrive 意为 "到达"，gain 意为 "获得"，facilitate 意为 "使容易"，reach 意为 "达到"。此处意为 "达成妥协"，要求填入一个及物动词，故首先排除 arrive。gain 和 facilitate 又不太符合句意，故选 D。

10. 选 A，此题为篇章逻辑题。wealthy 意为 "富裕的"，sensitive 意为 "敏感的"，poor 意为 "贫穷的"，rude 意为 "无礼的"。原句意为 "在国外的很多国际商务谈判中，美国人都被认为是有钱但不通人情的"。这里的 wealthy 实际上是和本段第三行中说的 multi-million-dollar 的近义词复现，故选 A。

11. 选 D，此题为篇章逻辑题。claim 意为 "宣称"，communicate 意为 "交流"，exchange 意为 "交换"，bargain 意为 "讨价还价"。原句意为 "国外的谈判者们通常觉得美国人代表了资产上亿的大公司，能够支付得起任何价钱，而且从来都不讨价还价"。整个文章的中心，都在说美国人不善于谈判，而且有钱，因此这里应该填入 bargaining。

12. 选 B，此题为语法结构题。这里考查了代词的指代，that 指的是 role。原句意为 "美国谈判者的角色演变成了一个不通人情的、到处传播信息、挥洒金钱的人"。

13. 选 A，此题为词义辨析题。study 意为 "研究"，discussion 意为 "讨论"，investigation 意为 "调查"，seminar 意为 "研究会"。原句意为 "在对于美国谈判者的研究中，人们发现了他们的许多性格特征，从而进一步证实了这种论调"。根据上下文，应选 A。

14. 选 D，此题为词义辨析题。assure 意为"保证"，secure 意为"保护"，guarantee 意为"保证，担保"，confirm 意为"证实"。confirm 和下文的 undermine 构成反义同现，为正确答案。

【考点归纳】

- assure 意为"向某人保证……"，一般搭配是 assure sb. of sth. 或者 assure sb. that...，如：I can assure you that it's perfectly safe. (我可以向你保证它绝对安全。)

- secure 指保护人或者物的安全，如：Despite making several good jokes, he could not secure the goodwill of the audience. (尽管他说了几个有趣的笑话，但仍无法确定观众是否接受他。)

- guarantee 意为"保证"，含义和 assure 比较像，一般说 guarantee that...，如：I guarantee that you'll like this book. (我保证你会喜欢这本书。)

- confirm 指进一步证实论断、猜测等，如：Please confirm your telephone message by writing to me. (请给我来封信，好进一步证实你在电话中传达的消息。)

15. 选 B，此题为词义辨析题。concept 意为"概念"，perception 意为"理解，感知"，realization 意为"实现"，feeling 意为"感情"。perception 和上一段开头的 perceive 构成同源词复现，故选 B。concept 指的是抽象、总称的概念，用在此处不合适。

16. 选 B，此题为固定搭配题。special 意为"特殊的"，particular 意为"特别的"，essential 意为"本质的"，private 意为"私人的"。in particular 是固定搭配，意为"尤其"，其他几个单词中，只有 private 的前面可以用 in，意为"私下的"，用在这里不合适。原句意为"尤其有两个特点导致了跨文化的误解，那就是美国谈判者的率直和急躁"，故选 B。

17. 选 A，此题为固定搭配题。on the part of 意为"在……那一方面"，句意见 16 题。

18. 选 B，此题为词义辨析和固定搭配题。disgusted 意为"厌恶的"，willing 意为"愿意的"，likely 意为"有可能的"，easy 意为"简单的"。原句意为"另一方面，外国的谈判者们却有可能非常重视谈判双方的关系，并且愿意为此投入大量的时间，以期取得长期的利益"。四个选项中只有 B 符合，be willing to do sth. 意为"愿意做某事"。

19. 选 D，此题为词义辨析题。strengthen 意为"巩固"，proceed 意为"进行"，tighten 意为"拉紧"，solidify 意为"巩固"。此处意为"巩固这种关系"，只有 strengthen 和 solidify 符合题意。但是 strengthen 一般指加强力量，所以排除，答案为 D。

20. 选 B，此题为词义辨析和篇章逻辑题。前文说到美国人的特点是直率，这里与其他国家的谈判者对比，可见他们比较喜欢委婉的方式，故答案为 B。indirect 和本段第三行的 directness 构成反义同现。direct 意为"直接的"，indirect 意为"间接的"，effective 意为"有效的"，efficient 意为"效率高的"。

Passage 14

【文章精要】

文章介绍了英国人口普查的发展历程。在 18 世纪至 19 世纪的英国，从事工业生产的人越来越多，同时英国的人口也飞速增长。由于担心快速的人口增长会导致贫穷和饥饿，英国开始了 10 年一次的人口普查。

【解析】

1. 选 A，此题为词义辨析和篇章逻辑题。continue 意为"继续"，decline 意为"下降"，maintain 意为"保持"，uphold 意为"支持"。文章第一句说到 18 世纪英国的很多家庭开始在工业领域工作赚钱。这句又说"这种趋势一直_____到 19 世纪"，可见是"持续，继续"。两句之间是递进关系，所以选 A。

2. 选 C，此题为词义辨析和篇章逻辑题。excellence 意为"优秀"，existence 意为"存在"，prominence 意为"突出，显著"，power 意为"力量"。空格所在分句和前一个分句——"这种趋势一直持续到 19 世纪"——构成转折关系，意为"虽然此时提供服务的工作早已超过制造产品的工作而突显出来"，所以选 C。

3. 选 A，此题为词义辨析和篇章逻辑题。此处句意为"人口增长比以前任何时候都快"，所以填 ever。

4. 选 B，此题为词义辨析题。existing 意为"存在"，occurring 意为"出现"，precipitating 意为"急落"，dating 意为"追溯到"。空格所在部分句子意为"（这是）在 18 世纪晚期以来出现的最明显的增长转折点"，可知选 B。

5. 选 D，此题为固定搭配题。be involved in 意为"卷入到……中，涉及……"。

【考点归纳】

- be included in 意为"包括在其中"，通常指比较具体的东西，如：My points are included in the report.（报告中包括了我的观点。）
- be absorbed in 意为"专心致志于"，如：He is absorbed in his work.（他专心致志地工作。）
- be indulged in 意为"沉迷于"，如：He is indulged in the Internet world.（他沉迷于网络世界。）
- be involved in 意为"卷入，涉及"，如：He was involved in the case.（他被卷入了这起案件中。）

6. 选 B，此题为词义辨析题。原句意为"维多利亚时代早期和乔治亚时代早期的情况相比，涉及商品制造业的人要多得多"。可见要填一个有表示"情况"之意的单词，所以选 B。

【考点归纳】
- affair 指国家大事或者公事，常见搭配有：international affair（国际事务），foreign affair（外交事务），business affair（商业事务）。
- incident 指小事或者事变，常见搭配有：exciting incidents on the trip（旅途中激动人心的事），vicious incidents（恶性事件）。
- event 指具有重大政治或者历史意义的事情或者活动，常见搭配有：political events（政治事件），historical events（历史事件），outdoor events（户外活动）。

7. 选 B，此题为词义辨析题。在第一段第四行曾经提到此时人口增长很快，这里又再次提到这个问题，但需要填名词。根据衍生词复现的线索，选择 rapidity。

8. 选 D，此题为篇章逻辑题。chaos 意为"混乱"，hit 意为"热点"，sympathy 意为"同情"，anxiety 意为"焦虑，担心"。四个单词各不相同。后句提到一个很悲观的人预言了一个不好的结果，根据同义词复现的线索，这里要填一个和 gloomy 同样性质的单词，所以选 D。人口增长过快可能让人担心或焦虑，却不太可能造成混乱，所以不选 A。

9. 选 A，此题为词义辨析题。predict 意为"预言"，suppose 意为"假设"，anticipate 意为"期待"，foretell 意为"预示"。根据上下文，应该选 A。

10. 选 A，此题为固定搭配题。in the event 是固定搭配，意思是"结果"。

11. 选 B，此题为词义辨析题。根据前文，该部分句子的意思应为"人们对人口增长的关心导致了 1801 年英国的第一次人口普查"，所以填 concern。passion 意为"热爱"，care 意为"（对人）关心照料"，grief 意为"悲伤"，均不符合题意。

12. 选 D，此题为词义辨析题。interruption 意为"打断，妨碍"，表示突然插入的某行动或过程，eruption 意为"爆发"，rupture 意为"裂缝"，disruption 意为"中断"，有"使之陷入混乱和杂乱无章"的意思。这里指的是人口普查在 1941 年因战争而"中断"，所以选 D。eruption 可以用在 war 后面，但不能用在 wartime 后面，所以不对。

13. 选 B，此题为词义辨析和篇章逻辑题。qualifications 意为"规格，素质"，occupations 意为"职业"，accomplishments 意为"造诣"，conditions 意为"条件"。空格后的半个分句是 and hence how people earned a living，根据同义词复现线索，这里应该是 earn a living 的同义词，所以选 B。

14. 选 A，此题为语法结构题。这里考查的是强调句 It is...that... 的用法。

15. 选 C，此题为词义辨析和篇章逻辑题。空格后的半个分句为 rather than of groups of people，根据反义同现的线索，可知这里应该填表示"个人"意义的单词，所以填 individuals。

16. 选 D，此题为词义辨析题。fundamental 意为"根本性的"，necessary 意为"必要的"，essential 意为"基本的"，crucial 意为"关键的"。根据上下文，填 crucial 最合适。

17. 选 A，此题为词义辨析题。issue 意为"发放"，exemplify 意为"举例证明"，attribute 意为"归结于"，subscribe 意为"订阅"。这里指给人们发放人口普查表，所以选 issue。

18. 选A，此题为词义辨析题。legally 意为"法律上地"，morally 意为"道德上地"，leg-islatively 意为"立法地"，compulsorily 意为"强迫地"。既然是"要求"，那么当然是 compulsorily，如果再选它，语义上就显得重复。morally 和 legislatively 显然不对，所以只能选A。

19. 选C，此题为词义辨析题。这里的意思是"1851年的人口普查要求填写的信息就更全面了"，所以选C。

20. 选D，此题为词义辨析题。assemble 意为"加工，组装"，accumulate 意为"积累（经验等）"，segregate 意为"隔离"，collect 意为"收集"。只有 collect 可以和空格后的 information 构成动宾搭配表示"收集信息"，所以是正确答案。

Passage 15

【文章精要】

文章主要探讨了美国人和亚洲人家庭观念的差异。亚洲人的家庭观念很强，非常尊重长辈，视赡养老人为自己的义务；与此相反，在青年人占主导地位的美国，赡养老人则被认为是一种负担。

【解析】

1. 选B，此题为词义辨析题。enlarge，extend 和 expand 均有"扩大"之意，lengthen 意为"加长"。原句意为"亚裔人的家庭一般是大家庭，好几代有血缘关系或者婚姻关系的人居住在同一个家庭里"。实际上，"大家庭"有固定的说法，即 extended family，所以正确答案是B。

【考点归纳】

- enlarge 指具体范围的"扩大"，是及物动词，如：enlarge a photo（放大照片）。
- extend 指比喻意义上的"延续"，或者范围的"扩展"，更偏向于"延续"，如：extend a road（延长公路）。它既可以作及物动词，又可以作不及物动词。
- expand 指"扩展"，既可以作不及物动词，又可以作及物动词，既可以指具体的东西，如：The field expands to the riverside.（这片田地一直延伸到河边。）又可以指抽象的东西，如：expand the business（扩大公司的业务）。

2. 选C，此题为篇章逻辑题。history 意为"历史"，interaction 意为"交流"，blood 意为"血缘"，bond 意为"合同"。在"家庭"这个场景下，连接人们的不是婚姻就是血缘了，故选C。

3. 选D，此题为词义辨析和固定搭配题。accuse，charge 和 blame 都有"谴责"之意，而 convict 意为"证明……有罪"。原句意为"一个亚洲人做错了事情，不仅仅他自己会受到谴责，他的整个家庭甚至包括死去的祖先都会受到谴责"，所以首先排除 convict；根据词法可知，正确答案为D。

【考点归纳】

- accuse 的固定用法为 accuse sb. of sth.，如：The man was accused of cheating. (那人被控欺诈。)
- charge 的固定用法为 charge sb. with sth.，如：The police charged him with car theft. (警方以偷车罪指控他。)
- blame 的固定用法为 blame sb. for sth.，或者 blame sth.，如：A freak storm was to blame for the power outage. (停电的起因是一场特大暴风雪。)

4. 选 A，此题为固定搭配题。原句意为"传统的中国人，和许多其他亚洲人一样，尊敬他们的长辈，而且觉得自己对他们负有责任"。"对……"在这里应该使用介词 toward，故选 A。

5. 选 C，此题为词义辨析题。contribution 意为"贡献"，suffering 意为"受难"，sacrifice 意为"牺牲"，tribute 意为"贡品"。原句意为"孩子们努力获得成功，在他们的父母年老的时候赡养他们，以此作为对父母为自己所作牺牲的回报"。根据句意，应该选择 C。

6. 选 B，此题为词义辨析题。formal 意为"正式的"，natural 意为"自然的，正常的"，regular 意为"经常的，规则的"，peculiar 意为"特殊的"。原句意为"这是中国人生活中的一个正常的部分"。根据上下文，应选 B。

7. 选 D，此题为篇章逻辑题。in comparison 意为"相比较而言"，to the same extent 意为"同等程度的"，in a way 意为"某种程度上"，in contrast 意为"相反"。前文说中国人都很尊敬和爱护自己的父母，后文说在美国照顾年老的父母被认为是一种负担，可见是"相反地"，故选 D。in comparison 虽然意思也可以，但是一般要说 in comparison with。

8. 选 C，此题为词义辨析和篇章逻辑题。relief 意为"减轻，免除"，responsibility 意为"责任，义务"，burden 意为"负担"，business 意为"事务"。根据前文出现的 a natural part of life in China 和反义同现的线索，这里应该指"负担"，故选 C。

9. 选 B，此题为词义辨析题。reward 意为"犒赏"，honor 意为"尊敬，给以荣誉"，regard 意为"认为"，compliment 意为"称赞"。此处意为"在美国，照顾老人不是一件多么光荣的事情"，所以用 honor。

10. 选 A，此题为篇章逻辑题。此处是进一步说明老年人在美国的地位，故选 in fact，意为"实际上"。

11. 选 B，此题为词义辨析题。accept 意为"接受"，receive 意为"收到"，deserve 意为"值得"，gain 意为"获得"。原句意为"实际上，在年轻人占统治地位的美国，变老被认为是一件坏事，许多老年人不会受到尊敬"，根据上下文，应选 B。

12. 选 B，此题为词义辨析和固定搭配题。confine 意为"限制"，dedicate 意为"致力"，correspond 意为"协调"，expose 意为"使曝光"。原句意为"他们为孩子作奉献，而且为了孩子能够受到教育宁愿牺牲一切"，be dedicated to 是固定搭配，意为"为……献身"，故选 B。

13. 选 A，此题为词义辨析和固定搭配题。devote 意为 "致力于"，contribute 意为 "奉献"，indulge 意为 "沉迷于"，observe 意为 "遵守，观察"。原句意为 "孩子们也会一切都为了他们的父母"。根据句意，首先排除 indulge 和 observe。contribute 不使用被动语态，也排除。be devoted to 意为 "为了……，致力于……"，和前文的 dedicated 构成同义词复现，故选 A。

14. 选 C，此题为词义辨析题。occasionally 意为 "有时"，intentionally 意为 "故意地"，typically 意为 "典型地"，steadily 意为 "平稳地"。原句意为 "为了经济原因而离开国家的孩子们最具代表性的做法就是把他们收入的一大部分寄回家给他们的父母"。根据上下文，只有 typically 符合题意。

15. 选 B，此题为词义辨析题。insist on 意为 "坚持"，consist of 意为 "由……组成"，persist in 意为 "坚持"，resist to 意为 "反抗"。原句意为 "越南的家庭由活着的人、死去的人和还未出生的人构成"，故选 B。

16. 选 B，此题为词义辨析题。incidence 意为 "影响范围"，decision 意为 "决定"，accident 意为 "事故"，expedition 意为 "远征"。此处选 decision，和后面的 action 构成了一定程度上的词汇同义词复现。原句意为 "任何决定或者行动都是为了家庭考虑，而不是为了个人欲望"。

17. 选 C，此题为词义辨析题。personal 意为 "私人的"，private 意为 "私人的"，individual 意为 "个人的"，own 意为 "自己的"。此处填 individual，和前面的 family 构成词汇反义同现。

18. 选 A，此题为词义辨析题。particularly 意为 "尤其"，naturally 意为 "自然地"，especially 意为 "特别地"，mentally 意为 "精神上地"。原句意为 "越南人尤其不相信所谓的自立，在这一方面，他们和美国人正好相反"，故选 A 最合适。

19. 选 B，此题为词义辨析和篇章逻辑题。counterpart 意为 "极其相似的人或物"，opposite 意为 "相反"，competitor 意为 "竞争者"，opponent 意为 "反对者"。根据文章的逻辑，这里说的是越南人和美国人大不相同，故选 B。

20. 选 B，此题为词义辨析题。station 意为 "车站"，status 意为 "地位，状况"，stature 意为 "身高"，state 意为 "状态"。这里考查的实际是近形词辨析。原句意为 "许多越南人认为他们此生中的行为会影响他们来生的状况"，故选 B。

Passage 16

【文章精要】

文章介绍了魔术大师 Houdini 和他的轶事。Houdini 非常擅长脱逃术，能够在几秒钟内解开任何的锁和结，曾经从警察的重重铁索下逃脱。最著名的一次是他被铁链锁住后装到箱子中，钉紧后投入了大海，但他还是奇迹般的在一分钟后就逃了出来。

【解析】

1. 选 B，此题为篇章逻辑题。上一句说了魔术师其实并不会什么神奇的法术，这句说这并不妨碍我们欣赏魔术，可见两者是转折关系，故选 B。

2. 选 A，此题为词义辨析题。produce 除了"生产"之外，还有"拿出"之意，get 意为"得到"，turn 意为"变成"，acquire 意为"得到"。原句意为"这并不妨碍我们欣赏魔术师从帽子里面变出兔子"，故选 A。

3. 选 C，此题为篇章逻辑题。根据上下文，作者的意思应该是"Houdini 可能是最伟大的魔术师"。首先排除 though 和 out of the question（决不可能），undoubted 是形容词，而此处要填副词，故答案为 C。

4. 选 A，此题为词义辨析和篇章逻辑题。四个单词的意思非常简单，无需解释。整篇文章其实都在说 Houdini 非常擅长"脱逃术"，因此和 escape 相关的词语如 free oneself from，famous escape 等出现了很多次。故此处答案为 A。

5. 选 A，此题为词义辨析题。complicated 意为"复杂的，难解的"，complex 意为"复杂的，综合的"，difficult 意为"困难的"，deliberate 意为"深思熟虑的"。此处选 complicated，这样 complicated locks 和前面的 tightest knots 构成词汇的场景同现。原句意为"他可以在几秒钟内从最紧的结和最复杂的锁中逃脱出来"。

6. 选 D，此题为语法结构题。名词性从句中各种成分齐全时，引导词用 that。

7. 选 B，此题为词义辨析题。create 意为"创造"，invent 意为"发明"，develop 意为"发展"，imagine 意为"想象"。此处意为"他曾经仔细研究过每一种发明出来的锁"，故选 B。

8. 选 D，此题为词义辨析题。此处意为"他们把他用链子_____了起来"，显然是"捆"，故选 D。

9. 选 C，此题为固定搭配题。in an instant 意为"立即"，此处意为"他立刻就把自己解开了"。instant 一般不和除了 in 外的介词搭配。

10. 选 C，此题为词义辨析题。原句意为"警察指责他使用了工具，再次把他锁了起来"，故选 C。accuse sb. of sth. 意为"指责、谴责、控告某人做了某事"。

【考点归纳】

- rid sb. of sth. 意为"摆脱……"，如：He was finally able to rid himself of all financial worries.（他终于使自己摆脱了所有的财政忧虑。）

- deprive sb. of sth. 意为"剥夺某人的……"，如：They were deprived of a normal childhood by the war.（由于战争，他们失去了正常的童年时代。）

11. 选 D，此题为词义辨析题。原句意为"Houdini 也许把他的针放在了蜡状物质中并且把它扔在了走廊的地板上"。candle 意为"蜡烛"，object 意为"物体"，material 意为"材料"，substance 意为"物质"，故选 D。

12. 选 C，此题为词义辨析题。process 意为"过程"，isle 意为"岛屿"，passage 意为"走廊"，room 意为"房间"。由句意（见 11 题）可知本题选 C。

13. 选 A，此题为词义辨析题。stick to 意为"粘住"，hold to 意为"坚持"，keep 是及物动词，不加介词，cling to 意为"依靠，坚持"。原句意为"当他从那里走过的时候，他踩在了这个蜡状物上，使它粘在自己的脚底"，故选 A。

14. 选 A，此题为语法结构题。此处应填入连接时间状语从句的引导词，选项中只有 A 合适。

15. 选 D，此题为词义辨析题。空格处修饰后面的形容词 surprising，可见要填入副词，故首先排除 overall。all but 意为"几乎"，no longer 意为"不再"，altogether 意为"完全，总而言之"。原句意为"他最著名的一次脱逃非常令人震惊"，故选 D。

16. 选 D，此题为词义辨析题。include 意为"包括"，locate 意为"位于"，circulate 意为"循环"，enclose 意为"装入"。原句意为"他身上锁着重重的锁链，被装入了一个空的木箱子中，箱子的盖子用钉子钉住了"，故选 D。

17. 选 B，此题为语法结构题。此处考查定语从句的引导词。因为空格前有介词，故只用 which，不用 that。

18. 选 B，此题为词义辨析题。四个单词均有"掉下，下降"之意，但是此处是被动语态，应填入一个及物动词，四个选项中只有 drop 是及物动词，故选 B。原句意为"箱子被扔入纽约港的海中"。

19. 选 B，此题为词义辨析题。face 意为"面部"，surface 意为"表面"，cover 意为"封皮，盖子"，horizon 意为"视野，地平线"。原句意为"一分钟后他就游到了水面"，故选 B。

20. 选 C，此题为词义辨析题。bring up 意为"养大"，bring out 意为"生产，说出"，break apart 意为"拆开"，break into 意为"闯入"。原句意为"当箱子被拆开的时候，它已经被打开而且里面放着原本用来锁住 Houdini 的铁链"，故选 C。

Passage 17

【文章精要】

文章主要探讨了阅读及其本质。专家们虽然都认为阅读是一项复杂的大脑功能，对于阅读的具体过程却看法不一。有人认为阅读就是将符号解码为声音的过程，有人却认为阅读是和思考紧密相连的，如果只是读出声音但却不加以理解，就不是真正的阅读。

【解析】

1. 选 B，此题为词义辨析题。substantively 意为"实质上"，substantially 意为"充分地，相当大地"，substitutively 意为"代用地"，subjectively 意为"主观地"。这道题考查近形词，原句意为"阅读的概念几个世纪以来变化＿＿＿＿＿＿"，自然是"相当大"，故选 B。

2. 选 C，此题为词义辨析题。focus 意为"聚焦"，direct 意为"指导"，devote 意为"致力于"，aim 意为"目标"。四个单词惯用的搭配为 focus on sth.，direct at sth.，devote to sth. 和 aim to do sth.，根据单词的用法，只能选 C。

3. 选 A，此题为篇章逻辑题。此句前半部分说"专家大都认为阅读涉及复杂而高级的大脑功能的组织问题"，后半部分说"他们在阅读的本质是什么上面却无法达成一致"，可见句子内部为转折关系，故选 A。

4. 选 A，此题为语法结构题。此处考查 involve 这个单词的用法，可以归为语法类题。involve 是及物动词，意为"涉及"，是正确答案。

5. 选 D，此题为词义辨析题。阅读是大脑的一项 function（功能），而非 quality（质量），meaning（意义）或者 value（价值）。故选 D。

6. 选 B，此题为词义辨析题。根据上下文，结合词汇同现的线索，前面提到 function（功能），这里自然是说 nature（本质，性质）了。

7. 选 A，此题为词义辨析题。此处 view 对应的就是句子前半部分的 regard，属于同义词复现。原句意为"有些专家认为语言就是用符号来代表声音的代码，他们认为阅读不过是将这些符号解码为它们所代表的声音的过程"。

8. 选 D，此题为固定搭配题。stand by 意为"支持，遵守"，stand to 意为"遵守，坚持，固执"，stand off 意为"疏远，避开"，stand for 意为"代表"。由句意（见第 7 题）可知本题选 D。

9. 选 B，此题为词义辨析题。此题考查近形词，content 意为"使满足"，contend 意为"主张"，contempt 意为"轻视"，contact 意为"接触"。contempt 是名词，应排除；content 和 contact 不符合句意。此处的 contend 和下一句的 maintain 构成同义词复现，故选 B。

10. 选 A，此题为词义辨析题。inexplicably 意为"到无法说明的程度地"，inexpressibly 意为"无法用语言表达地"，inextricably 意为"解决不了地"，inexpediently 意为"不适宜地"。前一句说"有专家认为思维过程和阅读的解码过程是没有关系的"，这句话则说"另外一些专家认为阅读和思维的关系_____"。显然是说关系很大，结合选项可知，只有 A 合适。

11. 选 A，此题为词义辨析题。interpret 意为"理解，将……解释为"，含有理解之意，explain 意为"解释"，也就是把你明白的东西向他人说明。此处句意为"一个孩子如果只是发出了声音，但是没有明白其含义，那么他并不是在进行真正意义上的阅读"，故选 A。

12. 选 C，此题为词义辨析题。这里要表达的意思是"真的阅读"，和"假的阅读"相对而言，故选 C。

【考点归纳】

- really 意为"实在地，真地"，表示程度，相当于 very，如：really fascinating（非常迷人）。

- definitely 意为"明确地，干脆地"，表示毫无疑问之意，相当于 surely，如：definitely wrong（绝对错了）。

- truly 意为"实在地，真正地"，和"虚假地"相对应，如：reported the matter truly（真实地报告这一事件）。

- indeed 含义和 really 类似，有 in fact 之意，如：very cold indeed（真是很冷）。

13. 选 D，此题为词义辨析和篇章逻辑题。此处主要考查语境理解，单词认识就行。

comprehensive 意为"综合的", practical 意为"实际的", fundamental 意为"基本的", theoretical 意为"理论上的"。原句意为"对于这些专家（认为阅读和思维是有很大关系的专家）来说，所谓读者不是那些仅仅具备_____的阅读能力的人，而是那些阅读的人"，显然，这里要说的意思是这些人不是光"理论上"会读，而要"真正"去读，故选 D。

14. 选 D，此题为词义辨析题。由句意（见 13 题）可知，本题选 D。

15. 选 C，此题为词义辨析题。class 意为"分班"，grant 意为"赋予"，classify 意为"分类，分等"，grade 意为"分级"。原句意为"对于一些专家来说，这些人（能读但是从来不读的人）不能归为真正意义的读者"，故空格应填入有"分类"之意的单词，故选 C。

16. 选 C，此题为词义辨析题。inclusive 意为"包括的"，inclinable 意为"倾向于……的"，conclusive 意为"无可置疑的，决定性的"，complicated 意为"复杂的"。此处意为"最_____和令人满意的定义"，根据同义词复现，应该是"无可置疑的"，故选 C。

17. 选 D，此题为词义辨析题。break up 意为"打碎"，elaborate 意为"详细阐述"，define 意为"定义"，unlock 意为"解开"。文章中一直说有人认为阅读就是解码，故根据同义词复现，此处应填 unlock。只不过此处作者给了一个折中的说法，即"阅读就是对语言符号进行解码，同时为了不同的目的，以不同的速度，在不同难度的情况下，主动地全面诠释其含义的能力"。

18. 选 A，此题为词义辨析题。由句意（见 17 题）可知本题选 A。

19. 选 C，此题为语法结构题。此处考查代词的指代，这里 to do so 指代前文的 to interpret meaning。

20. 选 B，此题为篇章逻辑题。此处是对前文的总结，故选 in short，意为"简而言之"。by the way 意为"顺便说一下"，so far 意为"迄今为止"，on the other hand 意为"在另一方面"。

Passage 18

【文章精要】

文章讨论了暴力解决种族矛盾的问题。再理智的人在这个问题上也难免走入极端，认为只有暴力才能解决问题，却没有意识到如果能把精力用在诸如提高生活水平和提供就业机会的问题上，情况就会好很多。

【解析】

1. 选 A，此题为词义辨析题。impose 意为"强加"，implement 意为"执行"，carry 意为"携带"，regulate 意为"规范"。文章这里是在举种族问题的反面例子，所以此处肯定是讲白人通过武力将自己的规则"强加"给其他民族的人，而不仅仅是"执行"，故选 A。

2. 选 C，此题为词义辨析题。几个单词很简单，都有"做，引起"的意思。然而"纵火"在英语中只能说成 set fire，故选 C。

3. 选 B，此题为固定搭配题。on both sides 意为"双方"。

4. 选 A，此题为词义辨析和篇章逻辑题。reasonable 意为"通情达理的"，reasonably 是其副词形式，reasonless 意为"无推理能力的，不合理的"，reason 意为"原因"。原句意为"双方的一些重要人物，他们在其他方面都是_____的，此时却大力支持暴力行动（来解决种族矛盾问题），就好像这种行为是合法的一样"。由于下一段开始讲 truly reasonable men（真正通情达理的人）会怎样，此处显然是在说那些其他方面 reasonable，遇到种族矛盾问题就变样的人，根据原词复现，应选 A。

5. 选 D，此题为篇章逻辑题。for the sake of 意为"为了……"，for fear of 意为"担心……"，in case of 意为"在……情况下"，in favor of 意为"支持"。由句意（见第 4 题）可知本题选 D。

6. 选 C，此题为固定搭配题。when it comes to the crunch 是一个习语，意为"当关键时刻到来时"，也可说成 if/when the crunch comes。

7. 选 B，此题为词义辨析题。improvement 意为"改进"，progress 意为"进展"，increase 意为"提高"，change 意为"改变"。原句意为"最让人担心和绝望的是，当提到关键性的问题时，我们一点进展也没有"，根据上下文，应选 B。

8. 选 A，此题为词义辨析题。basically 意为"基本上"，obviously 意为"明显地"，necessarily 意为"必须地"，eventually 意为"最终地"。原句意为"我们可能不用为了战争给身上涂抹颜料，可以穿西装打领带，但是我们的天性_____没有改变"。显然要填"基本上"，选 A。

9. 选 C，此题为语法结构题。此处考查 record 一词的非谓语动词形式，历史是被记录的，故应使用过去分词 recorded 表示被动的含义，选 C。

10. 选 D，此题为词义辨析题和篇章逻辑题。此题考查对上下文语境的理解。severe 意为"严厉的"，depressed 意为"沮丧的"，explicit 意为"明白的"，acute 意为"尖锐的"。原句意为"我们还没有意识到暴力并不能解决问题，只会让它更_____"，显然应填入"尖锐"，和前面的 solve the problem 构成反义同现，选 D。

11. 选 C，此题为词义辨析和语法结构题。bring to light 意为"发现，揭发"，come to light 意为"被发现，为人所知"。原句意为"在我们沮丧地凝视战争的硝烟和废墟，思考到底是什么袭击了自己的时候，依然没有任何解决的方法"，再加上主语为单数，故选 C。

12. 选 C，此题为词义辨析题。句意见 11 题。四个选项中，think 后接宾语从句，故排除；consider 作为"考虑"之意讲时，后面要用 doing sth.，此处显然不对；contemplate 意为"思考"，符合句意；regard 意为"认为"，意思不对，故选 C。

13. 选 A，此题为语法结构题。此处考查宾语从句的引导词，该引导词在从句中作主语，故只能选 A。

14. 选 B，此题为词义辨析题。really 意为"实际上"，truly 意为"真正地"，absolutely 意为"绝对地"，entirely 意为"完全地"。此处指"真正通情达理的人"，和"虚假"相对，故选 B。

15. 选 C，此题为词义辨析题。lay 意为 "放置"，lie 意为 "在于"，主语是复数，故选 C。

16. 选 D，此题为词义辨析题。原句意为 "由于支持用法律解决问题这种令人 (指他们民族的人) 无法忍受的事情，他们 (指不支持暴力解决问题的人) 被鄙视、被怀疑，甚至被他们民族自己的规则迫害"，故选 D。

17. 选 B，此题为词义辨析题。regulation 意为 "规则"，enforcement 意为 "执行"，imposition 意为 "强迫接受"，reform 意为 "改革"，此处指 "法律的执行"，即 law enforcement，故选 B。

18. 选 A，此题为词义辨析题。energy 意为 "精力"，attention 意为 "注意力"，time 意为 "时间"，support 意为 "支持"。此处意为 "如果用于暴力行为的精力得到正确的使用"，这里的 energy 和下文的 efforts 构成同义词复现，故选 A。

19. 选 A，此题为固定搭配题。几个单词惯用的搭配为 be focused on，be involved in，be attracted，be absorbed in。故选 A。

20. 选 C，此题为词义辨析题。原句意为 "我们就不会为找到解决方法而走冤枉路了"，实际上，go a long way to 是一种固定的表达方式，是 "为了达到……还有很长的路" 的意思，故选 C。

Passage 19

【文章精要】

　　文章主要探讨了近年美国人对体育运动非常热衷的现象。为了保持健康，大部分美国人每周都会抽出固定的时间用于锻炼，即使不喜欢运动的人，也会通过做柔软体操等来进行锻炼。

【解析】

1. 选 B，此题为词义辨析题。prosperity 意为 "繁荣"，popularity 意为 "流行"，density 意为 "密度"，intensity 意为 "强度"。文章开头即说近年美国人对体育运动有很大热情，这里自然是说体育运动和比赛越来越流行，故选 B。

2. 选 D，此题为词义辨析题。表示户外运动，要用 event，故选 D。affair 一般指国家大事，如 international affairs；case 一般指法律案件；incident 一般指突发事件。

3. 选 D，此题为词义辨析题。此处考查近义词的辨析，要求填入一个具有 "组成" 之意的单词。首先排除 construct (建设)，其次从词法角度考虑，只有 constitute 符合题意。

【考点归纳】

- compose 一般使用被动语态，即：A is composed of B and C。如果使用主动语态，主语应为多种不同的东西，即：B and C compose A，如：Water is composed of hydrogen and oxygen. (水是由氢和氧化合而成的。)

- consist 是不及物动词，使用固定搭配 consist of，如：Our class consists of 40 students. (我们班由 40 个学生组成。)

4. 选 C，此题为词义辨析及固定搭配题。ever after 意为 "从此以后一直……"，ever before 意为 "以前"，ever since 意为 "从那时到现在"，由句意可知此题选 C。

5. 选 B，此题为固定搭配题。in the aspect of 意为 "在……方面"，thanks to 意为 "由于"，in terms of 意为 "考虑到……"，by way of 意为 "作为……"。原句意为 "由于有了电视，孩子们在很小的时候就可以了解和欣赏体育运动节目"，选 B。

6. 选 A，此题为词义辨析题。schedule 意为 "日常安排"，plan 意为 "计划"，practice 意为 "实践"，job 意为 "工作"。原句意为 "大约 6000 万的男女每天从日程安排中抽出 25 分钟的时间锻炼，而且每周至少锻炼 3 次"，故选 A。

7. 选 D，此题为词义辨析题。additional 意为 "追加的"，substantial 意为 "大量的"，more 意为 "更多的"，extra 意为 "多余的"。原句意为 "大部分美国人都有多余的时间参加体育运动，也有多余的钱可以支付器械和指导"。此处应填 extra，和句子前半句的 extra 构成同义词复现。

8. 选 B，此题为词义辨析题。verify 意为 "证实"，justify 意为 "证明……是正当的"，demonstrate 意为 "示范，证明"，intensify 意为 "加强"。原句意为 "他们觉得为了保证身体健康，一切为了打保龄球、高尔夫球和网球的花销都是正当的"，故选 B。

9. 选 D，此题为词义辨析题。由句意（见第 8 题）可知，此处指 "花费"。cost 为 "花费，花销" 之意，但是没有复数；payment 指买了东西后的付款，表示一种行为或状态；fee 一般用于指学费、生活费，如：tuition and accommodation fee。而 expense 常用来指日常的花销或开支，故选 D。

10. 选 C，此题为词义辨析题。mentally 意为 "精神上"，psychologically 意为 "心理上"，physically 意为 "身体上"，emotionally 意为 "感情上"。文章讲的是体育运动，自然是 "身体上"，故选 C。

11. 选 A，此题为词义辨析题。follow 意为 "跟随，遵循"，observe 意为 "遵守（规则等）"，watch 意为 "观看"，simulate 意为 "模仿"。要想保持健康当然是要跟着一定的项目坚持锻炼，故选 A。

12. 选 A，此题为词义辨析和篇章逻辑题。空格处的词用来修饰动词 conduct，故应填副词，先排除 daily 和 weekly。regularly 意为 "经常性地"，irregularly 意为 "不经常地"，从篇章逻辑上看，应该选 A。

13. 选 D，此题为固定搭配题。be popular with 意为 "在……中很流行，很受欢迎"。

14. 选 B，此题为词义辨析题。原句意为 "走路是大概 4400 万美国人采取的主要锻炼方式"，故选 B。method 指解决问题的方法，所以不对。

15. 选 C，此题为词义辨析题。work 意为 "工作"，regularity 意为 "规律"，routine 意为 "常规，日常事务"，standard 意为 "标准"。此处大意为很多美国人都会每天散步 1 至 5 公里，可见这是他们的日常必修课，所以使用 routine。

16. 选 A，此题为篇章逻辑题。此句是说什么人会内部循环失调，4 个选项意思分别为：怠惰的、精力充沛的、闲散的、有精力的。显然应该选 A。

17. 选 B，此题为词义辨析题。4 个单词的含义虽然有类似之处，但是能和疾病搭配的只有 develop，如 develop an illness 是 "得病" 的意思。

18. 选 B，此题为词义辨析题。文章的中心就是讲美国人重视体育锻炼，因为他们想要保持健康的体魄，怕生病，因此他们会严肃认真地对待医生的警告，故选 B。severely 意为"严格地"，seriously 意为"严肃地，认真地"，seemingly 意为"表面上"，sensitively 意为"敏感地"。

19. 选 B，此题为固定搭配题。"在……上投资"就是 invest money in...。

20. 选 C，此题为词义辨析和固定搭配题。pay off 意为"还清"，pay back 意为"报答"，pay out 意为"付出"。根据上下文，他们在体育锻炼上投入了时间、精力、金钱，这种投资肯定会让他们有所收获，故选 C。

Passage 20

【文章精要】

文章介绍了一种关于人类外貌形成的新观点：人类外貌的形成并非完全由基因决定，相反，它很大程度上受到周围人和环境的影响。由此才可以理解为什么生活在一起的人或者同一个地区的人很多外貌特征都比较类似。

【解析】

1. 选 C，此题为词义辨析题。face 意为"脸"，complexion 意为"面色"，appearance 意为"外貌"，look 意为"面容"。原句意为"他相信人的外貌通常是受到文化的影响"。appearance 和 look 符合题意，但是 look 前面不用加 physical，故选 C。

2. 选 C，此题为篇章逻辑题。此句是由上句推出的，两句之间是因果关系，故选 C。accordingly 意为"因此，从而"。

3. 选 B，此题为词义辨析和篇章逻辑题。既然人的外貌是受到外部环境的影响，那么自然不是天生的 (not born with us)。

4. 选 D，此题为词义辨析和篇章逻辑题。changeable 意为"多变的"，formed 意为"成形的"，definite 意为"明确的，一定的"，unformed 意为"未成形的"。根据文章的前后语义逻辑，此处含义应为"婴儿的外貌特点是未定型的"，故选 D。文章的后面也多次出现 is not set at birth 和 not formed 等字眼，和此处构成同义词复现。

5. 选 D，此题为语法结构题。此处考查代词的指代，选 D。

6. 选 D，此题为语法结构题。此处考查宾语从句的连词。原句意为"这就解释了为什么美国一些地区的人会长得如此相似了"。

7. 选 A，此题为词义辨析和篇章逻辑题。alike 意为"相似的"，different 意为"不同的"，same 意为"相同的"，like 意为"像……一样"。由句意（见第 6 题）可知本题选 A，和下一句的 similar 构成同义词复现。

8. 选 B，此题为词义辨析题。character 意为"品质"，characteristic 意为"特点"，speciality 意为"特质，专业"，instinct 意为"本能"。原句意为"南方人有某些类似的面部特征，这些特征无法用遗传学来解释"。此处应选 B，与前文的 facial feature 构成词汇同义词复现。

9. 选 A，此题为词义辨析题。genetics 意为 "遗传学"，genesis 意为 "起源"，generation 意为 "一代人"，genealogy 意为 "族谱"。根据句意（见第 8 题），应选 A。

10. 选 C，此题为词义辨析题。concrete 意为 "具体的"，special 意为 "特殊的"，exact 意为 "准确的"，absolute 意为 "绝对的"。原句意为 "嘴巴的_____形状在出生时并未固定下来，而是后来形成的"。显然，应填入一个具有 "确切的，具体的" 之意的形容词。但 concrete 所指的 "具体的" 和 "抽象的" 相对应，而此处是说嘴巴 "确切的" 形状，故应选 C。

11. 选 C，此题为篇章逻辑题。此句是对上句的进一步说明，故选 C。in fact 意为 "实际上"。

12. 选 B，此题为词义辨析题。produce 意为 "生产"，set 意为 "固定"，make 意为 "制造"，develop 意为 "发展，发明"。原句意为 "实际上，嘴巴最终的形状要在恒齿形成后才会固定下来"，故选 B，和前文的 formed 构成词汇同义词复现。

13. 选 A，此题为词义辨析题。原句意为 "对于很多人来说，嘴巴的最终形状要直到他们进入青春期才会固定"，故选 A，此处 well 含有 "充分地，适当地" 之意。

14. 选 C，此题为词义辨析题。此句意为 "我们的长相是从旁边的人那里学到的"。前面曾经提到 A baby learns where to set the eyebrows...和 The exact shape of mouth...is learned after，故此处选 C，和前文构成词汇同义词复现。

15. 选 A，此题为词义辨析题。single 意为 "单一的"，only 意为 "唯一的"，separate 意为 "分开的"，lonely 意为 "孤独的"。原句意为 "这可能就是为什么在同一个国家内有些地区的人比另外一些地区的人更爱笑的原因"，故选 A。

16. 选 D，此题为篇章逻辑题。此处为举例说明上句话，故选 D。that is to say 意为 "换句话说，更确切地说"，用于进一步说明前面提到的问题。

17. 选 A，此题为词义辨析题。frequently 意为 "频繁地"，commonly 意为 "普通地"，usually 意为 "通常地"，regularly 意为 "有规律地"。原句意为 "例如在美国的南部，人们笑的频率最高"，故选 A，和前文的 more than 构成同义词复现。

18. 选 B，此题为篇章逻辑题。此处为递进关系，故选 B。still less 意为 "更少"。

19. 选 C，此题为词义辨析和篇章逻辑题。此处要求填入一个副词来修饰空格后的形容词 populated，故首先排除 A。从句意上来看，大城市自然是人口众多，故 barely（很少）和 sparsely（稀疏）都不对，选 C。densely populated 意为 "人口众多的"。

20. 选 A，此题为语法结构题。此处 do 代替前文的 smile and greet。原句意为 "在人口众多的大城市，人们相互微笑和打招呼的频率比乡村和小城镇上的人低很多"，故选 A。

第二章 短文改错

第一节 现状与趋势

大学英语六级考试的短文改错部分是运用心理语言学原理设计的一种测试题型，目的在于测试考生的语言知识及综合运用语言的能力。所选短文一般涉及考生较熟悉的科普、社科、人文历史等方面的内容，难度适中，字数在 200 字左右。它要求考生在 15 分钟内找出短文内的 10 处错误（不包括拼写或标点符号错误），并改正。这 10 处错误分别位于 10 行并对应 10 个题号，也就是说每一行（或题）仅有一个错误。考生在错误的地方增、删、改正、替换某一个词或短语，使短文语意连贯，结构正确。

在改革后的新题型中，短文改错属于"综合测试"的一部分，占总分的 10%，和完形填空构成二选一题型。从测试手段和测试形式来说，和旧题型相比没有太大变化。实际上，在旧题型中，短文改错出现的频率远远高于完形填空。以 2001 年至今的六级考试为例，13 次考试中只有 2001 年 1 月、2002 年 12 月和 2005 年 6 月考了完形填空，其余 10 次均考的是短文改错。究其原因，短文改错题的内容比较广泛，题目难度较大。无论是词法、句法还是篇章逻辑都可能成为改错设题的对象，做题时考生不仅要指出错误，还要能够改正才行（在原文中指出了错误之处并修改正确得 1 分；指出了错误但修改不正确得 0.5 分；未指出错误修改也不正确，或者虽然修改正确但是并未在原文中指出错误的，均是 0 分）。因此与完形填空相比，短文改错题明显增加了难度，更符合六级考试的难度要求。

总的说来，六级短文改错具有如下特点：

● 四级短文，六级难度。六级短文改错从文章内容和长度来说，比六级阅读理解部分的文章简单，相当于四级水平。但是由于考生在做题时不仅要理解单个句子并进行判断和改正，还需要在理解短文的结构，尤其是理解上下文逻辑关系发展的脉络后再进行判断和更正，所以短文改错的难度超越了文章本身的难度。

● 体裁上以说明文为主，逻辑性强。上面提到的 10 篇 2001 年至今的短文改错文章中说明文有 7 篇，议论文有 3 篇。这两种文体的共同点在于其行文的逻辑关系比较明确，而逻辑关系题也正是短文改错的一个重要考点。

● 检测综合运用语言的能力。从下表可以看出，六级短文改错的题型相对而言比较固定：词法错误在每套试题中都占了较大的比例，但与此同时，句法错误和逻辑错误也不可轻视。这恰恰印证了前文所说的，短文改错是从词法、句法、篇章逻辑三个层次上综合考查考生运用所学英语知识的能力。

2001~2006 六级短文改错全真试题题型分布表

年份 题型	2006	2005		2004	2003		2002		2001	总数	比例
	6	12	1	6	1	6	6	1	6		
词法错误	7	7	7	6	7	4	4	3	4	49	54.4%
句法错误	2	1	3	3	2	3	5	4	3	26	28.9%
逻辑错误	1	2	0	1	1	3	1	3	3	15	16.7%

注：考虑到 2003 年 9 月六级考试只在北京等 7 省市大学举行，具有一定局限性，上表并未纳入该年试题分析。

● 错误设置方面以错词为主。改错题的错误设置的形式一般有以下三类：

1）错词。在标有题号的一行中有一词在词法、搭配或词义等方面有错误，要求考生找出错误并换上正确的词。

2）缺词。在标有题号的一行的任何位置——包括该行首词前和末词后——缺了一词，要求考生按语法、搭配或上下文语义的需要找出缺词的位置并补上所缺的词。

3）多词。在标有题号的一行中有一词按语法、搭配或上下文语义纯属多余，要求考生找出该多余的词并划去。

历年考题的统计资料表明，绝大多数改错题均属于错词一类，而多词和缺词的错误在一篇改错题中加起来不超过 3 个。其主要原因在于这类题难度较大，更能考查考生实际的语言驾驭能力。

第二节 对策与技巧

第一节中提到，六级短文改错从词、句、篇三个不同的层次入手考查考生综合运用语言知识的能力。在本节中我们将六级短文改错的错误类型分为词法错误、句法错误和逻辑错误三大类，并针对这三类题分别剖析其应试技巧。

一、词法错误

六级短文改错中对词法的考查比较多，命题的时候考点很分散，实词、虚词都会有所涉及，不会集中考查某种词性的单词。

命题规律

1. 介词短语和固定搭配。**介词短语**就是由多个词构成的介词，如 because of, in spite of 等；**固定搭配**则指习语和一些常见的固定用法，即由名词、形容词、动词等和介词或者副词等构成的短语，如 influence on, different from, rely on 等。无论是介词短语还是固定搭配，考点常常对准介词，出现介词误用的情况；除此之外，对固定搭配的考查也常常涉及搭配中的冠词和名词单复数等问题，如将 in contrast 误用为 in the contrast，将 keep one's words 误用为 keep one's word 等等。

2. 动词。动词的考查主要集中在非谓语动词误用和及物动词、不及物动词混淆上。非谓语动词误用主要指现在分词和过去分词混淆，如将 a puzzling question 误用为 a puzzled question；遇到某些特殊的动词还要考虑它们后面要跟不定式还是动名词，还是两者都可以但是含义不同；还有动名词和不定式作句子的主语和宾语的问题，如有时原文中会直接使用动词原形作句子的主语，此时要改成动名词或不定式，但此类错误其实也可以归为句法错误中的句子结构混乱问题。**及物动词、不及物动词混淆**很好理解，如 survive（生存）一词是及物动词，因此"在地震中幸存下来"就是 survive the earthquake，而非 survive in the earth-quake，此时应去掉介词 in；有时候，在不及物动词后面又少了相应的介词，要加上。

3. 名词、冠词、代词。**名词单复数问题**也是考查的一个热点。**冠词**主要考查不定冠词和定冠词的混淆。**代词**主要考查其与所指代的名词是否一致，例如，若指代单数的物，要用 it，如果是复数，则要用 they；有时也会考查代词的混淆，例如作形式主语的话，要使用 it，而 that 等代词是没有这个功能的。

4. 易混词。主要就是**近义词混用**和**近形词混淆**的问题。如分不清 adopt 和 adapt，或者将 He is likely to do sth. 中的 likely 误用为其近义词 probable，但是 probable 前面的主语不能是人。

5. 词性。考查的重点是**词性混淆**，主要是名词与动词的误用、名词与形容词的误用以及形容词与副词的误用。例如说到某个问题的严重性，会用 increasingly serious（越来越严重），用副词修饰形容词，不能说 increasing serious。

答题技巧

1. 遇到特殊的介词短语或者固定搭配，要仔细辨别其形式是否正确，也就是其中的介词、冠词、名词的用法是否正确；对于介词短语，由于可能出现同一动词、名词、形容词后面可以跟不同的介词的情况，因此还要看看介词短语放在上下文中是否合适。如：break 可以和很多介词搭配表达不同的意思，break into 意为"非法闯入"，break off 意为"突然停止"，break up 意为"结束"，考生应根据上下文选择合适的搭配。

2. 遇到现在分词短语或者过去分词短语，一定要主动查找其逻辑主语，通过辨别该短语与其逻辑主语间的主被动关系来判断其用法是否正确，是否存在现在分词和过去分词混淆的情况。

3. 遇到某些用法比较有特色的动词，要充分考虑它后面的宾语。具体说来，就是这个动词到底能否直接跟宾语；如果它的后面可以跟非谓语动词作宾语，应用动名词还是不定式。

4. 遇到名词要考虑其单复数和前面所用冠词的问题；遇到代词，要考虑该词与它所指代的名词是否一致。

5. 学会从词法而不是单纯的汉语意思的角度辨别近义词，例如，同样有"导致"之意，cause 要用 cause sb. to do sth.，而 make 就要用 make sb. do sth.；同时在平时要多积累对近形词的认识，熟悉其拼写。

6. 认真辨别单词的词性，同时熟悉不同词性单词的用法。形容词用来修饰名词；副词用来修饰形容词、动词或者整个句子；主语、宾语要用名词而非动词或形容词。

二、句法错误

句法错误是六级短文改错中的又一大类。此类题中，考点主要集中在句子的基本语法状态（时态、语态、语气）、句子结构（主要是并列句和复合句）、主谓一致和某些特殊句型（倒装、强调、省略句）上。

命题规律

1. **句子的基本语法状态**。指句子的时态、语态和虚拟语气问题。具体说来，**时态问题**主要体现在某句话与整个篇章的时态不符；**语态问题**主要集中在该使用被动语态的时候却使用了主动语态或者漏了系动词；虚拟语气问题主要是该使用虚拟条件句时却使用了一般的条件状语从句，或者 suggest 等表示命令、建议、请求等词后面的从句中没有使用动词原形，以及 wish 或者 if only 等词后面的从句中没有根据具体情况使用一般过去时或者过去完成时。

2. **句子结构**。句子结构方面的问题可以分为以下几种：

   1）**句子结构不完整**。比较复杂的复合句最容易出现此类错误，因为句子较长，缺少了某个成分，如主语、谓语或者宾语，考生不容易发现。

   2）**句子结构混乱**。主要问题是一个简单句中出现了两个甚至更多的谓语，或者用动词作句子的主语或者宾语。

   3）**从句类型混淆**。最容易出现的是将强调句 It is...that... 与 that 引导的定语从句混淆，状语从句与 where 或 when 引导的定语从句混淆，同位语从句与定语从句混淆等。

   4）**定语从句关系词误用**。最容易出现的是将 which 与 that 误用，有时也会出现将 which 与 as 误用的情况。

   5）**并列句不对称**。and 连接的两个成分在语法状态上应当是对称的，也就是前面如果是动词的一般过去式，后面应该一样；前面如果是形容词比较级，其后也应如此；前面若为非谓语动词，后面也应是对应的形式。

3. **主谓一致**。当句子本身较长，主语和谓语之间有其他插入成分时，往往会出现**主谓不一致**的情况；另一种情况是如果主语不是通常的名词和代词，而是从句、非谓语动词短语或者一些特殊的短语等，也会出现**主谓不一致**的问题。

4. **特殊句型**。主要指倒装、强调和省略句中容易出现的一些问题。**倒装句问题**主要是句子部分倒装时漏掉了助动词；**强调句问题**集中在将 that 误认为是定语从句的关系代词 that 在句中作宾语的情况而漏掉；**省略句问题**一般出现在状语从句中：当状语从句的主语和主句相同，谓语为系动词时，要省略就要同时省略主语和谓语，而句中往往只省略了主语或者谓语。

答题技巧

1. 在做题之前先确定文章的基本时态，这样有助于发现短文中的时态问题。
2. 遇到比较特殊的动词如 suggest，wish 或连词 if 等时，要注意其后是否为虚拟语气。
3. 遇到比较复杂的复合句，即多重结构句时要充分注意句子有无缺少某个成分或者串句的情况。
4. 遇到状语从句、定语从句和同位语从句时，要仔细辨别从句类型，注意有无从句类型混淆的情况；定语从句要特别注意其关系词有无混用。
5. 遇到并列连词 and 要注意前后的成分从语法上说是否对称。
6. 遇到倒装、强调、省略等特殊句型一定要细心，看看是否符合相应的语法规则。

三、逻辑错误

逻辑错误主要是从篇章的层次考查考生对于上下文逻辑关系的理解。其考点相对于词法和句法错误来说相当地固定和集中，只有逻辑反义词和连接词误用两类。因此，虽然从题目的总数上来说逻辑错误无法和词法和句法错误相比，但是从小的考点来说，逻辑反义词和连接词误用在 10 道题目中所占的比率还是相当高的。

命题规律

1. 逻辑反义词。即短文中的错误单词和上下文的逻辑关系不符，恰巧是正确答案的反义词。例如将 buy 说成 sell，easy 说成 hard；还有就是按上下文语义，句中多用了 not 或 no，或必须添上 not 或 no。这是短文改错中出现频率较高也是短文改错中最具特色的一种错误类型，这类错误必须在透彻理解上下文语义的基础上才能发现并更正。

2. 连接词误用。逻辑错误中的连接词误用和句法错误中的从句类型混淆是不一样的，后者虽然也往往是连接词的问题，但是一般是由连接词引起的从句类型的混乱；而前者是指短文中前后两句话或者两个段落间的连接词未能正确地体现前后文之间的逻辑关系。常见的有并列连词 but，and，for，or 的混淆和误用；主从连词 because，as，if，unless，although，before，after 等的混淆和误用；连接性副词 however，moreover，therefore 等的混淆和误用；连接性介词 because of，despite，besides，instead of 等的混淆和误用。

答题技巧

1. 在做题之前要先弄清楚文章的基本态度，在做题的过程中遇到含义特征明显的动词和形容词如 buy，easy 等要充分注意。

2. 遇到表示明显逻辑关系如因果、转折、强对比和时间前后的连接性词语，要高度注意。

第三节 模拟练习

Directions: *This part consists of 40 short passages. In each passage, there are altogether 10 mistakes, one in each numbered line. You may have to change the word, add a word or delete a word. Mark out the mistakes and put the corrections in the blanks provided. If you change a word, cross it out and write the correct word in the corresponding blank. If you add a word, put an insertion mark (∧) in the right place and write the missing word in the blank. If you delete a word, cross it out and put a slash (/) in the blank.*

Passage 1

Animation (动画) means making things which are lifeless come alive and move. At earliest times, people have always been fascinated by   S1. _____

movement. And not until this century have we managed to capture   S2. _____

movement, to record it, and in the case of animation, to reinterpret it and recreate it. To do all this, we use a movie camera and a projector. In the world of cartoon animation, everything is impossible. You can make the characters you create do exactly what you want them to do. A famous early cartoon character was Felix the Cat, creating by Pat Sullivan in America in the early nineteen twenties. Fedix was a marvelous cat. He could do all sorts of things no natural cat could do as taking off his tail, using it for a handle and then putting it back. The famous Walt Disney cartoon characteristics came to life after 1928. Popeye the Sailorman and his girl friend Olive Oyl are born at the Max Fleischer studios in 1933. But to be an animator, you don't have to be a profession. It is possible for anyone to make a simple animated film without use a camera at all. All which you have to do is draw directly on to blank film and then runthe film through a projector.

S3. _____

S4. _____

S5. _____

S6. _____

S7. _____

S8. _____

S9. _____

S10. _____

Passage 2

More people than ever are drinking coffee these days—but in small quantities than they used to. Some manufacturers of coffee makers are trying to make advantage of this trend by developing diminutive machines that brew (煮) smaller amounts of coffee. Two U.S. appliance companies—Black & Decker, basing in Towson, Maryland, and Toastmaster Inc. of Columbia, Missouri—has recently introduced "drip" coffee makers that brew one or two cup servings of coffee. Neither of the products brew the coffee directly into a cup or mug, eliminating the need for a separate carafe. Since many people make a pot of coffee in the morning and drink only a single cup, the new coffee makers should reduce the wasted coffee. Black & Decker's Cup-at-a-Time spends $27, while Toastmaster's Coffee Break retails for $20.

S1. _____

S2. _____

S3. _____

S4. _____

S5. _____

S6. _____

S7. _____

Black & Decker also makes a coffee maker drips coffee directly into a carry-around thermal carafe. The carafe, a glass vacuum bottle, is supposed to keep the coffee fresh for hours. The product, called the Thermal Carafe Coffee-maker, comes with a built-in lid that opens during the brewing process, closes when it is completed. There are several models, including one that firs under the counter, ranging from $60 to $110 at price.

S8. _____

S9. _____

S10. _____

Passage 3

Unlike any earlier building complex anywhere in the world, Rocke-feller in New York City was built, not for a place where people could live in, but as a city in which they could work. It was one of the smallest building project of its kind, a city within city, and of the forerunner of projects that has sprung up all over the world. 30 architects, 120 drafts-men, and hundreds of other artists and technicians are employed just to draft the plans. Before the buildings could be erect, 229 old buildings had to be emptied of 4,000 tenants and razed. Just to buy up the leases took over two years and cost over $6,000,000. The unusual shape and setbacks of the 70-story RCA building resulted primary from practical considera-tions such as lighting, the movement of people and the building's services. The lower concourse and basement level were set aside for shops. A sunken plaza, complete with yards and fountains, were designed to provide access to these shops. Today the plaza, which used for ice-skating in winter and dining and dancing in summer, is one of the center's most popular attraction.

S1. _____

S2. _____

S3. _____

S4. _____

S5. _____

S6. _____

S7. _____

S8. _____

S9. _____

S10. _____

Passage 4

British anti-slavery was one of the most important reform movement of the 19th century. But its history is not without ironies. During the course of the 18th century the British perfected the Atlantic slave system. Indeed, what has been estimated that between 1700 and 1810 British merchants transported almost three million Africans across the Atlantic. That the British benefited from the Atlantic slave system is disputable. Yet, para-doxically, it was also the British who led the struggle to bring this system in an end.

The history of British anti-slavery can be divided into a number of distinct phases. The first of this stretched from 1787 to 1807 and was directed against the slave trade. Of course, there had been initiatives after this date. The Quakers, for instance, petitioned Parliament against the slave trade as early as 1783 and a similar petition submitted in 1785, this time from the inhabitants of Bridgewater in Somerset. But by and by these were piecemeal efforts, involved a relatively small number of people. It was the Society for the Abolition of the Slave Trade, organized in May 1787,

S1. _____

S2. _____

S3. _____

S4. _____

S5. _____

S6. _____

S7. _____

S8. _____

S9. _____

which set the movement on its modern course, evolving a structure and
organization that made it possible to mobile thousands of Britons.　　　　S10. _____

Passage 5

The *Mona Lisa* was one of Leonardo's favorite paintings, and he
carried it for him until he died. Today, it is regarded as the most famous
painting in the world, and is visited by thousand of people every year.

Who is this familiar figure? Many suggestions have made, but the most
alike candidate is Lisa Gherardini, the wife of a Florentine silk merchant.
Another more unlikely—and popular—theory is that the painting was a
self-portrait. There are certainly similarities between the face features of
the *Mona Lisa* and of the artist's self-portrait painted many years later.
Could this be why Leonardo gave the subject such an enigmatic smile?
Today, the *Mona Lisa* looks rather somber, in dull shades of brown and
yellow. This is due to a layer of varnish cover the paint, which has
yellowed over the years. It was possible that the painting was once
bright and more colorful than it is now.

The *Mona Lisa* was stolen from the Louver in 1911, by a former
employee who believed the painting belonged in Italy. The thief walked
out of the gallery with the picture underneath his painter's smock. He was
apprehended by police two years later, the painting was safely returned.

S1. _____
S2. _____
S3. _____
S4. _____
S5. _____
S6. _____

S7. _____
S8. _____
S9. _____

S10. _____

Passage 6

Psychology is the science of the mind. The human mind is the most
complex machine on Earth. It is the source of all thought and behavior. But
how can we study something more complex and mysterious as the mind?
Even we were to split open the skull of a willing volunteer and have a look
inside, we would only see the gray matter of the brain. We cannot see
someone thinking. Or can we observe their emotions, or memories, or
perceptions and dreams. So how do psychologists go about studying the
mind?

In fact, psychologists adapt a similar approach to scientists in other
fields. Nuclear physicists who interested in the structure of atoms cannot
observe protons, electrons and neutrons indirectly. Instead, they predict
how these elements should behave and devise experiments to confirm or
refute their expectations.

S1. _____
S2. _____

S3. _____

S4. _____
S5. _____
S6. _____

By a similar way, psychologists use human behavior as a clue to the workings of the mind. But we cannot observe the mind directly, everything we do, think, feel and say are determined by the functioning of the mind. So psychologists take human behavior as the raw data for test their theories about how the mind works.

S7. _____
S8. _____
S9. _____
S10. _____

Passage 7

Before Dr. Luther L. Terry, then the Surgeon General of the United States, issued his office first "Report on Smoking and Health" more than 30 years before, thousands of articles had already been written at the effects of tobacco use on the human body.

S1. _____
S2. _____
S3. _____

Tobacco companies had countered the reports, that purported to show links between smoking and cancer and other serious disease, with denials and competing studies. So in 1964, Terry and his Advisory Committee on Smoking and Health know they were stepping into a major pit of controversy when they announced "cigaret smoking is a health hazard of sufficient importance in the United States to warrant appropriate remedial action". It was America's first wide publicized acknowledgment smoking cigarets is a cause of serious diseases. But the issue wasn't settled in 1964, or was it settled in 1997, despite literally thousands more studies— and litigation that has forced at least one tobacco company to admit what some activists say they knew all along: cigaret smoke is hazardous to your health.

S4. _____
S5. _____

S6. _____

S7. _____
S8. _____
S9. _____

More than 30 years—and more than 20 Surgeon General reports—later, the issue appears headed for settlement in the courtroom rather than the laboratory.

S10. _____

Passage 8

Friendship is one of the greatest pleasures that people can enjoy. It is very difficult to find a best definition of friendship. A true friend does indeed find pleasure in our joy and share sorrow with our grief. In time of trial, he or she is always at our side to give us his or her help and comfort.

S1. _____
S2. _____

Knowing how valuable friendship is, we should be very careful in our choose of a friend. We must choose someone who has a good character, whose activities are good and who show kindness of heart. We should avoid from those shallow people who are easily

S3. _____
S4. _____
S5. _____

changing by adversities or misfortune.

A true friend can always be trusted, loved and respected. If you tell a friend your secrets, he or she will tell anyone else. Friends share each other joys and sorrows. They help each other when they are in trouble, and cheer each other when they are sad. The most important thing is that a friend always knows you. In conclusion, when you have made a good friend, don't forget him or her.

S6. _____
S7. _____
S8. _____
S9. _____
S10. _____

Passage 9

The factors that trigger migratory behavior in birds are difficult to explain. This behavior seems to be instinct, not learned. For example, many northern species leave their summer homes while the weather is still cold and the food supply plenty. Young arctic terns (燕鸥) born at the arctic breeding grounds will lake off with the flock for distant lands where they have never seen.

Bird migrations are probably regulating by the glandular (腺的) system. Scientists suspect that the changing length of the day is the factor that trigger migratory behavior. In an experiment, migratory birds were kept in artificially lighted rooms. It is found that if periods of darkness were lengthened proportionately, so the glands of the birds became active. These glands secrete hormones, which are chemicals that control numerous body functions. Shorter periods of daylight seem to change the hormone balance of birds, so that they retain more fat. This stored fat is the fuel provide the energy for a long flight. The same experiment revealed that the birds became more excited as the artificial night was lengthened. It is probably coincidence that most flocks begin their migratory flights at the night.

S1. _____
S2. _____
S3. _____

S4. _____

S5. _____
S6. _____
S7. _____

S8. _____

S9. _____
S10. _____

Passage 10

The agricultural revolution in the nineteenth century involved two things: the invention of labor-saving machinery and the developing of scientific agriculture. Labor-saving machinery naturally appeared first when labor was scarce. "In Europe," said Thomas Jefferson, "the object is to make the most of their land, labor being abundant; here it is to make the most of our labor, land being abundant." It was in the United States, therefore, the great advances in nineteenth-century agricultural machinery first come.

S1. _____

S2. _____

S3. _____
S4. _____

At the opening of the century, with the exception of a crude plow, farmers could have carried practically all of the existed agricultural imple-ments on their backs; by 1860, most of the machinery in usage today had been designed in an early form. The most important of the early inventions were the iron plow. As early as 1790 Charles Newbold of New Jersey had been working on the idea of a cast-iron plow and cost his entire fortune in introducing his invention. The farmers, therefore, were not interested in it, claiming that the iron poisoned the soil and made the weeds to grow. Nevertheless, many people devoted their attention to the plow, until in 1869 James Oliver of South Bend, Indiana, turned out the first chilled-steel plow.

S5. _____
S6. _____

S7. _____
S8. _____
S9. _____
S10. _____

Passage 11

Glacier National park in Montana shares boundaries with Canada, an American Indian reservation, and a national forest. Along the North Fork of the Flathead River, the park also border about 17,000 acres of private lands that currently used for ranching, timber, and agriculture. This land is an important part of the habitat and migratory routes for several endangering species that frequent the park. These private lands are essential the only ones available for development in the region.

S1. _____
S2. _____
S3. _____
S4. _____

With encouragement from the park, local landowners initiate a land-use planning effort to guide the future of the North Fork. The park is a partner in an interlocal agreement that calls for resource-managing agencies to work together and with the more than 400 private owners in an area. A draft plan has been prepared, with the objective of maintaining traditional economic uses though limiting new development that would damage park resources. Voluntary action by landowners, by cooperation with the park and the county, is helping to restrict small-lot subdivisions, maintain wildlife corridors, and minimize any harmful impact in the envi-ronment. The willingness of local landowners to participate in this protec-tion effort may have been stimulated by concerns which Congress would impose a legislative solution.

S5. _____
S6. _____

S7. _____
S8. _____

S9. _____

S10. _____

Passage 12

There are great many reasons for studying what philosophers have said in the past. One is that we cannot divide the history of philosophy

S1. _____

from which of science. Philosophy is large discussion about matters
in which few people are quite certain, and those few hold opposite
opinions. As knowledge increases, philosophy buds off the sciences.

For example, in the ancient world and the Middle Ages philosophers discuss motion. Aristotle and St. Thomas Aquinas taught that a
move body would slow down unless a force were constantly applied to it.
They were right. It goes on moving unless something slows it down. But
they had good arguments on their side, and if we study these and the
experiments proved them right, this will help us to distinguish truth
from false in the scientific controversies of today. We also see how
different philosopher reflects the social life of his day. Plato and Aristotle,
in the slave-owning society of ancient Greece, thought man's high state
was contemplation rather than activity. In the Middle Ages St. Thomas
believed a regularly feudal system of nine ranks of angels. Herbert
Spencer, in the time of free competition between capitalists, found the key
to progress as the survival of the fittest. Thus Marxism is seeing to fit into
its place as the philosophy for the workers, the only class with a future.

S2. _____
S3. _____

S4. _____
S5. _____
S6. _____

S7. _____

S8. _____

S9. _____

S10. _____

Passage 13

Most contemporary physicists reject the notion that man can ever
discover which mysterious forces like electricity, magnetism and gravita-
tion "really" are. Electricity, Bertrand Russell says, "is not a thing, like St.
Paul's Cathedral; it is a way on which things behave. When we have told
how things behave when they are electrified, and in what circumstances
they are electrified, we have told all there is to tell." Until recent scientists
would have approved of such an idea. Aristotle, for example, whose
natural science dominated western thought for two thousand years, believe
that man could arrive an understanding of reality by reasoning from
self-evident principles. He felt, for example, that it is a self-evident
principle that everything in the universe has their proper place, hence one
can deduce that objects fall to the ground because that's where they
belong, and smoke goes up because that's where it belongs. The goal of
Aristotelian science was to explain how things happen. Modern science
was born since Galileo began trying to explain how things happen and thus
originating the method of controlled experiment which now forms the
basis of scientific investigation.

S1. _____

S2. _____

S3. _____
S4. _____
S5. _____
S6. _____

S7. _____

S8. _____
S9. _____
S10. _____

Passage 14

The Industrial Revolution in Britain first began in the textile industry. England had been a major produce of wool for centuries. Ever since the enclosures, wool and then woolen cloth have been the principle exports of England. And cloth-making, though a domestic industry in the early years, had the characteristic of capitalist production separated the employer from the employee and introduced the division of labor, such as carding, spinning, weaving, falling and dye. With the expansion of market, the demand for cloth also increased. Although a spinner with a distaff (卷线杆) could only make one thread at a time. The short supply of yarn became the main obstacle to mass production of cloth. The general effort to improve thread-making techniques led to the invent of spinning Jenny in 1764, by the English spinner Hargreaves. The new instrument enabled a single workman to spin eight or ten threads in once. A year later, Richard Arkwright, a barber, patented a device for draw out thread by means of rollers. Then in 1779, Samual Crompton drew on these two new devices and invented a new kind of spinning machine known as the mule. It greatly decelerated the speed of production and improved the quality of thread.

S1. _____

S2. _____

S3. _____

S4. _____

S5. _____

S6. _____

S7. _____

S8. _____

S9. _____

S10. _____

Passage 15

Language learning begins with listening. Individual children vary greatly in the amount of listening they do after they start speaking, and late starters are often long listeners. Most children will "obey" spoken instructions some time before they can speak, though the word obey is hardly accurate like a description of the eager and delighted cooperation usually shown by the child. Before they can speak, many children will ask questions in gesture and by making questioning noises. Any attempt to trace the development from the noises babies make to their first spoken words lead to considerable difficulties. It is agreed they enjoy making noises, and that during the first few months one or two noise sort themselves out as particular indicative of delight, distress, sociability, and so on. But since these can be said to show the baby's intention to communicate, they can hardly be regarded as early forms of language. It is agreed, too, that from about three months they play with sounds for enjoyment, and that by six

S1. _____

S2. _____

S3. _____

S4. _____

S5. _____

S6. _____

S7. _____

S8. _____

months they are able to add new sounds to their repertoire. This self-imita-
tion leads on to deliberate imitation of sounds making or words spoken to   S9. _____
them by other people. The problem then arises as to the point which one   S10. _____
can say that these imitations can be considered as speech.

Passage 16

More attention was paid to the quality of production in France at the
time of Rene Coty. Charles Deschanel was then the financial minister. He
stressed that the French economy needs a larger share of the international   S1. _____
market to balance between its import and export trade.   S2. _____

French industrial and agricultural production then was still adequate to   S3. _____
meet the immediate needs of the people, let alone long-ranged developments.
Essential imports had stretched the national credit at the breaking point.   S4. _____
Rents were tightly controlled, though the extreme inflation affected general   S5. _____
population most severely through the cost of food. Food costs took as much
as 80 percent of the workers' income. Wages, it is true, had risen. Extensive
family allowances and benefits were paid by the state, and there were   S6. _____
full-time and overtime employment. Taking together, these factors enabled   S7. _____
the working class to exist but allowed them no sense of secure. In this   S8. _____
precarious (不稳定的) and discouraging situation, workmen were willing
to work overseas for higher wages. But the government reluctant to let   S9. _____
workers leave the country, because it was feared that this immigration of
workers would deplete the labor force, which might hinder the improve-
ment in the quality of industrious products produced and would only   S10. _____
increase the quantity of quality goods produced in foreign countries.

Passage 17

The most interesting architectural phenomenon of the 1970's was the
enthusiasm of refurbishing old buildings. Obviously, this was not an   S1. _____
entirely new phenomenon. Which is new is the wholesale interest in   S2. _____
reusing the past, in recycling, in adaptive rehabilitation (复原). A few trial
effort, such as Ghirardelli Square in San Francisco, proved their financial   S3. _____
viability in 1960s, but it was in the 1970's, with strong government
support through tax incentives and rapid depreciation. As well as growing
interest in ecology issues, that recycling became a major factor on the
urban scene.

One of the most comprehensive ventures were the restoration and transformation of Boston's eighteenth century Faneuil Hall and the Quincy Market, designed in 1824. This section has fallen on hard times, when beginning with the construction of a new city hall immediately adjacent, it has returned to life with the intelligence reuse of these fine new buildings under the design leadership of Benjamin Thomson. He has provided a marvelous setting for dining, shopping, professional offices, and simply walking.

S4. _____
S5. _____
S6. _____
S7. _____
S8. _____

Butler Square, in Minneapolis, exemplifies major changes in its complex of offices, commercial space, and public amenities (便利设施) carving out of a massive pile designed in 1906 as a hardware warehouse. The exciting interior timber structure of the building highlighted by cutting light courts through the interior and adding large skylights.

S9. _____
S10. _____

Passage 18

A painter hangs his or her finished pictures on a wall, and everyone can see it. A composer writes a work, and no one can hear it until it is performed. Professional singers and players have great responsibilities, for the composer is utterly independent on them. A student of music needs as long and as arduous the training to become a performer a medical student needs to become a doctor. Most training is concerned in technique, for musicians have to have the muscular proficiency of an athlete or a ballet dancer. Singers practice breathing every day, as their vocal chords would be inadequate with controlled muscular support. String players practice moving the fingers of the left hand up and down, while drawing the bow to and fro with the right arm—two entire different movements.

S1. _____
S2. _____
S3. _____
S4. _____
S5. _____
S6. _____
S7. _____

Singers and instruments have to be able to get every note perfectly in tune. Pianists are sparing this particular anxiety, for the notes are already there, wait for them, and it is the piano tuner's responsibility to tune the instrument for them. But they have their own difficulty: the hammers that hit the string have to be coaxed not to sound like percussion, and each overlapping tone has to sound clear.

S8. _____
S9. _____
S10. _____

Passage 19

Andrew Carnegie, known as the King of Steel, built the steel industry in the United States, and, in process, became one of the   S1. _____

wealthiest men in America. His success resulted in part in his ability   S2. _____

to buy the product and in part from his policy of expanding during periods S3. _____

of economical decline, when most of his competitors were reducing their   S4. _____

investments.

Carnegie believed that individuals should progress through hard

work, but he also felt strong that the wealthy should use their fortunes for S5. _____

the benefit of society. He opposed charity, prefer instead to provide educa- S6. _____

tional opportunities that would allow others to help them. "He who dies   S7. _____

rich, dies disgraced," he often said.

Among his more noteworthy contributions to society is those that bear S8. _____

his name, including the Carnegie Institute of Pittsburgh, which has a

library, a museum of fine arts, and a museum of national history. He also

founded a school of technology what is now part of Carnegie-Mellon   S9. _____

University. Other philanthropic gift are the Carnegie Endowment for   S10. _____

International Peace to promote understanding between nations, the

Carnegie Institute of Washington to fund scientific research, and Carnegie

Hall to provide a center for the arts.

Passage 20

For the last 82 years, Sweden's Nobel Academy has decided who will

receive the Nobel Prize in Literature, thereby determine who will be   S1. _____

elevated from the great and the near great to the immortal. But today the

Academy is coming with heavy criticism both from the without and from   S2. _____

within. Critics contend that the selection of the winners often have less to S3. _____

do with true writing ability as with the peculiar internal politics of the   S4. _____

Academy and of Sweden itself. According to Ingmar Bjorksten, the

cultural editor for one of the country's two major newspapers, the prize

continues to represent "that people call a very Swedish exercise: reflecting S5. _____

Swedish tastes."

The Academy has defended itself against such charges of provincialism

in its select by asserting that its physical distance from the great literary S6. _____

capitals of the world actually serves to protect the Academy from outside

influences. This may well be true, and critics respond that this very   S7. _____

distance may also be responsible for the Academy's ability to perceive   S8. _____

accurately authentic trends in the literary world. Regardless concerns over S9. _____

the selection process, however, it seems that the prize will continue to survive both as an indicator of the literature that we most highly praise for, and as an elusive goal that writers seek.

S10. _____

Passage 21

From Boston to Los Angeles, from New York City to Chicago to Dallas, museums are both planning, building, or wrapping up wholesale expansion programs. These programs already have radically altered facades and floor plan or are expected to do so in the not-too-distant future.

S1. _____

S2. _____

In New York City alone, six major institutions have spread up and out into the air space and neighborhoods around them or are preparing to do so. The reasons for this confluence of activity are complex, but one factor is a consideration somewhere—space. With collections expand, with the needs and functions of museums changing, empty space has become very precious commodity.

S3. _____

S4. _____
S5. _____
S6. _____

Probably nowhere in the country is this truer than in the Philadelphia Museum of Art, which has needed additional space for decades and which received its last significant facelift ten years ago. Because of the space crunch, the Art Museum has become increasingly cautious on considering acquisitions and donations of art, in some cases passing up opportunities to strengthen its collections.

S7. _____

S8. _____

Deaccession—or selling off—works of art has taken on new important because of the museum's space problems. And increasingly, curators have forced to juggle gallery space, rotating one masterpiece into public view while another is sent to storage.

S9. _____
S10. _____

Passage 22

Visitors to Britain may find the best place to sample local culture is in a traditional pub. Pub culture is designed to improve sociability in a society known as its reserve. Standing at the bar for service allow you to chat with others waiting to be served. The bar counter is possibly the only site in the British Isles which friendly conversation with strangers is considered entirely appropriate and real quite normal behavior. "If you haven't been to a pub, you haven't been to Britain." This tip can be found in a booklet, *Passport to the Pub: The Tourists' Guide to Pub Etiquette*, a customers' code of conduct for those want to sample "a central part of British life and culture". The trouble is that since you do not follow

S1. _____
S2. _____
S3. _____
S4. _____
S5. _____

S6. _____
S7. _____

the local rules, the experience may fall flatly. For example, if you are in a
big group, it is best only one or two people go to buy the drinks. Nothing
irritates the regular customers and bar staff less than a gang of strangers
blocking all access to the bar while they chat and dither about what to order.

S8. _____
S9. _____
S10. _____

Passage 23

Weddings in the United States vary as much as the people do. Because
many weddings, no matter where or how they are performed, include
certain traditional customers.

S1. _____

The wedding in itself usually lasts between 20 and 40 minutes. The
wedding party enters the church while the wedding march is played. The
bride carrying a bouquet enters lastly with her father who will "give her
away". The groom enters the church from a side door. When the wedding
party is gathering by the altar, the bride and groom exchange vows.
Following the vows, the couple exchange rings. Wear the wedding ring on
the fourth finger of the left hand is an old custom. After the ceremony it is
often a party, called a "reception" which gives the wedding guests an
opportunity to congratulate the newlyweds.

S2. _____
S3. _____
S4. _____
S5. _____
S6. _____
S7. _____

The car in which the couple leave the church is decorated in balloons,
streamers and shaving cream. The words "Just Married" are painted on
the trunk or back window. The bride and groom run to the car under
a shower of rice thrown by the wedding guest. When the couple drive
away the church, friends often chase them in cars, honking and drawing
attention to them. And then the couple go on their honeymoon.

S8. _____
S9. _____
S10. _____

Passage 24

The Japanese are fascinated by automata and new inventions.
Japanese children used to friendly robots in their comics, in toys, and in
TV animating cartoons. When as adults they join the workforce, robots
mean that there is no need to import cheap foreign labors, as happens in
many other parts of the world. There is no need for humans put up with
dirty, mind deadening mechanical work. The robot does it all with
complaint, around the clock. Robots don't go on strike over tea breaks—
they don't have tea, and any other kind of breaks. They work, day and
night, without having to be paid overtime, without making mistakes.
Human tasks subject to human error: robot error seldom occurs except as

S1. _____
S2. _____
S3. _____
S4. _____
S5. _____
S6. _____
S7. _____

result of human error!

In Japan, robots are almost respected for their virtues. When a new robot is introduced to a small suburb factory, a Shinto priest is invited to inaugurate them. He inaugurates the robot with words along the lines of "Welcome to our coworker. We hope you'll help him settle in." No one laughs.

S8. _____

S9. _____

S10. _____

Passage 25

General Electronic that now holds the title of the world's biggest company is an industrial giant which makes something from toasters to jet engines. GE has sales of $110 billion—nearly ten time that of Microsoft and 340,000 employees worldwide. It has seen its profits to grow by 15% a year to $11 billion. GE Capital Services, its financial subsidiary, makes up nearly half its sales. GE produces power generation systems, locomotive, medical imaging equipment and electrical appliances. It also owns the U.S. television network NBC and its financial news subsidiary, CNBC, and ironically, a joint venture with Microsoft provide news on the Internet.

Microsoft's shares now face a further period of certainty as the company's legal battle continues. It could also face difficulty in recruiting and retaining employees whose pay has boosted by their share options. The Seattle based firm is likely to go to an appeals court on any rulings. It could suffer further losses in lawsuits brought by competitors, who would be able to claim triple damages for any losses suffering. And with its energy and resources tied up in the lawsuits, the company may find it difficult to continue to innovate in the future, or move so aggressive to buy up competitors.

S1. _____

S2. _____

S3. _____

S4. _____

S5. _____

S6. _____

S7. _____

S8. _____

S9. _____

S10. _____

Passage 26

Americans love pets. And it's not just puppy love, either. Many pet owners treat their furry friends as part of the family. Sometimes they spice up their pets' living with entertaining videos and amusing toys. If they have an eye with fashion, pet owners can dress their pets in stylish clothes.

Beneath the fluffy luxuries, there lies a basic American belief: Pets have a right to be treated well. At least 75 animal welfare organizations exist in America, which provides care and adoption services for homeless and abused animals. Veterinarians can give animals incredible level of

S1. _____

S2. _____

S3. _____

S4. _____

medical care for an incredible price. To pay for the high-tech health care,
people can buy health insurance for their pets. And when it's time to say
good-bye, owners can bury their pets in a respectful pet cemetery.   S5. _____

    The average American enjoys having pets around, and for good
reason. Researchers have discovered that interacting with animals lower a   S6. _____
person's blood pressure. Dogs can offer protection from burglars and
unwelcome visitors. Cats can help to rid the home of unwanted pests. Little   S7. _____
creature of all shapes and sizes can provide companionship and love. In   S8. _____
many cases, have a pet prepares a young couple with the responsibilities of   S9. _____
parenthood. Pets even encourage social relationships: They give their owners
an appearance of friendly, and they provide a good topic of conversation.   S10. _____

Passage 27

    The most common reason for keeping a diary in the seventeenth
century is to keep an account of providence or God's ordering of the world   S1. _____
and for individual lives. Ralph Josselin called the diary he kept between   S2. _____
1641 and 1683 "a thankful observation of divine providence (神的眷顾)
and goodness towards me and a summary view of my life". As Isaac
Ambrose put in 1650, a diarist "observes something of God to his soul, and   S3. _____
of his soul to God". Diaries also allowed their authors to meditate regular   S4. _____
on personal failings—a type of writing confession in a protestant world   S5. _____
that had rejected the need for a catholic priest to mediate sins. Or the
diarist could count his blessings, and gave thanks for births or marriages or   S6. _____
seek consolation for illness and death. At an age when life in this world   S7. _____
and salvation in the next were both certain, diaries were a way of making   S8. _____
sense of and ordering existence. In short, they reflected the intensely intro-
spective and anxiety, self-examining religiosity of the seventeenth century,   S9. _____
particularly (so by no means exclusively) among the "hotter sort" of   S10. _____
protestants, such as the Presbyterians, independents, Baptists and Quakers.

Passage 28

    If you smoke and you still don't believe that there's a definite link
between smoke and bronchial troubles, heart disease and lung cancer,   S1. _____
and you are certainly deceiving yourself. No one will accuse you   S2. _____
with hypocrisy. Let us just say that you are suffering from a bad case of   S3. _____
wishful thinking. This needn't make you too uncomfortable because you

are in a good company. Whenever the subject of smoking and health is raised, the governments of most countries hear no evil, see no evil and smell no evil. Admittedly, a few governments have not taken timid measures. In Britain for instance, cigaret advertising has been banned on television. The conscience of the nation is appeased, while the population continues to puff its way to smoky, cancerous death.

    You don't have to look very far to find out that the official reactions to medical findings have been so lukewarm. The answer is simple money. Tobacco is a wonderful commodity to tax. It's almost like a tax on our daily bread. In tax revenue lonely, the government of Britain collect enough from smokers to pay for its entirely educational facilities. So while the authorities point out ever so discreetly that smoking may, conceivably, harmful, it doesn't do to shout too loudly about it.

S4. _____

S5. _____

S6. _____
S7. _____

S8. _____
S9. _____

S10. _____

Passage 29

    Dieters undertake starve themselves of their own free will, so why are they so miserable? Well, for one thing, they're always hungry. You can't be hungry and happy at the same time. All the horrible concoctions (调和物) what they eat instead of food leave them permanently satisfied. Wonderfood is a complete food, the advertisement says. "Just dissolve a teaspoonful in water..." A complete food it may be, although not quite as complete as a juicy steak. And, of course, they're always miserable because they feel so guilt. Hunger just proves too much for them and in the end they lash out and devour five huge guilt-inducing cream cakes at a sitting. And who can blame them? At least three times a day they are exposing to temptation. What utter torture is always watching others tucking into pile of mouth-watering food while you munch a water biscuit and sip unsweetened lemon juice!

    What's all this self-inflicted torture for? Saintly people deprive themselves with food to attain a state of grace. Unsaintly people do so to attain a state of misery. It will be a great day when all the dieters in the world abandon their slimming course; when they hold out their plates and demand second helpings!

S1. _____

S2. _____
S3. _____

S4. _____
S5. _____

S6. _____
S7. _____
S8. _____

S9. _____

S10. _____

Passage 30

Mass transportation revised the social and economic fabric of the
American city in three fundamental ways. It catalyzed (催化) physical
expansion, it sorted out people and land uses, it accelerated the inherent   S1. _____
stability of urban life. By opening vast areas of unoccupied land for   S2. _____
residential expansion, the omnibuses (公共汽车), horse railways, commuter
trains, and electric trolleys pulled settled regions outward two to four times
as distant from city centers than they were in the premodern era. In 1850,   S3. _____
for example, the borders of Boston lie scarcely two miles from the old   S4. _____
business district; by the turn of the century the radius extended ten miles.
Now those who could afford it could live far removed from the old city
center and still commute there to work, shopping, and entertainment. The   S5. _____
new accessibility of land around the periphery of almost every major city
sparked an explosion of real estate development and fueled that we now   S6. _____
know as urban sprawl. Between 1890 and 1920, for example, some
250,000 new residential lots were recorded within the borders of Chicago,
most of them locating in outlying areas. Over the same period, another   S7. _____
550,000 were plotted outside the city limits and within the metropolitan   S8. _____
area. Anxious to make advantage of the possibilities of commuting, real   S9. _____
estate developers added 800,000 potential building sites to the Chicago
region for just thirty years—lots that could have housed five to six million   S10. _____
people.

Passage 31

Lots of people pretend that they never read advertisements, but
this claim may be seriously doubt. It is hardly possible not to read   S1. _____
advertisements these days. And how fun they often are, too! Just   S2. _____
thinking what a railway station or a newspaper would be like without   S3. _____
advertisements. Would you enjoy gazing at a blank wall or reading
railway byelaws while wait for a train? Would you like to read only   S4. _____
close printed columns of news in your daily paper? A cheerful, witty   S5. _____
advertisement makes such difference to a drab wall or a newspaper full of   S6. _____
the daily ration of calamities (灾难).

We must not forget, either, that advertising makes a negative contri-   S7. _____
bution to our pockets. Newspapers, commercial radio and television
companies could not subsist without this resource of revenue. The fact that   S8. _____

we pay so little for our daily paper, or can enjoy so many broadcast
programs are due entirely to the money spent by advertisers. Just think
what a newspaper would cost if we have to pay its full price! Another
thing we mustn't forget is the "small ads", which are in virtually every
newspaper and magazine. What a tremendously useful service they
perform for the community! Just about anything can be accomplished
through these columns.

S9. _____

S10. _____

Passage 32

Not everybody reads the daily newspaper. People who do not read
newspapers are sometimes referred as "nonreaders". Early researchers
have shown that nonreaders are generally low in education, low in income,
either very young or very old. In addition, nonreaders are more likely to
live in rural areas, and have more contact with neighbors and friends.
Other studies show that nonreaders tend to isolating themselves from the
community and are less likely to own a home and usually belong to local
voluntary organizations.

S1. _____

S2. _____

S3. _____

S4. _____

Why don't these people read the daily paper? They say they don't
have the time, they prefer radio or TV, they have no interests in reading
after all, and besides they think newspapers are too expensive. Recent
surveys, however, have indicated that the portrait of the nonreader is
more complicated than first thinking. There appears to be a group of
nonreaders that does not fit the type mentioned above. They are high
in income and fall with the age group of 26 to 65. They are far more
probable to report that they don't have the time to read the papers and they
have no interests in the content.

S5. _____

S6. _____

S7. _____

S8. _____

Editors and publishers are reattempt to win them back. First, they are
adding news briefs and comprehensive indexes. This will help overcome
the time problem. And they are also giving the variety to newspaper
content to help building the readers' interests.

S9. _____

S10. _____

Passage 33

A "typical" British family used to consist of mother, father and two
children, and in recent years there have been many changes in family
life. Some of these have been caused by new laws and other are
the result of changes in society. For example, for the law made

S1. _____

S2. _____

S3. _____

easier to get a divorce, the number of divorces has increased. In fact, one marriage in every three now end in divorce. This means that there are a lot of one-parent families. Society is now more tolerant than it used to be with unmarried people, unmarried couples and single parents.

    Another change has been caused by the fact people are living longer nowadays, and many old people live alone following the death of their partners. As a cause of these changes in the pattern of people's lives, there are many families consist of only one person or one person and children. You might think that marriage and the families are not so popular as they once are. However, the majority of divorced people marry again and they sometimes take responsibility for a second family.

S4. _____

S5. _____

S6. _____

S7. _____

S8. _____

S9. _____

S10. _____

Passage 34

    The biggest safety threat facing airlines today may not be a terrorist with a gun, than the man with the portable computer in business class. In the last 15 years, pilots report well over 100 incidents that could have been caused by electromagnetic interference. The source of this interference remains confirmed, but increasingly, experts are pointing the blame to portable electronic devices such as portable computers, radio and cassette players and mobile telephones.

    RTCA, an organization advises the aviation industry, has recommended that all airlines banned such devices from used during "critical" stages of light, particularly take-off and landing. Some experts have gone further, calling for a total ban during all flights. Currently, rules on using these devices are left up to individual airlines. And although some airlines prohibit passengers from using such equipment during take-off and landing, most are willing to enforce a total ban, given that many passengers want to work during flights.

    The difficulty is predicting how electromagnetic fields might affect an aircraft's computers. Experts know that portable devices emit radiation which affect those wavelengths which aircraft use for navigation and communication. But, because they have not been able to reproduce these effects in a laboratory, they have no way of knowing whether the interference might be danger or not.

S1. _____

S2. _____

S3. _____

S4. _____

S5. _____

S6. _____

S7. _____

S8. _____

S9. _____

S10. _____

Passage 35

As researchers learn more about how children's intelligence develops, they increasingly surprised by the power of parents. The power of the school has been replaced with the home. To begin with, all the factors which are part of intelligent—the child's understanding of language learning patterns curiosity—is established well after the child enters school at the age of six. Study after study has shown that even after school begins, children's achievements have been less influenced by parents than by teachers. This is particularly true about learning that is language-related. The school rather than the home is given credit for variations in achievement in subject such as science.

In view of their power it's sad to see so many parents not taking the most of their child's intelligence. Until recently parents have been warned by educators who asked them not to educate their children. Many teachers now realize that children cannot be educated at school and parents are being asked to contribute both before and after the child enters school.

S1. _____
S2. _____
S3. _____
S4. _____
S5. _____
S6. _____

S7. _____
S8. _____
S9. _____

S10. _____

Passage 36

Geography is the study of the relationship between people and the land. Geographer compare and distinguish various places on earth. But they also go beyond the individual place and consider the earth like a whole. The word *geography* comes from two Greek words, *ge*, the Greek word for "earth" and graphein, means "to write". The English word *geography* means "to describe the earth". Some geography books focus on a small area like a town or a city. Other deal with a state, a region, a nation, or an entire continent. Many geography books deal with the whole earth. Another way to separate the study of geography is to distinguish between physical geography and cultural geography. The former focuses on the natural world; the latter starts with human beings and study how human beings and their environment act upon each other. But when geography is considered as a single subject, either branch can neglect the other. A geographer might be described as one who observes, records, and explains the differences between places. If all places were alike, there will be little need for geographers. We know, however, that no two places are exactly the same. Geography, then, is a point of view, a special way of looking at places.

S1. _____
S2. _____
S3. _____
S4. _____

S5. _____

S6. _____

S7. _____

S8. _____

S9. _____
S10. _____

答案与解析

Passage 1

【文章精要】

文章主要讲述了动画制作的产生和发展历程。在动画世界里，你可以让你创造的角色做任何事情；而且想要进行动画制作，你并不一定得是专业人士。

【解析】

S1. At→Since

介词误用，属词法错误题。此介词短语充当句子的时间状语，整个句子的时态是现在完成时，故介词应用 since 而非 at。

S2. And→But

连接词误用，属逻辑错误题。此句和上句间为转折关系，大意为"虽然人们很早就对运动着迷，但是直到 20 世纪才能够捕捉和记录运动"。

S3. everything→nothing

逻辑反义词，属逻辑错误题。根据上下文和文章中心内容，此处应该说的是"在卡通动画世界里，没有什么是不可能的"，所以要用 nothing。

S4. creating→created

非谓语动词误用，属词法错误题。此处的非谓语动词和它的逻辑主语 Felix the Cat（菲力克斯猫）是被动关系，所以要用过去分词 created。

S5. for→like 或 as

介词误用，属词法错误题。"把……当……用"应该说为 use...as/like...。

S6. characteristics→characters

近形词混淆，属词法错误题。characteristics 意为"特点"，而此处指"卡通人物"，故使用 characters。

【考点归纳】

- characteristics 意为"特性、特征"，如：Kindness is one of his characteristics.（和善是他的特性之一。）
- character 可以指"人格、品质"，还可以指"艺术作品中塑造的人物、角色"，如：personal attacks that damaged her character（损害她人品的人身攻击）。

S7. are→were

时态问题，属句法错误题。这里应该使用一般过去时。

S8. profession→professional

近形词混淆，属词法错误题。此处句意为"要想进行动画制作并不一定要是专业人士才行"，故此处要使用表示"专业人员"之意的单词。profession 是名词，含义为"职业"，所以不对，要改为 professional，此词可以作形容词和名词，作名词时含义为"专业人士"。

S9. use→using

非谓语动词误用，属词法错误题。介词后面应当使用动名词。

S10. which→that

定语从句关系代词问题，属句法错误题。定语从句的先行词如果是 all，那么从句关系代词只用 that，不用 which。

【考点归纳】

定语从句关系代词只用 that 而不用 which 的情况：

- 先行词前面有形容词最高级或序数词，如：This is the most interesting book that I've ever read. (这是我曾经读过的最有趣的一本书。)
- 先行词用 next, last, very, any, little, no 等修饰时，如：The last book that I read was a novel of a romantic love story. (我读过的上一本书是一本浪漫言情小说。)
- 先行词是 all, much, little, none 等时，如：All that we need is time. (我们需要的就是时间。)
- 先行词是不定代词 something, anything, everything 时，如：Everything that we need can be obtained. (我们需要的都可以得到。)

Passage 2

【文章精要】

文章讲述了可以煮少量咖啡的小咖啡壶的产生原因和工作原理。由于大多数人都是早上煮一大壶咖啡却只喝一小杯，于是一些公司发明了一种小咖啡壶，它可以保持咖啡新鲜数小时，因此大受欢迎。

【解析】

S1. small→smaller

形容词比较级问题，属词法错误题。该句后面有 than，所以前面应该是 smaller。

S2. make→take

固定搭配问题，属词法错误题。take advantage of 是固定搭配，意为"利用"。

S3. basing→based

非谓语动词误用,属词法错误题。base 和它的逻辑主语是被动关系,所以要用它的过去分词 based。

S4. has→have

主谓不一致,属句法错误题。句子的主语为 two U.S. appliance companies,故谓语动词用复数。

S5. Neither→Both

逻辑反义词,属逻辑错误题。根据文章的中心观点,这里是说两种产品都如何,所以要用 both。

S6. and→but

连接词误用,属逻辑错误题。并列句的前后显然是转折关系,意为"大部分人都是早上煮一壶咖啡但是却只喝一小杯"。

S7. spends→costs

近义词混淆,属词法错误题。spend 的主语必须是人,此处主语是物,而且是单数第三人称,故用 costs。

S8. 在 maker 后加 that

定语从句关系代词问题,属句法错误题。定语从句的关系代词在从句中作主语时不能省略,所以要在 drips 前加 that。

S9. 在 closes 前加 and

句子结构不完整,属句法错误题。closes 前的逗号连接了两个独立的主谓结构,这在英语中是错误的,因此必须要加上并列连词 and。

【考点归纳】

英语简单句的五种基本结构:

- SV(主+谓),如:The sun was shining.(阳光照耀。)
- SVP(主+谓+表),如:This is an English-Chinese dictionary.(这是一本英汉字典。)
- SVO(主+谓+宾),如:He enjoys reading.(他喜欢看书。)
- SVOO(主+谓+间接宾语+直接宾语),如:I gave him a book.(我给了他一本书。)
- SVOC(主+谓+宾+宾补),如:I paint my room pink.(我把屋子漆成了粉红色。)
  要注意的是,简单句的谓语动词只能有一个,若还要表达动词的意思,可以使用非谓语动词的形式,或者将简单句加上并列连词或者从属连词而变成并列句或者复合句才行。

S10. at→in

介词误用,属词法错误题。表示"在……方面",使用介词 in,即 in price。

Passage 3

【文章精要】

文章主要介绍了纽约市的洛克菲勒地区的建筑。该地区是一个城中城，其建造目的并非为了让人们居住，而是为了给人们提供便利的工作条件，因此其内的一切设施和布局都是为这一目的服务的。

【解析】

S1. for→as

介词误用，属词法错误题。此处表示"作为"之意，故用 as。

S2. 去掉 live 后的 in

句子结构混乱，属句法错误题。此处定语从句的引导词为关系副词 where，证明从句缺地点状语；live 后面如果使用 in，那么从句就只缺宾语，所以应该去掉 in。

【考点归纳】

定语从句关系词判断小窍门：先后再前。先看后面从句中缺什么，如果是主语或者宾语，就从关系代词中进行选择；如果缺状语，就从关系副词中进行选择。再看从句前面先行词的性质，是人还是物，是时间还是地点，然后再进行具体判断。

S3. smallest→biggest

逻辑反义词，属逻辑错误题。整篇文章讲的都是纽约城洛克菲勒地区的建设如何完善和巨大，因此它才能称为"城中城"，可见此处要说的是"它是同种类型项目中最大的一个"，故将 smallest 改为 biggest。

S4. has→have

主谓不一致，属句法错误题。定语从句的谓语动词应该和先行词保持一致，此处先行词是复数，所以谓语动词用 have。

S5. are→were

时态问题，属句法错误题。整个篇章的基本时态为一般过去时，此处依然讲过去的事情，故将 are 改成 were。

S6. erect→erected

非谓语动词误用，属词法错误题。此处是典型的被动语态，系动词后面要使用过去分词，故将 erect 改为 erected。

S7. primary→primarily

词性混淆，属词法错误题。该词用于修饰动词，所以应该使用副词 primarily。

S8. were→was

主谓不一致，属句法错误题。此处句子的主语是 a sunken plaza，而谓语前的 yards and fountains 只是主语后的插入语，所以谓语动词要用单数。

S9. 在 which 后加 is

语态问题，属句法错误题。此处定语从句的先行词为 plaza，和后面的 use 构成被动关系，所以从句应使用被动语态，故在 which 后增加系动词 is。

S10. attraction→attractions

名词单复数问题，属词法错误题。前面已经有了 one of，attraction 又是可数名词，故使用复数。

Passage 4

【文章精要】

文章主要介绍了英国反奴隶制的几个发展阶段。英国人在对待奴隶的态度上很矛盾：是他们完善了大西洋奴隶制，但这一制度也是在他们的领导下被推翻的。

【解析】

S1. movement→movements

名词单复数问题，属词法错误题。前面有了 one of，可见此处是复数，故使用 movements。

S2. what→it

句子结构混乱，属句法错误题。句子的开头不应该是主语从句，因为句子的主语实际上是后面 that 引导的那个从句，因此前面应该使用形式主语 it。

S3. disputable→indisputable

逻辑反义词，属逻辑错误题。根据上下文，此处句意显然为 "英国人从大西洋奴隶制中获利显然是无需争辩的事实"，所以将 disputable 改为 indisputable。

S4. in→to

固定搭配问题，属词法错误题。bring to an end 意为 "使结束"，故将 in 改为 to。

S5. this→these

代词指代问题，属词法错误题。此处代词指代上文的 phases，故应该使用复数形式 these。

S6. after→before

连接词误用，属逻辑错误题。此处用了过去完成时，显然指在这个日期之前，故将 after 改为 before。

S7. 在 petition 后加 was

语态问题，属句法错误题。"提交诉状" 应为 submit the petition 或者 the petition is/was submitted，此处应使用被动语态，故在 submitted 前增加 was。

S8. 第二个 by→large

固定搭配问题，属词法错误题。by and by 意为 "不久以后"，by and large 意为 "大体上"，根据句意，此处应该使用后者，故将第二个 by 改为 large。

S9. involved→involving

非谓语动词误用，属词法错误题。此处非谓语动词作定语修饰 efforts，且两者之间是主动关系，故使用现在分词。

S10. mobile→mobilize

词性混淆，属词法错误题。mobile 是形容词，意为"移动的"。此处显然要使用动词 mobilize，意为"动员"。

Passage 5

【文章精要】

文章主要介绍了关于达·芬奇的名画《蒙娜丽莎》的主人公身份的几种说法。许多人认为该画的原形是一名商人的妻子；也有人认为该画是画家的自画像。如今，这幅画由于年代久远，已经没有以前那么光彩照人了。

【解析】

S1. for→with

介词误用，属词法错误题。此句意为"他直到死都把这幅画带在身边"，应该使用介词 with。

S2. thousand→thousands

固定搭配问题，属词法错误题。"成千上万的"应为 thousands of。

S3. 在 have 后加 been

语态问题，属句法错误题。此处指"建议被提出"，应该使用被动语态，所以在 have 后加上 been。

S4. alike→likely

近形词混淆，属词法错误题。alike 意为"相似的"，likely 意为"可能的"。此处意为"最可能的候选人"，故使用 likely。

【考点归纳】

- alike 意为"相似的"，为表语形容词，如：The twins are alike as two peas in a pod. (这对双胞胎长得像一个豆荚里的两颗豆子一样相像。)
- likely 意为"有可能的"，是形容词，一般使用固定搭配 be likely to do sth. (有可能做某事)，如：We are likely to be late. (我们可能要迟到了。)

S5. and→but

连接词误用，属逻辑错误题。此处指"不太可能但是很流行的说法"，是转折而非并列关系，故使用 but。

S6. face→facial

词性混淆，属词法错误题。此处指"面部特征"，用来修饰 features 的只能是形容词

facial，而不能是名词 face。

S7. cover→covering

非谓语动词误用，属词法错误题。此处的 cover 用来修饰前面的名词 a layer of vanish，可见应使用其非谓语动词形式。另外，两者之间是主动关系，故使用现在分词。

S8. was→is

时态问题，属句法错误题。根据上下文，此处应为一般现在时。

S9. bright→brighter

形容词比较级问题，属词法错误题。此处明显是在进行比较，后面的 more colorful 更加说明了这一点，故将 bright 改为 brighter。

S10. 在 the painting 前加 and

句子结构混乱，属句法错误题。逗号前后是两个独立的主谓结构，故在第二个句子前加并列连词 and。

Passage 6

【文章精要】

本文主要讲心理学是一门非常艰深的科学，并介绍了心理学家是如何展开研究的。由于无法直接观察到人类大脑的活动，心理学家往往从人类的各种行为入手来分析和研究他们的心理。

【解析】

S1. more→as

比较状语从句问题，属句法错误题。根据句子后半部分的 as 可判断出此处应为平级比较，故将 more 改为 as。

S2. 在 Even 后加 if

句子结构混乱，属句法错误题。此句应为复合句，even 后面的应当是状语从句，但是没有从句的引导词，故在 even 后增加 if。

【考点归纳】

逗号不能连接两个独立的主谓结构，修改此类病句，根据具体情况，有三种方法：
- 在其中的一个句子前加引导词，将其变成从句；
- 在两个句子之间加并列连词，将它们连成一个并列句；
- 如果可能，将其中一个句子的谓语动词改成适当的非谓语动词形式。

S3. Or→Nor

连接词误用，属逻辑错误题。此处为否定，而且句子部分倒装，可见应该使用 nor。

【考点归纳】

有以下的任何一种情况，句子部分倒装：

- 表示否定的副词位于句首，如：Under no circumstances shall you lie to me. (你在任何情况下都不应该对我撒谎。)

- 由 only 构成的短语作状语位于句首，如：Only in this way can we solve the problem. (只有通过这种方法我们才能解决问题。)

- so...that 句型中的 so，such...that 句型中的 such 位于句首，如：So excellent was the boy that he was admitted to the university. (这个男孩是如此的优秀以致于他被大学录取。)

S4. adapt→adopt

近形词混淆，属词法错误题。adapt 意为"调整，使适应"；adopt 意为"采纳"。此处显然应该使用后者。

S5. 去掉 who 或在 who 后加 are

句子结构不完整，属句法错误题。如果将 who 后面的部分当作定语从句，那么它缺少谓语，故将 who 去掉，此时分词短语 interested in 直接作定语修饰前面的 physicists。或在 who 后加 are，补全定语从句。

S6. indirectly→directly

逻辑反义词，属逻辑错误题。根据逻辑，此处说的是不能直接如何，前面有了 cannot，那么此处应为 directly。

S7. By→In

固定搭配问题，属词法错误题。"以相同的方式"应为 in a similar way。

S8. But→Although

连接词误用，属逻辑错误题。此处表让步而非转折，故使用 although，句意为"虽然我们无法直接地观察大脑，我们所做的、想的、感觉到的一切都是由大脑功能所控制的"。

S9. are→is

主谓不一致，属句法错误题。句子的主语为 everything，谓语用单数。

S10. test→testing

非谓语动词误用，属词法错误题。此处 test 后有宾语，故 test 为动词；介词后要使用动词的动名词形式，故将 test 改为 testing。

Passage 7

【文章精要】

文章介绍了美国的第一份关于吸烟有害健康的报告——Luther L. Terry 博士的《关于吸烟和健康的报告》的产生和影响。

【解析】

S1. office→office's

词性混淆，属词法错误题。此处应该使用名词所有格，表示所属，故将 office 改为 office's。

S2. before→ago

近义词混淆，属词法错误题。从现在算起的过去，应该使用 ago。

【考点归纳】

- ago 的用法应注意两点：1) 用于一般过去时，2) 它所指的时间是从现在算起，所以从今天来看一天前就是 one day ago。
- before 的用法也应注意两点：1) 用于过去完成时，2) 它所指的时间不是从现在算起，而是从过去某一时刻算起，有时可以与 previously 换用，所以从昨天来看一天前就是 one day before。

S3. at→on

介词误用，属词法错误题。表示"在什么方面"应用介词 on。

S4. that→which

定语从句关系词问题，属句法错误题。此处应使用关系代词 which，因为这里是非限制性定词从句，这时只用 which 不用 that。

【考点归纳】

定语从句关系代词用 which 不用 that 的情况：

- which 可以引导非限定性定语从句，还可以放在介词后面，如：This is a very interesting book, which I bought last year. (这是一本非常有意思的书，去年我就买了。)
- 当先行词本身是 that 时，关系代词用 which，如：What I told him is that which I told you. (我告诉他的就是我告诉你的。)
- 关系词后面有插入语时，用 which，如：Here is the English grammar book which, as I have told you, will help you improve your English. (这就是那本我告诉你可以帮你提高英语的语法书。)
- which 引导定语从句时，先行词可以是一个完整的句子，而 that 引导定语从句时，先行词只能是一个单词，如：He is honest, which I have told you many times. (他很诚实，这一点我已经告诉过你很多次了。)

S5. disease→diseases

名词单复数问题，属词法错误题。other 的后面要用复数名词，故将 disease 改为 diseases。

S6. know→knew

时态问题，属句法错误题。前面的时间 1964 明确表明是过去时，故将 know 改为 knew。

S7. wide→widely

词性混淆，属词法错误题。此处单词用来修饰后面的动词 publicized，故使用副词 widely。

S8. 在 smoking 前加 that

名词性从句引导词问题，属句法错误题。此处是同位语从句，解释说明 acknowledgment。同位语从句的引导词 that 在从句中虽然不充当成分，但是不能省略。

【考点归纳】

需要注意的名词性从句引导词：

- 同位语从句的 that 不能省，如：Hearing the news that her son died, she fainted. (听到了儿子去世的消息，她晕倒了。)
- 主语从句的 that 不能省，如：It is obvious that China has been developing very fast these years. (显然，中国在近年来一直发展很快。)
- 引导主语从句表示"是否"之意只用 whether 不用 if，如：Whether he will come or not is still not clear. (他究竟是否回来仍不清楚。)

S9. or→nor

连接词误用，属逻辑错误题。此处为递进关系，而且是接着上句的否定往下说，故将 or 改为 nor。

S10. 在 the 前加 in

比较状语从句问题，属句法错误题。此处的 rather than 前后的两个成分应当是对等的，前面是介词短语 in the courtroom，后面自然就应该是介词短语 in the laboratory 了，所以要在 the laboratory 前加上 in。

Passage 8

【文章精要】

文章探讨了什么是真正的朋友的问题。真正的朋友无论何时都会站在我们的身边，分享快乐，分担痛苦。在择友时要注意，我们必须选择品行端正、心地善良的人作我们的朋友。

【解析】

S1. best→better

形容词比较级问题，属词法错误题。前面已经说了友谊的定义，这里应该是说没有办法找到更好的定义，故使用比较级 better。

S2. with→in

介词误用，属词法错误题。原句意为"一个真正的朋友在我们的喜悦中寻找欢乐，在我们的悲伤中分担哀愁"。将 with 改为 in，share sorrow in our grief 和前面的 find pleasure in our joy 构成并列关系。

S3. 第一个 choose→choice

词性混淆，属词法错误题。此处应该用名词，故使用 choice。

S4. show→shows

主谓不一致，属句法错误题。定语从句的谓语和先行词保持一致。从句的先行词为 someone，故从句谓语用单数形式。

S5. 去掉 from

及物动词和不及物动词混淆，属词法错误题。avoid 是及物动词，后面不需要任何介词。

S6. changing→changed

非谓语动词误用，属词法错误题。此处指"那些轻易就能被不幸改变的浅薄的人"。此处为被动语态，应使用过去分词 changed。

S7. will→won't

逻辑反义词，属逻辑错误题。根据上下文，真正的朋友不会把你的秘密告诉别人，故在 will 后加 not。

S8. 第一个 other→other's

代词指代问题，属词法错误题。此处应使用所有格形式，表示所属，故将 each other 改为 each other's。

S9. 在 other 后加 up

固定搭配问题，属词法错误题。cheer sb. up 意为"使某人振奋"。

S10. knows→understands

近义词混淆，属词法错误题。两个单词都有"知道"的意思，但是当宾语是人的时候，know 指"知道，认识"，而 understand 指"了解"。这里要表达的意思是"最重要的是朋友总是能够理解你"。

Passage 9

【文章精要】

　　文章解释了鸟类迁徙的问题。研究表明，鸟类的迁徙受到其体内腺状体的影响：如果白天的时间短而黑夜的时间长，它们体内的腺状体就会分泌较多的荷尔蒙从而储存较多的脂肪，为迁徙过程中的飞行提供足够的能量。

【解析】

S1. instinct→instinctive

词性混淆，属词法错误题。instinct 是名词，意为"本能"；instinctive 是形容词，意为"本能的"。此处作表语，修饰主语 behavior，应使用形容词，故将 instinct 改为 instinctive。

S2. cold→warm

逻辑反义词，属逻辑错误题。此处句意为很多北方的鸟类在夏天的时候就离开了家，此时天气还很暖和，食物的供应也很充足，故将 cold 改为 warm。

S3. where→which/that 或去掉 where

定语从句关系词问题，属句法错误题。定语从句缺宾语，故应使用关系代词而非关系副词，而关系代词在此时可以省略。

S4. regulating→regulated

非谓语动词误用，属词法错误题。此处为被动语态，故使用过去分词。

S5. trigger→triggers

主谓不一致，属句法错误题。从句先行词为单数，则定语从句的谓语用单数形式。

S6. is→was

时态问题，属句法错误题。此处所指的这个实验的发现，应该是一般过去时，故将 is 改为 was。

S7. 去掉 so

从句类型混淆，属句法错误题。前面已经有了 if 引导的条件状语从句，此处为主句，不再需要连接词，故去掉 so。

S8. provide→providing

句子结构混乱，属句法错误题。一个简单句中出现了两个谓语动词 is 和 provide，根据文意应将 provide 改为 providing，用现在分词作定语修饰 fuel。

S9. 在 probably 后加 no 或 not

逻辑反义词，属逻辑错误题。根据上下文逻辑，此处意为"大部分鸟在夜间开始迁徙不是巧合"，故在 probably 后加 no 或者 not。

S10. at→during 或去掉 the

介词误用，属词法错误题。"在夜间"可以用 during the night 或者 at night。

Passage 10

【文章精要】

文章主要介绍了 19 世纪农业机器的发明和影响。该时期的农业革命涉及两个方面：节省劳动力的机器的发明和科学农业的发展。在农业机器的发明方面，美国人做出了很大贡献。

【解析】

S1. developing→development

词性混淆，属词法错误题。这里应该使用 develop 的名词形式，表示"科技农业的发展"。此处的 development 与前面的 invention 是并列的。

S2. when→where

连接词误用，属逻辑错误题。从句意上看，两个单词都讲得通，但是下文说的是地方，故此处改为 where。

S3. 在 the great 前加 that

强调句问题，属句法错误题。此句是典型的强调句 It is...that...，其中 that 不能省略。

【考点归纳】

关于强调句：

- 如果句子去掉了 It is 和 that，依然成分齐全，是一句完整的句子，那么它就是强调句；
- 强调句中的 that 不能省略；
- 当强调的部分是人时可用 that 也可用 who。

S4. come→came

时态问题，属句法错误题。此处应为一般过去时，将 come 改为 came。

S5. existed→existing

非谓语动词误用，属词法错误题。此处指"现存的"，故使用 existing。此外，用过去分词作定语含有被动的意思，但 exist 是不及物动词，没有被动语态，故不用 existed。

S6. usage→use

固定搭配问题，属词法错误题。in use 为固定搭配，指"使用中"。

【考点归纳】

- use 意为"使用"，如：the use of the school library (使用学校图书馆)。
- usage 意为"用法"，如：the usage of a specific grammar item (一个具体语法条目的用法)。

S7. were→was

主谓不一致，属句法错误题。句子的主语是 the most important of...，应该按单数对待。

S8. cost→spent

近义词混淆，属词法错误题。cost 的主语是物，spend 的主语是人，此处主语是人，故用 spend。

S9. therefore→however

连接词误用，属逻辑错误题。此处是转折关系，故用 however。

S10. 去掉 to

非谓语动词误用，属词法错误题。make 的后面使用不带 to 的动词不定式，也就是 make sb. do sth.，故去掉 to。

Passage 11

【文章精要】

文章简要介绍了美加边界的"冰河国家公园"和一项有关公园发展的计划。该计划的目标是在确保公园所带来的经济利益的同时限制那些有可能损害公园资源的发展项目。

【解析】

S1. border→borders

主谓不一致，属句法错误题。句子主语为 park，是单数，故谓语也用单数。

S2. 在 that 后加 are

语态问题，属句法错误题。此句为被动语态，但是没有系动词，故在 that 后加上 are。

S3. endangering→endangered

非谓语动词误用，属词法错误题。"濒危物种"表状态，而非过程，用过去分词 endangered。

S4. essential→essentially

词性混淆，属词法错误题。修饰整个句子时，应用副词而非形容词，故将 essential 改为 essentially。

S5. initiate→initiated

时态问题，属句法错误题。根据上下文，此处为一般过去时，故将 initiate 改为 initiated。

S6. an→the

冠词误用，属词法错误题。此处特指该地区，用定冠词。

【考点归纳】

冠词用法小结：

- 泛指用 a，特指用 the；
- 第一次提到用 a，以后提到用 the；
- 专有名词如人名、地名、国名前不用冠词；
- 球类运动前不用冠词；
- 乐器前用 the；
- 山川、河流、海洋前用 the；
- 注意固定搭配中冠词的用法。

S7. though→but

连接词误用，属逻辑错误题。此处为转折关系，意为"起草好了新的草案，目标是维持传统经济用途，但是限制有可能破坏公园资源的新发展"。故将 though 改为 but。

S8. 第二个 by→in

固定搭配问题，属词法错误题。in cooperation with 意为"合作"。

S9. in→on

介词误用，属词法错误题。impact 后面只能用 on。

S10. which→that

从句类型混淆，属句法错误题。此处为同位语从句，而非定语从句，故不用 which 引导，只用 that。

【考点归纳】

同位语从句和由 that 引导的定语从句的区别在于：
- 同位语从句的引导词 that 在从句中不充当任何成分，如：We heard the news that our team won. （我们听到消息说我们队赢了。）
- 定语从句的引导词 that 在从句中充当主语或宾语，如：I'll tell you something that does sound strange. （我要告诉你一些听起来确实很奇怪的事。）

Passage 12

【文章精要】

文章简要探讨了哲学和科学之间的关系。作者认为哲学和科学是密不可分的：中世纪的很多哲学家都着手研究运动等自然科学的问题；此外他们对于自己的社会生活，即社会科学也有所研究。

【解析】

S1. divide→separate

近义词混淆，属词法错误题。divide 的意思是"划分"，用法为 divide into；separate 的意思是"分开"，用法是 separate from。此句后面有介词 from，可见要用 separate。

S2. which→that

代词指代问题，属词法错误题。此处并非任何从句，而应使用代词指代上文的 history，故用 that，which 没有这种指代的用法。

S3. in→about

介词误用，属词法错误题。be certain 后面只能使用介词 about，此处只是把这个介词提到了定语从句关系代词 which 的前面而已，故将 in 改为 about。

S4. discuss→discussed

时态问题，属句法错误题。此句的时间状语是 in the ancient world and the Middle Ages，所以谓语应为一般过去时。

S5. move→moving

非谓语动词误用，属词法错误题。此处用来修饰名词 body，应该使用现在分词，作形容词，表示正在进行的、主动的动作。故将 move 改为 moving。

S6. right→wrong

逻辑反义词，属逻辑错误题。根据上下文，这里指中世纪的很多科学家对于运动的观点都是错误的，其后还进一步说明错在哪里，故将 right 改为 wrong。

S7. 在 experiments 后加 which 或 that

定语从句关系词问题，属句法错误题。prove 及其后部分应该是用来修饰 experiments 的定语从句，但是缺少从句的关系代词和主语。关系代词在定语从句中作主语不能省略，故在 experiments 后加 which 或者 that。

S8. high→highest

形容词比较级问题，属词法错误题。此处指人类的最高境界，故用 highest。

S9. regularly→regular

词性混淆，属词法错误题。此处 regular 和 feudal 并列修饰 system，故用形容词形式。

S10. seeing→seen

语态问题，属句法错误题。此处是被动语态，所以应使用过去分词 seen。

Passage 13

【文章精要】

　　文章从人类到底能不能搞清楚电、磁、重力等神秘力量的本质入手，说明了古典科学和现代科学的区别：前者着重研究发生了什么，而后者着重研究事情是如何发生的。

【解析】

S1. which→what

从句引导词问题，属句法错误题。此处为宾语从句，引导词在句中作宾语，而且指物，故使用 what。which 不能引导名词性从句。

S2. on→in

介词误用，属词法错误题。此句中的 which 引导定语从句，指代先行词 a way。in a way 意为"以某种方式"，套用在定语从句中，此处应为 in which。

S3. recent→recently

词性混淆，属词法错误题。此处作整个句子的时间状语，应该使用副词而非形容词，所以将 recent 改为 recently。

S4. approved→disapproved

逻辑反义词，属逻辑错误题。根据上下文，此处指"不同意"，所以用 disapprove。

S5. believe→believed

时态问题，属句法错误题。此处应使用一般过去时。

S6. 在 arrive 后加 at

及物动词和不及物动词混淆，属词法错误题。arrive 是不及物动词，后面要使用介词 at。

S7. their→its

代词指代问题，属词法错误题。此处的物主代词指代前面的 everything in the universe，应该按单数对待，故使用 its，而非 their。

S8. how→why

连接词误用，属逻辑错误题。古典科学和现代科学的区别，就是前者解释是什么，而后者解释为什么。因此，此处应将 how 改为 why。

S9. since→when

从句引导词问题，属句法错误题。主句是一般过去时，后面是时间状语从句，故用

when 引导。since 表示时间时用作介词，引导从句时表示因果关系。所以这里要将 since 改为 when。

S10. originating→originated

并列句不对称，属句法错误题。and 后面的 thus 说明并列句的第二部分是和前面的 began 相对应，而非和 began 后的 trying 相对应，所以要使用 originate 的过去式 originated。

Passage 14

【文章精要】

文章简要介绍了英国 18 世纪中后期纺织工业的发展。由于该时期提高生产率的需要，相关的生产工具不断出现并得到改进。实际上英国的工业革命就是从纺织工业开始的。

【解析】

S1. produce→producer

近形词混淆，属词法错误题。此处是说英国是羊毛的主要产地，produce 作名词，意为"产物，农产品"，故用 producer "生产者"。

S2. have→had

时态问题，属句法错误题。此句的时间状语是 ever since the enclosures，故谓语应为过去完成时。

S3. principle→principal

近形词混淆，属词法错误题。principle 是名词，意为"原则"；principal 可以作形容词，意为"主要的"，也可以作名词，意为"（中学）校长"。此处意为"主要出口商品"，故将 principle 改为 principal。

S4. 在 production 后加 which 或 that

句子结构混乱，属句法错误题。此处 separated 后的句子应为定语从句，修饰前面的 capitalist production。但是定语从句缺少主语，可见要用关系代词，先行词为 production，故使用 which 或者 that。

S5. dye→dyeing

并列句不对称，属句法错误题。前面有 carding，spinning，weaving 等，相应地，dye 也应用其动名词。

S6. Although→But

连接词误用，属逻辑错误题。根据上下文，此处是转折关系。再者，although 是从属连词，引导的句子只能是从句，依附于主句；而 but 是并列连词，而并列句中的分句是可以独立存在的。此句是独立的，故将 although 改为 but。

S7. invent→invention

词性混淆，属词法错误题。the 后面要用名词，而 invent 是动词，故使用其名词形式 invention。

S8. in→at

固定搭配问题，属词法错误题。at once 意为 "一次性"。

S9. draw→drawing

非谓语动词误用，属词法错误题。for 是介词，后面不能用动词，故将 draw 改为其动名词形式 drawing。

S10. decelerated→accelerated

逻辑反义词，属逻辑错误题。根据上下文，此处指加快了生产速度，而非降低，故将 decelerated 改为 accelerated。

Passage 15

【文章精要】

文章主要探讨了婴儿 "语言" 的问题。婴儿学会说话前发出一些声音或者用手势来表示自己的感情，但是这些声音并不能算作语言，虽然它们和婴儿语言能力的发展是密不可分的。

【解析】

S1. after→before

连接词误用，属逻辑错误题。根据上下文逻辑，此处显然指孩子学会说话之前的听力，而非之后，故将 after 改为 before。

S2. like→as

近义词混淆，属词法错误题。like 和 as 都有 "像" 的意思，但是此处要求填入一个具有 "作为" 之意的单词，故将 like 改为 as。

S3. in→by

介词误用，属词法错误题。此处用 by，意为 "以某种方式"。

S4. lead→leads

主谓不一致，属句法错误题。此处句子的主语是上一行的 attempt，而不是动词前面的 words，所以要用动词单数第三人称的形式，将 lead 改为 leads。

S5. 在 they 前加 that

名词性从句引导词问题，属句法错误题。it 是句子的形式主语，而 they enjoy making noises 才是句子的逻辑主语，由于是主语从句，故引导词 that 是不能省略的。

S6. noise→noises

名词单复数问题，属词法错误题。one or two 按复数对待，所以后面是 noises。

S7. particular→particularly

词性混淆，属词法错误题。修饰形容词 indicative 应该使用副词 particularly。

S8. 第一个 can→cannot

逻辑反义词，属逻辑错误题。根据上下文，此处应为否定的，故使用 cannot。

S9. making→made

非谓语动词误用，属词法错误题。此处指 "发出的声音和说的话"，sound 和 make

之间是被动关系，故使用过去分词作定语。

S10. 在 point 后加 at

定语从句关系词问题，属句法错误题。定语从句的关系代词指代先行词 point，可是从句中缺少的是状语，因此在 which 前加上介词 at，那么 at which 在句子中作地点状语。注意"先后再前"的原则。

Passage 16

【文章精要】

文章简要描述了 Rene Coty 执政时期法国的工业生产情况。当时工人的待遇不好，而且各项物价还非常高，因此很多人宁愿到海外去打工，但是政府并不支持他们这样做。

【解析】

S1. needs→needed

时态问题，属句法错误题。根据主句从句时态一致的原则，此处应为一般过去时。

S2. 去掉 between

及物动词和不及物动词混淆，属词法错误题。balance 作动词时是及物动词，后面不用加介词，故去掉 between。

S3. adequate→inadequate

逻辑反义词，属逻辑错误题。根据上下文，当时法国的工农业生产还不足以满足人民短期的需要，更别说长期发展的需要了，故将 adequate 改为 inadequate。

S4. at→to

介词误用，属词法错误题。stretch sth.后面要使用介词 to，意为"把什么东西拉伸到了什么程度"，所以这里要将 at 改为 to。

S5. though→but

连接词误用，属逻辑错误题。根据上下文逻辑，此处为转折关系而非让步关系，故将 though 改为 but。

S6. 第二个 were→was

主谓不一致，属句法错误题。there be 句型的主谓一致问题依据"就近原则"，此处离 be 最近的是 full-time and overtime employment，按单数对待，故将 were 改为 was。

【考点归纳】

需要特别注意的主谓一致原则：

● 随前一致：together with，as well as，including，along with，with/of，accompanied with/by后的谓语动词单复数和短语前面的名词保持一致，如：My brother, together with my parents, comes to see me once a week. (我哥哥和我父母每周来看我一次。)

- 就近原则：either...or..., neither...nor..., not only...but also..., there be 结构中的谓语动词单复数和离它最近的名词保持一致，如：Not only my brother but also my parents come to see me once a week. (我哥哥和我父母每周来看我一次。)
- 百分比等结构：most, half, rest, some, majority, ...percent of sth. 谓语动词单复数和名词保持一致，如：Most of the water here is polluted. (这里大部分的水受到了污染。)
- a portion of sth., a series of sth., a pile of sth. 作句子主语时，谓语动词用单数，如：A series of programs has been carried on. (开展了一系列项目。)
- 若主语为非谓语动词或者名词性从句，谓语动词用单数，如：To go there or not hasn't been decided yet. (还没有决定到底去不去那里。)

S7. Taking→Taken

非谓语动词误用，属词法错误题。此处非谓语动词短语和主句主语 these factors 之间是被动关系，所以使用过去分词，将 taking 改为 taken。

S8. secure→security

词性混淆，属词法错误题。介词后面要用名词，故将 secure 改为 security。sense of security 即"安全感"。

S9. 在 government 后加 was

句子结构不完整，属句法错误题。句子缺少谓语动词，此处应使用系动词，故加上 was。

S10. industrious→industrial

近形词混淆，属词法错误题。industrious 意为"勤奋的"，industrial 意为"工业的"，此处要使用后者，表示"工业产品"。

【考点归纳】

改错中可能考到的几组近形词：

adopt 采纳，收养	adapt 调整，使适应
arise 出现	rise 升起
ashamed 感到羞愧的	shameful 可耻的
classical 古典的	classic 经典的，一流的
considerable 相当多的	considerate 体贴的
economic 经济的	economical 节俭的
effective 有效的	efficient 效率高的
personnel 人事	personal 个人的
principle 原则	principal 主要的
respectful 尊敬的	respectable 值得尊敬的

Passage 17

【文章精要】

文章简要介绍了 20 世纪 70 年代美国改造旧建筑的风潮。这种风潮的产生主要是出于经济和环保的考虑。这类改造中比较著名的几个建筑包括波士顿的 Faneuil 大礼堂和 Quincy 市场，以及明尼阿波利斯的 Butler 广场。

【解析】

S1. of→for

介词误用，属词法错误题。enthusiasm 后面要使用介词 for。

【考点归纳】

常用到 for 的情况有：

- 很多表示感情的名词后都使用介词 for，如：ambition，anxiety，affection，passion，sympathy 等；
- 表示"要求"的名词后也使用介词 for，如：requirement，request，demand，need；
- 表示"解释，原因"的名词后也要用 for，如：excuse，explanation，cause。

S2. Which→What

名词性从句引导词问题，属句法错误题。此处为主语从句，从句中缺主语，故使用 what。which 不能引导名词性从句。

S3. effort→efforts

名词单复数问题，属词法错误题。前面有 a few，可见是复数，故将 effort 改为 efforts。

S4. were→was

主谓不一致，属句法错误题。主语为 one of the...，应按单数对待，因此将 were 改为 was。

S5. has→had

时态问题，属句法错误题。此处 fall 这个动作发生在两行后的 return 之前，return 是过去发生的，所以 fall 就是过去的过去，这个时候应该使用过去完成时，故将 has 改为 had。

S6. when→but

连接词误用，属逻辑错误题。根据上下文逻辑，此处是转折关系，故将 when 改为 but。

S7. intelligence→intelligent

词性混淆，属词法错误题。修饰名词 reuse 应使用形容词 intelligent。

S8. new→old

逻辑反义词,属逻辑错误题。根据上下文逻辑,此处指旧楼,而非新楼,故将 new 改为 old。

S9. carving→carved

非谓语动词误用,属词法错误题。public amenities 与 carve 是被动关系,故使用过去分词。

S10. 在 building 后加 was

语态问题,属句法错误题。此处是被动语态,指大楼被突出,故加上系动词 was。

Passage 18

【文章精要】

文章主要讲述了主修音乐的学生的艰苦的学习训练方式以及他们在其中遇到的困难。主修声乐的学生必须保证自己的每一个音都准确无误,主修乐器的学生必须学会自己调音,使一种乐器的声音不至于听起来像另外一种乐器。

【解析】

S1. and→but

连接词误用,属逻辑错误题。根据上下文,此处应为转折关系,故将 and 改为 but。

S2. independent→dependent

逻辑反义词,属逻辑错误题。此处指"依靠",而非"独立",故使用 dependent。

S3. the→a

冠词误用,属词法错误题。此处所指的 training 为泛指,不确定的,故将 the 改为 a。

S4. 在 performer 后加 as

比较状语从句问题,属句法错误题。此处为同级比较,固定的结构为 as...as...,而原句比较的对象 a medical student 前面缺少连词 as,应加上。

S5. in→with

固定搭配问题,属词法错误题。和 concern 相关的固定搭配有两个,be concerned about 意为"关心,挂念";be concerned with 意为"参与,干预"。没有 be concerned in 这种用法。根据句意,此处应使用后者。

S6. with→without

逻辑反义词,属逻辑错误题。根据上下文逻辑,这里是说如果没有肌肉的支持,声带会如何,故使用 without。

S7. entire→entirely

词性混淆,属词法错误题。修饰形容词 different,应使用副词 entirely。

S8. sparing→spared

语态问题,属句法错误题。spare 在此为及物动词,指"使免遭、免于",原句意为"钢琴演奏者则没有此类焦虑",spare 应为被动语态。

S9. wait→waiting

非谓语动词误用，属词法错误题。此处应为非谓语动词短语作状语，而且由于其和逻辑主语是主动关系，应使用现在分词。

S10. difficulty→difficulties

名词单复数问题，属词法错误题。后面解释时提到了两个困难，可见此处应使用复数。

Passage 19

【文章精要】

文章简要介绍了钢铁大王 Carnegie 的人生信条和主要贡献。Carnegie 的成功主要来自于他的销售能力和在经济衰退时扩张事业的策略。Carnegie 坚信成功来自于努力，认为财富应当用于造福社会，所以他为社会福利事业做了很大贡献。

【解析】

S1. 在 process 前加 the

冠词误用，属词法错误题。"在此过程中"应为 in the process。

S2. 第三个 in→from

固定搭配问题，属词法错误题。result in 的意思是"导致"，result from 意为"由……产生"。此处显然是说他的成功来自于他的什么能力，故将 in 改为 from。

S3. buy→sell

逻辑反义词，属逻辑错误题。根据上下文逻辑，Carnegie 是钢铁大王，应该是销售产品的，故将 buy 改为 sell。

S4. economical→economic

近形词混淆，属词法错误题。economical 意为"节俭的"，economic 意为"经济的"，此处说经济滑坡，自然是 economic decline。

S5. strong→strongly

词性混淆，属词法错误题。修饰动词 felt 应使用副词 strongly。

S6. prefer→preferring

非谓语动词误用，属词法错误题。此处应使用分词短语作状语，否则一个简单句中就有两个独立的主谓结构。prefer 和逻辑主语 he 之间是主动关系，故使用现在分词。

S7. them→themselves

代词指代问题，属词法错误题。Carnegie 不主张施舍，他更喜欢给那些需要帮助的人提供受教育的机会，使他们能够自己帮助自己，所以此处应使用反身代词 themselves。

S8. is→are

主谓不一致，属句法错误题。主语为 contributions，谓语动词用复数形式。

S9. what→that 或 which

从句引导词问题，属句法错误题。此处是定语从句，修饰先行词 a school of technology，而非名词性从句。定语从句缺主语，且先行词为物，故使用关系代词 that 或者 which。

S10. gift→gifts

名词单复数问题，属词法错误题。other 后面要使用复数名词，另外，gift 后的谓语动词 are 也表明 gift 应为复数。

Passage 20

【文章精要】

文章介绍了近年来诺贝尔文学奖的评审委员会受到了很多批评和谴责的情况。很多人认为奖项的评选不能够反映出作者真正的写作能力，而只是反映了瑞典人自己的口味而已，认为委员会对世界文学界的趋势不够敏感。

【解析】

S1. determine→determining

句子结构混乱，属句法错误题。thereby 是副词，而非连词，故后面不能连接一个独立的主谓结构，故将 determine 改为 determining，用现在分词短语作状语。

S2. with→under

介词误用，属词法错误题。要表示"在……的批评下"，criticism 前只能使用介词 under。

S3. have→has

主谓不一致，属句法错误题。主语为 selection，故谓语动词用单数。

S4. as→than

比较状语从句问题，属句法错误题。前面有比较级 less，后面自然是 than 而不是 as。

S5. that→what

名词性从句引导词问题，属句法错误题。此处为宾语从句，而且引导词在从句中作宾语，故使用 what。引导宾语从句时 that 和 what 的区别就是，that 在从句中不充当任何成分，是可以省略的，而 what 在从句中要充当主语或者宾语，不能省略。

S6. select→selection

词性混淆，属词法错误题。its 是物主代词，后面要使用名词，故将 select 改为 selection。

S7. and→but

连接词误用，属逻辑错误题。根据上下文，此处为转折关系，故用 but。

S8. ability→inability

逻辑反义词，属逻辑错误题。根据上下文，有人批评评奖委员会无法感知最新的流行趋势，所以是 inability。

S9. 在 Regardless 后加 of

固定搭配问题，属词法错误题。regardless of 为介词短语，意为"不管……"。

S10. 去掉 for

及物不及物动词混淆，属词法错误题。praise 是及物动词，后面不用介词。

Passage 21

【文章精要】

文章主要介绍了博物馆缺乏空间的问题和博物馆为此采取的相应措施。由于缺乏足够的空间，很多博物馆不得不放弃了很多扩大自己收藏的机会，还有一些博物馆只能展出一些展品，而把其余的收藏起来。

【解析】

S1. both→either

固定搭配问题，属词法错误题。此处考查固定搭配 either...or... 和 both...and...。文中提到的博物馆的做法不止两种，故使用 either...or... 这种搭配。

S2. plan→plans

名词单复数问题，属词法错误题。根据并列对称的原则，and 之前为 facades，那么 and 之后也应该是复数，故将 plan 改为 plans。

S3. them→it

代词指代问题，属词法错误题。此处代词指代上文的 the air space，故使用单数形式 it。

S4. somewhere→everywhere

逻辑反义词，属逻辑错误题。根据上下文逻辑，这个因素是无论何地均要考虑的，故使用 everywhere。

S5. expand→expanding

非谓语动词误用，属词法错误题。with 是介词，后面要用动名词，故将 expand 改为 expanding。

S6. 在 become 后加 a

冠词误用，属词法错误题。commodity 是可数名词单数，故在前面加不定冠词 a。

S7. 第二个 in→at

介词误用，属词法错误题。Philadelphia Museum of Art 是相对而言的小地点，前面使用介词 at。

S8. on→in

介词误用，属词法错误题。"很谨慎地做某事"用英语表达为 be cautious in doing sth.，故将此处的 on 改为 in。

S9. important→importance

词性混淆，属词法错误题。take on 后面应使用名词，故将 important 改为 importance。

S10. 在 have 后加 been

语态问题，属句法错误题。此处为被动语态，却缺少系动词，故 have 后加上 been。

Passage 22

【文章精要】

文章简要介绍了英国的酒吧文化和酒吧中应遵守的礼仪。酒吧是保守的英国人进行社交的一个场合，也是最能反映英国文化的地方。在酒吧买饮料时不要一群人围堵吧台，而最好是派一两个代表去买。

【解析】

S1. improve→promote

近义词混淆，属词法错误题。improve 一般指提高水平，如 improve English level；promote 可以指"提拔"，也可以指"增进交流"等。此处应将 improve 改为 promote。promote sociability 意为"促进社交"。

S2. as→for

介词误用，属词法错误题。be known as 意为"作为……而为人所知"；be known for 意为"因为……而著名"。此处意为英国社会因其保守而著名，故将 as 改为 for。

S3. allow→allows

主谓不一致，属句法错误题。主语为动名词，谓语用单数。

S4. which→where 或在 which 前加 in

定语从句关系词问题，属句法错误题。定语从句缺少状语，从句先行词为地点，故从句的关系词应使用 where 或者 in which。

S5. real→really

词性混淆，属词法错误题。修饰后面的形容词 quite，应使用副词 really。

S6. want→wanting 或者在 want 前加 who

句子结构混乱，属句法错误题。for 为介词，后面的宾语是代词 those，不可再跟主谓结构。故将 want 改为 wanting，用现在分词短语作定语修饰 those，或者在 want 前加 who 构成定语从句修饰 those。

S7. since→if

连接词误用，属逻辑错误题。根据上下文，此句意为"问题是如果你不遵守规则，那么这就会是一次失败的经历"，显然此处为条件关系，而非因果关系，故将 since 改为 if。

S8. flatly→flat

固定搭配问题，属词法错误题。fall flat 是固定搭配，意为"达不到预期效果"。

S9. 在 best 后加 if

句子结构混乱，属句法错误题。It is best 为主句，后面应该是条件状语从句，故在 only 前面增加从句引导词 if。

S10. less→more

逻辑反义词，属逻辑错误题。根据上下文，此处是说没有什么比一大堆人堵在吧台前商量买什么更让一般的顾客和酒吧工作人员恼怒的了。故将 less 改为 more。

Passage 23

【文章精要】

文章简要介绍了美国婚礼的习俗和过程。在结婚仪式中，新娘的父亲会将她交到新郎手中，然后两人宣誓，互换戒指。仪式后，会有招待来宾的餐会，而新婚夫妇则会坐上有"新婚"字样的汽车开始自己的蜜月旅行。

【解析】

S1. Because→But

句子结构混乱和连接词误用，属句法错误题和逻辑错误题。从句法角度看，because 是从属连词，而该句却没有主句，只有从句，显然不对。从逻辑角度看，此处是转折关系，故将 because 改为 but。

S2. customers→customs

近形词混淆，属词法错误题。custom 意为"习俗"，customer 意为"顾客"，该句意为"很多婚礼无论举办的地点和形式如何，都包括一些传统的习俗"，故将customers 改为 customs。

S3. 去掉 in

代词指代问题，属词法错误题。此处使用反身代词强调前面的 wedding，无需使用任何介词。

S4. lastly→last

近形词混淆，属词法错误题。last 和 lastly 均为副词：last 意为"最后地"，也可作形容词；lastly 通常用于列举，意为"终于"。此处指新娘最后进来，故使用 last。

S5. gathering→gathered

非谓语动词误用，属词法错误题。此处表示人群都聚集到圣坛前后，新郎和新娘开始交换誓言，故 gather 应使用过去分词，表示一种状态而不是正在进行的动作。

S6. Wear→Wearing

句子结构混乱，属句法错误题。动词不能作句子的主语，要使用其相应的动名词形式，故将 wear 改为 wearing。

S7. it→there

句子结构混乱，属句法错误题。此处指婚礼后有一个派对，应用 there be 句型。

S8. 第二个 in→with

介词误用，属词法错误题。be decorated with... 意为"用……装饰"。

S9. guest→guests

名词单复数问题，属词法错误题。婚礼的客人不可能只有一个人，故为 guests。

S10. 在 away 后加 from

词性混淆，属词法错误题。away 有 "离开" 之意，但是是副词；此处应加上介词 from，表示开车离开教堂。

Passage 24

【文章精要】

文章简要介绍了日本人对机器人的钟爱以及机器人的好处。机器人可以替人类干很多枯燥而又危险的工作，而且从来不需要休息，也很少出错。因此，日本人很喜欢机器人，每当工厂有新的机器人加入时，他们甚至会举行一个小小的欢迎仪式。

【解析】

S1. 在 children 后加 are

固定搭配问题，属词法错误题。此处指日本小孩很适应机器人的存在，应该使用固定搭配 be used to。

【考点归纳】

与 use 有关的常考固定用法有：

- be used to sth. 为固定用法，意为 "适应……"，to 是介词，如：I am not used to getting up early. (我不习惯早起。)
- used to do sth. 为固定用法，意为 "过去经常做……"，to 是不定式符号，如：I used to get up late. (我过去常常起床很晚。)
- be used to do sth. 是动词 use 的被动语态，意为 "被用来做……"，如：An axe can be used to cut trees. (斧子可以用来砍树。)

S2. animating→animated

非谓语动词误用，属词法错误题。animate 意为 "赋予生命"，其过去分词 animated 意为 "栩栩如生的"，现在分词 animating 意为 "鼓舞士气的"，此处指栩栩如生的卡通，故将 animating 改为 animated。

S3. labors→labor

名词单复数问题，属词法错误题。labor 是不可数名词，没有复数形式。

S4. 在 put 前加 to

句子结构混乱，属句法错误题。此句已经有了谓语动词 is，不可能在一个简单句中出现两个谓语动词，而且 put up with dirty 是用来补充说明 need 的，在这里应该使用动词不定式表示目的，故在 put 前增加 to。

S5. with→without

逻辑反义词，属逻辑错误题。机器人做什么都是毫无怨言的，故使用 without。

S6. 第一个 and→or

连接词误用，属逻辑错误题。此句意为"他们没有下午茶休息时间，也没有任何的休息时间"，否定句中并列连接两个成分应该使用 or 而不是 and。

S7. 在 subject 前加 are

句子结构不完整，属句法错误题。subject 此处为形容词，而句子明显缺少谓语动词。be subject to 的意思是"受支配，属于"，句子的主语 tasks 为复数，故在 subject 前增加系动词 are。

S8. 在 result 前加 a

固定搭配问题，属词法错误题。as a result of 意为"作为……的后果，由……导致"。

S9. suburb→suburban

词性混淆，属词法错误题。修饰后面的名词 factory 应使用形容词 suburban。

S10. them→it

代词指代问题，属词法错误题。此处代词指代上文的 a new robot，故使用单数 it。

Passage 25

【文章精要】

文章简要介绍了世界最大的公司 GE（通用）的基本情况及其业务所涉及的领域。同时文章也指出，GE 的竞争对手微软则因为牵扯到了法律问题而面临困境，甚至有可能蒙受很大损失。

【解析】

S1. something→everything

逻辑反义词，属逻辑错误题。根据上下文，此处意为"任何事物"，故使用 everything。

S2. time→times

近形词混淆，属词法错误题。此处句意为通用的销售额几乎是微软的 10 倍，表示倍数应该用 times。

S3. 去掉 to

非谓语动词误用，属词法错误题。感观动词后使用不带 to 的不定式，故去掉 to。

【考点归纳】

使用不带 to 的不定式的情况：

- 感观动词 see，smell，hear，feel 后使用不带 to 的不定式，如：I saw him work in the yard yesterday.（昨天我看到他在花园里工作。）
- 使役动词 make，let，have 后使用不带 to 的不定式，如：The teacher made naughty boy stand there all the class.（老师让那个淘气的男孩在那里站了一整节课。）
- help 后也使用不带 to 的不定式，如：Mary helped John clean the house.（玛丽帮助约翰打扫屋子。）

S4. makes→make

主谓不一致，属句法错误题。句子主语为 GE Capital Services，故谓语动词用复数。

S5. 在 provide 前加 to

句子结构混乱，属句法错误题。逗号不可能连接两个独立的主谓结构，故后一个主谓结构需进行修改。provide news in the Internet 在这里显然是作定语修饰 a joint venture with Microsoft 的，故应使用其动词不定式的形式，所以在 provide 前增加 to。

S6. certainty→uncertainty

逻辑反义词，属逻辑错误题。根据上下文，微软公司由于吃官司，情况应该是"不确定"，故将 certainty 改为 uncertainty。

S7. 在 has 后加 been

语态问题，属句法错误题。此处为被动语态，却没有系动词，故在 has 后增加 been。

S8. in→from

介词误用，属词法错误题。"由……造成的损失"使用介词 from。

S9. suffering→suffered

非谓语动词误用，属词法错误题。损失是被人承受的，故 loss 和 suffer 间是被动关系，所以使用过去分词 suffered。

S10. aggressive→aggressively

词性混淆，属词法错误题。修饰动词 move 应使用副词 aggressively。

Passage 26

【文章精要】

文章主要讲述了美国人对宠物的喜爱，以及养宠物带来的好处。美国人把宠物当作自己的家人对待，给它们悉心的照料。研究人员发现养宠物可以有效降低人的血压，还可以帮助年轻夫妇尽快学会照顾别人，还能促进社会交往。

【解析】

S1. living→lives

近义词混淆，属词法错误题。living 是 live 的动名词，意为"生存"，而此处指宠物们的丰富多彩的生活，故使用 life 的复数 lives。

S2. with→for

固定搭配问题，属词法错误题。have an eye for 意为"很能鉴赏，很能看出"。

【考点归纳】

与 eye 有关的常考短语还有：

● all eyes 意为"全神贯注地"，如：He listened to the lecture all eyes. (他全神贯注地听讲座。)

- eye to eye 意为"见解一致"，如：We're eye to eye on all the vital issues. (对于重大问题我们的观点一致。)
- have one's eye on 意为"注视，密切注意"，如：I always have my eye on the latest trend in this area. (我总是密切注意该领域的最新流行趋势。)
- with an eye to 意为"着眼于"，如：I've just watched the film with an eye to my history class and found it very good dramatically. (我以着眼于历史课的角度观看了那部影片，发现那片子棒极了。)

S3. provides→provide

主谓不一致，属句法错误题。定语从句的先行词为 organizations，故从句的谓语用复数。

S4. 在 animals 后加 an

冠词误用，属词法错误题。level 是单数可数名词，应在之前加上不定冠词 an。

S5. respectful→respectable

近形词混淆，属词法错误题。respectful 意为"尊敬（别人）的"，respectable 意为"值得尊敬的，体面的"。此处句意为"主人把自己的宠物埋葬在体面的宠物墓地中"，故使用 respectable。

S6. lower→lowers

主谓不一致，属句法错误题。动名词作主语，谓语动词用单数。

S7. 去掉 to

非谓语动词误用，属词法错误题。help 后面使用不带 to 的不定式，也就是动词原形，故应该去掉此处的 to。

S8. creature→creatures

名词单复数问题，属词法错误题。由定语 of all shapes and sizes 可以推出被修饰词应该是复数，故使用 creatures。

S9. have→having

句子结构混乱，属句法错误题。简单句不能有两个独立的主谓结构，而此处的 have a pet 显然要作句子的主语，故应该使用其动名词形式 having a pet。

S10. friendly→friendliness

词性混淆，属词法错误题。of 是介词，后面要跟名词，故使用形容词 friendly 的名词 friendliness。

Passage 27

【文章精要】

文章简要讲述了 17 世纪人们喜欢记日记的原因。人们记日记主要是为了记录上帝对自己的启示，自己的一些忏悔、感恩等。总之，记日记是一个自我反省的过程。

【解析】

S1. is→was

时态问题，属句法错误题。in the seventeenth century 表明此处应为一般过去时。

S2. for→of

固定搭配问题，属词法错误题。keep an account of 意为"记录，记载"。这里的 of individual lives 和前面的 of providence 并列对称。

S3. 在 put 后加 it

句子结构不完整，属句法错误题。此处 as 引导方式状语从句，从句缺少宾语，故增加 it 来指代逗号后面的部分。as 引导的从句意为"正如 Ambrose 在 1965 年写的那样"。

S4. regular→regularly

词性混淆，属词法错误题。修饰动词 meditate 应使用副词 regularly。

S5. writing→written

非谓语动词误用，属词法错误题。confession（招供）是被人写出来的，故使用 write 的过去分词表示被动。written 在此意为"书面的"。

S6. gave→give

并列句不对称，属句法错误题。此处的动词和前面的 count 对称，也使用原形。

S7. At→In

介词误用，属词法错误题。"在……时代"，使用介词 in。

S8. certain→uncertain

逻辑反义词，属逻辑错误题。根据上下文，此句意为"在此生的生命和来生的救赎都不确定的年代，日记可以让人们搞清楚存在的意义"。故使用 uncertain。

S9. anxiety→anxious

词性混淆，属词法错误题。and 的前面是形容词，根据对称原则，and 后也使用形容词，故将 anxiety 改为 anxious。

S10. so→though

连接词误用，属逻辑错误题。根据上下文，此处为让步关系，意为"尤其是（尽管并不绝对是）"，故使用 though。

Passage 28

【文章精要】

吸烟有害健康，会导致肺癌等疾病，这是毫无疑问的事情。文章认为很少有政府对此采取有利措施的原因是如果一旦全面禁烟，政府的经济收入会大大减少。

【解析】

S1. smoke→smoking

词性混淆，属词法错误题。smoke 作动词时，意为"吸烟"，作名词时，意为"烟雾"。此处指吸烟和肺部疾病的关系，故使用 smoke 的动名词 smoking。

S2. and→then 或者去掉 and

句子结构混乱，属句法错误题。and 是并列连词，连接两个对称的分句。但是此处前面是条件状语从句，不对称，故应去掉 and 或将 and 改为 then，使后面变成主句。

S3. with→of

固定搭配问题，属词法错误题。accuse sb. of sth.意为"为……谴责或控告某人"，不能使用介词 with。

S4. 去掉 a

冠词误用，属词法错误题。此处显然不是"在一家好公司"（in a good company）之意，而是说"有人和你做伴"（in good company）。此处 company 意为"陪伴"，抽象名词，前面不用冠词。

S5. 去掉 not

逻辑反义词，属逻辑错误题。根据上下文，此处句意为"的确，有很少的一部分国家采取了一些畏首畏尾的做法，例如英国……"，所以此处的意思是"采取了"而不是"没有采取"，所以应该去掉 have 后的 not。

S6. that→why

连接词误用，属逻辑错误题。此处不是要找到事实的真相，而是要找到"为什么官方对医学发现反应冷淡"，故将 that 改为 why。

S7. simple→simply

词性混淆，属词法错误题。此处句意为"答案仅仅是钱"，故使用副词 simply。

S8. lonely→alone

近形词混淆，属词法错误题。lonely 意为"孤独的"，alone 意为"单独，一个"，此处意为"单税收一项"，故使用 alone。

【考点归纳】

几组常考同源异义词：

- alone 意为"单独的"，lonely 意为"孤独的"，如：I always feel lonely when I am alone.（当我一个人的时候我总会感到孤独。）
- shameful 意为"可耻的"，shameless 意为"无耻的"，ashamed 意为"感到羞耻的"，如：A shameless man will never feel ashamed of the shameful things he has done.（一个无耻的人从来不会为他所作的无耻的事情感到羞耻。）
- considerable 意为"相当大量的"，considerate 意为"体贴人的"，considering 意为"考虑到"，如：Considering that you are not considerate, it will take you considerable time to find a girlfriend.（考虑到你不是很体贴，你要花相当长的时间才能找到一个女朋友。）

S9. collect→collects

主谓不一致，属句法错误题。句子的主语为 the government of Britain，故谓语动词使用单数。

S10. 在 harmful 前加 be

句子结构不完整，属句法错误题。此处只有主语和表语没有系动词，故在 harmful 前加 be。

Passage 29

【文章精要】

文章描述了节食者们所要经历的痛苦：他们总是处于饥饿之中，因而不快乐；同时他们一旦抵制不住诱惑吃了东西，又会有很大的负罪感。

【解析】

S1. 在 starve 前加 to

句子结构混乱，属句法错误题。句子的宾语只能是名词、代词、动名词或者不定式，而此处的 starve 显然要作 undertake 的宾语，而 undertake 后面只能使用不定式，所以在 starve 前增加 to。

S2. what→that

从句类型混淆，属句法错误题。此处是定语从句修饰先行词 concoctions，故将 what 改为 that。

S3. satisfied→dissatisfied

逻辑反义词，属逻辑错误题。吃不饱这些人自然不满意了，所以是 dissatisfied。

S4. although→but

连接词误用，属逻辑错误题。此处意为"或许这是一种（营养）全面的食物，但也不可能像……"，逗号后为转折关系，故将 although 改为 but。

S5. guilt→guilty

词性混淆，属词法错误题。feel 后面使用形容词，故将 guilt 改为 guilty。

S6. exposing→exposed

语态问题，属句法错误题。此处是被动语态，应使用过去分词。be exposed to sth. 意为"受到……的影响，暴露于……"。

S7. 在 torture 后加 it

句子结构不完整，属句法错误题。此处为感叹句，缺少主语，所以加上 it 作形式主语。

【考点归纳】

- what 引导的感叹句：what＋n.＋主语＋谓语，如：What a good girl she is!（她是一个多么好的女孩啊！）
- how 引导的感叹句：how＋adj./adv.＋主语＋谓语，如：How nice this place is!（这个地方多么漂亮啊！）

S8. pile→piles

固定搭配问题，属词法错误题。"一堆堆的"就是 piles of。

S9. with→of

固定搭配问题，属词法错误题。deprive of 意为"剥夺"。

S10. course→courses

名词单复数问题，属词法错误题。此处句意为"放弃他们的减肥课程"，名词 course 前有物主代词 their，可见应该使用名词的复数形式 courses。

Passage 30

【文章精要】

文章简要介绍了美国公共交通体系的发展、现状和影响。汽车、地铁、火车和电车构成了美国的公共交通体系，在它的带动下，城市加速扩张，土地资源的配置日趋合理化，城市生活日趋稳定。

【解析】

S1. 第二个 it 前加 and

句子结构混乱，属句法错误题。三个简单句不能用逗号连接，故在第三个分句前加 and，把它们连成并列句。

S2. stability→instability

逻辑反义词，属逻辑错误题。根据上下文，这里指城市生活的不稳定性，故将 stability 改为 instability。

S3. as→more

比较状语从句问题，属句法错误题。后面有 than，前面当然是 more。

S4. lie→lay

时态问题，属句法错误题。此处为一般过去时，应使用 lie 的过去式 lay。

【考点归纳】

● lie 指"躺下，位于"时，是不及物动词，过去式为 lay，过去分词为 lain。

● lie 指"撒谎"时，是不及物动词，规则变化，过去式和过去分词均为 lied。

● lay 意为"放下"，是及物动词，过去式和过去分词均为 laid。

S5. to→for

介词误用，属词法错误题。work 既可以作动词，又可以作名词，但是根据并列对称的原则，后面的 shopping 和 entertainment 均为名词，那么此处 work 也是名词，前面只能使用介词 for。

S6. that→what

名词性从句引导词问题，属句法错误题。此处为宾语从句，从句中缺宾语，故使用

what，不用 that。

S7. locating→located

非谓语动词误用，属词法错误题。them (residential lots) 与 locate 是被动关系，用过去分词。

S8. and→but

连接词误用，属逻辑错误题。and 前是 outside the city limits（在城市分界以外），后是 within the metropolitan area（在市区以内），前后显然是转折关系，故将 and 改为 but。

S9. make→take 或 advantage→use

固定搭配问题，属词法错误题。take advantage of 为固定搭配，意为"利用"。此句也可以将 advantage 改为 use，因为固定搭配 make use of 可表达同样的含义。

S10. for→in

介词误用，属词法错误题。此处指 30 年内，使用介词 in。

Passage 31

【文章精要】

文章探讨了广告的优点：有趣的广告给我们阅读报纸带来了乐趣和调剂，同时报纸上的广告不单给报社的收入带来保证，使我们付很少的钱就可以阅读报纸，而且我们从中也可以找到有用的信息，从而给我们的生活带来了很大便利。

【解析】

S1. doubt→doubted

语态问题，属句法错误题。此处为被动语态，不能使用动词原形，要用过去分词形式。

S2. how→what 或 fun→funny

词性混淆，属词法错误题。此处考查 how 和 what 引导感叹句的区别，how 感叹形容词，what 感叹名词，fun 是名词，故将 how 改为 what 或将 fun 改成形容词 funny。

S3. thinking→think

句子结构混乱，属句法错误题。句子没有谓语，故将 thinking 改为 think。

S4. wait→waiting

句子结构混乱，属句法错误题。此处考查省略句，当状语从句的主语和主句主语相同，谓语是系动词时，可以同时省略主谓。此句原本是 while you are waiting，省略了 you are，故应将 wait 改为 waiting。

S5. close→closely

词性混淆，属词法错误题。此处修饰过去分词 printed，应使用副词 closely。

S6. 在 such 后加 a

冠词误用，属词法错误题。difference 为单数可数名词，前面要用 a。

S7. negative→positive

逻辑反义词，属逻辑错误题。根据上下文，此处是说广告还是有好处的，故将 negative 改为 positive。

S8. resource→source

近形词混淆，属词法错误题。resource 意为"资源"，source 意为"来源"，此处指税收来源，故使用后者。

S9. are→is

主谓不一致，属句法错误题。主语为 the fact，故谓语动词用单数。

S10. have→had

句法错误，属虚拟语气问题。此处考查虚拟条件句，表示对现在的虚拟，从句中用一般过去时，故将 have to 改为 had to。

【考点归纳】

几类常见的虚拟语气：

● 虚拟条件句：

表示对现在的虚拟，从句用一般过去时，主句用"would＋v."，如：If I were you, I would study hard. (如果我是你，我就好好学习。)

表示对过去的虚拟，从句用过去完成时，主句用"would have＋v-ed"，如：If I had studied hard, I would have passed the exam. (如果我当时好好学习的话，我的考试就通过了。)

● 形式为"should＋v."类的虚拟语气：

表示命令、建议、请求、要求的动词、形容词或名词(如 advise, advice, advisable)后面的从句中使用此类虚拟语气，should 可以省略，如：I suggested that we (should) climb the mountain this weekend. (我建议我们这周末去爬山。)

表示"以防、万一"的连词如 in case 和 lest 引导的从句中使用此类虚拟语气，should 可以省略，如：Bring an umbrella with you in case that it (should) rain. (带把伞，以防下雨。)

● wish 后宾语从句中的虚拟语气：表示对现在的虚拟用一般过去时，表示对过去的虚拟用过去完成时。很多单词都和 wish 有类似的用法，如：would rather, if only, as if 等后面都用此种类型的虚拟语气，如：I wish I were not here. (真希望我现在不在这里。)

He talked as if he had been abroad for many years. (他说的好像他出国了很多年一样。)

Passage 32

【文章精要】

文章简要介绍了 non-readers (不读报的人) 的特点，分析了他们不喜欢阅读报纸的原因，并指出编辑和出版商已经着手改革以激发这些人对报纸的兴趣。

【解析】

S1. 在 referred 后加 to

及物动词与不及物动词混淆，属词法错误题。refer 是不及物动词，后面要用介词 to。

S2. more→less

逻辑反义词，属逻辑错误题。此处说不读报的人很少和人接触，故将 more 改为 less。

S3. isolating→isolate

非谓语动词误用，属词法错误题。tend to 中的 to 是不定式符号，而非介词，故将 isolating 改为动词原形 isolate。

S4. usually→seldom/rarely

逻辑反义词，属逻辑错误题。根据上下文逻辑，这些人很少属于任何志愿性组织，故将 usually 改为其反义词。

S5. after→at

固定搭配问题，属词法错误题。此处是固定搭配 not...at all，意为"根本不……"。

S6. thinking→thought

非谓语动词误用，属词法错误题。此处应使用过去分词表被动。

S7. with→into

介词误用，属词法错误题。fall into 意为"属于……"。

S8. probable→likely

近义词混淆，属词法错误题。两者都有"可能的"之意，但是用 probable 时，主语只能是物或者形式主语 it，而使用 likely 对于主语没有特别要求。

S9. reattempt→reattempting

句子结构混乱，属句法错误题。are 和 reattempt 两个谓语动词同时出现，显然有问题，故将 reattempt 改为 reattempting，将句子变为现在进行时。

S10. building→build

非谓语动词误用，属词法错误题。help 后面使用不带 to 的不定式。

Passage 33

【文章精要】

文章简要介绍了近年来英国人家庭生活的主要变化——单亲家庭增多及老年人在另一半去世后独居——并探讨了造成这些变化的原因。

【解析】

S1. and→but

连接词误用，属逻辑错误题。根据上下文，此处应为转折关系。

S2. other→others

固定搭配问题，属词法错误题。some...others 是固定用法。

S3. 第二个 for→since

近义词混淆，属词法错误题。for 和 since 都可以表示"因为"，但是 for 表示原因引导的从句一般放在句末，所以用在此处不对。

S4. 在 easier 前加 it

句子结构不完整，属句法错误题。句子的主语为 law，谓语为 made，easier 是宾语补足语，逻辑宾语是 easier 后面的不定式 to get a divorce，可见此句缺少形式宾语 it。

【考点归纳】

- 使用 it 作形式主语或者形式宾语：英语句子结构和汉语不同，其中一个主要的区别是英语的句子习惯前短后长，凡是较长的成分一律后置，因此当句子的主语过长，如主语为不定式短语、动名词短语或者主语从句时，会使用 it 作形式主语，而将真正的主语后置，成为逻辑主语，如：That he will come is no doubt. 这句话一般情况下会说成 It is no doubt that he will come. (毫无疑问他会来的。)

- 如果句子的宾语是复合宾语，即"宾语＋宾语补足语（宾补）"的形式，而宾语是不定式短语、动名词短语或宾语从句，宾补很短时，则使用 it 作形式宾语，真正的宾语放在宾补的后面，成为逻辑宾语，如：I think it a good idea to ban smoking in public places. 一般情况下就不会说成 I think to ban smoking in public places a good idea. 虽然后者在语法上也是正确的。

S5. end→ends

主谓不一致，属句法错误题。one in every three，按单数对待，故将 end 改为 ends。

S6. with→of

介词误用，属词法错误题。形容词 tolerant 后面只能使用介词 of。

S7. 在 fact 后加 that

名词性从句引导词问题，属句法错误题。fact 之后的部分为同位语从句，补充说明 fact，其引导词不能省略。

S8. cause→result

逻辑反义词，属逻辑错误题。as a cause of 意为"作为……的原因"，as a result of 意为"作为……的结果"，根据上下文语义，此处应该使用后者。

S9. consist→consisting 或在 families 后加 that

句子结构混乱，属句法错误题。简单句中不能出现两个谓语动词，故将后者 consist 改成现在分词 consisting 或者改为定语从句 that consist。

S10. are→were

时态问题，属句法错误题。此处应为一般过去时。

Passage 34

【文章精要】

文章主要说明了电脑对飞机的飞行可能产生影响。但是文章同时又说，至今还没有明确证据表明这种影响是否达到危险的程度，航空公司也不愿意在飞行的过程中全面禁止乘客使用电脑。

【解析】

S1. than→but

连接词误用，属逻辑错误题。此处为固定句式 not...but...，此句大意为"最大的飞行隐患不是持枪的恐怖分子，而是商务舱中携带手提电脑的人"。

S2. report→reported

时态问题，属句法错误题。句子的时间状语 in the last 15 years 表明其基本时态应该是一般过去时，所以将 report 改为 reported。

S3. confirmed→unconfirmed

逻辑反义词，属逻辑错误题。根据上下文，电脑对飞机影响的原因还不大清楚，故使用 unconfirmed。

S4. to→at

介词误用，属词法错误题。point to 和 point at 均有"指向"之意，但是使用 point 时，直接说 point to sth./sb.，point 后面不跟宾语，故此处不对，应将 to 改为 at。

S5. 在 organization 后加 which

句子结构混乱，属句法错误题。句子后面有谓语 has recommended，可见前面只是主语部分。故在 organization 后加 which 引导定语从句。

S6. banned→ban

句法错误，属虚拟语气问题。recommend 后面的宾语从句中要使用形式为"should＋v."的虚拟语气，should 可以省略，此处直接使用动词原形 ban。

S7. 在 used 前加 being

非谓语动词误用，属词法错误题。from 是介词，后面不能直接使用过去分词 used，如果要表示相同的意思，应该使用动名词才行，故在 used 前加上 being。

S8. willing→reluctant 或者在 willing 前加 not

逻辑反义词，属逻辑错误题。此句意为"尽管一些航空公司禁止乘客在飞机起飞和着陆时使用那些电子产品，但由于很多乘客想在飞行时继续办公，所以很多航空公司也不愿意彻底实施禁令"。因此应将 willing 改为与其相反的意思。

S9. affect→affects

主谓不一致，属句法错误题。定语从句先行词 radiation 是单数，故从句谓语动词用单数。

S10. danger→dangerous

词性混淆，属词法错误题。此处应使用形容词补充修饰主语，故将 danger 改为 dangerous。

Passage 35

【文章精要】

文章主要说明了在教育孩子的过程中，父母的作用是非常大的。研究表明，无论孩子在开始上学前还是上学后，他们智力的发展在很大程度上都受父母的影响，因此父母必须在教育孩子方面作出更多努力。

【解析】

S1. 在 increasingly 前加 are

句子结构不完整，属句法错误题。此句是被动语态，意为"为……感到惊讶"，但是却只有过去分词 surprised，没有系动词，故应加上对应的系动词 are。

S2. with→by

介词误用，属词法错误题。"用 A 代替 B"的英语表达为 replace B with A 或者 B be replaced by A，此处是被动语态，故使用后者。

S3. intelligent→intelligence

词性混淆，属词法错误题。of 为介词，后面要用名词 intelligence 而非形容词 intelligent。

S4. is→are

主谓不一致，属句法错误题。主语为第三行的 factors，故谓语动词用复数。

S5. 第二个 after→before

连接词误用，属逻辑错误题。根据上下文，很多影响孩子智力的因素在他们上学之前就已经形成，故将 after 改为 before。

S6. less→more

逻辑反义词，属逻辑错误题。根据上下文，即使在孩子上学后，父母对孩子的影响也要超过老师对他们的影响，故将 less 改为 more。

S7. subject→subjects

名词单复数问题，属词法错误题。原句大意为"学生在诸如科学等学科中取得的成就都归功于学校，而学生在学校学习的科目一定不只有科学一门"，所以应将 subject 改为其复数 subjects。

S8. taking→making

固定搭配问题，属词法错误题。make the most of 是固定搭配，意为"充分利用"。

S9. have→had

时态问题，属句法错误题。过去的过去发生的事情用过去完成时。recently（最近）指过去，until recently 则指过去以前，所以将 have 改为 had。

S10. 在 educated 后加 only 或者 just

逻辑反义词，属逻辑错误题。此处句意应为"孩子们不应该仅仅在学校接受教育"，而不是"孩子们不应该在学校接受教育"，所以在 educated 后增加 only 或者 just。

Passage 36

【文章精要】

文章简要介绍了地理学的两个分支——自然地理学和文化地理学，以及两者间的关系。前者主要研究自然界，后者主要研究人与自然的关系，这两个分支是密不可分的。

【解析】

S1. distinguish→contrast

近义词混淆，属词法错误题。两者都有对比不同之处的意思，但是 contrast 是及物动词，而 distinguish 是不及物动词，一般说 distinguish between A and B，故将 distinguish 改为 contrast。

S2. place→places

名词单复数问题，属词法错误题。此处指地球上的各个地方，应用复数。

S3. like→as

介词误用，属词法错误题。consider 后面要用介词 as。

S4. 在 means 前加 which

句子结构混乱，属句法错误题。前面已经有了谓语，在没有连接词的情况下，此处不应出现另一个主谓结构，故在 means 前加 which 将这部分变为非限定性定语从句。

S5. Other→Others

固定搭配问题，属词法错误题。前一句有 some，这一句对应的就是 others。

S6. separate→divide

近义词混淆，属词法错误题。separate 指将两者分开，divide 指将一个东西分成两半，此处应该用后者。

S7. study→studies

主谓不一致，属句法错误题。句子主语为 the latter，是单数，故将 study 改为 studies。

S8. either→neither

逻辑反义词，属逻辑错误题。根据上下文，地理学的两个分支，谁也不能忽略谁，故将 either 改为 neither。

S9. will→would

句法错误，属虚拟语气问题。表示对现在情况的虚拟，主句用"would＋v."。

S10. however→therefore

连接词误用，属逻辑错误题。前一句用虚拟语气说"如果所有的地方都是相似的，那么就不需要地理学家了"，此句显然是接着往下说"因此我们知道没有任何两个地方是完全一样的"，故此处为因果关系，使用连接副词 therefore。

【考点归纳】

- 表示因果关系的副词：therefore，thus，accordingly，consequently，hence
- 表示因果关系的连词：because，since，for，so
- 表示转折关系的副词：however，nevertheless，whatsoever，notwithstanding
- 表示转折关系的连词：but，notwithstanding，yet

第三章 汉英翻译

第一节 现状与趋势

在《改革方案》中，综合测试部分的另一重要题型是汉英翻译。该题型要求用汉英翻译的方法补全五个句子，每个句子的平均长度约为 15 个单词，需填入的部分为 6 到 10 个单词，占总分值的 5%。

通过对《大学英语六级考试试点考试样卷》(以下简称《六级样卷》) 样题的分析，我们发现新题型在放弃专门的词汇语法结构题型后，把相关知识点设置到了汉英翻译部分。以六级样卷中的汉译英题目为例：

72. It was essential that _____ (我们在月底前签订合同).

标准答案： we sign the contract before the end of the month

考查重点： 虚拟语气的用法。

73. To our delight, she _____ (进大学一个月就适应了校园生活).

标准答案： adapted (herself) to campus life a month after entering college

考查重点： 短语和搭配；六级高频考词 adapt。

74. The new government was accused _____ (未实现其降低失业率的承诺).

标准答案： of failure to fulfill its promise to reduce the unemployment rate

考查重点： 短语和搭配；不定式短语作同位语。

75. The workmen think _____ (遵守安全规则很重要).

标准答案： it very important to comply with/follow the safety regulations

考查重点： it 作形式宾语；短语和搭配。

76. The customer complained that no sooner _____ (他刚试着使用这台机器，它就不运转了).

标准答案： had he tried to use the machine than it stopped working

考查重点： 倒装结构；过去完成时。

从给出的这五个翻译样题不难看出，其中重点考查的各类短语及语法知识与六级旧题型中词汇与结构题目中的测试重点不谋而合，即六级旧题型中词汇与结构中重点考查的知识点，将会成为新题型中汉英翻译的重点。此外，由于汉英翻译考查的方式更为灵活，范围更为广泛，而且能够综合地、全面地考查考生把握汉英两种语言句子结构和关键词汇的能力，这一新题型必将成为六级考试的重点和难点之一。

<h2 style="text-align:center">第二节 对策与技巧</h2>

在上一节中提到，六级的汉英翻译和旧题型中的词汇与结构部分相比，从测试的手段和效果来说实现了一个较大的飞跃。但是归根到底，它考查的是考生的语言基础知识，即重点语法知识、高频词汇运用和句子结构辨析，并不会涉及过多的翻译技巧。这一节我们将从这三个考查重点入手来点拨应试技巧。

一、重点语法知识

 命题规律

1. 定语从句。作为整个英语语法体系中的一个难点，定语从句的考查是必不可少的。而对于定语从句的考查，无疑又会集中在关系词上，即根据不同的先行词和从句本身的结构要求，判断应该选择关系代词还是关系副词，以及具体选择哪个关系代词或者关系副词。

2. 状语从句。对于状语从句的考查主要集中在让步状语从句和比较状语从句上面。具体说来，经常会考到的句式有"无论……"，"A 是 B 的多少倍"，"与其……不如……"等。

3. 倒装句。对倒装句的考查往往会给出句子的开头，例如介词短语表示地点、方向或者表示否定意义的短语，让考生翻译其后的部分，而这部分有可能是完全倒装也有可能是部分倒装，要视题干给出的句子开头而定。

4. 强调句。强调句结构 It is/was...that/who...也是考查的热点。一般会让考生翻译 that/who 后的部分。

5. 虚拟语气。虚拟条件句，表示命令、建议、请求等动词及其衍生词后所跟的"(should)＋v."形式的虚拟语气，还有 wish，if only 等词后的虚拟语气一直是六级考试各种题型的热门考点。

6. 非谓语动词和独立主格。主要考查分词、不定式以及其独立主格在句子中作状语的情况。

7. 句子的基本时态、语态和主谓一致问题。该项在大部分情况下并非题目的主要考点，但是不论什么句子都要考虑其时态、语态和主谓一致问题。往往考生在做题的过程中虽然能够注意到主要考点如定语从句、虚拟语气等，但却在这些地方丢分。

 答题技巧

1. 一旦确定所译部分为定语从句，要遵循"先后再前"的原则。即先看后面，就是看从句本身缺少什么成分，若缺少主、宾语，可以确定此题用关系代词，若缺少状语，则要使用关系副词。关系副词比较简单，若是关系代词，则还要进一步区分 that，which，who，as。具体内容可以参见第二章短文改错第三节中相关的【考点归纳】部分。

2. 对于状语从句，一定要熟悉"no matter＋疑问代词或者疑问副词"的用法，以及表示倍数、平级比较的特定句型和短语，特别要注意状语从句中的省略问题，如果没有把握，就不要省略。具体内容可以参见本章第三节中相关的【考点归纳】部分。

3. 熟悉常见的倒装、强调和虚拟语气的类型和用法。需要注意的是部分倒装句在翻译的时候不要忘记了助动词，强调句切勿和定语从句混淆，虚拟语气的虚拟条件句中会有一些特殊的情况如条件句倒装、含蓄条件句和错综时间条件句的情况。具体内容参见本章第三节中相关的【考点归纳】部分。

4. 非谓语动词和独立主格是中国学生在学习英语时的一个弱项，因此一定要特别注意，尤其是现在分词和过去分词以及不定式的区别；还有就是非谓语动词的逻辑主语问题。不过考试中涉及的非谓语动词和独立主格大部分是作状语的情况，而此时往往可以用状语从句代替。考生若没有把握，建议使用状语从句。具体内容可参见本章第三节中相关的【考点归纳】部分。

5. 翻译完每一道题后，请检查句子的基本时态、语态是否正确，主谓是否一致。

二、高频词汇运用

六级高频词汇也是汉英翻译的一个重点。对于这些单词，要掌握的不仅仅是它们的汉语意思，最重要的是要掌握它们的用法。在这一点上，历年的考题给了我们很大的提示，因此用历年的词汇结构部分考题来做练习并非像许多人想象的那样在新题型出来后就没有用了，相反，这种练习可以帮助大家更好地预测汉英翻译部分的考点。

命题规律

1. 常见近形词可能成为考点。汉英翻译无法考查两个近形词的区别，但是却并不排除考生由于分不清楚两个单词而用错词的情况。如 attribute 和 contribute 这两个单词，考生就非常容易混淆。

2. 常见近义词可能成为考点。很多单词含义相近用法却完全不同，例如要翻译"坚持做某事"这个结构，使用 persist，就要用 persist in doing sth.；而使用 insist，就要用 insist on doing sth.。

3. 重点短语可能成为考点。

答题技巧

1. 准确选词，确切表达意思。这一点，光靠临场发挥显然是不行的，有赖于考生平时的日积月累，上文中提到的做以前旧题型中的词汇结构部分真题，应该算是一个非常有效的方法。

2. 旁敲侧击，达到目的。有时所要翻译的那个确切的单词不会用或是不知如何拼写，这时要学会开动脑筋绕着说，能表达句子的核心意思即可。翻译是一种比较灵活的题型，答案的可能性比较多。例如"让某人失望"这个短语的翻译，比较地道的说法是 let sb. down，但是如果不会这么用，完全可以使用 make sb. disappointed 来替代；还有"洪水的受害者"，准确的说法就是 flood victims，可是如果不知道 victim 这个词，就可以考虑翻译成 those who suffered from the flood。

三、句子结构辨析

汉英翻译部分考查的是句子中一部分的翻译，因此考生必须特别注意这一部分在整个句子中充当的成分。然后根据它所充当的特定语法成分来判断所填的到底应该是从句还是短语，是谓语动词还是非谓语动词。如果不顾句子结构，而是根据括号中的汉语乱译一气，就很容易出错。

命题规律

1. 所译部分有可能是完整的从句。
2. 所译部分有可能是起修饰整个句子作用的短语。
3. 所译部分有可能是主句或者从句中的一个成分。

答题技巧

1. 若所译部分是完整的从句，那么问题就会简单许多。只需确定究竟是什么从句，选择合适的连接词进行翻译，然后检查从句的时态是否和主句一致，语态是否正确，主谓是否一致即可。
2. 若所译部分是起修饰整个句子作用的短语，问题也不是很大。此时该短语其实在整个句子中充当状语，只要保证其逻辑主语和主句主语一致即可，若不一致，则考虑是否可以使用独立主格结构。
3. 若所译部分是主句或者从句中的一个成分，则一定要注意其前后题干中的英语单词。首先确定是什么成分：主语和宾语要用名词性的，定语要用形容词性的，状语则要使用介词短语或者不定式、分词等；介词后面无疑要用动名词，而不定式符号 to 后肯定要用动词原形。然后再根据提示进行翻译，否则很有可能因为语法问题丢分。

第三节 模拟练习

Directions: *Complete the sentences by translating into English the Chinese given in brackets.*

Unit 1

1. _____ (设计出一种新的技术), the yields as a whole increased by 20 percent.

2. My father did not go to New York, _____ (医生建议他不要去那里).

3. We have been told that under no circumstances _____ (我们可以因为私事使用办公室的电话).

4. The book _____ (教授和我们谈到过的) was not in the school library.

5. _____ (尽管我承认存在问题), I don't think that they can be solved.

Unit 2

6. _____ (和整个地球的尺寸相比), the highest mountain does not seem high at all.

7. _____ (我希望我去过) Stockholm when I was in Sweden. I hear it's a beautiful city.

8. _____ (我们一到山顶) than we all sat down to rest.

9. _____ (许多困难出现了) as a result of the change over to a new type of fuel.

10. _____ (尽管你的观点值得考虑), the committee finds it unwise to place too much importance on them.

Unit 3

11. The children went there to watch _____ (铁塔被竖立起来).

12. By signing this application, I ask that _____ (为我开一个户头) and a credit card issued as I request.

13. Only under special circumstances _____ (允许新生参加补考).

14. A season ticket _____ (使持有者有权) make as many journeys as he wishes within the stated period of time.

15. _____ (尽管人类现在可以创造出放射性物质), there is nothing he can do to reduce their radioactivity.

Unit 4

16. The manager promised to keep me _____ (知道我们业务的进展情况).

17. The judge recommended that _____ (三年之内不得释放他).

18. Only by shouting at the top of his voice _____ (他才能让别人听见他说的话).

19. Features such as height, weight and skin color _____ (在个人和个人之间都是不同的).

20. Once they had fame, fortune, secure future, all _____ (剩下的只有贫穷).

Unit 5

21. Mrs. Brown is supposed _____ (上周已经去了意大利).

22. One of the requirements for a fire is that _____ (材料加热至它的燃点).

23. She never laughed, _____ (也从来没有发过脾气).

24. Don't _____ (把消息透露给公众) until we give you the go-ahead.

25. Recycling wastes slows down _____ (我们用尽地球有限资源的速度).

Unit 6

26. The match was cancelled because most of the members objected _____ (在没有标准场地的情况下进行比赛).

27. It is of the utmost importance that _____ (你准时到达这里).

28. I could not persuade him to accept it, nor _____ (能让他看到它的重要性).

29. American football and baseball are _____ (通过电视转播而变得为英国人所知).

30. What a good listener is able to do is to process what he hears _____ (在它出现的上下文的基础上).

Unit 7

31. The speaker, _____ (因为她精彩的演讲而著名), was warmly received by the audience.

32. He must have had an accident, _____ (否则他那时应该已经到达这里了).

33. The organization had broken no rules, but neither _____ (负责任地行动起来).

34. The soldier _____ (被控逃跑) when the enemy attacks.

35. The fire started on the first floor of the hospital, _____ (医院的大部分病人是老人).

Unit 8

36. _____ (无论演出多么频繁), the works of Beethoven always attract large audiences.

37. It was essential that the application forms _____ (在截止日期前寄回).

38. We don't need air conditioning, nor _____ (负担得起).

39. Over a third of the population was estimated _____ (无法接受医疗服务).

40. Water enters into a great variety of chemical reactions, _____ (其中的一些在前几页书中提到过).

Unit 9

41. _____ (在其他条件均等的情况下), a man who expresses himself effectively is sure to succeed more rapidly than a man whose command of language is poor.

42. We desire that the tour leader _____ (立刻通知我们任何计划的改变).

43. It was in the 1960's _____ (两国的贸易达到了最高点).

44. The lawyer advised him _____ (放弃这件案子) since he stood little chance to win.

45. Without facts, we cannot form a worthwhile opinion for we need to have factual knowledge _____ (把我们的思想建立在其上).

Unit 10

46. _____ (被给予了这么好的一个机会), he planned to learn more.

47. We didn't know his telephone number, _____ (否则我们就给他打电话了).

48. It was from Stephen _____ (她第一次听说那个被称为专家的人).

49. _____ (看到血) always makes him feel sick.

50. I suggested he _____ (调整自己以适应新环境).

Unit 11

51. If I correct someone, I will do it as if _____ (我才是那个被纠正错误的人).

52. I don't think it advisable that Tom _____ (被指派负责这个任务) since he has no experience.

53. In the southern part of the United States _____ (有许多废弃的矿镇) built in the last century.

54. _____ (经理大发脾气) just because his secretary was ten minutes late.

55. The world's greatest sporting event, the Olympic Games, upholds the amateur ideal _____ (重在参与，而非胜利).

Unit 12

56. There's a man at the reception desk who seems angry and I think _____ (他打算制造麻烦).

57. _____ (如果没有提前计划整个手术), a great deal of time and money would have been lost.

58. So _____ (他变得很困惑) that he didn't know how to start his lecture.

59. They claim that _____ (大约1000家工厂在经济危机的时候倒闭).

60. The problem of _____ (选谁作为他的继承人) was quickly disposed of.

Unit 13

61. If the ocean were free of ice, storm paths would move further north, _____ (夺去北美洲平原的降雨).

62. As commander-in-chief of the armed forces, I have directed that _____ (采取一切措施) for our defense.

63. On no account _____ (给小孩子任何钱).

64. Although they plant some trees in this area every year, _____ (有些山顶依然是光秃秃的).

65. Physics is the present-day equivalent of _____ (过去被称为自然哲学的东西).

Unit 14

66. When I woke up, I found myself _____ (躺在床上).

67. We are all for your proposal that _____ (取消讨论).

68. So _____ (机器人很聪明) that they may eventually reduce the amount of the labor needed by 90 percent.

69. The man to whom we handed the forms pointed out that _____ (表格没有正确填写).

70. We grow all our own fruit and vegetables, _____ (这很省钱).

Unit 15

71. _____ (开始只是一个有着 17 个孩子的家庭中的一个可怜的小男孩), Benjamin Franklin became famous as a statesman, scientist, and author.

72. To be frank, I'd rather _____ (你没有牵扯到这件案子中).

73. The doctor warned his patient that on no account _____ (他回来工作) until he had completely recovered.

74. The relationship between employers and employees _____ (透彻地研究过).

75. _____ (太阳而不是地球是中心) in our planetary system was a difficult concept to grasp in the Middle Ages.

Unit 16

76. At last she left her house and I got to the airport, only _____ (看到飞机飞走了).

77. The mad man was put in the padded cell lest _____ (他会伤害他自己).

78. I have two boys, _____ (没有一个喜欢吃糖).

79. _____ (是我们的长期政策) that we will achieve unity through peaceful means.

80. _____ (一旦某些化学物质相互混合), heat is produced.

Unit 17

81. Henry Ford's introduction of the assembly line vastly reduced _____ (制造一辆汽车所需的时间).

82. It's high time _____ (你意识到自己并非这个世界上最
重要的人).

83. Neither of the young men who had applied for a position in the university _____
(被录取了).

84. _____ (很有雄心), my brother wants to master English,
French and Spanish before he is sixteen.

85. They assured us that _____ (不管等待我们的是什么),
they were there to share it.

Unit 18

86. The information was later admitted _____ (是通过不可
靠的来源得到的).

87. But for his courage, the battle _____ (会失败).

88. According to the schedule, three-fourths of the dyke (堤坝) _____
(将在今年年底完工).

89. The author of the report is well _____ (熟悉医院中的问
题) because he has been working there for many years.

90. He never hesitates to make such _____ (被认为是对他人
有用的批评).

Unit 19

91. The chairman threatened to _____ (如果他的政策不被
采纳的话就退休).

92. But for the flood, _____ (船就及时到达终点了).

93. Joe's father, along with his two uncles, _____ (要求他在
纽约多呆一天).

94. We are interested in the weather because _____ (它对我
们的影响如此直接) —what we wear, what we do and even how we feel.

95. By 2010, production in the area is expected _____ (是
2000 年产量的两倍).

Unit 20

96. The mother didn't know _____ (谁该因为打破的玻璃
而受到责备).

97. You did tell me what to do. If only _____ (我采纳了你的建议).

98. If law and order _____ (没有受到保护), neither the citizen nor his property is safe.

99. They _____ (采取有效措施) to prevent poisonous gases from escaping.

100. This is one of the rarest questions _____ (在这样一次会议中被提出的).

Unit 21

101. The police accused him of setting fire to the building but he _____ (否认在失火那天晚上曾经在那个地方呆过).

102. It's high time _____ (我们把注意力转向这个问题).

103. Not until the game had begun _____ (他才到了运动场).

104. I want to buy a new tie _____ (和这套棕色西装相配).

105. Some companies have introduced flexible working time with less emphasis on pressure _____ (更强调效率).

Unit 22

106. Sometimes very young children have trouble _____ (区分事实和虚构的故事) and may believe that such things actually exist.

107. If only _____ (你没有告诉他我说了什么). Everything would have been all right.

108. Only when the war was over _____ (他才能愉快地去工作).

109. A lorry _____ (撞到了简) and sped away.

110. Output is now _____ (是 1990 年之前的 6 倍).

Unit 23

111. Buck Helm, a retired salesman, survived _____ (在车内被活埋了 90 个小时).

112. He is less _____ (适合当经理) than a school boy would be.

113. On the hay _____ (躺着一个不到 17 岁的受伤的男孩).

114. I always _____ (坚持我所说的).

115. Just as the builder is skilled in the handling of his bricks, _____ (有经验的作家也很擅长运用他的语言).

Unit 24

116. There _____ (对迈克的诚实存有怀疑), the company asked him to resign.

117. Were they to cease advertising, _____ (价格将会大大降低).

118. Only with hard work _____ (你才能指望加薪).

119. Before payday I have _____ (和我哥哥一样少的钱).

120. We preferred to postpone the meeting _____ (而不是在没有总统出席的情况下召开它).

Unit 25

121. A large fish was slowly swimming through the water, its tail _____ (前前后后地游来游去，像钟摆一样).

122. It is important that _____ (筹集足够的钱) to fund the project.

123. Not only _____ (他们带了小吃和饮料), but they also brought cards for entertainment.

124. It is difficult _____ (在周围这么多噪音的情况下继续进行对话).

125. Everyone asked me where he was but it was _____ (对我来说同样是个谜) as to them.

Unit 26

126. All flights _____ (均因暴风雪取消), they decided to take the train.

127. _____ (如果昨天我们没有被打断), we would have finished our work.

128. The trip _____ (按照花销和时间来计划).

129. The trumpet player was certainly loud but I wasn't bothered by his loudness _____ (而是他的缺乏天分).

130. Tom should know _____ (明事理，不至于找迪克帮忙).

Unit 27

131. All things considered, _____ (计划的行程不得不取消).

132. He is working hard for fear _____ (他会落后).

133. They are building the dam _____ (和另一家公司联合).

134. Everyone in the world should be regarded more _____
     (在运动中而不是在静止中).

135. Codes are a way of writing something in secret; _____
     (也就是说，任何不知道密码的人都无法读它).

Unit 28

136. A Dream of the Red Chamber is said _____ (译成了十
     几种语言) in the last decade.

137. The driver looked over the engine carefully lest _____
     (它会在路上出故障).

138. Throughout his life, Henry Moore _____ (保持着对艺
     术的兴趣).

139. _____ (正如今天报纸上宣布的那样), the Shanghai
     Export Commodities Fair is also open on Sunday.

140. We have done things we ought not to have done and _____
     (应该做的事情却没有做).

Unit 29

141. _____ (相信地球是扁平的), many feared that Colum-
     bus would fall off the edge of the earth.

142. It is highly desirable that _____ (选一个新主席) for the
     committee.

143. I hope that all the precautions against air pollution will be seriously considered here, _____
     _____ (当地政府也是如此建议的).

144. Language can be defined as a tool _____ (人们通过它
     和其他人交流).

145. All _____ (需要的) is a continuous supply of the basic
     necessities of life.

Unit 30

146. _____ (没有钱也不想让任何人知道), he simply said he would go without dinner.

147. He doesn't dare to leave the house in case _____ (他会被认出来).

148. Many Europeans _____ (考察非洲) in the 19th century.

149. _____ (是和汤姆) that Mary talked yesterday.

150. Helen was much kinder to her younger child than she was to the other, _____

_____ (这让另一个孩子很嫉妒).

Unit 31

151. After the Arab states won independence, great emphasis was laid on expanding education, with _____ (女孩和男孩都被鼓励去上学).

152. The coming of the railways in the 1830s _____ (改变了我们的社会和经济生活).

153. The goals _____ (他终生为之奋斗的) no longer seemed important to him.

154. How close parents are to their children _____ (对孩子的性格有巨大的影响).

155. Due to his excellent performance in work, he is _____ (升为经理).

Unit 32

156. This crop has similar qualities to the previous one, _____ (两者都适应同一种土壤).

157. I hate people _____ (揭露电影的结尾) that you haven't seen before.

158. _____ (全世界都知道), Mark Twain is a great American writer.

159. In some countries, _____ (所谓的平等) does not really mean equal right for all people.

160. The result _____ (把他从压力中解脱出来).

Unit 33

161. _____ (在最近的一次科学比赛中被评为最好的), the three students were awarded scholarship totaling 21,000 dollars.

162. The computer revolution may well change society _____ (和工业革命一样彻底).

163. I've never been to Beijing, but it's the place _____ (我最想去的).

164. They are teachers and don't realize _____ (要经营一家公司要花费多少).

165. I have kept that portrait _____ (我每天能看到的地方), as it always remind me of my university life.

Unit 34

166. _____ (从盘子上标注的日期), we decided that they were made in Song Dynasty.

167. When people become unemployed, it is _____ (闲散往往比缺少薪水更糟).

168. _____ (正如我们所料), the response to the question was very mixed.

169. By success I don't mean _____ (通常所想) when that word is used.

170. There's little chance that mankind _____ (能在核战中存活下来).

Unit 35

171. It _____ (已经相当晚了), we took our things and retired to our room.

172. You should hire a _____ (比现在这个效率更高的经理).

173. Living in the central Australian desert has its problems, _____ (其中获得水只是一个最小的问题).

174. _____ (在那个地区展开了一项关于人们业余活动的调查), the results of which were surprising.

175. Americans eat _____ (两倍的蛋白质) as they actually need every day.

Unit 36

176. The old man came upstairs with great strength, _____ (右手拿着一根手杖) for support.

177. Frankfurt, Germany, is in one of the _____ (西欧人口最密集的地区).

178. There are few electronic applications _____ (更容易引起有关未来就业机会的恐惧) than robots.

179. She is _____ (更像一个音乐家) than her brother.

180. Nuclear science should be developed to _____ (造福人类而不是危害人类).

Unit 37

181. While _____ (因为发明电话而被人们记住), Alexander Graham Bell devoted his life to helping the deaf.

182. _____ (我过去吸烟很厉害), but I gave it up three years ago.

183. _____ (年轻人而非老年人) are more likely to prefer pop songs.

184. Cancer _____ (仅次于心脏病) as a cause of death.

185. The computer has brought about surprising technological changes _____ _____ (我们组织和输出信息的方式).

Unit 38

186. _____ (被警察包围), the kidnappers had no choice but to surrender.

187. _____ (虽然长期效果无法预料), the project has been approved by the committee.

188. He is _____ (与其说是作家) as a scientist.

189. The destruction of these treasures was loss for mankind that _____ (多少金钱都无法弥补).

190. _____ (会节约很多人力) if the electronic computers had been invented earlier.

Unit 39

191. There _____ (没有新鲜的饮用水) and no good farm land, it was not a comfortable place in which to live.

192. In most of the United States, the morning newspaper _____ (由学龄儿童递送).

193. So, as you see, _____ (斗争远未结束).

194. This crop does not do well in soils other than _____ (那个它一直生长的土壤).

195. _____ (除了英国再没有任何一个国家) can one experience four seasons in the course of a single day.

Unit 40

196. Peter is a good student, English _____ (是他最擅长的一门课).

197. It is quite necessary for a qualified teacher _____ (有优雅的举止和广博的知识).

198. When he arrived, he found _____ (家里除了老人和病人什么人都没有).

199. _____ (没有足够的钱也不想从父亲那里借), he decided to sell his watch.

200. Although he knew little about the large amount of work done in the field, he succeeded _____ (在其他同类实验都失败的地方).

答案与解析

Unit 1

【解析】

1. When a new technique had been worked out/A new technique having been worked out

   分析句子结构，题干中给出的英文部分是简单句，那么需要翻译的部分要么译成从句，要么译成非谓语动词短语。此处"设计出"有"解决"之意，故译作 work out。由于没有明确的施动者，故使用被动语态。

2. because the doctor suggested that he (should) not go there

   本题考查虚拟语气的用法。suggest 表示"建议"之意，后面宾语从句中使用虚拟语气"should＋v."，should 可以省略，故"建议他不要去那里"就是 suggested that he (should) not go there。此外，由于和题干中英语部分是明显的因果关系，句子前面要使用表示原因的连词 because。

3. shall we use the telephone in the office for personal affairs

   本题考查 under no circumstances 位于句首时，句子主谓倒装的情况。"应该"使用情态动词 shall，倒装时把它提前；"私事"译作 personal affairs。

4. that the professor referred to us

   分析句子结构，所译部分作定语修饰句子的主语 the book，故使用定语从句。"教授和我们谈到过的"就是 the professor referred to us。

5. While I admit that there are problems

   本题考查让步状语从句。"尽管"可以译作 although 或者 while，由于主句使用一般现在时，所以从句也要使用相同的时态，"承认"就是 admit。

Unit 2

【解析】

6. When compared with the size of the whole earth

   本题考查英文中比较句式的表达。"A 与 B 相比"可用 compare A with B 的结构，题干中给出的英文部分已是完整的句子，故翻译时可采用过去分词短语的结构 Compared with the size of the whole earth 或者 When compared with the size of the whole earth。

7. I wish I had been to

本题考查虚拟语气。后面的从句用一般过去时，可见是对过去发生事情的虚拟，所以 wish 后面用过去完成时。

8. No sooner had we reached the top of the mountain/We had no sooner reached the top of the mountain

本题考查 no sooner...than...（一······就······）的用法。no sooner 的后面要用过去完成时，than 的后面使用一般过去时。如果 no sooner 位于句首，那么主句部分倒装。

【考点归纳】

表示"一······就······"的几种说法：

● as soon as，如：As soon as we reached the top of the mountain, we all sat down to rest.

● hardly...when...，如：Hardly had we reached the top of the mountain when we all sat down to rest.

● no sooner...than...，如：No sooner had we reached the top of the mountain than we all sat down to rest.

9. Many difficulties have arisen

"困难出现"可以译作 difficulties arise，因为是"出现了"，所以使用现在完成时。这里主要考查的就是 arise 的用法，注意不要和 rise 混淆。

10. While your opinion is worth considering

此处考查让步状语从句和 worth 的用法。worth 是介词而非动词，故"值得"要用 be worth...；此外，worth 的后面要用动名词的主动形式表示被动，故"考虑"在这里译作 considering。

Unit 3

【解析】

11. the iron tower being erected

本题考查 watch 后动词的用法。感观动词后面用动词原形表示已经完成的动作，用动词的现在分词表示正在进行的动作。此处表示正在进行的动作，而且是被动语态，所以使用 being erected。要注意的是，这里不能直接说 the iron tower erected，否则句意就变为"看那个被立起来的铁塔"，此时 erected 修饰 tower，而且"看"也不能用 watch，要用 see。

12. a bank account (should) be opened for me

本题考查虚拟语气的用法。ask 此处表示"要求"之意，后面使用虚拟语气，形式为"(should) + v."。此外，"开户头"就是 open an account，变成被动语态就是 an account be opened。

13. **are freshmen permitted to take the make-up test**

   本题考查句子的倒装。题干中 only 修饰的介词短语 under special circumstances 位于句首，句子需部分倒装。"允许某人做某事"可以译为 allow/permit sb. to do sth.，"补考"就是 make-up test。

【考点归纳】

几种常考的倒装句：

● 以 never, hardly, not, not only, little, seldom, often, many a time, not until, rarely, in vain, scarcely/hardly...when, no sooner...than 等词开头的句中，常用倒装语序，如：
   Never have I seen him before. (我过去从来没有见过他。)
   Hardly had I reached the bus stop when the bus started. (我刚到车站，公共汽车就开了。)

● 在 only 所修饰的副词、介词短语或状语从句放在句首时，常用倒装语序，如：
   Only then did I realize that I was wrong. (只有在那时我才意识到自己错了。)
   Only in this way can you learn from your friends. (只有这样你才能向你的朋友学习。)

● 宾语中含有某些具有强调意义的限定词，如 not a, nothing, nobody, no one, many a, many, 且位于句首时，常用倒装语序，如：
   Not a single word did Mr. Li speak. (李先生一句话也没说。)
   Nothing did I know about the matter. (关于这件事我一点儿也不知道。)

14. **entitles the holder to**

   本题考查动词 entitle 的用法。entitle sb. to sth. 意为"使某人有权……"。

【考点归纳】

表示"对……享有权利"时，entitle 的两种用法：

● entitle sb. to sth.，如：Every citizen is entitled to equal protection under the law. (每个公民都有权依法受同等保护。)

● entitle sb. to do sth.，如：This preferential ticket entitles you to travel first class. (凭这张优惠票，你可以坐头等舱旅行。)

15. **While man can create radioactive elements now**

   所填部分的基本结构为让步状语从句，"创造"可译为 create，"放射性物质"译作 radioactive elements。

Unit 4

【解析】

16. **informed of how our business is getting along**

   分析句子结构，在这里 keep 后面应当接复合宾语，因此所填部分应当使用分词短语作

me 的宾语补足语。"知道"在此处译作 inform of，因为 inform sb. of sth.意为"让某人获悉某事"，keep sb. informed of sth.具有相同的含义。"进展"译作 get along。

17. he (should) not be released within three years

本题考查虚拟语气的用法。recommend 后面使用虚拟语气，形式为"(should) +v."，"释放"的被动形式是 be released。

18. was he able to make himself heard

本题考查 only 位于句首时的倒装情况。此处时态没有很大限制，但使用一般过去时要好一些；"让别人听到他说的话"译作 make himself heard。

19. vary from individual to individual

分析句子结构，缺少谓语，所以此处"不同"译作动词 vary，那么后面接介词 from。

20. that is left is poverty

此处考查定语从句的用法。分析句子结构，题干部分是从句，缺少主句。主句的第一个单词是 all，那么此处"剩下的"应译作一个定语从句，先行词是 all，从句关系代词用 that，所以就是 all that is left；主句的谓语动词用单数；"贫穷"为 poverty。

Unit 5

【解析】

21. to have left for Italy last week

此处考查动词不定式的用法。分析句子结构，be supposed 后面要跟 to do sth.；此外，这里说"上周已经去了"，而不定式原形表示的是未来，故使用不定式完成时表示过去，即 to have done sth.。

【考点归纳】

● 不定式的一般时 to do sth.表示将来，如：He decided to work harder. (他决定更努力地工作。)

● 不定式的完成时 to have done 表示已经完成的动作，如：He pretended not to have seen me. (他假装没有看见我。)

22. the material (should) be heated to its burning temperature

此处考查虚拟语气的用法。requirement 意为"要求"，此时用来解释说明 requirement 内容的从句要用虚拟语气，形式为"(should) +v."，没有明确施动者，故使用被动语态，即 the material be heated to。"燃点"就是 burning temperature。

23. nor did she ever lose her temper

本题考查"也没有……"的说法。"发脾气"译作 lose one's temper。题干中用了 She never laughed，那么此空最简单的填法就是 and never lost her temper either。但同时也可以使用 nor，nor 位于句首句子要部分倒装，因此就是 nor did she ever lose her temper。

24. release the news to the public

"透漏，泄漏"用动词 release，"把消息透漏给某人"就是 release the news to sb.。

25. the rate at which we use up the finite resources of the earth

本题考查定语从句的用法。分析句子结构，题干是一个简单句，但是缺少宾语。因此，所填部分首先是句子的宾语 rate，其余内容作定语修饰 rate，由于从句中缺少状语，而 rate 的前面又使用介词 at，故从句关系词就用 at which。"用尽"就是 use up，"有限的资源"译作 finite resources。

Unit 6

【解析】

26. to holding the match without a standard court

分析句子结构，题干是简单句，但是缺少宾语。object 作动词用，表示"反对"之意，而且是不及物动词，后面要跟介词 to，其后再跟动名词作 to 的宾语。"进行比赛"就是 hold the match，不过这里要用动名词，就是 holding the match。

27. you (should) be here on time

本题考查虚拟语气的用法。此处应该使用形式为"(should) ＋v."的虚拟语气。"准时"就是 on time。

28. could I make him realize the importance of it

此题考查 nor 位于句首时句子的部分倒装。"让某人做某事"就是 make sb. do sth.，所以此空就是 could I make him realize the importance of it。

29. known to the British through televised transmissions

"为……所知"就是 known to sb.，"电视转播"就是 televised transmission。

【考点归纳】

与 known 有关的常考短语有：

● be known for...意为"因……而著名"，如：He is known for his talent for music. (他的音乐才能众所周知。)

● be known as...意为"作为……而著名"，如：Lu Xun is known as a writer. (鲁迅是著名作家。)

● be known to...意为"为……所知"，如：The fact is known to all. (这一事实大家都知道。)

30. on the basis of the context in which it occurs

分析句子结构，此处要填的是一个介词短语，在句子中作状语。"在……的基础上"可以译作 on the basis of...，"它出现的上下文"就是 the context in which it occurs。

Unit 7

【解析】

31. (who is) known for her splendid speeches

分析句子结构，要翻译的句子可以是分词短语作定语，也可以是定语从句。"因……而著名"就是 be known for...，"精彩的"可以译作 splendid 或者 wonderful。

32. or he would have been here

本题考查虚拟语气的用法。此处是虚拟条件句。题干为 he must have had an accident，用"must＋现在完成时"表示对过去事情的推测，所以所译部分也是表示对过去事情的虚拟，那么在此时应使用"would＋现在完成时"。

【考点归纳】

几种常见的虚拟条件句：

● 一般虚拟条件句：

对现在的虚拟：If I were you, I would study hard. (如果我是你，我一定会好好学习。)

对过去的虚拟：If I had studied hard, I would have passed the exam. (如果我努力学习了，就不会考试不及格了。)

对将来的虚拟：If you were to go to the party, you would enjoy it. (如果你去参加聚会，一定会玩得很高兴。)

● 错综时间条件句，即条件句说过去，主句说现在：If I had studied hard, I would pass the exam now. (如果我努力学习，现在就不会考试不及格了。)

● 含蓄条件句：Without/But for your help, I would not have succeeded. (如果没有你的帮助，我是不会成功的。)

● 条件句中去掉 if，则条件句部分倒装：Were I you, I would study hard. (如果我是你，我一定会好好学习。)

33. had it acted responsibly

本题考查 neither 位于句首句子的部分倒装。并列句的第一个分句用的是过去完成时，那么此处所译的第二个分句也应是过去完成时，部分倒装时，had 提前。"负责任地行动"就是 act responsibly。

34. was accused of running away/was charged with running away

本题主要考查"指控"的说法。常见的有两种：accuse sb. of sth. 和 charge sb. with sth.。此处使用的是被动语态，故为 be accused of sth. 或者 be charged with sth.。注意 of 后应为名词或动名词。

35. most of whose patients are the elderly

本题考查定语从句的用法。题干是主句，那么此处应为从句，由于和主句的 hospital 相关，故使用定语从句，"大部分病人"就是 most of whose patients，"老人"可译作 the elderly。

Unit 8

【解析】

36. No matter how frequently performed

本题考查让步状语从句的用法。作品是"被演出",因此应使用被动语态,即 be performed。"频繁地"译作 frequently。此外,由于状语从句的主语和主句相同,谓语是系动词,因此可以同时省略主语和谓语。

37. (should) be sent back before the deadline

本题考查虚拟语气的用法。It is essential that 后面要使用形式为"(should) +v."的虚拟语气。此外,由于没有明确的施动者,所填部分要使用被动语态。"截止日期"可以译为 deadline。

38. can we afford it

本题考查 nor 位于句首时句子的部分倒装。"负担得起"就是 can afford it,部分倒装时则将 can 提到主语 we 的前面。

39. to have no access to medical care

分析句子结构,be estimated 后面应该使用动词不定式。"无法接受"此处可以译作 to have no access to,"医疗服务"就是 medical care。

40. a few of which have been mentioned in previous pages

本题考查定语从句的用法。由于题干中的英语部分是独立的简单句,可见要翻译的部分是从句。"其中的一些"指的是主句中 chemical reactions 中的一些,译作 a few of which,"前几页"就是 in previous pages。此外,由于此句没有明显的施动者,所以应使用被动语态。

Unit 9

【解析】

41. When other things are equal 或 Other things being equal

分析句子结构,缺少状语。那么所填部分可以使用状语从句,也可以使用独立主格结构。"均等"就是 equal,所以此处可以译作 When other things are equal 或者 Other things being equal。

42. (should) inform us immediately of any changes in the plan

本题考查虚拟语气的用法。desire 后的宾语从句中使用"(should) +v."形式的虚拟语气。"通知某人某事"译作 inform sb. of sth.。

43. that the trade between two countries reached its highest point

本题考查强调句的用法。所译部分是强调句的从句部分,前面用 that 引导。"达到最高点"就是 reach its highest point。

【考点归纳】

强调句的特点：

● 强调句就是将一个普通的句子所需强调的部分提到句首，前面用 It is/was 来加以强调；剩余的部分放在后面用 that/who 引导。

● 强调句去掉 It is/was 和 that/who 后，剩余的部分依然是一个完整的句子。

● 强调句一般使用 It is/was...that 的形式，但如果所强调的部分是人，则既可以用 that 也可以用 who。

● 一个句子，除了谓语部分外，其他任何成分都可以加以强调，变成强调句，如：

Yesterday my mother threw a bad egg at the manager. →

It was yesterday that my mother threw a bad egg at the manager.

It was my mother who/that threw a bad egg at the manager.

It was a bad egg that my mother threw at the manager yesterday.

It was at the manager that my mother threw a bad egg yesterday.

44. to drop the case

分析句子结构，advise 后面可以使用从句或者不定式，此处 advise 后面已经有了 him，可见要使用 advise sb. to do sth.的用法。"放弃这件案子"就是 drop the case。

45. on which our thinking is based

本题考查定语从句的用法。所填部分的"其"指的就是前文的 factual knowledge，可见此处的翻译要使用定语从句，将两者联系起来。所填部分可以使用主动语态，即 on which to base our thinking，因为主句的主语是 we；也可以使用被动语态，即 on which our thinking is based。

Unit 10

【解析】

46. Since he had been given such a good chance 或 Having been given such a good chance

分析句子结构，所填部分应该是状语从句或者非谓语动词短语作状语。所填部分的动作应该发生在"他打算"（he planned）之前，故使用过去完成时，译作 Since he had been given such a good chance；或者使用分词短语的被动形式，译作 Having been given such a good chance。

47. otherwise we would have telephoned him

本题考查虚拟语气的用法。"否则"就是 otherwise，其后的情况不是真的，故使用虚拟语气；题干中的英语部分使用一般过去时，故所译部分的虚拟语气应表示和过去的事实相反，使用"would＋现在完成时"形式。

48. that she first heard of the man referred to as the expert

本题考查强调句的用法。"听说"就是 hear of，"那个被称为专家的人"可以译作 the

man referred to as the expert。

49. The sight of blood

分析句子结构，题干中的英语部分为句子的谓语和宾语部分，可见所填部分应该充当句子的主语，那么应该是名词性质的。"看到"在此处就应该采用名词短语 the sight of。

50. (should) adapt/adjust/accustom himself to the new environment

本题考查"调整"的英文说法和虚拟语气的用法。"调整自己以适应"可以译作 adapt/adjust/accustom oneself to。suggest 后面要使用虚拟语气，should 可以省略，故此处为 (should) adapt/adjust/accustom himself to the new environment。

Unit 11

【解析】

51. I were the man being corrected

as if 后面的从句中应使用虚拟语气。题干中的英语部分使用一般现在时，所以 as if 后面的虚拟语气表示的是和现在相反的情况，故用一般过去时。"被纠正错误的那个人"就是 the man being corrected，man 后面使用分词短语的被动形式作定语。

52. (should) be assigned the task

本题考查虚拟语气的用法。advisable 后的从句中要使用形式为"(should) ＋v."的虚拟语气。"指派给某人某事"就是 assign sb. sth.，assign 的后面要使用双宾语。此处没有明确表明动作的主动者，故使用被动语态。

53. are many abandoned mining towns

本题考查介词短语作状语位于句首时句子的完全倒装。"废弃的"就是 abandoned。

【考点归纳】

● 完全倒装指将句子中的谓语动词全部置于主语之前；而部分倒装则只将相应的助动词提到主语的前面（参见短文改错第三节 Passage 6 解析中的【考点归纳】），如：

In came a man with a white beard. (忽然进来一个长白胡子的男人。) (完全倒装)

Hardly did I think it possible. (我几乎认为这是不可能的。) (不完全倒装)

● here, there, now, then, thus, out, in, up, down, away 等副词置于句首，谓语动词是 be, come, go, lie, run, rush 等时句子完全倒装，如：

There comes the bus. (汽车来了。)

Away went the boy. (那男孩走了。)

Out rush the children. (孩子们跑了出来。)

● 全部倒装的句型结构的主语必须是名词，如果主语是人称代词则不能倒装，如：

Here it is. (这就是。)

There she comes! (她来了！)

54. The manager lost his temper

"大发脾气" 就是 lose one's temper。此外，从句中使用的一般过去时，那么主句也应该使用一般过去时。

55. that what matters is participating rather than winning

本题考查同位语从句的用法。分析句子结构，所译部分的作用是解释说明空格前的名词 the amateur ideal，故使用同位语从句，引导词是 that。"重要的是"可以译作主语从句 what is important is 或者 what matters，"重在参与而不是胜利"在句子中作表语，因此使用动名词形式 participating rather than winning。

Unit 12

【解析】

56. he means to make trouble

"打算做"不怎么光彩的事情的时候，我们倾向于使用 mean to do sth. 而非 plan to do sth.，"制造麻烦"就是 make trouble。此处需注意主语是 he，谓语 mean 要使用第三人称单数。

57. If the whole operations had not been planned in advance

本题考查虚拟条件句。题干中的英语部分是主句，使用"would＋现在完成时"，可见此处虚拟语气指和过去的事实相反，因此所译部分的条件句要使用过去完成时。此外，所译部分未出现明确的施动者，应使用被动语态。"手术"就是 operation，"提前计划"可译作 plan in advance。

58. confused did he become

本题考查 so 位于句首时句子的修饰性倒装。"变得困惑"就是 become confused，题干中的英语部分使用一般过去时，可见整个句子指过去发生的事情，因此所译部分将助动词 did 放在主语 he 的前面，实现句子的部分倒装。

【考点归纳】

一些比较特殊的部分倒装：

- so...that 句型中的 so，such...that 句型中的 such 位于句首时，需倒装，如：So frightened was he that he did not dare to move an inch. (他如此恐惧，不敢移动一步。)
- 在某些表示祝愿的句型中要用倒装，如：May you all be happy. (祝你们全都幸福。)
- 在虚拟语气条件句中从句谓语动词有 were，had，should 等词，可将 if 省略，把 were，had，should 移到主语之前，采取部分倒装，如：Were I you, I would try it again. (如果我是你，我就会再试一试。)

59. approximately/about 1,000 factories closed down during the economic crisis

"倒闭"就是 close down，"经济危机"可译作 economic crisis。此处指过去发生的事情，故使用一般过去时。

60. whom to choose as his successor

本题考查宾语从句的用法。空格前是介词 of，可见所译部分要使用宾语从句。"继承人"就是 successor。"选谁"在此处可以使用"疑问代词＋不定式"的方式来翻译成 whom to choose，当然，也可以使用宾语从句 whom he would choose。

Unit 13

【解析】

61. depriving the plains in North America of its rainfall

分析句子结构，题干中的英语部分分别是句子的主句和从句，可见要翻译的部分应该是非谓语动词短语作句子的状语。主句的主语是 storm paths，也正是所译部分的逻辑主语，故所译部分使用现在分词短语作结果状语。"夺去"就是 deprive of。

62. all measures (should) be taken

本题考查虚拟语气的用法。表示"命令"之意的动词 direct 后面的从句中要使用形式为"(should) ＋v."的虚拟语气。"采取措施"可译作 take measures，由于所译部分没有表明施动者，故使用被动语态 measures be taken。

63. should any money be given to a child

本题考查 on no account 这个含有否定意义的短语作状语位于句首时句子的部分倒装。由于未表明动作的主动者，所译部分使用被动语态，译作 should any money be given to a child。

64. tops of some of the hills are still bare

分析句子结构发现，题干中的英语部分为一个让步状语从句，所填部分是该句的主句，其时态与从句一致。形容山顶"光秃秃的"要使用形容词 bare。

65. what used to be called natural philosophy

本题考查宾语从句的用法。空格前为介词 of，则所译部分应为宾语从句。"过去被称作"可译为 what used to be called。

Unit 14

【解析】

66. lying on the bed

本题主要考查动词 find 后使用复合宾语的情况。"躺在床上"和其逻辑主语 myself 是主动关系，故应使用现在分词 lying on the bed。

【考点归纳】

复合宾语的特点总结：
- 复合宾语就是"宾语＋宾语补足语"，宾语补足语是用来补充修饰宾语的。
- 宾语补足语可以是形容词、介词短语或者非谓语动词短语。

- 当使用分词短语作宾语补足语时，如果它和宾语是主动关系，用现在分词；如果是被动关系，用过去分词。
- 复合宾语判断小窍门：动词后的两个单词之间如果加上相应的系动词，可以构成一句语法、语义均正确的话，那么这两个单词就是宾语和宾语补足语的关系。以本题为例，I found myself lying on the bed 其实就是 I was lying on the bed。

67. the discussion (should) be cancelled/the discussion (should) be called off

本题考查虚拟语气的用法。proposal 是动词 propose 的名词形式，两者后面的从句中均要使用形式为 "(should) +v." 的虚拟语气。"取消讨论" 就是 call off the discussion 或者 cancel the discussion，此处根据需要使用被动语态。

68. smart are the robots

本题考查 so 位于句首时句子的修饰性倒装。"机器人很聪明" 就是 robots are so smart，此处由于题干中已经给出 so，而且位于句首，所以句子要倒装，将系动词 are 提到主语 robots 的前面。

69. the forms are not properly filled in

分析句子结构，所译部分是宾语从句。"表格没有正确填写" 应当是被动的，因此 "填表" 在此处译为 the forms are filled in，"正确地" 就是 "适当地"，译作 properly。

70. which saves money

本题考查定语从句的用法。所译部分使用定语从句，关系代词要使用 which，有两个原因：其一，空格前的逗号表明这里是非限定性定语从句；其二，此处的 which 指代前面的整句话，that 没有这个功能。

【考点归纳】

- which 引导定语从句时可以指代前文的整句话，因此不仅仅是一个先行词，如：He is very honest, which I told you long ago.（我很早就告诉过你，他很诚实。）
- as 也可以引导定语从句，指代一句话，但是这句话可以在定语从句的前面，也可以在定语从句的后面，而 which 引导的定语从句只能放在主句之后，如：As I told you long ago, he is very honest.（正如我早就告诉过你的，他很诚实。）此处的 as 不能用 which 替换，但是上面例子中的 which 可以用 as 替换。

Unit 15

【解析】

71. Starting as a poor boy in a family of seventeen children

分析句子结构，题干中的英语部分为主句，可见所译部分为状语部分。此处使用分词短语更为简洁，因为所译部分的逻辑主语就是主句的主语 Benjamin Franklin，故使用现在分词 starting。

72. you were not involved in the case 或 you had not been involved in the case

　　本题考查虚拟语气的用法。would rather 后面要使用虚拟语气，表示对现在的虚拟，用一般过去时；表示对过去的虚拟，用过去完成时。此处由于没有上下文，两者均可。"牵扯其中"就是 be involved in，故此句可以译为 you were not involved in the case 或者 you had not been involved in the case。

73. should he go back to work

　　本题考查介词短语位于句首时句子的部分倒装情况。所译部分为宾语从句中的主句部分，句首是 on no account，故使用部分倒装，将 should 提到主语 he 的前面。"回来工作"可译作 go back to work。

74. has been studied intensively/thoroughly

　　"研究过"在翻译时应当使用被动语态的现在完成时，就是 has/have been studied。由于主语是 relationship，故谓语动词用单数 has。"透彻地"可以译作 intensively 或者 thoroughly。

75. That the sun instead of the earth is the center

　　分析句子结构，所译部分作整个句子的主语，故在这里应该使用主语从句，用 that 引导。

Unit 16

【解析】

76. to see the plane flying away

　　分析句子结构，此处使用动词不定式作结果状语。see 后面使用现在分词表示动作进行的过程。

77. he (should) injure himself

　　本题考查虚拟语气的用法。表示"唯恐、万一"的连词 lest 和 in case 的后面使用形式为"(should) ＋v."的虚拟语气。"伤害"译作 injure。

78. neither of whom likes sweets 或 and neither of them likes sweets

　　由于题干中的英语部分是独立的简单句，那么此处所译部分根据具体情况可以译为定语从句 neither of whom likes sweets 或者并列句 and neither of them likes sweets。需要特别注意的是 neither of 按单数对待。

79. It is our consistent policy

　　分析句子结构，题干中的英语部分应当是主语从句，但是由于所译部分位于它的前面，因此所译部分中要使用形式主语 it 来代替这个主语从句。"长期政策"译作 consistent policy。

【考点归纳】

it 可以用作句子的形式主语，代替较长的逻辑主语，如：

● 逻辑主语为动词不定式时：We find it difficult to prevent people from doing that. (我们发现要阻止人们那样做简直太难了。)

- 逻辑主语为动名词时：It's no use talking without doing.（光说不做是没有用的。）
- 逻辑主语为名词性从句时：It's a well-known fact that the development of a country depends on the quality of its younger generation.（众所周知，一个国家的发展取决于该国年轻人的素质。）

80. Whenever some chemicals are mixed

分析句子结构，此处要翻译的是一个条件状语从句。"一旦"在这里就是 whenever，"相互混合"就是 are mixed。

Unit 17

【解析】

81. the time it takes to make a car

分析所需翻译的部分，"制造一辆汽车所需要的"作定语修饰"时间"，故所译部分的中心词是时间（time），作空格前动词 reduced 的宾语。"花时间做某事"用英语表达就是 It takes/took some time to do sth.，time 作先行词，那么它的定语就是 that it takes to make a car，其中 that 指代 time，可以省略。

82. you realized that you are not the most important person in the world

本题考查虚拟语气的用法。It's high time 后面要使用虚拟语气，形式为动词的一般过去时，所以"意识到"在此处译为 realized。

83. was admitted/accepted/enrolled

句子的主语为 neither of...，按照单数对待。所译部分为被动语态，"被录取"就是 was admitted/accepted/enrolled。

84. Since he is ambitious 或 Being ambitious

分析句子结构，所译部分为状语，和主句之间是因果关系，可以译作 Since he is ambitious。也可以使用分词短语 being ambitious，这样显得更简洁。

85. whatever was waiting for us

分析句子结构，所需翻译部分为让步状语从句，用 whatever 引导。题干中的英语部分都是一般过去时，故此处使用过去进行时更为合适。

Unit 18

【解析】

86. to have been obtained from unreliable sources

分析句子结构，be admitted 后面要使用动词不定式。题干中的英语部分使用了一般过去时，故所译部分的不定式中要使用完成时表示过去。此外，所译部分没有明确的施动者，故使用动词的被动语态，"得到"译作 to have been obtained。"来源"是 sources 而非 resources。

87. would have been lost

本题考查虚拟语气的用法。这里是典型的含蓄条件句，也就是说句子中没有明显的虚拟语气标志词 if，但是 but for his courage 的意思就是"要不是他的勇气"，表明此处是虚拟语气。主句中用一般过去时表示对现在的虚拟，用过去完成时表示对过去的虚拟，此处指的应当是过去，故译作 would have been lost。

88. will have been finished by the end of this year

本题考查的重点是句子的时态问题。"今年年底"是将来，译作 by the end of this year，此时句子的时态应使用将来完成时。另外，要注意所译部分的语态是被动语态。

89. acquainted with problems in the hospital

本题考查短语 be well acquainted with（熟悉）的用法。be familiar with 虽然意思也对，但是 familiar 的前面一般不使用副词 well。

90. criticisms which are considered as helpful to others

"批评"就是 criticism，作空格前动词 make 的宾语。"被认为是对他人有用的"在此处译作定语从句，修饰 criticism，其中"认为……是"译作 consider sth. as...。

Unit 19

【解析】

91. resign if his policies were not adopted

"退休"译作 resign，"采纳政策"就是 adopt the policies，但是此处要使用被动语态。

92. the ship would have reached its destination on time

本题考查虚拟语气的用法。从题干中英语部分的 but for 可以看出，本句是虚拟语气中的含蓄条件句。所译部分中使用"would＋现在完成时"表示对过去事实的虚拟。

93. demanded that he (should) stay in New York another day

要求就是 demand，此处使用一般过去时，其后要使用形式为"(should) ＋v."的虚拟语气。"多呆一天"译作 stay another day。

94. it affects us so directly

"影响"就是 affect，此处使用一般现在时的单数第三人称。"直接地"译作 directly。

95. to double that of 2000

分析句子结构，be expected 后面要使用动词不定式。"两倍"可以直接使用 double，或者 become double of。此外"2000 年产量"中的"产量"由于前文已有，此处应用代词 that 来替代。

【考点归纳】

表示倍数的词还有：

● double 作动词，意为"成为两倍"，如：This country has doubled her annual output of steel during the post-war years.（战后，该国的钢年产量是以前的两倍。）

- treble 作动词，意为"成为三倍"，如：The enemy's force trebles ours.（敌人的力量是我们的三倍。）

Unit 20

【解析】

96. who to blame for the broken window

   分析句子结构，缺少宾语。故此处使用疑问代词 who 引导的宾语从句。从句中可以使用"who＋不定式"的形式，即 who to blame，这样比 who she should blame 更为简洁。

97. I had adopted/taken/followed your advice

   本题考查虚拟语气的用法。if only 后使用虚拟语气。题干中的英语部分使用一般过去时，可见此处是对过去的虚拟，故使用过去完成时的形式。"采纳意见"可以译作 adopt your advice，take your advice 或者 follow your advice。

98. is not preserved

   此处"保护"译作 preserve，而且要使用被动语态。需要注意的是，这里 law and order 指的是同一事物，故按单数对待。

99. adopt effective measures

   "采取措施"译作 adopt measures，也可以说 take measures，"有效的"是 effective，而非 efficient。

100. that have been raised in such a meeting

   分析句子结构，所译部分是定语从句，从句中应使用被动语态的现在完成时。"提出问题"中的"提出"译作 raise。

Unit 21

【解析】

101. denied that he had been in the area on the night of the fire/denied having been in the area on the night of the fire

   本题考查动词 deny 作为"否认"之意时的用法。deny 的后面可以跟宾语从句，也可以跟动名词或者名词短语。跟宾语从句时，由于题干中的英语部分用的是一般过去时，而所译部分的动作发生在之前，故使用过去完成时；跟动名词时，则要用动名词的完成时形式。

102. we turned our attention to the problem

   本题考查虚拟语气的用法。It's high time 后面使用虚拟语气，形式为动词的一般过去时。"把注意力转向……"译作 turn one's attention to。

103. did he reach the sports ground

   本题考查 not until 位于句首时句子的部分倒装。由题干中给出的英文部分可知，所译部分为一般过去时；由于要部分倒装，故将助动词 did 提到主语 he 的前面。"到达"可以译为 reach 或者 arrive at。

104. to go with this brown suit

   分析句子结构，所译部分应该是动词不定式表示目的。"和……相配"译为 go with。

105. and more on efficiency

   本题考查比较级。这里的"更强调效率"不用译为动宾结构，因为题干中的英语部分已经有了 less emphasis on pressure，根据并列句的对称原则，此处应该译为 and more on efficiency。

Unit 22

【解析】

106. separating reality from fiction

   分析句子结构，have trouble 后面要跟 doing sth.；"区分 A 和 B"使用固定搭配 separate A from B，"事实"为 reality，"虚构"则译为 fiction。故此处译为 separating reality from fiction。

107. you hadn't told him what I said

   本题考查虚拟语气的用法。if only 后面使用虚拟语气，而题干中的英语部分使用了"would＋现在完成时"，可见指过去，故 if only 后面使用过去完成时表示对过去发生事情的虚拟。

108. was he able to go happily to work

   本题考查 only 位于句首时句子的倒装。从题干中的英语部分可以得知句子的时态是一般过去时，"能够"是 be able to，故此处将 was 提到主语 he 的前面。

109. ran over Jane

   本题考查动词短语 run over（撞到）的用法。

110. six times that of before 1990

   本题考查倍数的表达方法。"六倍"就是 six times。

【考点归纳】

要表达"据推测去年工业产值总额为 2000 年的 2.5 倍"有以下三种方式：

- A is X times B，如：The gross value of industrial output last year was estimated to be 2.5 times that of 2000.

- A is X times more than B，如：The gross value of industrial output last year was estimated to be 2.5 times more than that of 2000.

- A is X times as + adj. + as B，如：The industrial output last year was estimated to be 2.5 times as much as that of 2000.

Unit 23

【解析】

111. having been buried alive for 90 hours in his car

分析句子结构，survive 是及物动词，则后面只能跟名词或者动名词短语。他被活埋发生在 survived 之前，故此处用动名词的完成式形式表示过去的过去，即 having been buried alive。

112. fit to be a manager

本题考查表示比较的说法。句意为"他还不如一个小学生适合当经理"，故使用 less... than... 的说法，"适合"译为 fit。

113. lied a wounded boy of no more than seventeen years old

本题考查介词短语作状语位于句首时句子的倒装。如果表示方向、地点的副词或者介词短语位于句首，而句子的主语是代词，则不倒装，但若句子的主语是名词，则句子要完全倒装。所译部分的主语是 a wounded boy of no more than seventeen years old，属于名词短语，故这里要完全倒装，将谓语"躺（lied）"提到主语的前面。

114. hold to what I have said

"坚持"译作 hold to，to 是介词，后面要用名词、动名词或者宾语从句。此处"我所说的"译为宾语从句 what I have said。"坚持"也可译作 stick to，adhere to，persist in 等。

115. the experienced writer is skilled in the handling of his words

分析句子结构，题干中的英语部分为方式状语从句，由 just as 引导，那么所译部分的主语在结构上和从句要保持对称，故"擅长运用"也译作 be skilled in the handling of...。"有经验的"译作 experienced。

Unit 24

【解析】

116. being some doubts about Mike's honesty

本题考查独立主格的用法。分析句子结构，逗号后面为主句，则逗号之前应该是从句或者非谓语动词短语作状语；空格前已有了 There，故此处不可能是从句，只能是分词短语构成的独立主格，逻辑主语为 there，后面使用现在分词短语 being some doubts about。

117. the price would be reduced sharply

本题考查虚拟语气的用法。题干中的英语部分为虚拟条件句没有 if 时的倒装，使用一般过去时表示对现在的虚拟，那么对应的主句，也就是所译部分应当使用"would＋v."的形式。此外由于所译部分没有明确的施动者，要使用被动语态，"降低"译作 reduce。

118. **can you expect to get a pay raise**

   本题考查 only 位于句首时句子的部分倒装。因此，can 提到主语 you 之前。"指望做某事" 就是 expect to do sth., "加薪" 译作 get a pay raise。

119. **as little money as my brother has**

   本题考查比较的表达。"钱" 为不可数名词，因此修饰它的形容词就是 little。

120. **rather than hold it without the presence of the president**

   本题考查 prefer to do sth. rather than do sth.的表达方式。"召开" 译作 hold，"出席" 译作 presence。

【考点归纳】

要表达 "宁愿做某事" 有以下两种方式：

- prefer to do sth. rather than do sth.，如：He preferred to die rather than surrender. (他宁死不屈。)

- prefer doing sth. to doing sth.，如本题还可以表达为：We preferred postponing the meeting to holding it without the presence of the president.

Unit 25

【解析】

121. **swimming back and forth like the pendulum of a clock**

   分析句子结构，逗号前是主句，则所译部分不可能是独立的句子，应该是从句或者分词短语，但是空格前有了 its tail 的限制，那么只能是分词短语构成的独立主格了。swim 和 its tail 间是主动关系，故使用现在分词 swimming，"前前后后" 就是 back and forth，"钟摆" 译作 pendulum of a clock。

122. **enough money (should) be collected**

   It is important that 后面要使用虚拟语气，形式为 "(should) ＋v."，"筹钱" 译为 collect money，由于此处没有明确的施动者，所以使用被动语态。

123. **did they bring snacks and drinks**

   本题考查 not only 位于句首时句子的部分倒装。由于是一般过去时，故将 did 提到主语 they 的前面。

124. **to carry on the conversation with so much noise around**

   分析句子结构，所译部分为不定式短语，是句子的逻辑主语，而题干中的 it 只是形式主语。"进行对话" 可译作 carry on the conversation，"在周围这么多噪音的情况下" 译作 with so much noise around。

【考点归纳】

与 carry 有关的常考短语还有：

- carry off 意为"拿走，赢得，轻易地完成"，如：Tom carried off all the school prizes. (汤姆轻而易举地获得了学校的所有奖项。)

- carry on 意为"继续，进行"，如：The couple carried on a thriving business. (夫妻俩生意兴隆。)

- carry out 意为"实行，执行，贯彻"，如：The team carried out the mission successfully. (那个团队成功地完成了使命。)

- carry away 意为"使失去理智（自我控制力）"，如：The officer was carried away by desire. (那位官员被欲望冲昏了头脑。)

125. as much mysterious to me

所译部分的"谜"并非谜语的意思，而是指"不知道的，不清楚的，神秘的"，故使用形容词 mysterious，"同样"则译作 as much。

Unit 26

【解析】

126. being cancelled because of the storm/being called off because of the storm

分析句子结构，逗号后为主句，空格前有名词 all flights，可知所译部分为独立主格中的分词部分，"取消"可译作 cancel 或者 call off，但要注意的是应该使用被动语态。

127. If we had not been interrupted yesterday

本题考查虚拟语气的用法。逗号后是主句，用"would＋现在完成时"，可见是对过去的虚拟，因此所译部分使用过去完成时。

128. is planned in terms of expenses and time

此处"计划"应使用被动语态 is planned，"按照"译作 in terms of，"花销"即 expenses。

129. so much as by his lack of talent

本题考查短语 not...so much as... 的用法。该短语意为"与其……不如……"，省略号的部分可以是任何词性，但是两部分必须对称。

【考点归纳】

表示"与其……不如……"的说法有：

- not so much A as B 或者 not A so much as B，如本句。

- more B than A，如：I was bothered more by his lack of talent than by his loudness.

- less A than B，如：I was bothered less by his loudness than by his lack of talent.

130. better than to ask Dick for help

　　本题考查短语 know better than to do sth.（明事理而不至于做某事）的用法。

【考点归纳】

　　一些貌似比较级的特殊短语有：

- none other than 意为"不是别人，而正是……"，如：The first speech was given by none other than Mr. Smith.（第一个演讲的不是别人正是史密斯先生。）
- not so much as 意为"甚至不；连……都没有……"，如：I have not so much as heard of him, much less know him.（我都没听说过他，更别提认识他了。）
- other than 意为"远非……"，如：The truth is quite other than what you think.（事实并非你想象的那样。）
- still less 意为"更不必说……"，如：He knows little of mathematics, and still less of chemistry.（他对数学知之甚少，更别提化学了。）
- much more 意为"更……"，如：John likes music, much more dancing.（约翰喜欢音乐，更喜欢跳舞。）
- as good as 意为"相当于……一样"，如：The house was as good as sold.（这所房子相当于出售一样。）
- as good as or better than 意为"和……一样好，甚至更好"，如：The facilities of the older hospital are as good as or better than those of the new hospital.（这家老医院的设备跟新医院的一样好，甚至更好。）
- as good as, if not better than 意为"如果没有……更好，也至少决不差"，如：Ann's work is as good as, if not better than, ours.（安的工作如果不比我们的好，至少也不会比我们差。）

Unit 27

【解析】

131. the planned trip will have to be called off/cancelled

　　分析句子结构，逗号前为独立主格，故所译部分为主句，"计划的行程"译作 the planned trip，"取消"要使用被动语态，译作 be called off 或者 be cancelled。

【考点归纳】

　　与 call 有关的常考短语有：

- call for 意为"邀约，要求"，如：This news calls for champagne.（这个消息值得开香槟酒庆祝。）
- call on/upon 意为"访问，拜访（某人），号召"，如：I call upon you to tell the truth.（我要求你说真话。）

- call up 意为 "打电话，召集，使人想起"，如：Those stories call up old times. (那些故事使人想起昔日时光。)
- call at 意为 "拜访（某地）"，如：The train on platform 3 is for London, calling at Reading. (第三站台的火车开往伦敦，在雷丁停车。)

132. that he (should) fall behind

本题考查虚拟语气的用法。for fear 后面的从句要用 that 引导，而且要使用虚拟语气，形式为 "(should) ＋v."，"落后" 译作 fall behind。

133. in association with another company

分析句子结构，题干中给出的英语部分是主句，那么所译部分只能是方式状语。"和……联合" 译作 in association with。

134. as in motion than as at rest

本题考查 more...than... 表示 "与其……不如……" 的用法，可参见 129 题的【考点归纳】。需要注意的是 "在运动中" 译作 in motion，"在静止中" 译作 at rest。be regarded as 意为 "当作，看作"。

135. that is to say, anyone who don't know it will not be able to read it

"也就是说" 可译作 that is to say 或者 in other words。"任何不知道密码的人" 在翻译时要使用定语从句，译作 anyone who don't know it。

Unit 28

【解析】

136. to have been translated into dozens of languages

分析句子结构，所译部分为动词不定式短语。由于句子有时间的限制 in the last decade，可见 "译成了十几种语言" 是指在过去译成，故使用不定式的完成式，而且要使用被动语态。"十几种" 就是 dozens of。

137. it (should) break down on the way

本题考查虚拟语气的用法。lest 后的从句中使用形式为 "(should) ＋v." 的虚拟语气，"出故障" 译为 break down。

【考点归纳】

与 break 有关的常考短语有：

- break down 意为 "（机器）出故障，（健康）垮掉，崩溃"，如：The elevator broke down. (电梯出毛病了。)
- break out 意为 "爆发，突然出现，逃脱"，如：Fighting broke out in the prison cells. (牢房里发生了斗殴。)

- break through 意为 "突围，取得突破"，如：The sun broke through at last in the afternoon. （下午，太阳终于从云层后面钻出来了。）
- break up 意为 "打碎，驱散，终止"，如：An impromptu visit broke up the long afternoon. （突然的造访打破了漫长的午后时光。）

138. maintained an interest in art

"保持兴趣" 可以译作 maintained an interest in 或者 kept an interest in。

139. As is announced in today's newspaper

本题考查定语从句的用法。分析句子结构可知所译部分要使用定语从句，关系词指代逗号后的整句话，但是由于所译部分位于主句之前，故关系词只能使用 as 不能用 which。"宣布" 译为 announce。此外，消息是 "被宣布"，故从句中使用被动语态。

140. left things we ought to have done

此处 "没有做" 可以译作 did not do，但是译作 left 更为简洁。"应该做的事" 译作 things we ought to have done 或者 things we should have done，根据并列句对称原则，使用前者更好些。

Unit 29

【解析】

141. Believing the earth was flat

分析句子结构，所译部分作主句的状语。翻译时可以使用现在分词短语，因为 believe 和它的逻辑主语，也就是主句的主语 many (people) 间是主动关系；也可以根据所译部分和主句逻辑关系（因果）将其译成原因状语从句 Since they believed that the earth was flat。

142. a new chairman be elected

desirable 来自动词 desire，其后的从句中要使用形式为 "(should) ＋v." 的虚拟语气。由于所译部分没有明确的施动者，故使用被动语态。

143. as is suggested by the local government

本题考查定语从句的用法。分析句子结构，所译部分为定语从句，关系词指代 all the precautions against air pollution will be seriously considered 这句话，且在从句中作主语。由此可知，关系词应该使用 as 或者 which，且从句中要使用被动语态。"当地政府" 译作 local government。

144. by which people communicate with others

分析句子结构，所译部分中的 "其" 指的就是空格前的 a tool，那么翻译时最好使用定语从句，"通过其" 就是 by which，"交流" 译作 communicate with。

145. that is needed

分析句子结构，所译部分为定语从句，由于先行词是 all，故从句的关系代词用 that 而不用 which，且要使用被动语态。

Unit 30

【解析】

146. Having no money but not wanting anyone to know

分析句子结构，所译部分作状语。由于"没有钱"和"不想让别人知道"的主语都是主句的主语 he，可知此处翻译使用现在分词短语最为简洁。

147. he (should) be recognized

本题考查虚拟语气的用法。连词 in case 后面的从句中要使用形式为 "(should) ＋v." 的虚拟语气。"被认出"译作 be recognized。

148. explored Africa

"考察"在此处就是"探测，探究"的意思，译作 explored。

149. It was with Tom

本题考查强调句的用法。如果不强调，句子应为 Mary talked with Tom yesterday，此处强调 with Tom，而且时态是过去时，故空格部分译作 It was with Tom。

150. which made the other jealous

本题考查定语从句的用法。"这"指 Helen was much kinder to her younger child than she was to the other 这句话所陈述的事实，故所译部分定语从句的引导词只能用 which 或者 as；"嫉妒"译作 jealous。

Unit 31

【解析】

151. girls and boys being encouraged to go to school

分析句子结构，空格前为介词 with，可知所译部分为动名词短语，由于是"被鼓励"，所以翻译时要使用动名词的被动形式 being encouraged。

152. transformed/changed our society and economic life

此处的"改变"有"变革"之意，故既可以译作 changed，又可以译作 transformed。

153. that he sought for all his life

分析句子结构，所译部分为定语从句。"奋斗"为 seek for，从句中使用一般过去时，就是 sought for，"终生"就是 all one's life。

154. has strong influence on characters of the children

"影响"此处译为 have influence on，由于句子的主语是从句，故谓语动词用单数，即 has influence on。"巨大的"可以译作 strong 或者 great，"性格"译作 characters。

155. promoted to manager

本题考查 promote 的用法。promote sb. to sth. 意为"提升某人为……"。

Unit 32

【解析】

156. both of which are adapted to the same kind of oil

分析句子结构，所译部分为定语从句，"两者"就是 both of which，which 指代前文中提到的 this crop 和 the previous one。"适应"译作 be adapted to。

157. who reveal the end of the movie

所译部分为定语从句，"揭露"译作 reveal，"电影的结尾"可译作 the end of the movie。

158. As is known to the world

本题考查 as 引导的定语从句位于主句前的用法。此处 as 指代逗号后的整句话所陈述的事实。

159. what is called "equality"

本题考查主语从句的用法。分析句子结构可知，所译部分是句子的主语，"所谓的"可译作 what is called，"平等"这里用名词 equality。

160. relieved him from pressure

本题考查 relieve 的用法，"解脱"就是 relieve sb. from...。

Unit 33

【解析】

161. Judged the best in a recent science competition

分析句子结构，所译之处为句子的状语，由于其逻辑主语为主句的主语 the three students，故可以使用分词短语作状语。"评为"可译作 judge，和逻辑主语间是被动关系，因此使用过去分词 judged。

162. as fundamentally as the Industrial Revolution

本题考查副词的同级比较 as...as... 的用法。"彻底地"译作 fundamentally。

163. that I want to visit most

本题考查定语从句的用法。"最"在此处译作 most，不可译作 mostly，因为后者的意思是"大多数地"。

164. what it takes to run a company

本题综合考查了宾语从句和固定句式 it takes sb. some time/money to do sth. 的用法。what 是宾语从句的引导词，但同时也在从句中作动词 takes 的宾语。

165. where I can see it every day

分析句子结构，本句缺少状语，因此可以译作 where 引导的地点状语从句；当然，也可以在翻译的时候首先使用 in the place 作句子的地点状语，然后加上定语从句 where/in which I can see it every day。

【考点归纳】

定语从句和其他从句的区别：

● 定语从句和状语从句：

He found the books <u>where he had put it</u>. (状语从句)

He found the books <u>in the place where he had put it</u>. (先行词＋定语从句)

(他在他原来放那本书的地方找到了它。)

● 定语从句和同位语从句：

The news that we heard is not true. (定语从句，that 在从句中作宾语)

(我们听到的那个消息不是真的。)

The news that he won the prize is not true. (同位语从句，that 在从句中不充当任何成分)

(说他赢了的那个消息不是真的。)

● 定语从句与强调结构：

It is the place where they lived before. (先行词＋定语从句)

(这就是他们生活过的地方。)

It is in the place that they lived before. (强调句，强调 the place)

(他们以前就是在这个地方生活的。)

Unit 34

【解析】

166. From the date marked on the plate

分析句子结构，所译部分为句子的状语。"从"此处译为 from，"标注的"使用过去分词 marked，作定语修饰前面的 date。

167. idleness that is even worse than lack of salary

本题考查强调句。此句中强调的是"闲散"，即 idleness，故将 idleness 放在 it is 之后，句子的其余部分放在 that 引导的从句后，"缺少薪水"译为 lack of salary。

168. As had been expected/As we had expected

本题考查定语从句的用法。此处定语从句位于主句之前，而且定语从句的引导词指代整个主句表示的内容，故只能用 as。"预料"译为 expect，由于"预料"发生在主句之前，故使用过去完成时表示过去的过去。

169. what is usually thought of

分析句子结构，mean 是及物动词，后面直接跟宾语，故此处所译部分为宾语从句。"想到"译为 think of，由于所译部分没有明确的施动者，故使用被动语态。

170. can survive a nuclear war

"存活"可译作 survive，是及物动词，故后面直接跟宾语 nuclear war。

Unit 35

【解析】

171. being rather late now

题干中的英语部分是独立的句子，所译部分前有代词 it，由此推知所译部分为独立主格结构中的分词部分，逻辑主语就是 it。"已经相当晚了"译为简单句则是 It is rather late now，此处使用独立主格结构则是 It being rather late now。

172. more efficient manager than the one you have now

本题考查比较状语从句的用法。"效率高的"译作 efficient。那么"比……效率高的经理"就是 a more efficient manager than...。

173. of which obtaining water is the least

本题考查定语从句的用法。"其中"的"其"指代题干中的 its problems，翻译时使用关系代词 which，"其中一个"则是 of which。"最小的"译作 the least。

174. A survey was carried out in the area about people's leisure time activities

"展开"此处译为 carry out，"一项调查"译作 a survey，"业余活动"译作 leisure time activities。分析句子结构，题干中的英语部分为定语从句，则所译部分为主句。

175. twice as much protein

本题考查比较的表达方式。"两倍"译作"twice as + adj."，由于"蛋白质"（protein）是不可数名词，故对应的形容词就是 much。所以此处译为 twice as much protein。

Unit 36

【解析】

176. holding a stick in his right hand

分析句子结构，所译部分为状语，其逻辑主语为"右手"，而非主句的主语 the old man，故翻译时使用独立主格，holding a stick in his right hand。

177. most densely-populated areas in Western Europe

"人口密集的地区"可以译作 densely-populated areas 或者 areas with dense population。形容人口的稠密程度，要使用形容词 dense。

178. more likely to raise fears concerning future job opportunities

分析句子结构，所译部分的基本结构为动词不定式。注意，此处"更容易"应译作 more likely，不能译作 more probable，因为后者主语不能是人；"引起恐惧"就是 raise fears，"关于"此处译作 concerning。

【考点归纳】

几个分词介词的用法总结：

- respecting，regarding，concerning 意思均为"关于"，如：I wrote a letter respecting/regarding/concerning my daughter's school examinations. (我就女儿学校考试的问题写了一封信。)

- provided 意为"倘若"，如：We will pay you the bonus provided the job is completed on time. (倘若工作能够准时完成，我们就给你发奖金。)

- supposing 意为"假如"，如：Supposing it rains tomorrow, what will you do? (假如明天下雨，你会干什么？)

179. more of a musician

分析此句，意思为"她比她的哥哥更像一个音乐家"。"音乐家"（musician）是名词，故前面要加上介词 of。

180. benefit people rather than harm people

此处"而不是"译为 rather than，或者使用 not to 也可以。"造福"译作 benefit，"危害"译作 harm。

Unit 37

【解析】

181. being remembered for his invention of telephone

"因为……而被人记住"译作 be remembered for...，"发明电话"译作 invention of telephone。while 可以直接放在分词短语的前面，故此处可以译为 being remembered for his invention of telephone；也可以将此句译作由 while 引导的状语从句，就是 he is remembered for his invention of telephone。

182. I used to smoke heavily

表示过去常做某事而现在已经不做，要用 used to do sth. 的结构。注意，"吸烟很厉害"用 smoke heavily，不能用副词 seriously。

183. Young people rather than the elderly

此处"而非"没有取代的意思，故不能译作 instead of，只能使用 rather than，或者用一个简单的 not 就可以。"年轻人"译作 the young 或者 young people，"老年人"则是 the elderly 或者 elderly people，还有一种说法，就是 senior citizens。

184. is second to heart attack

"仅次于"此处译为 be second to sth.，需要注意的是这里说的是一般性事实，故在翻译的时候使用一般现在时。

185. the way we organize and produce information

本题考查定语从句的用法。the way 作定语从句的先行词时，省略定语从句的关系词。"组织"译作 organize，"输出"译作 produce 或者 output。

【考点归纳】

定语从句中的省略：

- 从句的关系代词在从句中作宾语，可以省略，如：This is the book (that) I bought yesterday. (这就是我昨天买的那本书。)
- 先行词为 the moment，the way，the second，the day，the instance 时，定语从句的关系词可以省略，如：I will never forget the moment (that) I first met her. (我永远也不会忘记我初次遇见她的那一刻。)

Unit 38

【解析】

186. Surrounded by the police

分析句子结构，所译部分为句子的状语，它和其逻辑主语也即主句主语 the kidnappers 间是被动关系，故使用过去分词。因此译作 surrounded by the police。

187. Although its long-term effect cannot be predicted

分析句子结构，所译部分为让步状语从句。"长期效果"译作 long-term effect，"预料"译作 predict 或者 anticipate。由于所译部分没有明确的行为主动者，故使用被动语态。

188. not so much a writer

本题考查"与其……不如……"的说法。表示此意可以使用三个短语 less...than...，more...than...，或 not so much...as...，详见第 129 题的【考点归纳】。但是由于题干中的英语部分已经给出了 as a scientist，故只能使用 not so much...as...的用法。

189. no amount of money can make up for

本题考查定语从句的用法。分析句子结构，此处定语从句的关系代词在从句中作"弥补"（make up for）的宾语。此处"多少金钱"是"多少钱都不够"之意，因此在这里不能译作 how much money，而应译作 no amount of money。

【考点归纳】

与 make 有关的常考短语有：

- make for 意为"朝……前进，促成……"，如：The large print makes for easier reading. (大号字体容易阅读。)
- make out 意为"辨认出，理解，写出"，如：I could barely make out the traffic signs through the rain. (在雨中我几乎看不清交通标志。)
- make up 意为"整理，化妆，捏造"，如：Stop making things up! (不要胡编乱造了！)
- make up for 意为"补偿，弥补"，如：Hard work can make up for intelligence. (勤能补拙。)

190. A lot of labor would have been saved

本题考查虚拟语气的用法。题干中的英语部分是从句，使用了过去完成时，可见此处是对过去事实的虚拟，故所译部分使用"would＋现在完成时"。"人力"译为 labor，不可数名词，"节约"译作 save。

Unit 39

【解析】

191. being no fresh drinking water

分析句子结构，逗号之后为主句，而所译部分前面有主语 there，故所译部分是独立主格结构的一部分。"没有新鲜的饮用水"若直接译为简单句，就是 There is no fresh water，此处使用独立主格，译为 being no fresh water。

192. is delivered by school age children

分析句子含义，此处表示被动，故应使用被动语态，由于指的是一般性的行为，故使用一般现在时。"递送"译作 deliver，"学龄儿童"就是 school age children。

193. the fight is far from finished/the fight is all but finished

"远未"在翻译时可以使用固定短语 far from 或者 all but，后面要使用形容词，故"结束"使用其过去分词 finished。

194. the one it has been growing in

本题考查定语从句的用法。先行词为 the soil，但是由于前面已经有了 soil 一词，故为了避免重复，使用 the one 来指代。"一直生长的"此处译为定语从句，in which it has been growing 或者 which/that it has been growing in，后者由于介词在句末，而没有放在关系代词前，故既可以使用 which 又可以使用 that，而且关系代词可以省略。此处指某状态的持续，故翻译时使用完成进行时。

【考点归纳】

现在完成进行时和现在完成时的区别：

● 当核心动词是延续性动词如 stay，work，live 等时，两者没有区别，如：I have worked in the factory for twenty years. （我已经在这家工厂工作了 20 年了。）这句话也可以说成 I have been working here for twenty years。

● 当核心动词为动作性动词时，两者有区别：完成时指在过去某个不确定时间已经完成了某动作，如：I have finished my homework already. （我已经做完家庭作业了。）完成进行时指在某时间内一直反复地进行某个动作，有可能进行下去，也有可能终止，如：I have been doing my homework all the morning. （我一早上都在做家庭作业。）

195. In no country other than Britain

分析句子结构，题干中的英语部分为主谓倒装的形式，故所译部分可能是表示地点的状语位于句首。"除……外再没有"译作 no other than...。

Unit 40

【解析】

196. being his best subject

分析句子结构，所译部分为独立主格结构中的一部分，由于和逻辑主语 English 间是主动关系，故使用现在分词 being his best subject。

197. to have good manners and expansive knowledge

分析句子结构，所译部分应采用动词不定式的形式。"优雅的举止"可以译为 good manners 或者 elegant manners，"广博的知识"译作 expansive knowledge。

198. none but the elderly and sick

"除了……外什么都没有"，如果指人，则译为 none but...，如果指物，则译为 nothing but...，此处显然使用前者。"老人和病人"可以使用形容词指代一类人，就是 the elderly and the sick。

199. Having not enough money and not wanting to borrow from his father

所译部分为句子的状语。逻辑主语为主句主语 he，此处翻译可使用分词短语。由于分词和主语间为主动关系，故使用现在分词短语。

200. where other experiments of the same kind failed

本题考查地点状语从句的用法。succeed 为不及物动词，可见句子缺少状语。"其他同类实验"译作 other experiments of the same kind，"失败"就是 fail。

第四章 短句问答

第一节 现状与趋势

短句问答（简答题）要求考生阅读一篇字数为 450 字左右的文章，文章后附有 5 个问题或不完整的句子，要求考生在阅读完短文后用不超过 10 个词的简短英文（可以是句子，也可以是单词或短语）回答所提出的问题或补充不完整的句子。

在《六级样卷》中，短句问答与篇章词汇理解构成二选一题型，占总分的 5%。从测试手段和测试形式来说，和旧题型相比没有太大变化。但在旧题型中，短句问答一般作为阅读理解部分的最后一篇文章出现，而在新题型中则放在篇章阅读理解之前考查。在以往的六级考试中，该题型出现频率并不高，在 1997 年 1 月的六级考试中第一次出现，接连考了五次之后，从 1999 年 6 月至今都为短文改错或者完形填空所替代，没有再出现过。尽管如此，在《六级样卷》中仍然将此类题型列出，可见它还是相当重要的。

总的说来，六级短句问答具有如下特点：

- 体裁上以说明文为主，记叙文也出现过。内容涉及考生所熟悉的科普、人文、历史等方面，难度与六级的阅读理解相当。

- 综合考查考生的阅读能力和书面表达能力。一方面，短句问答题的本质是阅读理解，其考点与阅读理解题中的考点非常接近。另一方面，此类题还要求考生根据对文章的准确理解填写答案，而且不能照抄原文中的句子，其实质是考查考生的语言表达能力和概括能力，这在本质上与作文的考查完全一致。这两点从以往的评分标准上也可以看出。短句问答总共 10 分，有 5 个题目。每题满分为 2 分，最低为 0 分。评分时同时考虑内容和语言。答出全部内容，语法正确给满分；答出部分内容但语法正确根据具体情况扣分。扣分标准为：1）语言错误扣 0.5 分，每题语言错误扣分不超过 0.5 分，标点符号和大小写错误不计；2）无关内容扣 0.5 分，答案中有相互矛盾的内容，矛盾的两部分均不得分；3）整句照抄扣分，照抄一句扣 0.5 分，照抄两句或两句以上不得分。

- 重点考查考生对篇章细节的理解和通过细节进行合理推断的能力。从下表可以看出，在历年的六级短句问答题目中，细节题占了绝对多数，推断题位居其次，但是主旨题和语义题则很少甚至没有。

六级短句问答全真试题题型分布表

题型＼年份	1999		1998		1997	总数	比例
	1	6	1	6	1		
主旨题	0	0	0	0	1	1	4%
细节题	4	4	3	3	3	17	68%
推断题	1	1	2	1	1	6	24%
语义题	0	0	0	1	0	1	4%

第二节 对策与技巧

这一节我们将对以上各个题型进行深入剖析，针对不同的题型点拨应试技巧。

一、细节题

对文章的细节提问是短句问答中出现频率最高的题型。由于是对文章细节的提问，提问的形式是多种多样的，对象涉及文章中的各种细节，如人物、时间、地点、事件等等，题目的答案一般可以在文章中直接找到。和阅读理解中的细节题不同的是，短句问答中的细节题更易通过关键信息词的对应而回原文定位，很少出现题干中的词在原文中找不到，而需要寻找同义词的现象。在解答这种题目的时候，考生最应该注意的是不要照抄原文，而应将文中相关的短语或句子修改后作答。

📖 命题规律

1. 举例处常考。句中由 as，such as，for example，for instance 等引导的短语或句子为举例处，这些地方通常会设问题。
2. 隐蔽处常考。隐蔽处即指句子中容易被考生忽略之处，包括插入语、同位语、长句后半句、定语、副词和不定式等。
3. 特殊标点处常考。破折号、冒号、括号和引号处通常会出细节性问题。
4. 引用他人论述处常考。论述处的命题往往会询问此论述的含义或者目的。
5. 绝对性词汇处常考。文章中若出现 first，most，all，only，anyone，always，never，none 等绝对性词汇或形容词、副词最高级，或 only，sole，unique，simply（只要），just（只要）等表示"唯一"的词汇往往是考点。

📖 答题技巧

1. 通过题干中的关键词回原文定位，往往只需要读关键词所在的那一句或者两句话即可找到答案。
2. 确保答案语法正确，在结构上符合题目要求。例如，题目问 What made John depressed? 根据关键词 depressed 回原文定位后原句是 John was depressed because he lost the game。此时，很多考生容易回答成 Because he lost the game。然而仔细检查就会发现题目要求回答的是 what，因此应该使用名词性的短语或者从句作答，故答案应为 That he lost the game。

3. 可以照抄原文中的单词，但不可整句照抄。细节题的定位容易带来的另一个问题就是照抄原句导致扣分。此时一定要注意，可以用原文中的单词，但不可整句照抄。考生可以通过同义词替换、改变语态、由短语变从句或者由从句变短语的形式对原文信息进行"改头换面"。

二、推断题

推断题考查考生根据自己从文中获得的信息进行合理推断的能力。和细节题不同，这类题的答案一般不会直接出现在文章中，而需要考生根据相关细节，依靠自己的逻辑判断能力去分析作者隐含的意思。此类题型主要集中在对因果关系、观点和态度等的判断上。

提问方式

1. 针对文章的内容、结构和逻辑关系等进行推断：

◆ What can be implied about...from the...paragraph?

◆ It can be inferred/concluded from the...paragraph that...is _____.

◆ What does the paragraph preceding/following this one probably discuss?

◆ Paragraph...indicates that the cause of...is probably _____.

◆ What conclusion can you draw about...from the passage?

2. 针对作者的观点、态度、语气等进行推断：

◆ What does the author think about...?

◆ What can be concluded from the...sentence of paragraph...?

◆ What does the author imply in the passage?

◆ The passage is most likely written for _____.

命题规律

1. 转折与强对比处常考。转折处常常是语义（语句）的重点，转折一般通过 however, but, yet, in fact 等引导。强对比常由 unlike, until, however, but 等引导。命题模式如下：文章中说 A 具有 X 属性，B 与 A 不同。问：B 有何属性？答案为非 X 属性。一般转折和强对比处的推断题都比较容易解答。

2. 因果关系处常考。标志性的词语如下：连词有 because, since, for, as, therefore, so, consequently 等；动词有 cause, result in, result from, originate, lead to, bring about 等；名词有 base, basis, result, consequence 等。这些地方也常常受到出题者的青睐，考查因果关系的推断。

3. 评论处常考。此处由于往往暗含了作者对某事物的观点、态度，因此有可能出现有关观点态度的推断题。

答题技巧

1. 根据文章内部的逻辑关系进行合理推断，注意明显的标志性逻辑关系词语。

2. 文章或者段落的中心往往会给推断提供有力依据，因此推断一定要紧紧抓住文章中心，切莫主观臆断或毫无根据地进行推断，也不可依据自己的常识而非文章本意进行推断。

3. 学会区分事实与观点，熟悉相关的表示观点的词语。

三、语义题

语义题也就是对一个生词、短语（句）或者某个代词进行提问，一般需要考生知道或能够推断出该生词的近义词、该短语（句）的引申意义，或者找出该代词的指代对象。

提问方式

◆ What does the word "..." mean?

◆ Who does the word "..." refer to in Line...?

◆ The phrase "..." means _____.

◆ In Line..., the word "..." could be correctly replaced by _____.

命题规律

1. 逻辑关系较为明显的句子易考。这样可以考查考生根据上下文逻辑关系推测生词含义的能力。

2. 一词多义的单词易考。有些词一词多义，要求考生能通过阅读来理解该词的确切含义。

3. 含有指示代词的句子中，常会考查指示代词所指的对象，尤其是结构复杂，指代关系也复杂的句子，往往容易出现此类题目。

答题技巧

1. 通过上下文合理推测单词的含义：根据上下文中的重述、同义词、解释、举例、定义等推测单词的含义；根据上下文的对比、转折、因果等逻辑关系推测单词的含义；根据构词法推测单词的含义。

2. 寻找代词指代对象时，可以结合文章的中心，还有代词本身的单复数、指人还是指物等性质进行分析，往往可以取得较好的效果。

四、主旨题

主旨题主要测试应试者对整篇文章的理解和对文章或者段落中心的把握能力。

提问方式

◆ What is the passage mainly about?

◆ What is the main purpose of the passage?

◆ This passage tells us _____.

◆ In the...paragraph we're told that _____.

命题规律

1. 段首、段尾句处常考。这里往往会出现和段落中心相关的题目。

2. 文章的首、末段常考。这里往往会考查和整个文章中心相关的题目。

3. 转折、因果等表明逻辑关系处常考。转折之后、因果之后往往会出现文章或者段落的中心。

答题技巧

1. 快速浏览文章，把握结构，查找文章主题句。由于六级的短句问答题以说明文为主，因此文章的中心句往往出现在第一段的首句或者末句。

2. 关于段落的主题，可能出现的地方有段落的开头、结尾、转折后、举例后。

3. 如果没有明确的主题句，那么就要寻找有无具体事例、细节、论述表明或者暗含了文章主题。

第三节 模拟练习

Directions: *In this part there is a short passage with five questions or incomplete statements. Read the passage carefully. Then answer the questions or complete the statements in the fewest possible words (not exceeding 10 words).*

Passage 1

Carbon dioxide makes up less than one percent of the Earth's atmosphere. But the gas is very important to life on Earth. Scientists are finding that processes involving carbon dioxide affect our climate in ways that are difficult to understand. Last month, a committee of the National Academy of Sciences in Washington released a report. It confirmed that world temperatures increased about six-tenths of a degree Celsius in the last one hundred years. The report also confirmed evidence that the level of carbon dioxide is increasing.

The best information about climate in the past comes from tests of ice many kilometers deep in Antarctica and Greenland. The tests show changes in temperature during the past four-hundred-thousand years. These tests show that levels of carbon dioxide today are the highest ever measured. These findings have led scientists to believe that carbon dioxide is a major cause of climate warming.

Carbon dioxide is released into the atmosphere when fuel is burned. Oil, coal and wood are all fuels that release the gas. When biological waste breaks down, it also releases carbon dioxide.

However, plants use carbon dioxide in the process called photosynthesis. This process provides food for almost all life on Earth. Some groups that support burning oil and coal want to increase the amount of carbon dioxide in the atmosphere. They oppose international efforts to control carbon dioxide.

Some scientists believe that forests and trees are able to capture large amounts of carbon dioxide from the air. Some groups even suggest that an increase in carbon dioxide could cause plants to grow faster.

A recent study in North Carolina found that more carbon dioxide in the air could cause trees to grow faster. But the researchers found the effect appears to last for only three years. Another study showed that much of the carbon dioxide that is taken in by trees is released within three years. The study noted that leaves release carbon dioxide when they fall from trees and break down in the soil. Plants also naturally release carbon dioxide through the process of respiration.

The natural balance of gases in the atmosphere is a complex scientific issue. The debate over carbon dioxide is only one part of efforts to understand world climate change.

S1. The committee report of National Academy of Sciences in Washington reveal that level of carbon dioxide increases with _____ .

_____

S2. What conclusion has the author drawn from tests results of ice in Antarctica and Greenland?

_____

_____

S3. According to the passage, sources of carbon dioxide include (1) _____ and (2) _____ .

(1) _____

(2) _____

S4. Why do some people disagree with the control of carbon dioxide according to the passage?

_____

_____

S5. What do studies carried out in North Carolina suggest about trees' function for absorbing carbon dioxide?

_____

_____

Passage 2

An American scientist has found that many images of dinosaurs may be wrong. For years, pictures of the ancient creatures have shown their nose openings near the top of the head. The new study suggests the dinosaurs' nostrils (鼻孔) were just above the mouth.

Dinosaurs used their nostrils to breathe, smell and control their body temperature. The new theory could help explain how the huge creatures were able to survive by using their sense of smell to find food, a mate and possible enemies.

Lawrence Witmer of Ohio University in Athens, Ohio led the study. The publication *Science* reported his findings.

Many of the early dinosaur remains recovered by scientists were from huge creatures called sauropods. Scientists believed that sauropods must have lived in water because their bodies were so huge and their necks were so long.

Nostrils high on the head would have permitted the dinosaurs to breathe while partly under water. The discovery of a sauropod head bone in 1884 added support for this belief. The skull had a large hole at the top of the head.

Professor Witmer says experts learned years later that sauropods generally were not sea creatures. But he says the earlier theory about nostril position was extended to other dinosaurs.

Only dinosaur bones have survived as fossil remains. Scientists have never recovered dinosaur remains of soft tissue. Scientists interested in the physical appearance of dinosaurs often study birds and animals similar to the ancient creatures. Professor Witmer examined forty-five kinds of birds, crocodiles and lizards that are the closest living relatives to dinosaurs. He noted the placement of soft tissue through hundreds of x-ray images and by cutting pieces of tissue. Soft tissue leaves markings on bone. Professor Witmer used this information to make a map of the likely position of soft tissue in the dinosaurs' noses. He found that the birds and reptiles he studied share a common nostril position.

Professor Witmer found that the hole scientists once thought was a nostril in dinosaurs is just one part of the larger nasal (鼻的) passage. He found that the nostrils were farther forward and closer to the mouth. He says this new nostril position was true for all dinosaurs.

S1. What is the passage mainly about?

_____

_____

S2. What can be inferred from the passage about the possible relationship between sauropods and dinosaurs?

_____

S3. According to the passage, although experts learned that sauropods were not sea creatures, they still believe that dinosaurs have nostrils high on the head, probably because _____ had a large hole on the head.

_____

S4. Professor Witmer made a map of the likely position of soft tissue in the dinosaurs' noses by studying _____.

_____

S5. The underlined word "passage" in the last paragraph probably means _____.

_____

_____

Passage 3

By the mid-nineteenth century, the term "icebox" had entered the American language, but ice was still only beginning to affect the diet of ordinary citizens in the United States. The ice trade grew with the growth of cities. Ice was used in hotels, taverns (酒馆), and hospitals, and by some forward-looking city dealers in fresh meat, fresh fish, and butter. After the Civil War (1861-1865), as ice was used to refrigerate freight cars, it also came into household use. Even before 1880, half of the ice sold in New York, Philadelphia, and Baltimore, and one-third of that sold in Boston and Chicago, went to families for their own use. This had become possible because a new household convenience, the icebox, a precursor of the modern fridge, had been invented.

Making an efficient icebox was not as easy as we might now suppose. In the early nineteenth century, the knowledge of the physics of heat, which was essential to a science of refrigeration, was rudimentary (未发展的). The commonsense notion that the best icebox was one that prevented the ice from melting was of course mistaken, for it was the melting of the ice that performed the cooling. Nevertheless, early efforts to economize ice included wrapping up the ice in blankets, which kept the ice from doing its job. Not until near the end of the nineteenth century did inventors achieve the delicate balance of insulation and circulation needed for an efficient icebox.

But as early as 1803, and ingenious Maryland farmer, Thomas Moore, had been on the right track. He owned a farm about twenty miles outside the city of Washington, for which the village of George-town was the market center. When he used an icebox of his own design to transport his butter to market, he found that customers would pass up the rapidly melting stuff in the tubs of his competitors to pay a premium price for his butter, still fresh and hard in neat, one-pound bricks. One advantage of his icebox, Moore explained, was that farmers would no longer have to travel to market at night in order to keep their produce cool.

S1. What is the topic of the passage?

_____

S2. Where was ice used after the Civil War?

_____

_____

S3. What was essential to a science of refrigeration according to the passage?

_____

_____

S4. It can be inferred from the passage that the theoretical foundation of ice box should be that _____.

S5. Without an ice box, farmers had to go to the market at night because _____.

_____

Passage 4

Although we now tend to refer to the various crafts according to the materials used to construct them-clay, glass, wood, fiber, and metal-it was once common to think of crafts in terms of function, which led to their being known as the "applied arts." Approaching crafts from the point of view of function, we can divide them into simple categories: containers, shelters, and supports. There is no way around the fact that containers, shelters, and supports must be functional. The applied arts are thus bound by the laws of physics, which pertain (适合) to both the materials used in their making and the substances and things to be contained, supported, and sheltered. These laws are universal in their application, regardless of cultural beliefs, geography, or climate. If a pot has no bottom or has large openings in its sides, it could hardly be considered a container in any traditional sense. Since the laws of physics, not some arbitrary decision, have determined the general form of applied-art objects, they follow basic patterns, so much so that functional forms can vary only within certain limits.

Fine-art objects are not constructed by the laws of physics in the same way that applied-art objects are. Because their primary purpose is not functional, they are only limited in terms of the materials used to make them. Sculptures must, for example, be stable, which requires an understanding of the properties of mass, weight distribution, and stress. Paintings must have rigid stretchers so that the canvas (画布) will be taut (拉紧的), and the paint must not crack, deteriorate, or discolor. These are problems that must be overcome by the artist because they tend to intrude upon his or her conception of the work. For example, in the early Italian Renaissance, bronze statues of horses with a raised foreleg usually had a cannonball under that hoof (蹄). This was done because the cannonball was needed to support the weight of the leg. In other words, the demand of the laws of physics, not the sculptor's aesthetic intentions, placed the ball there. That this device was a necessary structural compromise is clear from the fact that the cannonball disappeared when sculptors learned how to strengthen the internal structure of a statue with iron braces (iron being much stronger than bronze).

S1. Applied-art objects are bound by laws of physics in both their (1) _____ and (2) _____.

(1) _____

(2) _____

S2. Why does the author mention the example of a pot with no bottom in paragraph 1?

_____

_____

S3. In which aspect are fine-art objects limited by laws of physics?

_____

_____

S4. Artists engaged in fine-arts must overcome limitations of laws of physics in order to _____.

_____

_____

S5. It can be inferred from the passage that while artists engaged in fine arts will overcome the limitations of laws of physics, those engaged in applied arts will probably _____.

_____

_____

Passage 5

Many of the most damaging and life threatening types of weather torrential rains, severe thunderstorms, and tornadoes-begin quickly, strike suddenly, and disappear rapidly, destroying small regions while leaving neighboring areas untouched. Such event as a tornado struck the northeastern section of Edmonton, Alberta, in July 1987. Total damages from the tornado exceeded $250 million, the highest ever for any Canadian storm.

Conventional computer models of the atmosphere have limited value in predicting short lived local storms like the Edmonton tornado, because the available weather data are generally not detailed enough to allow computers to study carefully the subtle atmospheric changes that come before these storms. In most nations, for example, weather-balloon observations are taken just once every twelve hours at locations typically separated by hundreds of miles. With such limited data, conventional forecasting models do a much better job predicting general weather conditions over large regions than they do forecasting specific local events.

Until recently, the observation intensive approach needed for accurate, very short-range forecasts, or "Nowcasts", was not feasible. The cost of equipping and operating many thousands of conventional weather stations was extremely high, and the difficulties involved in rapidly collecting and processing the raw weather data from such a network were hard to overcome. Fortunately, scientific and technological advances have overcome most of these problems. Radar systems, automated weather instruments, and satellites are all capable of making detailed, nearly continuous observation over large regions at a relatively low cost. Communications satellites can transmit data around the world cheaply and instantaneously, and modern computers can quickly compile and analyze this large volume of weather information. Meteorologists (气象学者) and computer scientists now work together to design computer programs and video equipment capable of transforming raw weather data into words, symbols, and vivid graphic displays that forecasters can interpret easily and quickly. As meteorologists have begun using these new technologies in weather forecasting offices, Nowcasting is becoming a reality.

S1. It can be inferred from the passage that the value of damages from torrential rains, severe thunderstorms and tornadoes is _____.

_____

_____

S2. Why do conventional models of the atmosphere fail to predict such a short-lived tornado?

_____

_____

S3. It can be inferred from the passage that conventional forecasting models are now mostly used for

_____.

_____

_____

S4. What does "Nowcasts" mean according to the passage?

_____

_____

S5. According to the passage, what makes "Nowcast" a reality?

_____

_____

Passage 6

For many years the agricultural revolution in England was thought to have occurred because of three major changes: the selective breeding of livestock; the removal of common property rights to land; and new systems of cropping, involving turnips (芜菁甘蓝) and clover (苜蓿). All this was thought to have been due to a group of heroic individuals, who, according to one account, are "a band of men whose names are, or ought to be, household words with English farmers: Jethro Tull, Lord Townshend, Arthur Young, Bakewell, Coke of Holkham and the Collings".

These men are seen as having triumphed over a conservative mass of country bumpkins. They are thought to have single-handedly, in a few years, transformed English agriculture from a peasant subsistence economy to a thriving capitalist agricultural system, capable of feeding the teeming millions in the new industrial cities.

All these details are in some dispute, but there is general agreement that the role of the "Great Men" as pioneers and innovators has been exaggerated. "Turnip" Townshend, for example, was a boy when turnips were first grown on his estate, and he could not, as the textbooks tell us, have introduced them from Hanover. Jethro Tull was something of a crank and not, as we have been told, the first person to invent a seed drill, which in any case was not used by farmers on any scale until a century after his treatise *Horse Hoeing Husbandry* was first published in 1731.

To continue, Coke of Holkham was a great publicist (especially of his own achievements), but some of the farming practices he encouraged (such as the employment of the Norfolk four-course rotation in unsuitable conditions) may have been positively harmful. And Arthur Young, the agricultural writer, has been described as a "a mountebank (骗子), a charlatan and a scribbler" by one author, although others see him as a proto-social scientist. Finally, Bakewell's New Leicester sheep was a success, but his Longhorn cattle were not. It seems that only the Collings brothers, who developed the shorthorn cattle breed, can escape criticism. Despite this evidence, the myths associated with these individuals have proved extremely difficult to dislodge from literature not directed at a specialist historical audience.

S1. For many years, the three major changes leading to the agricultural revolution in England were attributed to _____.

_____

_____

S2. What kind of agriculture system used to exist in England before the agricultural revolution according to the passage?

_____

_____

S3. What is generally agreed about the "Great Men"?

_____

_____

S4. What's the author's attitude towards some of the farming practices Coke of Holkham encouraged?

_____

_____

S5. According to the passage, only _____ will not believe the myths of those "Great Men".

_____

_____

Passage 7

About ten men in every hundred suffer from color blindness in some way; women are luckier only about one in two hundred is affected in this manner. There are different forms of color blindness. A man may not be able to see deep red. He may think that red, orange and yellow are all shades of green. Sometimes a person cannot tell the difference between blue and green. In rare cases an unlucky man may see everything in shades of green—a strange world indeed.

In certain occupations color blindness can be dangerous and candidates are tested most carefully. For example, when fighting at night, soldiers use lights of flares to signal to each other. A green light may mean "Advance" and a red light may mean "Danger! Keep back!" You can see what will happen if somebody thinks that red is green! Color blindness in human beings is a strange thing to explain. In a single eye there are millions of very small things called "cones". These help to see in a bright light and to tell the difference between colors. There are also millions of "rods" but these are used for seeing when it is nearly dark. They show us shape but not color. Wait until it is dark tonight, and then go outside. Look round you and try to see what colors you can recognize.

Birds and animals which hunt at night have eyes which contain few or no cones at all, so they cannot see colors. As far as we know, bats and adult owls cannot see colors at all only light and dark shapes. Similarly cats and dogs cannot see colors as well as we can.

Insects can see ultra-violet rays which are invisible to us, and some of them can even see X-rays. The wings of a moth may seem gray and dull to us, but to insects they may appear beautiful, showing colors which we cannot see. Scientists know that there are other colors around us which insects can see but which we cannot see. Some insects have favorite colors. Mosquitoes like blue, but do not like yellow. A red light will not attract insects but a blue lamp will.

S1. According to the passage, color blindness can be dangerous in certain occupations like _____.

_____

S2. When millions of rods in our eyes are at work in darkness, we can see _____.

_____

S3. Why can't bats and adult owls see colors according to the passage?

_____

S4. According to the passage, insects can see _____ which humans can't see.

S5. What might be the reason that a blue lamp will attract insects but a red light won't according to the passage?

_____

Passage 8

Some people are born with the belief that they are masters of their own lives. Others feel they are at the mercy of fate. New research shows that part of those feelings are in the genes.

Psychologists have long known that people confident in their ability to control their destinies are more likely to adjust well to growing old than those who feel that they drift on the currents of fate. Two researchers who questioned hundreds of Swedish twins report that such confidence, or lack of it, is partly genetic and partly drawn from experience. They also found that the belief in blind luck—a conviction that coincidence plays a big role in life—is something learned in life and has nothing to do with heredity.

The research was conducted at the Karolinska Institute-better known as the body that annually awards the Nobel Prize for medicine by Nancy Pedersen of the Institute and Margaret Gatz, a professor of psychology at the University of Southern California in Los Angeles. Their results were recently published in the United States in the *Journal of Gerontology*. People who are confident of their ability to control their lives have an "internal locus of control", and have a better chance of being well adjusted in their old age, said Pedersen. An "external locus of control", believing that outside forces determine the course of life, has been linked to depression in latter years, she said. "We are trying to understand what makes people different. What makes some people age gracefully and others have a more difficult time?" she said. The study showed that while people have an inborn predilection (爱好) toward independence and self-confidence, about 70 percent of this personality trait is affected by a person's environment and lifetime experiences.

Pedersen's studies, with various collaborators, probe the aging process by comparing sets of twins, both identical and fraternal, many of whom were separated at an early age. The subjects were drawn from a roster first compiled about 30 years ago registering all twins born in Sweden since 1886. The complete list, which was extended in 1971, has 95,000 sets of twins.

S1. According to the passage, new research shows that people's confidence or lack of it comes from (1) _____ and (2) _____.

(1) _____

(2) _____

S2. According to the research, people who feel that they drift on the currents of fate tend to feel _____ in their latter years.

_____

_____

S3. "Internal locus of control" means that believing that _____.

_____

S4. It can be inferred from the passage that Nancy Pederson probably believes that people's feeling of independence and self-confidence mainly comes from his _____.

_____

S5. The main purpose of Pederson's research is to study people's _____.

_____

_____

Passage 9

After resting on the ocean floor for nearly three-quarters of a century, a great ship seemed to come alive again. The legend of the White Star liner Titanic, which struck an iceberg and sank on its maiden voyage in 1912, carrying more than 1,500 passengers to their death, has been celebrated in print and on film, in poetry and song. But last week what had been legendary suddenly became real. As they viewed videotapes and photographs of the sunken leviathan (巨物), millions of people around the world could sense her mass, her quiet and the ruined splendor of a lost age.

Watching on television, they joined the undersea craft Alvin and Jason Jr. (J.J.) as they toured the wreckage of the luxury liner, wandering across the decks past corroded bollards (系船柱), peering into the officer's quarters and through rust-curtained portholes (舷窗). Views of the railings where doomed passengers and crewmembers stood evoked images of the moonless night 74 years ago when the great ship slipped beneath the waves.

The two-minute videotape and nine photographs, all in color and shot 12,500 ft. under the North Atlantic, were a tiny sample of 60 hours of video and 60,000 stills garnered during the twelve-day exploration. They are released at a Washington press conference conducted by Marine Geologist Robert Ballard, 44, who led the teams from the Wood Hole Oceanographic Institution that found the Titanic last September and revisited it this July.

Recounting the highlights of what has already become the most celebrated feat of underwater exploration, Ballard revealed some startling new information. His deep-diving craft failed to find the 300-ft. gash (很深的裂缝) that, according to legend, was torn in the Titanic's hull when the ship plowed into the iceberg. Instead, he suggested, the collision had buckled the ship's plates, allowing water to pour in. He also brought back evidence that the ship broke apart not when she hit bottom, as he had thought when viewing the first Titanic images last September, but as she sank: the stern, which settled on the bottom almost 1,800 ft. from the bow, had swiveled 180 on its way down.

S1. The phrase "the sunken leviathan" in paragraph 1 refers to _____.

_____

S2. How did the ship sink?

_____

_____

S3. The passage was probably written in _____.

_____

_____

S4. According to the legend of Titanic, how did the 300-ft. gash come into being at the time of collision?

_____

S5. According to Ballard's finding, the ship broke apart when _____.

_____

_____

Passage 10

Home. Few words in the English language have such a special meaning. Home is a place where you can relax, kick back and just be yourself. Just about everyone has a strong opinion of what makes a house a home. And for most people in America, home should be, above all, comfortable.

Americans like their homes to reflect their personal tastes. Many do-it-yourselfers enjoy fixing up their house and making it more "livable". They often try to create a cozy atmosphere so that when they're at home, they'll really feel "at home". Sofas and lounge chairs may be heavily padded and arranged in groupings conducive (有益于) to relaxed conversation. The bathroom even receives special attention. Carpeted floors, scented soaps, colorful wallpaper and decorative curtains adorn the "comfort room" in many homes. And on average, Americans have more bathrooms than any other people in the world.

Americans try to make the most of their space, too. The majority of homes have built-in closets and shelves, and people spare no pains to add dressers, filing cabinets and closet organizers to maximize their storage space. Although keeping the house neat is often a constant battle, Americans feel it's a battle worth fighting.

People in America keep an eye on the latest trends in interior design. In the 80s, the "country" look dominated the home decorating scene. Rustic furniture and shelves full of old-fashioned knick-knacks created a homey atmosphere reminiscent of rural America several generations back. The 90s have brought in another longing for the past: the retro (怀旧的) 50s and 60s look-plain and simple furniture with square backs and arms and block-style legs.

With all this attention to their homes, you would think Americans place a high premium on house-keeping. In fact, however, keeping house doesn't receive as much attention as it used to. Why? The fast-paced lifestyles of the 90s allow little spare time for dusting, vacuuming and scrubbing the tub. Ironically, however, even though more and more women work outside the home, women still do twice as much house work as men. Modern conveniences like the washing machine, the vacuum cleaner, and the dishwasher have taken some of the drudgery (苦差事) out of household chores. But in general, Americans these days take their cue from books like How to Avoid Housework.

S1. Which word in the first paragraph describes the ideal home for most Americans?

_____

S2. According to the passage, Americans' homes usually can reflect _____.

_____

_____

S3. Why do most American homes have built-in closets and shelves, added dressers, etc.?

_____

_____

S4. Popularity of rustic furniture in 1980s and plain and simple furniture in 1990s reflect Americans' attention to _____.

_____

_____

S5. Keeping house doesn't get so much attention today due to _____.

_____

_____

Passage 11

History gives several clues to explain American attitudes toward the law. The U.S. Constitution, the basis for all laws in America, reflects many historical influences. The Magna Carta, or "Great Charter", was one. King John of England was forced to sign this document in 1215. It placed the king under the authority of the law. No longer was the king law; rather, the law was king. America's Christian heritage has also shaped how people view the law. For one thing, the Bible reveals God's unchanging laws which people must obey. It also teaches people to respect human authority as established by God.

Of course, not everyone in America abides by the law. Crime is a growing problem. For that reason, law enforcement officials will never be out of a job. Police officers have their hands full trying to arrest lawbreakers. Detective agencies spend countless hours trying to figure out unsolved crimes. Nevertheless, most Americans still like to believe that the "long arm of the law" will eventually nab the bad guys.

But even bad guys in America have the right to a fair trial. When a person is brought to an American court, he is presumed innocent until proven guilty. Many ancient Eastern systems, in contrast, viewed an accused person as guilty until proven innocent. They used torture and other extreme measures to find out the truth. The American system tries to protect the rights of the accused. Still, the system is far from perfect. Court cases involving celebrities like O.J. Simpson can become media circuses. Skilled lawyers sometimes use minor issues to get their clients set free. And prison inmates may live even better than many poor citizens.

No one believes a perfect legal system is possible. Yet every society has laws. Whether people follow the letter of the law or just the spirit of the law, they recognize the need for laws to keep order in society. Without them, chaos would result. If every man were a law unto himself, no man would be free.

S1. According to the passage, the law became the king in the U.S. when _____.

_____

_____

S2. According to the passage, what kind of law does the Bible represent?

_____

_____

S3. Most Americans still believe in the power of law, although _____.

_____

_____

S4. According to the passage, the accused in America is viewed _____ when first brought to court.

_____

_____

S5. What does the author probably think of the legal system according to the last paragraph?

_____

_____

Passage 12

A look at the history of the United States indicates that this country has often been called "a melting pot", where various immigrant and ethnic groups have learned to work together to build a unique nation. Even those "original" Americans, the Indians, probably walked a land bridge from Asia to North America some thousands of years ago. So, who are the real Americans? The answer is that any and all of them are! And you, no matter where you come from, could also become an American should you want to. Then you would become another addition to America's wonderfully rich "nation of immigrants".

The United States is currently shifting from being a nation of immigrants of mainly European descent to one of immigrants from other parts of the world. The number of recent immigrants has skyrocketed. They desire to escape economic hardship and political oppression in their native countries as well as the desire to seek a better education and a more prosperous life in America, "the land of opportunity". Although there are frequent conflicts between the cultures they have brought with them from the "old country" and those found in America, most immigrants learn to adjust to and love their adopted land.

Americans have also learned much from the customs and ideas of the immigrants and are often influenced by them in subtle and interesting ways. Immigrants bring their native cultural, political, and social patterns and attitudes, varied academic and religious backgrounds, as well as their ethnic arts, sports, holidays, festivals, and foods. They have greatly enriched American life.

For immigrants from all parts of the world, the United States has been a "melting pot" in which the foreigners have sometimes remained culturally and linguistically what they were in their native lands even as they move toward becoming citizens of the United States, a country whose people share a common cultural outlook and set of values. The melting pot does not melt away all recollections of another way of life in another place—nor should it. On the contrary, immigrants should maintain the languages, skills, religions, customs and arts of their own heritage, even while they are working towards entering the mainstream of American culture.

S1. The U.S. is called "a melting pot" because it is a nation of _____.

_____

_____

S2. Where did most of the immigrants in America come from according to the passage?

_____

_____

S3. In paragraph 2, the underlined "adopted land" refers to _____.

_____

S4. In what way do immigrants influence Americans?

_____

_____

S5. What should immigrants do to their own heritage in American culture according to the passage?

_____

_____

Passage 13

Architecture is about evolution, not revolution. It used to be thought that once the Romans pulled out of Britain in the fifth century, their elegant villas, carefully-planned towns and engineering marvels like Hadrian's Wall simply fell into decay as British culture was plunged into the Dark Ages. It took the Norman Conquest of 1066 to bring back the light, and the Gothic cathedral-builders of the Middle Ages played an important part in the revival of British culture.

However, the truth is not as simple as that. Romano-British culture—and that included architecture along with language, religion, political organization and the arts—survived long after the Roman withdrawal. And although the Anglo-Saxons had a sophisticated building style of their own, little survives to bear witness to their achievements as the vast majority of Anglo-Saxon buildings were made of wood.

Even so, the period between the Norman landing at Pevensey in 1066 and the day in 1485 when Richard III lost his horse and his head at Bosworth, ushering in the Tudors and the Early Modern period, marks a rare flowering of British building. And it is all the more remarkable because the underlying ethos (民族精神) of medieval architecture was "fitness for purpose". The great cathedrals and parish churches that lifted up their towers to heaven were not only acts of devotion in stone; they were also fiercely functional buildings. Castles served their particular purpose and their battlements and turrets were for use rather than ornament. The rambling manor houses of the later Middle Ages, however, were primarily homes, their owners achieving respect and maintaining status by their hospitality and good lordship rather than the grandeur of their buildings.

Fitness for purpose also characterized the homes of the poorer classes. Such people didn't matter very much to the ruling elite and so neither did their houses. These were dark, primitive structures of one or two rooms, usually with crude timber frames, low walls and thatched roofs. They weren't built to last. And they didn't.

S1. According to the passage, if architecture was about revolution, Romano-British culture should _____ after the Roman withdrawal.

S2. Why couldn't Anglo-Saxon buildings survive a long time according to the passage?

S3. When did British buildings enjoy their most splendid time according to the passage?

S4. The buildings in the Early Modern Period were remarkable because of their _____.

S5. Structures of homes of the poorer classes in the later Middle Ages were generally _____.

Passage 14

Black people were the only "immigrants" who didn't choose to come to America. For hundreds of years, Africans were taken from their homes to be slaves in the New World. Even George Washington and Thomas Jefferson had slaves. The phrase "all men are created equal" didn't apply to blacks in their day. The end of the Civil War finally brought freedom to the slaves in 1865, but blacks still had a lower position in society. Many Southern states practiced segregation to "keep blacks in their place". Blacks and whites went to different schools, ate at different restaurants, even drank from different water fountains.

The Civil Rights Movement in the 1950s and 1960s helped black people secure many of the rights promised in the Constitution. A 1954 Supreme Court decision ruled that segregation (种族隔离) had no place in public schools. Gradually, American education became more fair. In 1955, Rosa Parks refused to give up her seat on a bus for a white man. Her courage sparked a bus boycott in Montgomery, Alabama, that ended segregation on city buses. Martin Luther King Jr. encouraged black people to use nonviolent means to achieve their goals of equal treatment. Finally, Congress passed the Civil Rights Act of 1964 to stop discrimination in all public places.

In spite of the gains of the Civil Rights Movement, racial problems still exist. The laws have changed, but some people—on all sides of the color spectrum—remain prejudiced. Tensions sometimes erupt in violence. The 1992 Los Angeles riots sprang from the verdict of a racially-charged court case. Moreover, blacks and whites are not the only racial groups struggling to get along. Multicultural America has numerous minority groups that argue for equal treatment. Some contend that current immigration laws unfairly discriminate against certain racial groups.

Even so, in the past 40 years, race relations in America have greatly improved. Minority groups now have equal opportunities in many areas of education, employment and housing. Interracial marriages are becoming more accepted. Children of different races—and their parents—are learning to play together and work together.

S1. How did Africans first come to America?

_____

_____

S2. What happened to slaves in 1865?

_____

_____

S3. What is the Civil Rights Act of 1964 for?

_____

_____

S4. Not only blacks but also _____ struggle to get equal treatment.

_____

S5. What is the current situation of race relations in America?

_____

_____

Passage 15

To Americans, the goal of parents is to help children stand on their own two feet. From infancy, each child may get his or her own room. As children grow, they gain more freedom to make their own choices. Teenagers choose their own forms of entertainment, as well as the friends to share them with. When they reach young adulthood, they choose their own careers and marriage partners. Of course, many young adults still seek their parents' advice and approval for the choices they make. But once they "leave the nest" at around 18 to 21 years old, they want to be on their own, not "tied to their mother's apron strings".

Most young couples with children struggle with the issue of childcare. Mothers have traditionally stayed home with their children. In recent years, though, a growing trend is to put preschoolers in a day care center so Mom can work. Many Americans have strong feelings about which type of arrangement is best. Some argue that attending a day care center can be a positive experience for children. Others insist that mothers are the best caregivers for children. A number of women are now leaving the work force to become full-time homemakers.

Disciplining children is another area that American parents have differing opinions about. Many parents feel that an old-fashioned spanking helps youngsters learn what "No!" means. Others prefer alternate forms of discipline. For example, "time outs" have become popular in recent years. Children in "time out" have to sit in a corner or by a wall. They can get up only when they are ready to act nicely. Older children and teenagers who break the rules may be grounded, or not allowed to go out with friends. Some of their privileges at home—like TV or telephone use—may also be taken away for a while. Although discipline isn't fun for parents or children, it's a necessary part of training.

Being a parent is a tall order. It takes patience, love, wisdom, courage and a good sense of humor to raise children and not lose your sanity (心智健全). Some people are just deciding not to have children at all, since they're not sure it's worth it. But raising children means training the next generation and preserving our culture. What could be worth more than that?

S1. The goal of American parents is to help children become _____.

_____

_____

S2. What does "tied to their mother's apron strings" in paragraph 1 mean?

_____

S3. Why are a number of women leaving the work force to become full-time homemakers according to the passage?

_____

_____

S4. What does the author think of discipline?

_____

_____

S5. It can be inferred from the passage that the author probably thinks raising children is _____.

_____

_____

Passage 16

Growing old is not exactly pleasant for people in youth-oriented American culture. Most Americans like to look young, act young and feel young. As the old saying goes, "You're as young as you feel." Older people joke about how many years young they are, rather than how many years old. People in some countries value the aged as a source of experience and wisdom. But Americans seem to favor those that are young, or at least "young at heart".

Many older Americans find the "golden years" to be anything but golden. Economically, "senior citizens" often struggle just to get by. Retirement—typically at age 65—brings a sharp decrease in personal income. Social Security benefits usually cannot make up the difference. Older people may suffer from poor nutrition, medical care and housing. Some even experience age discrimination. In 1987, American sociologist Pat Moore dressed up like an older person and wandered city streets. She was often treated rudely—even cheated and robbed. However, dressed as a young person, she received much more respect. Of course, not all elderly Americans have such negative experiences. But old age does present unique challenges.

Ironically, the elderly population in America is expanding fast. Why? People are living longer. Fewer babies are being born. And middle-aged "baby boomers" are rapidly entering the ranks of the elderly. America may soon be a place where <u>wrinkles</u> are "in". Marketing experts are already focusing on this growing group of consumers. And even now the elderly have a great deal of political power. The American Association of Retired Persons (AARP), with over 30 million members, has a strong voice in Washington.

A common stereotype of older Americans is that they are usually "put away" in nursing homes and forgotten about. Actually, only about 5 percent live in some type of institution. More than half of those 65 or older live with or near at least one of their children. The vast majority of the elderly live alone and take care of themselves. According to the U.S. Census Bureau, 75 percent own their own homes. Over a million senior adults live in retirement communities. These provide residents with meals, recreation, companionship, medical care and a safe environment.

S1. According to the passage, people in some countries consider old people _____, but this is not the case in America.

_____

_____

S2. What happens to people's income when they retire in the U.S.?

_____

_____

S3. Pat Moore's test is to show the _____ in American society.

S4. According to the passage, the number of old people in America is _____.

S5. What does the underlined word "wrinkles" in paragraph 3 refer to?

Passage 17

Without doubt, erupting volcanoes are the most awesome and terrifying sights in nature. In fact, their untamed destructive firepower has shaped and influenced many ancient cultures from Pompeii, to Japan. It's estimated that one in ten of the world's population live within "danger range" of volcanoes. According to the Smithsonian Institute, there are 1,511 "active" volcanoes across the globe, and many more dormant ones that could recharge (再次袭击) at any moment.

Like earthquakes, volcanoes form at weak points in the Earth's crust, known as "fault-lines". When two tectonic plates collide, the event can provide the catalyst for volcanic activity. As one section slides on top of the other, the one beneath is pushed down into the mantle. Water trapped in the crust can cause reactions within the mantle. Why? Well, it's thought that when the water mixes with the mantle, it lowers the mantle's melting point, and the solid mantle melts to form a liquid, known as "magma" (岩浆).

Since liquid rock is less dense than solid rock, magma begins to rise through the Earth's crust. It forces its way up, melting surrounding rock and increasing the amount of magma. Magma only stops rising when the pressure from the rock layer above it becomes too great. It gathers below the Earth's surface in a "magma chamber". When the pressure increases in the chamber, the crust finally gives way and magma spews out onto the Earth's surface forming a volcano. When it reaches the surface, magma becomes known as "lava" (熔岩).

Volcanic eruptions vary in intensity and appearance depending on two factors: the amount of gas contained in the magma and its viscosity—how runny it is. In general, the explosive eruptions come from high gas levels and high viscosity in the magma. Whilst lava floes result from magmas with low gas levels and low viscosity.

S1. Volcanoes' firepower is destructive in that _____.

S2. What leads to reactions within the mantle according to the passage?

S3. What is magma?

_____

_____

S4. What does magma turn into when it reaches the earth's surface?

_____

_____

S5. The amount of gas contained in magma and its viscosity influence volcano eruptions'
   (1) _____ and (2) _____.
   (1) _____
   (2) _____

Passage 18

Old people are always saying that the young are not what they were. The same comment is made from generation to generation and it is always true. It has never been truer than it is today. The young are better educated. They have a lot more money to spend and enjoy more freedom. They grow up more quickly and are not so dependent on their parents. They think more for themselves and do not blindly accept the ideals of their elders. Events which the older generation remembers vividly are nothing more than past history. This is as it should be. Every new generation is different from the one that preceded it. Today the difference is very marked indeed.

The old always assume that they know best for the simple reason that they have been around a bit longer. They don't like to feel that their values are being questioned or threatened. And this is precisely what the young are doing. They are questioning the assumptions of their elders and disturbing their complacency (自满). Office hours, for instance, are nothing more than enforced slavery. Wouldn't people work best if they were given complete freedom and responsibility? And what about clothing? Who said that all the men in the world should wear drab gray suits and convict haircuts?

These are not questions the older generation can shrug off lightly. Their record over the past forty years or so hasn't been exactly spotless. Traditionally, the young have turned to their elders for guidance. Today, the situation might be reversed. The old-if they are prepared to admit it-could learn a thing or two from their children. One of the biggest lessons they could learn is that enjoyment is not "sinful". Enjoyment is a principle one could apply to all aspects of life. It is surely not wrong to enjoy your work and enjoy your leisure. It is surely not wrong to live in the present rather than in the past or future.

S1. The underlined word "it" in paragraph 1 refers to the comment _____.

_____

_____

S2. What's the relationship between parents and children today according to the passage?

_____

_____

S3. Why do the old think that they know best according to the passage?

_____

_____

S4. Young people think that people would work best with _____.

_____

_____

S5. According to young people, enjoyment is a principle instead of _____.

_____

_____

Passage 19

It is commonly believed in the United States that school is where people go to get an education. Nevertheless, it has been said that today children interrupt their education to go to school. The distinction between schooling and education implied by this remark is important.

Education is much more open-ended and all-inclusive than schooling. Education knows no bounds. It can take place anywhere, whether in the shower or in the job, whether in a kitchen or on a tractor. It includes both the formal learning that takes place in schools and the whole universe of informal learning. The agents of education can range from a revered grandparent to the people debating politics on the radio, from a child to a distinguished scientist. Whereas schooling has a certain predictability, education quite often produces surprises. A chance conversation with a stranger may lead a person to discover how little is known of other religions. People are engaged in education from infancy on. Education, then, is a very broad, inclusive term. It is a lifelong process, a process that starts long before the start of school, and one that should be an integral part of one's entire life.

Schooling, on the other hand, is a specific, formalized process, whose general pattern varies little from one setting to the next. Throughout a country, children arrive at school at approximately the same time, take assigned seats, are taught by an adult, use similar textbooks, do homework, take exams, and so on. The slices of reality that are to be learned, whether they are the alphabet or an understanding of the working of government, have usually been limited by the boundaries of the subject being taught. For example, high school students know that it is not likely to find out in their classes the truth about political problems in their communities or what the newest filmmakers are experimenting with. There are definite conditions surrounding the formalized process of schooling.

S1. According to the passage, schooling and education are _____.

S2. What does education include according to the passage?

S3. According to the passage, when does education start?

S4. What are the features of schooling?

S5. According to the passage, boundaries of the subject being taught often limit _____.

Passage 20

The preservation of embryos and juveniles is a rate occurrence in the fossil record. The tiny, delicate skeletons are usually scattered by scavengers or destroyed by weathering before they can be fossilized. Ichthyosaurs (鱼龙) had a higher chance of being preserved than did terrestrial creatures because, as marine animals, they tended to live in environments less subject to erosion. Still, their fossilization required a suite of factors: a slow rate of decay of soft tissues, little scavenging by other animals, a lack of swift currents and waves to jumble and carry away small bones, and fairly rapid burial. Given these factors, some areas have become a treasury of well-preserved ichthyosaur fossils.

The deposits at Holzmaden, Germany, present an interesting case for analysis. The ichthyosaur remains are found in black, bituminous marine shale deposited about 190 million years ago. Over the years, thousands of specimens of marine reptiles, fish and invertebrates have been recovered from these rocks. The quality of preservation is outstanding, but what is even more impressive is the number of ichthyosaur fossils containing preserved embryos. Ichthyosaurs with embryos have been reported from 6 different levels of the shale (页岩) in a small area around Holzmaden, suggesting that a specific site was used by large numbers of ichthyosaurs repeatedly over time. The embryos are quite advanced in their physical development; their paddles, for example, are already well formed. One specimen is even preserved in the birth canal. In addition, the shale contains the remains of many newborns that are between 20 and 30 inches long.

Why are there so many pregnant females and young at Holzmaden when they are so rare elsewhere? The quality of preservation is almost unmatched and quarry operations have been carried out carefully with an awareness of the value of the fossils. But these factors do not account for the interesting question of how there came to be such a concentration of pregnant ichthyosaurs in a particular place very close to their time of giving birth.

S1. What are the causes of tiny skeleton's not being fossilized?

_____

_____

S2. It can be inferred from the passage that ichthyosaurs usually live in _____.

_____

_____

S3. What is the most impressive of the ichthyosaur remains found in the deposits at Holzmaden according to the passage?

_____

_____

S4. How is the physical development of the embryos of the ichthyosaur remains?

_____

_____

S5. What can be inferred from the passage about the reason why there are so many pregnant females and young at Holzmaden?

_____

_____

答案与解析

Passage 1

【文章精要】

文章主要讲述了学术界关于二氧化碳多了到底对环境有无好处的争论，并指出这是一个复杂的问题。

【解析】

S1. global temperatures

推断题。由题干中的关键词 National Academy of Sciences 定位第一段的后半部分。由倒数第二句中的 the world temperatures increased about... 和最后一句中的 the level of carbon dioxide is increasing 可以推知，该报告表明空气中二氧化碳的含量是和全球气温一同升高的。

S2. Carbon dioxide is a major cause of global warming.

细节题。由题干中的关键词 tests results of ice in Antarctica and Greenland 定位第二段。该段的最后一句话 These findings have led scientists to believe that carbon dioxide is a major cause of climate warming 直接给出了答案。

S3. (1) fuels; (2) biological waste

推断题。题目问二氧化碳的来源有哪两种，可以定位原文的第三段。第一句话说 Carbon dioxide is released into the atmosphere when fuel is burned；第二句话又进一步举例说明了几种 fuel，例如 oil，coal 和 wood，可见第一种来源是 fuels。第三句说 When biological waste breaks down, it also releases carbon dioxide，可见第二种来源是 biological waste。

S4. Because they support burning oil and coal.

细节题。题干中的关键词 disagree with the control of carbon dioxide 对应第三段末句的 oppose international efforts to control carbon dioxide。由该段倒数第二句可知这些人反对的原因是 they support burning oil and coal。

S5. It can last for only three years./It is limited.

推断题。根据题干中的关键词 studies in North Carolina 定位原文的第六段。第一句话中说空气中的二氧化碳多可以 cause trees to grow faster，但是第二句又接着说 the effect appears to last for only three years，第三句又举了另一个例子证明这一点，即树木吸收的二氧化碳大都会在三年内释放出来，由此可以推知，研究结果表明树木吸收空气中二氧化碳的能力是有限的，即 It can last for only three years 或者说 It is limited。

Passage 2

【文章精要】

文章主要讲述了一项有关恐龙鼻孔位置的研究及其发现。恐龙的鼻孔并非像以前的研究所说的那样位于头顶，而是在靠近嘴巴的位置。

【解析】

S1. Position of dinosaurs' nostrils.

主旨题。文章从头到尾都在讨论恐龙鼻孔的位置问题，可见答案是 position of dinosaurs' nostrils。

S2. Sauropods are a kind of dinosaurs.

推断题。由题干中关键词 sauropods and dinosaur 可以定位原文第四段。第一句话说许多早期发现的恐龙遗骸都是来自于 huge creatures called sauropods。由此可以推知，sauropods 是 dinosaurs 的一种。

S3. the sauropod head bone found in 1884

推断题。由题干中的关键词 nostrils high on the head 可以定位原文中的第五段。第二句话说 the discovery of a sauropod head bone in 1884 证实了这种说法，第三句话中又说这个 head bone 的 skull 上有个大洞，可见就是恐龙鼻孔的位置。由此可以直接得到答案就是 the sauropod head bone found in 1884。

S4. soft tissue markings on (fossil remains of) dinosaur bones.

推断题。由题干中的 professor Witmer 和 to make a map of...the dinosaurs' noses 可以定位到原文倒数第二段倒数第二句话。此句的前两句说到 He noted placement of soft tissue through hundreds of X-ray images and by cutting pieces of tissue 以及 Soft tissue leaves markings on bone，可见 Witmer 得出的关于恐龙鼻孔位置的结论是通过研究这些 markings on the bone。

S5. channel

词语释义题。题目中明确定位了本题的答案在最后一段。此句说科学家原先以为是鼻孔的地方不过是 nasal passage 的一部分，可见 nasal passage 意为"鼻腔"，故 passage 的意思应当是 channel。

Passage 3

【文章精要】

文章主要介绍了冰盒——现代冰箱的前身——的产生及其作用。冰盒的产生没有人们想象的那么容易，因为最初人们对其原理存在误解，没有意识到实际上冰的融化才是制冷的原理，因此直到 19 世纪末才制造出了有效的冰盒。

【解析】

S1. Icebox.

主旨题。文章从头到尾都在讲 icebox 是如何产生的，其工作原理和优点，可见 icebox 是这篇文章的中心。

S2. In refrigerate freight cars and households.

细节题。题目询问在内战后冰被用在哪些地方。根据题干关键词 Civil War 可以定位至文章第一段第四句话，由...ice was used to refrigerate freight cars...into house hold use 可知问题的答案。

S3. Knowledge of the physics of heat.

细节题。由题干关键词 a science of refrigeration 可以直接定位至原文第二段第二句话，...the knowledge of the physics of heat, which was essential to a science of refrigeration 直接给出了问题的答案。

S4. the melting of ice performed cooling

推断题。题目询问冰盒的理论原理是什么，可以定位至文章第二段的第三句话，...for it was the melting of the ice that performed the cooling，此句大意说当时人们以为阻碍冰融化才能有效制冷，但实际上这是错误的观点，因为只有在冰的融化过程中才能有效制冷。可见冰盒的理论原理就是 the melting of ice performed cooling。

S5. they want to keep their produce cool

推断题。由题干关键词 farmers had to go to the market at night 定位至原文最后一句话 ...was that farmers would no longer have to travel to market at night in order to keep their produce cool，大意是有了冰盒，他们不用再为了保证产品新鲜而半夜赶路去市场了。可见目的是 to keep their produce cool。

Passage 4

【文章精要】

文章探讨了应用艺术和美术（用于欣赏的艺术）的一个主要区别：两者受物理规则影响的程度不同。前者在功能和材料方面都受到影响，而后者只是在材料方面受到限制而已。

【解析】

S1. (1) materials; (2) functions

推断题。根据题干中的关键词 applied arts 和 laws of physics 可以定位到第一段的中间部分。根据第四句可以推知，物理规则对应用艺术的影响体现在材料和功能两个方面。

S2. To illustrate laws of physics are universal in their application.

推断题。题干中明确定位了本题的答案在第一段。具体的位置应该是在举例之前或者之后。而该例子就是为了证明它前面的那句话 These laws are universal in their application, regardless of...，由此可以得出答案。

S3. In the materials used to make them.

细节题。根据题干中的关键词 fine-art objects 可以定位到文章的第二段。第二句话中提到 they are only limited in terms of the materials used to make them，由此可以得出答案。

S4. intrude upon his or her conception of the work.

细节题。由题干中的关键词 overcome 可以直接定位到文章第二段的第五句话，答案就是该句的后半部分 because they tend to intrude upon his or her conception of the work。

S5. compromise to these laws/work according to these laws

推断题。题目问在物理规则带来的一系列限制方面，从事美术的艺术家们竭尽全力克服它们，与此相比，应用艺术的艺术家们会怎样做。由题干中的关键词 applied arts 可以定位到第一段。由最后一句中的 so much so that functional forms can vary only within certain limits 可以推知这些艺术家会妥协于物理规则带来的局限性。

Passage 5

【文章精要】

文章主要介绍了天气预报技术的发展。传统的天气预报在预测较大范围内长期的天气变化趋势时比较有效，但对短期内天气变化情况的即时预测在过去由于各方面因素的影响而无法实现。现在，随着电脑技术的发展，即时预测已经成为现实。

【解析】

S1. very high

推断题。题目问飓风等自然灾害带来的损失情况如何。根据题干中的 torrential rains, severe thunderstorms 和 tornadoes 可以定位至文章第一段。最后一句说到损失的总值 exceeded $250 million，可见非常大，故答案为 very high 或者 every great。

S2. Because the available data are not detailed enough.

细节题。题目问传统的天气预报为何不能有效预报短期内天气的变化。由题干中的关键词 conventional models of atmosphere 可以定位至第二段的开头。第一句话的后半句 because the available weather data are generally not detailed enough 直接给出了答案。

S3. predicting general weather conditions over large regions

推断题。题目问传统的天气预报现在的主要用途。由题干中的关键词 conventional models 定位第二段。最后一句说到 conventional forecasting models do a much better job predicting general weather conditions over large regions than...。既然如此，那么传统的方式现在自然也主要是用来预测大范围内的总体天气情况。

S4. Accurate, short-range forecasts.

词语释义题。题干中明确定位了本题的答案在第三段。第一句话就给出了解释 accurate, very short-range forecasts。

S5. Computer programs and video equipment.

细节题。题目询问是什么使得 Nowcast 变成了现实，可以定位至文章的最后一句话

... using these new technologies in weather forecasting offices, Nowcasting is becoming a reality，可见是 these new technologies 使得 Nowcasting 成为现实。而 these new technologies 显然指代的是上句话中的 computer programs and video equipment。

Passage 6

【文章精要】

文章主要探讨了英国农业革命期间几位有重大发明的"英雄"及其事迹。一直以来，英国的农业革命被归功于这些人。文章则通过举例证明，事实上他们的作用被夸大了，但这一点除了专家，一般人很难了解。

【解析】

S1. a group of heroic individuals

细节题。由题干中的关键词 agricultural revolution 可以直接定位第一段。由第二句话 All this was thought to have been due to a group of heroic individuals 可直接得出答案。

S2. A peasant subsidence economy.

推断题。题目问英国农业革命前是什么样的农业体系。由文章第二段的第二句话 transformed English agriculture from a peasant subsistence economy to a thriving capitalist agricultural system 可以推知在此之前英国是小农经济。

S3. That their role as pioneers and innovations has been exaggerated.

细节题。由题干关键词 generally agreed 可以定位文章第三段。由该段第一句话的后半部分可以得出答案。

S4. Negative.

推断题。题目问作者对于 Coke of Holkham 所鼓励的一些农业实践的看法。由题干关键词 Coke of Holkman 定位原文第四段。第一句的结尾给出了评论 positively harmful，可见作者的态度是否定的，即 negative。

S5. specialist historical audience

推断题。题目问谁不会相信那些"英雄"的传说。定位原文第四段。最后一句说 the myths...have proved extremely difficult to...at a specialist historical audience，可以推知只有这些 specialist historical audience 才不会相信这些传说。

Passage 7

【文章精要】

文章主要探讨了色盲的问题，并指出导致人或动物色盲的原因是眼球内的视锥细胞数量过少或者根本没有。然而，有些颜色虽然人类看不到，但昆虫却可以看到。

【解析】

S1. soldiers

细节题。由题干关键词 dangerous 定位原文第二段。第二句所举的 soldiers 的例子显然就是为了证明主题句所说的对于某些职业来说色盲会造成危险。

S2. shapes only

细节题。由题干关键词 millions of rods 定位原文第二段。由该段倒数第二句话中的 They show us shape but not color 可知，答案是 shapes only。

S3. Because they have no cones.

细节题。题目问为何蝙蝠和成年猫头鹰无法分辨颜色。根据关键词 bats 和 adult owls 定位第三段。该例是为了说明此段的主题句，即 Birds and animals which hunt at night have eyes which contain few or no cones at all, so they cannot see colors，由此得出答案。

S4. ultra-violet rays and even X-rays

细节题。题目问什么是昆虫能看见而人类却看不到的。定位原文最后一段第一句话，可得出答案。

S5. Insects' favorite color is blue.

推断题。由题干关键词 blue lamp 和 red light 可定位原文最后一段。倒数第二句话说 Some insects have favorite colors，可以直接得出答案。但是注意本题的提问方式是 What might be the reason...? 因此答案应该是一个名词短语。

Passage 8

【文章精要】

文章介绍了心理学家 Nancy Pedersen 的一项关于人类变老过程的对比性研究。其结果表明，有些人觉得自己能主宰自己的命运，有些人则觉得自己受到命运的捉弄，这些感觉来自遗传和生活经历两个方面。在逐渐变老的过程中，前者可以调节自己，后者则往往感到沮丧。

【解析】

S1. (1) genes; (2) experience

细节题。由题干关键词 confidence or lack of it 定位原文第二段。第二句话中的 such confidence, or lack of it, is partly genetic and partly drawn from experience 直接给出答案。要注意，问题的两个空在介词 from 的后面，因此要将原文中的 genetic 和 drawn from experience 改成相应的名词形式。

S2. depressed

推断题。题干中关键信息 people who feel that they drift on the currents of fate 与第三段中的 believing that outside forces determine the course of life 相对应。由该句后半部分可知，这种感觉 has been linked to depression in latter years，可见这种人容易感到 depressed。

S3. they can control their destinies/lives

词语释义题。由题干关键词 internal locus of control 可将答案明确定位在第三段。第三句说 People who are confident of their ability to control their lives have an "internal locus of control"，由此可以得到答案。

S4. environment and lifetime experiences

推断题。题干中的关键词 feeling of independence and self-confidence 可以定位文章第三段最后一句。此句说研究表明虽然大部分人生来就有 independence and self-confidence 的趋势，但是 70％的人的这种性格都是来自后天的环境和生活经历的影响。既然是 70％，自然具有代表性，由此可以推知答案。

S5. aging process

细节题。答案在最后一段的第一句，Pedersen's studies, with various collaborators, probe the aging process by...。

Passage 9

【文章精要】

　　文章主要介绍了一次对泰坦尼克号沉船的探索之旅。一个地理研究小组重返泰坦尼克的残骸，拍摄了一系列录影带，并获得了一些有关该船沉没过程的新发现。

【解析】

S1. Titanic

词语释义题。由题干直接定位第一段，最后一句中的 the sunken leviathan 显然指代前文的 Titanic。

S2. By striking an iceberg

细节题。答案在第二句话中，The saga of the White Star liner Titanic, which struck an iceberg and sank on its maiden voyage in 1912，可见 Titanic 是因为撞击冰山才导致沉没的。

S3. 1986

推断题。题目问本文写于那一年。第一段中说 Titanic 于 1912 年沉没，第二段的最后一句说那是 74 年前的事情，可见文章写于 1986 年。

S4. It was torn in the ship's hull.

细节题。由题干关键词 the 300-ft. gash 定位文章最后一段。第二句话中说裂痕 was torn in the Titanic's hull when the ship plowed into the iceberg，由此可以得出答案。

S5. she sank

细节题。由题干关键词 broke apart 定位最后一段的最后一句话，由 the ship broke apart not when she hit bottom...but as she sank 可以得出答案。

Passage 10

【文章精要】

　　文章主要介绍了美国人装饰自已的家时的一些理念：舒适、反映个人品味、充分利用空间及随时与潮流保持一致。同时指出，由于生活节奏的加快，今天的美国人不再也无法在家居装饰上投入太大精力了。

【解析】

S1. Comfortable.

细节题。由题干直接定位第一段。最后一句话说 And for most people in America, home should be, above all, comfortable，可见美国人装饰自己家的第一原则就是要 comfortable。

S2. their personal tastes

细节题。答案在第二段的第一句话，美国人希望自己的家可以反映个人品味，就是 their personal tastes。

S3. Because Americans want to make the most of their space.

推断题。由题干关键词 built-in closets and shelves 定位原文第三段第二句。而此句的举例恰是为了证明本段主题句，也即第一句话 Americans try to make the most of their space。

S4. the latest trends in interior design

推断题。由题干中的关键词 popularity of rustic furniture in 1980s 可以定位第四段第三句话。而此例是为了支持本段的主题句，也就是第一句话 People in America keep an eye on the latest trends in interior design，由此可以推知答案。

S5. little spare time caused by the fast-spaced lifestyles

细节题。由题干可以定位文章最后一段的第二句话。而第三句就接着解释了他们无法在家庭装饰上倾注太多心力的原因：The fast-paced lifestyles of the 90s allow little spare time for dusting, vacuuming and scrubbing the tub。要注意，此题为补全句子，空格前为介词短语 due to，因此要将原文信息改为相应的名词短语形式。

Passage 11

【文章精要】

这是一篇探讨美国法律制度的作用的文章。美国一直以来都是一个尊重法律的国家，尽管违法的事情时有发生，但人们仍然对法律笃信不已。文章认为，美国现行的法律制度尚不完善，但它仍是维护社会安定所必需的。

【解析】

S1. the Magna Carta was assigned (by King John) in 1215

推断题。由题干关键信息 the law became the king 定位原文第一段。根据原文，在 King John of England was forced to sign this document 后，国王不再是法律，法律才是国王，而这一 document，就是第三句中提到的 the Magna Carta，由此可以得出答案。

S2. God's unchanging laws.

细节题。由题干关键词 the Bible 定位原文第一段的最后。由倒数第二句 the Bible reveals God's unchanging laws which people must obey 直接给出了答案。

S3. there are many crimes

推断题。由题干关键信息 most Americans still believe in the power of law 定位原文第二段最后一句。而此句话之前一直在说美国的犯罪行为猖獗，由此可以推知答案。

S4. innocent

细节题。题干关键词 the accused 对应原文第三段第一句中的 bad guys，由此可定位至第二段。第二句话 he is presumed innocent until proven guilty 直接给出了答案。

S5. Not perfect but necessary/important.

推断题。题目问作者对美国法律体系的态度。由最后一段第一句话 No one believes a perfect legal system is possible 和第三句话中的 they recognize the need for laws to keep order in society 可以推知答案。

Passage 12

【文章精要】

文章主要探讨了美国这个移民国家到底是不是民族文化"大熔炉"的问题。文章指出，其实美国并未将这些来自不同文化背景的人融为一体，也不应这样做。移民们应当在保留自己的文化传统的同时融入美国社会。

【解析】

S1. immigrants

推断题。题目问美国被称为 melting pot 的原因，可定位至第一段的第一句话。由 melting pot 后的定语从句 where various immigrant and ethnic groups have learned to work together to build a unique nation 可以推出原因是美国是一个 nation of immigrants。

S2. Europe.

细节题。题目问美国移民主要来自哪里。由第二段第一句话中 a nation of immigrants of mainly European descent 可知答案。

S3. America/the U.S.

词语释义题。由题干定位第二段。文章的中心都是在讲移民在美国的生活，由此可知 the adopted land 指的是美国。

S4. In subtle and interesting ways.

细节题。题目问移民如何影响了美国，由题干关键词 influence 定位原文第三段的第一句话。Americans...are often influenced by them in subtle and interesting ways 直接给出了答案。

S5. They should maintain their own heritage.

细节题。由题干中的关键词 immigrants 和 heritage 定位文章最后一段的最后一句话。由 On the contrary, immigrants should maintain the languages, skills, religions, customs and arts of their own heritage 可得出答案。

Passage 13

【文章精要】

　　文章主要介绍了英国建筑风格的发展。在罗马人撤离后很长一段时间内，其建筑风格依然在英国占主导地位，但在 1066 至 1485 年间，英国建筑逐步发展并有了自己的风格——功能型建筑，即以建筑的目的为主导的风格。

【解析】

S1. fell into decay/disappear

推断题。题目问如果建筑的发展是一个突变的过程，那么 Romano-British 文化在罗马人撤离后会怎样。定位至第一段的开头。第一句话表明主题，建筑的发展是渐进的（evolution）而非突变的（revolution）。第二句和第三句说过去人们认为罗马文化在罗马人撤离后就会消亡，实则不然，以此例来支持、证明第一句话。由此可以推知答案。

S2. Because most of them were made of wood.

细节题。题目问为什么 Anglo-Saxon 建筑存在的时间不长。定位第二段最后一句，little survives...as the vast majority of Anglo-Saxon buildings were made of wood 直接给出了答案。

S3. Between 1066 and 1485.

细节题。题目问英国建筑的辉煌时期是在什么时候。题干中的 splendid 对应文章第三段第一句话中的 a rare flowering，故可以定位于此。由 between...in 1066 and the day in 1485...at Bosworth 可知答案。

S4. fitness for purpose/functions

细节题。由题干中关键词 the Early Modern Period 和 remarkable 可定位至文章第三段的第二句话，由 And it is all the more remarkable because the underlying ethos of medieval architecture was "fitness for purpose" 可知此阶段英国建筑繁荣的原因。此外，下一句中说到这些建筑是 functional buildings，也可以作为答案。

S5. dark and primitive

细节题。由题干中关键词 homes of the poorer classes 定位至最后一段。第二句中的 These were dark, primitive structures... 直接给出了答案。

Passage 14

【文章精要】

　　文章主要介绍了美国在解决种族问题方面所付出的努力。民权运动和一系列相关法律的出台在缓解种族矛盾方面起到了很大作用。今天，美国白人和其他民族间的关系已经得到很大改善。

【解析】

S1. They were taken there as slaves.

细节题。题目问第一批非洲人是如何到美国的，可定位至文章第一段。该段第二句话 For hundreds of years, Africans were taken from their homes to be slaves in the New World 直接给出了答案。

S2. They were freed but had a lower social position.

细节题。由题干中的 1865 年可定位至第一段的倒数第二句话。这句话说明了当时黑奴的状况。

S3. Stopping discrimination in public places.

细节题。由题干关键词 Civil Rights Act of 1964 可定位至第二段结尾部分。Congress passed the Civil Rights Act of 1964 to stop discrimination in all public places 说明了此项法案的目的。要注意，原文中用动词不定式表示目的，但回答本题时需要用名词性质的短语。

S4. minority groups

细节题。题目问除了黑人还有什么人力争获得平等的对待。由第三段的倒数第二句 Multicultural America has numerous minority groups that argue for equal treatment 可以得出答案。

S5. They have greatly improved.

细节题。由题干中的关键词 race relation 可以定位文章最后一段。第一句话中 race relations in America have greatly improved 直接给出了答案。

Passage 15

【文章精要】

文章主要探讨了美国人教育孩子的目的——教会他们独立，以及在教育孩子的过程中遇到的问题——母亲是否应该辞职来全职教育孩子，以及如何教训孩子。同时，文章还指出许多人由于觉得无法承担养育后代的重大责任而选择不生孩子。

【解析】

S1. independent

推断题。由题干关键词 the goal of American parents 可以定位至第一段。第一句说 the goal of parents is to help children stand on their own two feet，可以推知美国父母教育孩子的目的是教会他们独立。

S2. Dependent on their parents.

词语释义题。由题干定位到第一段最后一句。该句前半部分说 they want to be on their own，后半部分又说 not "tied to..."，可见 tied to...和 on their own 含义相反，所以它的意思应该是 dependent on their parents。

S3. Because mothers are the best caregivers for children.

细节题。由题干关键词 full-time homemakers 可以定位第二段最后一句。倒数第二句解释了很多女性做全职主妇是因为 Others insist that mothers are the best caregivers for children。

S4. It's necessary although isn't fun.

细节题。由题干关键词 discipline 可以定位至原文第三段。此段讲了父母教训孩子的方式。最后一句话给出了对于 discipline 的评价，即 Although discipline isn't fun for parents or children, it's a necessary part of training，由此可以得出答案。

S5. something worth doing

推断题。题目问作者对养育孩子的看法。定位至最后一段。作者说很多人因为害怕承担责任而选择不生孩子。但最后一句使用了反义疑问句 What could be worth more than that? 由此可以推知作者觉得养育孩子是一件非常值得做的事情。

Passage 16

【文章精要】

文章主要探讨了美国社会老年人经济收入下降、老龄人口增多及老年人的生活状况等问题。在美国这个年轻人占主导地位的社会，一旦退休、变老，生活就会出现很多的问题，而老年人本身也不愿被看作老年人，他们喜欢年轻的感觉。

【解析】

S1. as a source of experience and wisdom

细节题。题目问在有些国家人们对老年人的态度。定位至第一段的倒数第二句。People in some countries value the aged as a source of experience and wisdom 直接给出了答案。

S2. Their income decreases sharply.

细节题。题目问美国的老年人退休后的经济状况。由题干中关键词 retire 定位至第二段第三句。Retirement...brings a sharp decrease in personal income 表明退休后他们的经济收入大大下降。

S3. age discrimination

推断题。本题询问美国社会学家 Pat Moore 的小实验的目的。可以定位至文章第二段的倒数第三句话。Pat 打扮成老年人时处处受到不公平的对待，但当她打扮成年轻人时就受到了尊敬。可见这个小实验的目的是为了反映倒数第四句话中说的 age discrimination (年龄歧视)。

S4. increasing

细节题。题目问美国老年人口的发展趋势，对应原文第三段的第一句话 the elderly population in America is expanding fast。由此可知老年人口迅速增长。

S5. Old people.

词语释义题。由题干可明确定位本题的答案在第三段。此段主要讲美国老年人增多的问题，这里说 wrinkles are in，意思就是老年人增多。wrinkles 指"皱纹"，这里作者使用老年人的这一特点来指代老年人。

Passage 17

【文章精要】

这是一篇有关火山的说明文。文章首先指出火山给人类带来的危害，接着又讲述了火山的形成及爆发过程。

【解析】

S1. it has shaped and influenced many ancient cultures

细节题。由题干中关键词 destructive 定位至第一段。根据第二句的 their untamed destructive firepower has shaped and influenced many ancient cultures，可以找到火山破坏性力量的有力证明。

S2. Water trapped in the crust.

细节题。题目问是什么导致了地幔内的反应。由题干中关键词 reactions within the mantle 可以定位至第二段。第四句话 Water trapped in the crust can cause reactions within the mantle 直接给出了答案。

S3. Liquid formed when solid mantle melts.

细节题。由第二段最后一句话 the solid mantle melts to form a liquid, known as "magma" 可以得知 magma 的定义就是 liquid formed when solid mantle melts。

S4. Lava.

细节题。题目问 magma（岩浆）到达地表的时候会变成什么。由题干中关键信息 when it reaches the surface 可以定位至第三段。最后一句话 When it reaches the surface, magma becomes known as "lava" 直接给出了答案，即 magma 变成了 lava（熔岩）。

S5. (1) intensity; (2) appearance

推断题。题目问岩浆中的气体及岩浆的粘度如何影响火山爆发。由题干关键词 gas 和 viscosity 定位至最后一段。第一句话 Volcanic eruptions vary in intensity and appearance depending on two factors:...，其大意就是火山爆发的强度和出现依赖于两个因素，即岩浆中的气体和岩浆粘度。反过来说，后面的两个因素就是从强度（intensity）和是否出现（appearance）两个方面影响火山爆发的。

Passage 18

【文章精要】

文章主要探讨了老年人应该如何对待年轻人的问题。老年人总觉得自己经验丰富，很权威，但年轻人却总爱质疑他们的价值观。文章指出，对于年轻人的质疑，老年人不要觉得难以接受，相反，他们确实可以从年轻人那里学到一点东西。

【解析】

S1. that young people are not what old people were

词语释义题。由题干直接定位第一段。第三句话中画线的 it 和第二句话中的 it 指代同一个内容，就是第一句中的 that the young are not what they were，这个 they 就是 old people。

S2. Children are not so dependent on their parents.

细节题。题目问今天孩子和父母间的关系如何。根据题干内容可以定位至第一段。第五句说 They grow up more quickly and are not so dependent on their parents，可见孩子和父母的关系就是孩子不再那么依赖父母了。

S3. Because they have been around longer.

细节题。题目问为什么老年人总是觉得自己知道的最多最正确。根据题干内容可以定位至第二段。第一句中的 they have been around longer 指出，原因就是他们觉得自己年长，经验丰富。

S4. complete freedom and responsibility

推断题。题目问年轻人对于人们何种情况下工作效率最高的看法。由题干内容可以定位至第二段。由倒数第三句的反问句 Wouldn't people work best if they were given complete freedom and responsibility? 可以推知，年轻人认为自由和责任感才是高效工作的保证。

S5. a sin

推断题。由题干的关键词 enjoyment 可以定位至最后一段。由第六句话 One of the biggest lessons they (the old) could learn is that enjoyment is not "sinful" 可以推知，年轻人认为享受不是一种罪过（a sin）。

Passage 19

【文章精要】

文章主要探讨了教育和上学两者的区别。文章指出，教育包括了正式和非正式的学习，而上学则指具体的、正式的学习过程。

【解析】

S1. different

推断题。由题干关键词 schooling and education 定位至第一段。最后一句中的 the distinction between schooling and education 暗示了两者是不同的。

S2. Formal and informal learning.

细节题。题目问教育（education）包括了什么。由题干内容可以定位至第二段，此段的主要内容就是关于 education。第四句话 It includes both the formal learning...informal learning，其大意就是 education 既包括正式学习（formal learning），也包括非正式学习（informal learning）。

S3. Long before schooling.

细节题。题目问教育这个过程是何时开始的。根据题干关键信息 education starts 定位至第二段最后。最后一句中的 a process that starts long before the start of school 直接给出了问题的答案。

S4. Specific and formalized.

细节题。本题问上学（schooling）的特点。根据题干内容定位至第三段，因为此段的主要内容就是 schooling。第一句话说上学是一个 specific，formalized process，可知其特点就是具体的、正式的（specific and formalized）。

S5. the reality to be learned

细节题。由题干关键词 boundaries of the subject being taught 定位至第三段的中间。倒数第三句话 The slices of reality...have usually been limited by the boundaries of the subject being taught 指出，所学的事实经常会受到所学学科的限制，由此可知答案。

Passage 20

【文章精要】

文章主要讲述了在德国 Holzmaden 发现的鱼龙化石的一些情况。其最引人瞩目的特点就是化石中有很多未出生的鱼龙的胚胎，但为什么此地会有如此多的怀孕及年幼鱼龙的化石，原因还不太清楚。

【解析】

S1. Being scattered by scavengers or destroyed by weathering.

细节题。由题干关键词 tiny skeleton not being fossilized 可定位至第一段。第二句话说 The tiny, delicate skeletons are usually scattered by scavengers or destroyed by weathering...，可见它们没有石化的原因是受到食腐动物（scavengers）或者天气的破坏，由此可知答案。

S2. water

推断题。题目问鱼龙一般居住在哪里。第一段的第三句说鱼龙是 marine animals（海洋动物），由此可推知它们一般居住在水里。

S3. The number of ichthyosaur fossils containing preserved embryos.

细节题。由题干关键词 ichthyosaur remains 和 Holzmaden 可定位至第二段。由第四句中的 but what is even more impressive is the number of ichthyosaur fossils containing preserved embryos 可知，化石中居然有胚胎，这一点是这些鱼龙化石最引人瞩目的地方。

S4. Quite advanced.

细节题。由题干关键词 physical development 可定位至第三段。倒数第三句说到 The embryos are quite advanced in their physical development，可知这些化石从体格上来说是 quite advanced。

S5. It is still not clear.

推断题。题目问为什么此地会有如此多的怀孕及年幼鱼龙的化石，因此可以定位至第四段，该段的第一句即提出了此问题。由最后一句中的 But these factors do not account for the interesting question 可以推知，原因并不明确。